FARIDEH HEYAT

Land
OF FORTY TRIBES

London, 2015

Published in United Kindom
Hertfordshire Press Ltd © 2015

9 Cherry Bank, Chapel Street
Hemel Hempstead, Herts.
HP2 5DE, UK

e-mail: publisher@hertfordshirepress.com
www.hertfordshirepress.com

Land of Forty Tribes
© Farideh Heyat

Editor: Carole Mitchell
Design: Aleksandra Vlasova

hard back edition

---

*British Library Catalogue in Publication Data
A catalogue record for this book is available from the British Library
Library of Congress in Publication Data
A catalogue record for this book has been requested*

ISBN: 978-0-9930444-6-5

CONTENTS

About Author

Farideh Heyat is a writer and researcher based in London, born
in Iran. She received her PhD in social anthropology from SOAS,
University of London. Her focus of research for many years was
on women and gender in Azerbaijan. She is the author of numerous
articles on the subject and a book, *Azeri Women in Transition:
women in Soviet and post-Soviet Azerbaijan*, published in 2002.

Following this, she took on a year's teaching post in Bishkek,
Kyrgyzstan. During that year and in 2008 she travelled extensively
in Kyrgyzstan and Uzbekistan. She has published a number
of articles on women in Kyrgyzstan. The present book is based
on her observations and experience of working and travelling
in those countries, and her research on the history of Central Asia.

Chapter I

The charm of an ex-Soviet city

It is 6 a.m. on a Sunday morning, and I am sitting here in the VIP
lounge of Bishkek airport. I was ushered through the arrivals by an
airport official, past a large crowd queuing patiently to get through
the controls. There were so many Chinese-looking faces around; I
wondered if I had landed in Beijing airport. I am supposed to be
picked up by someone from the Central Asia Charitable Education
who employed me to teach at a university here. Instead, I have spent
the past hour sitting on one of the sofas in this dull, empty room with
only the airport officials poking their heads in and out, discreetly
checking my as yet unverified presence; my passport still remains in
their possession. Having travelled all night from London via Istanbul,
on a noisy, overbooked plane, I am desperate for sleep. But dressed
as I am in a professional suit, I can't quite lie down on this sofa in the
manner of one of those stranded tourists at Gatwick airport.

Land of Forty Tribes

What if nobody comes to pick me up? Where will I go then? It is the start of the weekend. My hosts' offices must be closed. I have never been so far away in the East, never to the east of Tehran. Yet here I am sitting in the hinterland of Central Asia, in one of the poorest countries in the world. A colleague who had recently returned from a trip to Bishkek told me about a mugging attempt on him in the city centre. As a foreigner from the West, he warned, I could be a prime target for the newly dispossessed, who fill the streets in the capital and loiter around its shiny new stores. But I had already arranged my trip and bought my plane ticket. Now I am half-expecting my arrival here to turn nasty at some point, still haunted by the dream I had a few days ago.

I was flying with a flock of birds, huge white creatures, moving in a triangular formation. I was seated atop one in the centre. Their flight took us over vast forests, deep blue lakes and high barren mountains. There were thin clouds above and pleasant cool air around us. Then, all of a sudden, the sun came out and the head bird made a sharp turn to the east, followed by all the others in the flock. Panic and terror struck me as I looked down and realised that beneath me was only the far distant ground, with the flock of birds speeding away.

The next day I had received an e-mail from the Central Asia Charitable Education, telling me I was going to be met at the airport by a colleague. He would take me to the VIP lounge for some refreshment, before driving me to my apartment in the city. I felt reassured and impressed by the reception they were going to offer me, a lowly-paid academic. Now I wish that my host, a local employee, had just turned up on time, holding a sign with my name on it. I don't want to be a VIP; I would rather be an OP, an Ordinary Person.

The charm of an ex-Soviet city

But what is 'ordinary' here, in this recently opened-up world of ancient mysteries? Or for that matter, in my taking up a job at my stage in life, and travelling half-way across the world, for yet another 'experience'. I wonder how many westerners have come here since the days of Marco Polo. He probably never got this far anyway, trekking from the shores of the Persian Gulf, through the Pamir Mountains of Tajikistan, and onto the court of the Mongol emperor in Beijing. In those days, Central Asia, lying en route to the silk farms of China was not dissected by national borders. It was only under Stalin that Bolsheviks drew up arbitrary lines on a map and divided this vast corner of the Turkic world into nations. Among the nationalities that emerged were the Kyrgyz, originally known as *kirk iz*, people of forty tribes. They will be my host nation for the coming year. My introduction to the newly sovereign Kyrgyzstan came via reading the philosophical novels of Chingiz Aytmatov, the great Kyrgyz author. Reading him I wanted to see the majestic mountains of Tien Shan with their sacred waterfalls, the scheming wolves that lured wicked men to the edge of a precipice and to their death, and the nomads of high pastures who revered the God of the blue sky, *gok tangri*. This was to be a journey back to my own Turkic roots, a journey of discovery and enlightenment. But for now, I have to wait, sitting on this tacky velour sofa, happy to be considered a VIP.

Finally, someone comes in and calls for me, a stocky young man with short black hair and slanted eyes. He introduces himself as Talay, an employee of CACE. "Sima? Your luggage is ready next door," he tells me in a foreign American accent. He collects 20 dollars from me for the use of the VIP lounge and walks off, leaving me trailing behind, carrying my heavy hand luggage. I am surprised with his informality. He looks not much older than my son, who is twenty.

But he talks to me as if we are college buddies, none of the courtesies I would expect from a young man in Asia. Later, I find out that a few years ago he had been on a high school exchange programme in the US, after which he took an undergraduate degree at the American University here.

Next door is the point of delivery of luggage for the VIP passengers; they are not expected to go through the customs. But much to my surprise, my various suitcases are lined up to be scanned by an X-ray machine, much in the way of pre-boarding a flight. No problem, I assume, just a little more delay. I am certainly not importing any drugs from Europe to Central Asia, where much of it originates from. No guns in my bags, either. The uniformed official who is inspecting the images on the screen lets the first two cases go past; then with the third one he points to an object and enquires its identity. It is a small rectangular box, the content of which I can't remember. Everything had been packed a few days earlier in London, in a mad rush to vacate and rent out my flat, and to prepare my son to leave home for his first year at university. This job had come up suddenly and I expected to be living away for at least a year.

When the bag is unzipped it turns out to be a box of needles my physician friend had given me in case I fall ill and need an injection. They were all individually sealed, unused needles. "Hepatitis and HIV are rife in the region" he had warned. It takes a while to convince the official of my need to carry this box. He insists there are good private clinics in Bishkek, taking care of foreigners. I tell Talay I will not argue medicine with this man. I am not parting with my needles; it is my peace of mind for the coming year.

The charm of an ex-Soviet city

The officer finally gives in, then moves onto another item. It is a sealed box of tampons. He demands to know what is inside and opens it without permission. He pulls one out and demands to know what it is for.

I feel the tension rising in me. How am I going to explain it to this idiot?

"Tell him it is for sanitary use by women," I say to Talay.

"What is sani...?" he asks. As I ponder a reply the customs man tears the wrapping off one long tampon, holds it by the attached string, dangles it in the air, and looks at me curiously.

"This is getting ridiculous", I protest, feeling the heat of a blush on my cheeks.

Talay giggles, having finally clicked. But his explanations do not generate any humour in the others. The official has been joined by two other uniformed men and a woman. Everyone maintains a solemn face. The woman in uniform also has a blank expression. Finally, I am told to zip up my bag. There are now two more cases to be checked. But the guy has lost interest and just waves them through, still pondering the application of a tampon.

Outside in the car, Talay tells me this was not normal procedure. They should have just brought my bags to the VIP lounge and let me leave. But as it happens, the entry date for my visa was a day later, which made them suspicious. In my annoyance, I remember an anecdote an Azeri friend visiting London had told me, just before my departure for Kyrgyzstan. He was a businessman I had first met during a research trip to Baku, capital of Azerbaijan. He had business dealings in Bishkek and had been there many times since before the breakup of the Soviet Union. When he found out I was on my way here, he said to me, "You know, Bishkek is no Baku", and proceeded with the following, "If a conman goes out onto the streets in Europe, claiming to be the new prophet, he may convince ten people. If he does that in Baku, perhaps a hundred will follow him. But in Bishkek, he is likely to gather a thousand heeding his message."

"You are just echoing the Russian prejudices," I said, recalling the way Azerbaijanis always considered themselves more developed than the Central Asian Muslims.

"You wait and see" he replied.

Now finally on the road to the city, I decided I wasn't going to let a silly incident at the airport cloud my vision of my future here. We were travelling on a newly-built road, well paved, with hardly any traffic. It was lined on either side by a row of tall birch trees and green fields. The sun was shining bright across a blue sky. I was happy to get away from the cold and damp of London in September. The past month had been so damn hectic. Getting ready for the teaching, as well as the trip, in a matter of one month had been a race against time. I needed to physically gather all the material for the various courses I was to teach: locating and photocopying, page by page, almost every source I was to refer to, book chapters, journal articles, the lot. The library of the International University in Bishkek was very poorly resourced and students could not afford to purchase foreign books. I had to assemble my own little library and carry it in a suitcase. After all, I was to take western knowledge to Central Asia, as demanded by CACE's mission statement. A colleague at my university, watching me curse by the side of a failed photocopier, had smiled and said,

"You're doing pioneering work. It can't be easy."

"Yes, I am heading for the Wild East" I told him.

The charm of an ex-Soviet city

***

After a 30 kilometre ride into town past fortress America, the new US embassy building constructed last year following September 11, we arrived at my designated apartment in central Bishkek. The Soviet-style block of low-rise apartments, built around a courtyard, was in a state of total dilapidation: washed out, cracked plaster on the walls, chipped and fading doors and window frames, and broken paving stones with lots of protruding weeds. Inside my apartment, the tiny bedroom was off the barely furnished small lounge with an old sofa that turned into a double bed. The floors of my apartment were of polished wood, but there were no carpets or curtains, except for the yellowing white lace hanging over the bedroom window. In that room there was a very small walk-in closet, but otherwise, there were no storage cupboards, except for a locked cabinet in the sitting room. No doubt it contained the landlady's personal belongings she could not store elsewhere.

From my time in Baku a couple of years ago, when I was there for three months on a research trip, I was familiar with the problems of renting a furnished apartment in the former Soviet Union. People rented their home and moved in with relatives to earn badly needed cash. The notion of a tenant having sole use of the furnishings inside a rented home had not yet been established. Sometimes the owners even left clothing and other personal items behind as a pretext to check up on their tenants. Despite the introduction of free market economy a decade ago, the rental sector here does not seem to have changed much.

With no sleep all night, I was desperate to use the bedroom, uninviting as it looked. The single bed was jammed against a wall to create more space for a pathway to the walk-in closet. But worst of all was the bright sunlight that streamed through the window facing the bed. At home I hung heavy curtains across my bedroom windows. Now how could I ignore the blazing light on my face? I needed to get some help, but Talay was out of reach. He left very quickly after my luggage was dropped off. But he did tell me that the Russian couple next door were very friendly. If I needed anything, I could call on them. So I went to my neighbours and rang the bell. Tanya, a woman in her forties, responded with a smile and invited me in. She then offered me a cup of tea and some cake. Her apartment was identical to mine, except for a slightly larger bedroom and kitchen, accommodating a few more items of furniture. Her two daughters slept on a bunk-bed in the sitting room, partitioned with a curtain. I did not have enough vocabulary in Russian to fully explain my predicament. But no sooner did she come into my bedroom than she realised the problem with the lack of curtains. She returned with a few nails, a hammer, and a dark bedspread which she fixed on the window frame. But still, I could not relax and fall asleep yet. I was curious and impatient to see more of the neighbourhood, and needed to buy some groceries. After journeying 6000 miles across the sky, and the ride through so many alien streets, I had to use my legs and feel the ground beneath my feet.

The view from my sitting room window revealed a line of noisy vehicles passing by. There were not many people about. The few who came past were young, mostly Slavic looking, dressed in western fashion. Once outside on the street, I could see no sign of shops nearby, only housing and wide dusty roads. After a few minutes of walking I returned to where my apartment was. I had noticed a kiosk across the road that looked like a tiny shop. You could buy bread, water, vodka, sweets, biscuits and cigarettes here. The man serving looked around forty, with greying, dark hair and Caucasian features. He told me he was an Azerbaijani from across the border in Kazakhstan; his parents had been forced to settle there in the 1930s. He had moved to Bishkek in the early 1980s, soon after marrying a fellow Azeri from Kazakhstan. He spoke perfect Azeri, a variant of Turkish, despite living all his life away from Azerbaijan. This was also the language spoken in my home. My parents had originated from Tabriz, the provincial capital of Iranian Azerbaijan, though we lived in Tehran and spoke in Farsi to outsiders. Now meeting an Azeri couple in the neighbourhood, I felt more at ease about my environment. As we were chatting, the wife arrived to take over the kiosk. She was a Middle Eastern looking, tall, shapely woman with long, wavy hair and beautiful, sad eyes. Her Azeri was equally flawless. She told me they only socialised with their own ethnic group.

"It is the same with the Kyrgyz and the Kazaks here. They don't like to mix with other nationalities. It is difficult to make friends among them," she concluded in a resigned voice. I felt sorry for her; life in a box can't be easy. Her family were second generation forced migrants, and still unassimilated.

Ethnicity was certainly a major issue in the lives of all former Soviet citizens. Lenin had devised a nationality policy that granted all the people of the Union equal status, rights and benefits. But what had emerged in reality was an obsession with ethnic belonging that divided people far more than it united them. This was reinforced by the Soviet passport system that recorded every citizen's nationality, or ethnic grouping. For example, a Jewish, a Kyrgyz, a Kazak and a Ukrainian resident of Kyrgyzstan were clearly distinguished. At the same time, the citizens of the 15 Union republics who resided in their own territory did relatively well, whilst the smaller nationalities and those who had been displaced suffered discrimination and loss of opportunities. The exception was the Russians. They dominated everyone else. Their mother tongue was the language of inter-republic communication, as well as that of higher education. With Russian language schools attaining higher standard than others, the local elite everywhere adopted it as their common tongue. This was certainly the case in Azerbaijan, and, as I found out later, true for the Kyrgyz elite.

***

The city of Bishkek, originally known as Pishpek, was built in the 1920s by an Uzbek khan, a clay fort that watched over the caravans on the Silk Road heading for the Tien Shan mountains bordering China. In the second half of the 19th century the Russian Army invaded the region and sacked the place. The garrison town they built in its place soon swelled in numbers with migrating Russian peasants fleeing dire poverty and landlessness. Serfdom in Russia had not long been abolished. By 1926, the Bolshevik General Frunze, who had defeated the White Army, as well as the local rebellion, the Basmachi movement, brought the whole region under communist rule. The young city, growing rapidly in population, most of them Russians, was designated the capital of the Soviet Socialist Republic of Kyrgyzia. It was then renamed Frunze, a name it held until the country's independence in 1991. Frunze was constructed and developed as a modern Soviet city, along the principles of scientific socialism, where wide boulevards accommodated mass ceremonies and parades that displayed the might of the state. Numerous public parks afforded comfort and relaxation to the citizens in the heat of the summer, and, most significantly, an opera house and a theatre offered high culture at very low prices.

In the afternoon of my first day here I took a walk around central Bishkek, and was struck by the calm of the place. It had a tranquillity I associated with a bygone age: little traffic on the roads, and no bicycles or scooters whooshing past. The wide pavements, bordered with tall poplars and old oaks, had few pedestrians strolling along them; such a far cry from the hustle and bustle of London, or those other major cities in the Middle East, such as Tehran and Istanbul. This was certainly neither East, nor West. It was a new world, one that was also very different from that other new world I had known, the American big city with its consummate energy, speed, and abundance of material goods. Here there were mostly mini markets, grocery shops and street stalls selling some essentials. The one department store, the old *tsum*, had been turned into a collection of individually run little shops, offering all manner of consumer goods, imported mainly from China. The population of the city was a mix of Central Asians, mostly Kyrgyz, and Slavic people. Russians and Ukrainians, a majority before independence, now constituted half the population. In addition today, there were westerners and a few Turks and South Asians living here or travelling through.

Lenin Square, renamed Ala Too, after the high mountain range in the distance was the central square of the city. It was a huge expanse of space hemmed in by low rise buildings. The pride of the place, a concrete statue of Lenin that pointed to Ala Too, marked the lack of willingness by Kyrgyz authorities to obliterate signs of their Soviet past. On another site nearby, seated bronze statues of Marx and Engels deep in conversation, were plotting the overthrow of capitalism in the century to come. But the 20th century had come and gone; with people of this region currently experiencing a new wave of free enterprise they called *diki* capitalism. This was an entrepreneurship of the greedy and the unscrupulous, who through personal connections, had bought up former state assets at giveaway prices. Nonetheless, a memorial to the fallen defenders of the October Revolution, a red granite obelisk, was still standing a hundred metres away from the Lenin statue on Erkendik Boulevard. A small park with a central walkway and benches stretched along the middle of this, set apart from the traffic on either side by a row of tall trees and shrubs. In the past, it was called Drezhinsky, the name of the powerful and brutal head of *cheka*, the Bolsheviks' secret police, feared and resented by millions in the 1930s. He had been responsible for the show trials, exiles and executions of thousands of men and women under Stalin. Following independence, the name was changed to Erkendik, meaning freedom in Kyrgyz.

Bina, a woman of Indian origin who ran the CACE office in Bishkek, had come to pick me up and take me along to meet other colleagues for dinner. As we walked along the Erkendik Boulevard, I marvelled at the autumnal colours around us. The yellowing leaves, high up the treetops, reflected the golden rays of a late summer sun, whilst the lower barks, painted white, contrasted sharply with the greenery on the ground. Bina seemed a very friendly type, as with the group of fellow teachers who had come via CACE this summer to teach at the International University. The meeting venue was the Fat Boy, a café/restaurant favoured by students and staff at the university. It was a cheap joint, furnished with plastic chairs and tablecloths with a whiff of a Mediterranean cafe. It was run by a Greek Cypriot from London, serving mainly pizzas, burgers, and beer.

My colleagues included three Europeans, a Pakistani man and an American woman, Julie. After we finished with the meal we sat around drinking and chatting. The sun had just gone in but the air was pleasantly warm. Sipping the cool beer at this pavement café, I could not believe that it was still the same day I had journeyed half-way across the world to Central Asia. I was happy not to have to spend my first evening here alone in that pokey little flat.

***

My second day in Bishkek was another beautiful sunny day. I visited a number of the parks, some with massive willows and old oak trees. The most interesting of them was the one situated right in the vicinity of the university. This was a sculpture park. Among the masses of tall trees, there were stone sculptures of wolves, horses and owls, totemic symbols for the Kyrgyz people. In the late afternoon sun they cast long shadows on the shrubbery and the surrounding rough grounds.

After visiting the park I went to Julie's birthday party. She was another anthropologist, a blue-eyed Southerner with a broad smile and grey hair that flew in all directions. She had a friendly demeanour, but when, at the end of her party, I suggested we meet soon to discuss our teaching, she just said, "Maybe" and moved on to talk to Bina. Those two seemed to have already formed a close friendship in the couple of weeks Julie had been in the country. At this gathering I also met Roger, an American ex-hippy, who had in the previous year taught at our university. He now worked with an American NGO in the city of

Osh, in southern Kyrgyzstan. He wore a pony tail under his Central Asian embroidered cap, and kept one hand busy flicking the beads on his rosary set, in the manner of Middle Eastern men idling at a tea house. When he discovered I was originally from Iran, he began to tell me about his journey a few years ago to Mashhad, the provincial capital of Khorasan, north east of Iran; he had been detained by the morality police there. The city was the site of the shrine of Imam Reza, the eighth descendent of the Prophet Mohamed, whose tomb was one of the holiest sites for the Shiites.

"How did you get a visa with an American passport?" I asked.

"I didn't," he replied with a glint in his eyes. "I used my British passport, my mother is Scottish".

Roger had been living in Tajikistan at the time and had picked up some Tajik, a language very close to Farsi. He had been travelling with his Tajik fiancée and her brother. One night, on the road in Mashhad, their taxi had been stopped by the morality police, who had spotted him in the back seat of the car with his arm around the girl. They were all taken to a detention centre and kept overnight. The couple were then charged with the crime of fornication, for which they could have been whipped 80 lashes, had they been Iranian nationals. As it was, the offending party got away lightly. The policeman took away all the travel money Roger had left on him before escorting them to the Turkmenistan border. Here they were met by dead-eyed, long faced Turkmen officials repeatedly checking the details on their passports, in between, staring at them. This had gone on for hours, before they could finally catch a bus to leave. What infuriated him was that on the way to the border one of the policemen had given him a cheeky smile and said in English: "you come again. I find you much beautiful girls." Then turning to Roger's male companion with whom he could communicate in Farsi, he had added: "*sighe*, temporary marriage, is very cheap. You can have for one day, or one month, as you wish."

Hearing his story, I could understand the lingering resentment in Roger's voice as he proclaimed: "Iranian police are fascists". I now wondered if there had been more complications than he was letting on. I guessed that Central Asia, despite being a poor and underdeveloped region of the world was quite a fun place for him, both as a male and as an American. Still, I wondered how he had managed to conduct an affair with a Tajik girl in the company of her brother. Tajiks are the most conservative of Central Asians when it comes to gender relations and female chastity. Although with the promise of a marriage and the hope of a new life in the West, attitudes could be relaxed. Roger insisted that he knew the local custom and had behaved correctly towards the girl. I did not ask why he had not finally married her.

That evening I returned to my apartment at the end of a happy and hopeful day. But as soon as I got inside, a sense of foreboding overtook me. The ride home in the taxi was an anxious affair. Bina had earlier warned me to be careful using taxis alone at night. As a foreign woman, and being unfamiliar with city streets, I was particularly vulnerable to being kidnapped and robbed. Taxis were not properly licensed here. Anyone could obtain the luminous sign on the black market, place it atop the vehicle, and remove it later as they wished. Side streets were very dark at night. Electric lighting in public places had not been maintained in recent years. The breakup of the Soviet Union had left most of the peripheral republics bankrupt, and the inter-republic exchange of goods and services had almost ceased to exist. Public services had never been much good by western standards, but what there was had deteriorated sharply in the first years of independence. This included the road surfaces and pavements of all but a few highways. Certainly the pavements and side streets around my place required a watchful gaze when walking, even in daylight. In those moonless nights, avoiding the potholes was an art to be mastered. That is, if fear of an approaching stranger did not jolt you into taking the wrong step and twisting an ankle.

I had the sense that Bishkek was a Jekyll and Hyde of a city: pleasant, joyful, and serene in the day; fearful, anxious, and full of mystery at night. Although my next door neighbours seemed a friendly lot, I had not met anyone else from this block. More importantly, what if I was to move? Who would I be living next to? My suitcases were still laid out on the floor, unpacked, as I did not have adequate storage space for all my belongings. I could not imagine this place as my home for a whole year. For one thing, the noise of the traffic outside my window every morning and evening made it hard to concentrate on academic work. I needed to find alternative accommodation and move soon. I could see that Talay was not going to be sympathetic. I had been the last of the foreign teachers to arrive and was assigned the only remaining apartment CACE had contracted for the year.

"I hope you like it here," he had said yesterday in a self-satisfied tone as he brought me in. Then went on to say: "The landlady put in a new fridge and TV because we agreed to rent it for a whole year."

I knew such imported goods were very expensive over here, but I did not feel I should be obliged by any deals Talay had made with the owner. No doubt the guy had lots of deals going on locally. But I was not going to let him make my life a misery for the coming year. I would offer to find another flat myself. But how?

The charm of an ex-Soviet city

***

The university is housed in a new building next to one of the nicest parks in central Bishkek. There is a shine to the fresh paint on the walls and polished parquet on the floors, paid for through grants from western donors and the Kyrgyz government. My students are ethnically a mixed bunch: Russians, Ukrainians, Koreans, Kyrgyz, one Kazak and an Uzbek among them. They seem eager to learn, friendly and polite, the kind of students every teacher dreams of. Was this too good to be true? They were all in their final year, with reasonable command of English. The department of Kyrgyz Ethnology, on the other hand, was a non-English speaking environment. Only the head, a Kyrgyz woman in her forties spoke some English. She doubled as the academic vice-principal, housed on the top floor of the building with the other bosses of the university, remote from the day-to-day running of her department. Her secretary, Aida, with whom I was to have a lot of dealings in the year to come, spoke her own version of English. If I made her repeat every sentence at least twice, I could just make sense of what she was trying to convey. As I found out later, Aida, the Wagnerian heroine, was a popular name with the Kyrgyz; I met at least two more on our campus that week.

Among the students who came to see me about the supervision of their final year thesis was Jamila, a rather demure, softly spoken Kyrgyz girl. She had been waiting for my arrival over the past two weeks to start her project. It was to be on women and Islam, a subject I had researched and published on.

"Miss, you can help me do a great project", she said rather excitedly as we sat down.

"Sure", I replied, "but you'll have to show me an outline of your ideas, and do a lot of relevant reading".

However, this was easier said than done, given how poorly the library was resourced. We went on to discuss different sects of Islam in relation to women. She knew very little about it since religion had been outside most people's sphere of interest until recently. There was now a growing awareness of, and interest in Islam as a basis for national identity. Jamila had enrolled on her anthropology degree, having failed to get into the politics department.

"You know Miss," she said in a frustrated voice, "in this university they look down at us doing ethnology. Politics students consider themselves the brightest and we, the dumbest."

I expected already that over here there was a lack of understanding of social/cultural anthropology as an academic discipline. Unlike in the West, where anthropology is preoccupied with the study of conflict, the Soviets had turned the subject into glorified folklore studies, labelling it *etnografiia*. Delving into the complexities of divisions and hierarchies among the innumerable multi-ethnic, multi-lingual communities of the Soviet empire was considered destabilising. The Soviet system, according to the Leninist ideology, would give rise to a New Man/Woman evolving out of tribal, ethnic and national antagonisms and discord; a harmonious future was deemed the logic of the communist system. The tragedy of this high minded Soviet idealism was the many inter-ethnic wars that flared up in the Caucasus and Central Asia, once the party had loosened its iron grip; Armenians and Azeris, Georgians and Abkhazians, Uzbeks and the Kyrgyz, were all at each other's throat once the Union collapsed. Lenin and his Bolshevik colleagues had clearly underestimated the mass of contradictions and pressures, internally and from abroad, that undermined the plans and idealism of the vanguard of the party.

The charm of an ex-Soviet city

***

It is Friday afternoon and the end of my first week in Bishkek. I am to meet Jamila to go and view some more apartments. The three flats I visited the other day were all shabbily furnished, their buildings in a derelict state. I tried not to get depressed about it, wondering how far I will have to compromise to eventually find a place. Jamila is half an hour late, and I am getting hot and bothered waiting for her outside the main entrance to the university. The sun is very strong in the early afternoon and there are no shady areas in the large square facing the entrance to the building. The tall trees in the park on the edge of the square are a fair distance away. Finally, as I decide to leave, I notice one of my Kyrgyz students, Jildiz, coming out of the building, accompanied by another girl who is holding a baby. She comes to greet me, introducing her sister who is carrying Jildiz's infant son. Jildiz has a moon-shaped face, and rough skin. Though not particularly pretty, she radiates warmth through her charming smile and manners. I tell her about Jamila not turning up to our appointment and my disappointment with the flats I have seen so far. She offers to take me to visit other accommodation agencies that may offer better places. She sees off her sister and the baby. We walk to the main road and get into a *marshutka*. These are an assortment of mini vans that cover set routes, costing much less than taxis. So far I have never been on one, since a taxi ride only costs a dollar.

We look at two more apartments. One, in particular, impresses me. It has the best bathroom I have seen so far, and nicely polished wood floors in all the rooms. The landlord tells us he had an American engineer for a tenant, who did the renovation.

"There are nice apartments around," Jildiz says, "but they are more expensive than what the university will pay for. This one is within budget."

When we step onto the small balcony I am stunned with the panoramic view. The lights of the city are just coming on. It is dusk, but you can still see the edge of the tall mountains in the far distance.

"It is lovely to have breakfast here in the mornings," the landlord tells us.

"I am going to take it," I tell Jildiz.

I leave the apartment feeling relieved. I have finally found a lovely place to call home for a year.

Outside on the landing, however, I begin to doubt. We wait a number of minutes for the lift to come up to the top floor. We enter the tatty old cubicle, where no more than two or three slim people can fit, and begin a slow, noisy descent down the nine floors. I now wonder about the maintenance of these old Soviet lifts and how often they break down. I don't fancy the idea of having to walk up and carry shopping at such times. In addition, there is the security problem of getting into this lift, alone at night. The entrance to the block is at the back of the building, facing dimly lit rough grounds, with shrubs and a few trees.

"I am sorry," I say to Jildiz, "It's a lovely apartment but I can't see myself living here."

"Never mind," she says. "There is another agency we can try tomorrow."

Outside on the main road, there is busy traffic. We are by a junction, where there are food stalls, shops and local restaurants offering Kyrgyz food. I invite Jildiz to have dinner with me. We choose a place with seats outside and ask the waiter what is available.

Kyrgyz food is similar to Chinese but not as sophisticated. There are plenty of soup dishes with meat, vegetables and noodles, or dumplings. I decide to try a *lahman*, a typical Kyrgyz dish of spicy noodles, shredded beef and carrots, served in a soup bowl. These days, the internationalisation of Bishkek has extended the range of cuisine in the city. There are a few Italian, Chinese, Indian, and Turkish restaurants around. In particular, the arrival of the Turks has brought the kebab culture to Bishkek, though, as yet, there are not many doner kebab stalls. Most local people seem to frequent Kyrgyz or Russian restaurants that are very inexpensive.

It is now getting dark, and the street lights are coming on. There is a fresh breeze about; the temperature feels perfect. A few more diners have taken seats outside. As we begin our meal, Jildiz tells me about her life. She is twenty one, from a village in Talas, in the north of Kyrgyzstan. She has been living in Bishkek for over four years now, hoping to graduate next summer. Last year she had to take a year off her studies, to have her son. I am quite curious about the child's origins. The baby had quite a dark skin and fuzzy hair. The father must have been of African descent, which is unusual here. I ask if he was one of the African-American GIs in Bishkek? There is a fair-sized American Army presence here.

"No," she says. He's never been to Kyrgyzstan. He is a technician from California. She had gone to visit him the summer before last, and stayed on for a few months after the birth of her son.
"How on earth did you meet him?"
She chuckles and says "Internet dating."
"Was this one of those mail order bride arrangements?" I ask.
A few months ago I had read about this in an academic article.

But those cases were mostly ethnic Russians from Bishkek, hoping to marry an American.

"No, no," she shakes her head, "I wanted to meet someone interesting, and we seemed to get on well in our correspondence. We exchanged messages for a few months. Then I went over there to meet him."

Wow! This country has certainly reached the age of globalisation, if village girls are on the Internet, dating foreigners and conducting long distance relationships.

"It must have cost him a lot to fund your trip, all that way," I remain sceptical.

"Oh, he could afford it. He had a house with a swimming pool in it."

From what she says about him, I gather he is well into his forties, more than twice her age.

"But why did you let yourself get pregnant in the middle of your studies? You are so young."

I realise I sound like her mother, which puts her on the defensive.

"Kyrgyz men are jealous and demanding; and they can be violent," she says with a terse look. "My father was like that. He used to beat my mother at the slightest excuse. Eventually he got into a fight with someone in our neighbourhood and ended up in jail." She pauses for a moment, then her face lights up, "But John is very different. He is kind and considerate. We had good time together. I wanted to have a child with him and was praying to get pregnant quickly. I wanted my child to be born in the US."

"What did he think about it?"

"I think John was not happy with the idea at first. He already had a teenage son and daughter. Then later when my son was born, he accepted it. He sends us regular money and tells me to take good care of the baby. I have told him it is my sister who is looking after him, while I am studying. I really hope John is going to help my sister move with us over there."

"Well, …" I want to tell her that she is hoping too much. But not to upset her, I just advise her to focus on her studies, which may provide more certain prospects for her future. I don't think she has a clue how much alienation, degradation and violence the poor in the US may suffer. If she moves over there and before long he abandons her, she will be a single parent foreigner, no family support, and very little money. She could be in for a hell of a hard life.

***

The following day, Jamila phoned. She told me she had been waiting for me at the wrong spot, even though I made it quite clear where to meet. She had now located an agency dealing in good quality housing, "the best one" she insisted. This time we met after class and set off together. There was a taxi just outside the university building, an old Lada, with its driver having a quiet snooze. He was a Kyrgyz man of middle years with a long moustache, dressed in very shabby clothes. He spoke the local dialect in the usual rapid manner that I couldn't catch from my knowledge of Turkish. After a short ride around the central streets it became clear the guy was lost. Following a couple of u-turns and enquiring from a number of passersby, a short exchange followed between Jamila and the driver. She was talking in her gentle manner, but the man's voice suddenly began to raise, his tone getting quite angry as he glared at us through his front mirror.
"What is the matter?" I asked.

"He is stupid," Jamila scorned. "He says I gave him wrong directions, the street doesn't exist. He is telling me, 'don't talk to me like that, I am your elder.'"

"Why, what did you? … ."

But before I could finish my sentence, the guy had suddenly stopped the vehicle and turned round facing us. Another short exchange followed between him and Jamila. He was now shouting and waving a fist in the air. A moment later he opened the door on his side, got out of the car, and rushed around towards the back passenger seat, where Jamila was sitting.

In a reflex action, I opened the door on my side and jumped out, pulling Jamila by the arm as hard as I could. If we were going to be assaulted, I did not want to be inside the vehicle.

"What the hell?" I shouted once on the pavement, "What is the matter with him?"

Jamila was obviously shaken, and followed my lead, quickly stepping away from the cab. She then said, "He wanted us to leave his car."

"Is that all? He could have just said so."

The man now gave us a stern look and mumbled something, before getting back into his seat and driving off. He had not collected his fare from me. Not that I was in a hurry to pay after such a display of senseless rage. The man's behaviour had made me think of the wild Kyrgyz tribesmen who roamed the mountains of this land for centuries, waging war on neighbouring tribes. But in reality he was just a tired old taxi driver, having to face a cocky young female at the end of a long day. Fortunately, we did not have to worry about finding the address we were looking for. Soon a boy serving at a kiosk nearby pointed us in the right direction.

The charm of an ex-Soviet city

The agency office was on the ground floor of a three storey building. The patch of pavement outside had the shine of new white tiles and the front door and windows were in white PVC. This place was clearly upmarket, as reflected in their fees, far higher than the other agencies with their poorly furnished offices. But luck was not on our side. On arrival we were told it was only ten minutes to closing time. On a Saturday they shut early. The woman attending us didn't think she had enough time to search through her list and arrange for visits.

"Please tell her I am short of time," I pleaded. "I need to view the places this weekend. I can't return on Monday just to register."

The woman seemed oblivious to my request, maintaining a blank expression as if she had not heard a word. Just at this point her phone rang and she began a lengthy chat. Some minutes later, she turned to us and said briefly, "I am sorry. You have to come back on Monday." Clearly there was no arguing with her.

Outside on the street, I felt angry and disappointed. Noticing this, Jamila said, "They are lazy and selfish. They don't want to help people." She then gave me a sympathetic look and added, "It must be difficult for you coming from London. I think people there are very kind and polite."

"Not always. But over there, employees of a shop or an agency know they are selling something, so they have to work for it."

Here, on the other hand, I could see that the legacies of poor Soviet service industry still lingered on. In the past all retail business used to be owned and managed by the state.

We now hovered around for a while wondering what to do next. It was another very warm, sunny day, with little traffic on the road.

I bought a packet of cigarettes and a couple of soft drinks from the little kiosk on the corner and took a break on an old wooden bench under the tall birch trees. We sat down, balancing ourselves carefully. As I lit a cigarette, I told Jamila, I was well aware of women smoking in public being considered immoral over here. But since there was no one to notice us, and I looked clearly a foreigner, I thought I could get away with it.

"I already guessed you were an open-minded lady from the way you dress. You are easy to talk to," Jamila said with a sincere look.

Whether it was this or some other motive impelling her, she then began to tell me her life story.

Jamila's family lived in Osh, the second largest city of Kyrgyzstan. It was far in the south of the country separated by mountain ranges that took some twelve hours to cross by car. Jamila was ten years old when her father died. Her mother, a school teacher, had struggled to raise her and her younger brother on her meagre income. State employees' salaries kept diminishing in value in the post-Soviet era. Jamila had come to Bishkek upon the invitation of an aunt, who lived here with her own family of three daughters and a son. Passing the entry exam of the International University was a great achievement for her; it gave her the chance to be educated at the most prestigious university in the country, and hopefully a well-paid job at the end. The first couple of years had been tough and unhappy. She was spending most of her spare time cooking, cleaning and being ordered around by her older cousins. But as her English improved she was able to get jobs that paid her relatively well, and eventually move out. In the third year she had her lucky break when an American teacher, Roger, who had just taken a year's appointment at the university, fell in love with her and proposed to marry her. She now lived in an apartment rented by him. He had moved to Osh city, in the south of the country, working for an NGO over there; he came to visit her from time to time. Jamila had the looks of a cute Chinese doll with shiny black hair and flawless skin. Her gentle voice and manners were most endearing.

With no prompting, she began to discuss her relationship with her American fiancé. She seemed anxious about his commitment to her, despite the engagement. "I have told him that he was the first man I slept with. I hope he believed me."

"Why is that important to you?"

"I don't want him to think I was not a good girl because I was not a virgin. This is very important in our culture."

"But he is not from your culture."

"Oh, he knows a lot about it, even speaks some Kyrgyz."

"So, did you have other boyfriends before him?"

"No, he was the first."

"Then how did you ...?"

"Shall we go, Miss?" Jamila now suggested. We had both finished our drinks.

We walked down the road in the direction we had come from, looking for a taxi. With her head lowered, Jamila began in a hesitant voice.

"You, you see Miss, ... a couple of years after my father died, my uncle came to live with us, and ..." She stopped mid-sentence. I had a feeling that something awful was to follow, but did not want to delve into it. Catching a glimpse of my eyes, she averted hers and continued, "My uncle was a bad man, very bad man." She stopped again and sighed, then added in a solemn voice, "Basically, he abused me, and that is how I lost my virginity."

"Did you tell your mother about it?" I asked her after a silence.

"No, I did not want to upset her too much. He was her brother."

"How old were you when this happened?"

"I was twelve."

"Did you tell anyone else?"

"Only my fiancé. I have not talked to anyone else about it."

So now I was privy to her deep secret, something I had to carry with me in confidence. If this had happened in the UK, I could have referred her to a whole host of counsellors and psychologists. But in these countries, even if worse things happened to children, they just had to salvage the rest of their lives and get on with it.

***

Later that evening, sitting alone at home, I am wondering what the heck I am doing in this Godforsaken country. On a Saturday night I was always out with friends, or if my German prince was around, we would go out to the theatre, or for a meal at a nice restaurant. Now I am sitting here among my over-filled bags and suitcases, most of them still unpacked. I had anticipated that by now I would have found another apartment. For entertainment, I only have the cable TV with a couple of English language channels. They broadcast mostly news programmes: hours of war footage, politicians being economical with the truth, and coverage of natural and man-made disasters. Worst of all is the American Fox News channel that I had never viewed before coming here. Around the clock, they beam out a concoction of ignorance and distortions. Oh if only I could phone home and see what is happening over there? But to phone Europe from here is very expensive. The old Soviet telecom system has barely changed. I have to strictly ration my calls.

The charm of an ex-Soviet city

Now, after so many years of worrying about my son's schooling, and keeping him immune from the problems of street violence, drink and drugs, I am free once more to focus on my career. For years, I had dreamt of coming to Central Asia, the land of my ancestors, to live, work and travel. But now that I am finally here I miss London. That microcosm of every colour, race, and nationality; a place where migrants and refugees alike could melt away, alleviate the pain of displacement and exile. I miss the sounds and smells of the local markets, the high streets with their familiar chain stores, and the countless cinemas, theatres and art galleries. Then there is that house of culture, the arts complex on the south bank of the River Thames, and the beautiful walkway to Shakespeare's Globe theatre with its pavement cafes and views of the river. It is a district I regard as a place of nourishment for the soul.

Tonight, gripped with nostalgia, I survey my unpacked bags and have a strong desire to book the first available flight back home. But this thought brings a sense of defeat as I imagine the disappointment on the faces of my students if they hear of my sudden departure. Finally, to change my mood I step out onto the little balcony off the sitting room. There is a full moon above and a canopy of stars blinking in the dark velvet sky. The street below is finally quiet, hardly any cars pass by. It must be close to midnight. I lean on the metal railings around the edge of the balcony and look up. It must be magical on nights like this to stroll on the high mountain pastures of this land and gaze at the stars. I have an inkling of it from a tourist advert frequently shown on local TV: a landscape of green hilly pastures under a bright blue sky with snow-capped mountains in the distance. There are a number of traditional yurts, round tents made of felt, dotted around. Among them a few horses quietly graze on the meadow. A Kyrgyz rider wearing the tall embroidered white felt hat gallops in the distance. Two little boys run to greet him, playfully tumbling and laughing along the way. A young woman in her ankle length, flowing dress and embroidered, cone-shaped hat emerges from a yurt. She leaves the front hatch open for the viewers to glance at the elegantly crafted rugs and tapestries that adorn the interior of the tent. Their design depicts elements of nature: the sun, the moon, the stars, birds and flowers.

As I reflect on these enchanting images of rural life, the quiet of the night is suddenly broken with the phone ringing. I am startled and feel apprehensive. Who is calling me so late at night? "Hello ?" I say hesitantly.

"Ah, hello Sima," a familiar male voice greets me.

"Gerhard,…" I almost shout, delighted to be contacted by someone from that other world.

"I have been trying to call you for hours but couldn't get a line. … now the connection is perfect."

Indeed, Gerhard sounds as if he is on the next street, but he is at home in Bonn. After a brief conversation, I ask when he is coming over.

"I have a meeting at the Ministry in two weeks time. I will try to come over the week after."

"But you are supposed to be retired now, why do you have to attend meetings every week?" I say in an agitated tone.

"I am tied up at present with this consultancy project. I *told* you about it already".

I sense a row is brewing up long distance, making this an expensive call for him. I should take it easy; he'll be doing me a favour, I tell myself.

The charm of an ex-Soviet city

In the rush to leave London, I have left my laptop behind, along with my boots and my winter coat. He has promised to go over there to my flat to pick them up for me. At the same time, I wish he wasn't coming. This trip was partly to get away from him and our cul-de-sac relationship that has been going on for over a decade. But I can hardly tell him 'Don't come'. Already, in the weeks I was getting ready for the trip, he had gone to the university bookshop in Bonn and bought himself a large volume on Central Asia. His initial scepticism, following my surprise announcement that I had landed a job at such a remote location, did not last long. He certainly never said "But what about me?" Over the years, with our differing commitments, we had settled into a seasonal affair of the heart. The strong attraction we felt for each other had to meander its way through a maze of logistic complexities in different countries and across different cultures.

***

I first met Gerhard during a visit to my aunt in Istanbul. She was a student there in the 1970s, married a Turkish national and settled in the city. Gerhard was at the start of a week's sightseeing tour of the city and we met by chance at the Topkapi palace. The distinguished looking, smartly dressed tall German with a warm smile had fixed his gaze on me for some time before we began to chat. That evening he invited me to have dinner with him, and in the following days I became his companion, translator and guide to life in the East. He was an economist by training and held a top executive post in the Finance Ministry in Bonn. Many years earlier, he had done a Master's degree at a British university. Since then he visited the UK several times for meetings or holidays. In the week that I toured the city with him I was dazzled with his suave, gentlemanly, manners, his tastes and interests in the arts, and his kindness. He told me that he had been separated from his wife a decade ago and I told him I had a boy of ten who lived with me. Otherwise, we did not discuss our private lives. In the two months that followed our parting, Gerhard Von Stein, the *ministerial direktor*, the most eminent man I had ever kissed, rarely let an evening go by without phoning me at length. But a kiss was all that it was for me, and only after copious amounts of wine on our last evening together. At first I had been highly flattered with the attention, though the thought of a sexual affair with a man eighteen years my senior was unappealing. But by the end of our two months of telephone romance, I had dumped the rocky relationship I was in at the time, and taken off the first available weekend to be with him in Bonn. I had imagined he would want nothing better than to spend every hour of those two days and nights with me. Foolish thoughts, as it turned out.

On the Friday afternoon when I arrived in Bonn, my first visit to the city, he did not even have time to pick me up at the airport. I had to make my own way to his office. He welcomed me to a plush suite with a large leather sofa and a fancy new bathroom. He had an emergency meeting, he said, and would be back within the hour. Meanwhile, he told me, I could browse through his large bookcase that included a number of English language books, or take a nap on the sofa if I felt tired. He had been wooing me for weeks, long distance. I expected a more attentive reception. When he finally appeared in the room, two hours later, I was ready to chuck the bouquet of pink roses he had given me in the bin, and take a cab back to the airport.

Later that evening, impressed with the charm of his beautiful art deco house close to the banks of the river Rhine, and his warm welcome, I forgot my earlier disappointment. Then the following day, a Saturday, I was mostly on my own among his countless collection of paintings, sculptures and other works of art. It felt like a solitary museum visit with the doors firmly shut and no human warmth inside. His son and daughter who normally lived with him were away at the time and the cleaner who came in for her twice weekly round, only spoke German, a language as yet unfamiliar to me. Then in the evening, he tried to make up for it by taking me on a lovely walk by the river, after which we dined at a plush restaurant. Later, when we got home, he impressed me with his exquisite collection of art work. But come Sunday morning, I was again on my own; he had to attend an emergency meeting.

Finally that afternoon, I began to think, this was going to be a relationship full of frustration, more trouble than it was worth. I then told him, "I am sorry, this is not going to work. You don't have any room in your life for a woman."

He paused for a moment, never a man of quick reactions, then took my hand in his, looked me in the eye and said calmly, "You see, every woman dreams of a prince charming who will come and sweep her off her feet. What she does not realise is that for him to remain a prince, he has to devote himself to his domain. And therein lies the dilemma."

Yes, he could be that modern day German prince who had come for me in his shiny white Mercedes. But was this what I wanted? A prince in a distant land in whose domain I would lose myself, give up my own dreams? I was already smitten with his charm. Perhaps it was not too late for me, though aged forty, to have a new start in life and tackle a new language in a new country. But my better judgement told me, I should get out now before I sank too deep. When I left him at Bonn airport I made no arrangements for a future meeting. Two weeks later however, Gerhard was at the door of my London flat, wishing to spend the weekend with me, and no distractions. The following month, he had talked me into joining him for a holiday in a luxury villa in the Alps, my young son in tow. And that was how our saga began; one that does not seem to end, even with me escaping to the mountains of Central Asia.

Chapter II

My Kyrgyz family

My new two-bedroom apartment in Bishkek is superb, beyond my expectation. It is in a three storey grand old block, on the corner of Erkendik and Toktogul, only a ten minute walk from the university. Built in the 1930s and referred to as *Stalinka*, these were the preserve of the old elite, the communist party hierarchy. They have some of the charm of Old Europe, distinct from the boxy apartment blocks constructed in later years. Inside, the rooms are spacious with tall windows and very high ceilings decorated with ornate plaster work. It's a shame about the fading 1970s furnishings. They mar the building's opulence. The minimalist kitchen also leaves a lot to be desired. It's a bright spacious room with an old gas cooker, a sink, a few formica cupboards and a small table and three chairs. The outdated, meagre interior of this apartment contrasts sharply with its grand structure; a feature not uncommon in many early Soviet buildings. Still, I am happy. I have a wardrobe to hang clothes in and a decent size desk to work at. What is more, there is a small balcony off the kitchen overlooking a large courtyard. It's covered in shrubbery, delineated by rough ground. There are a number of acacia and birch trees dotted around. The snow-capped peaks of Tien Shan are just about visible from the vista afforded on the balcony. On a sunny day I can sit here for a quiet smoke and marvel at the distant view.

Big Clara, my new landlady, comes on a Friday to do the cleaning and laundry. She even irons my underwear and T-shirts; a luxury I associate with colonial ladies. When I took the flat, I told her that living on my own I had no need for a cleaner. But she insisted. I bartered her down from 30 to 20 dollars a month. Later I felt a bit mean, but I have to live on a monthly salary of 200. That is what the university pays its foreign professors; the locals only get 120. The rent is another 200 a month, paid by the university. The owner's family of five live on that.

Clara is tall, big and tough, in the way of a Russian peasant, but with the face of a noble Kyrgyz woman. She has almond eyes, an elegant nose and a rose bud of a mouth. Her short hair, greying at the temples, is always neatly groomed. She is polite and pleasant, doesn't talk much. Despite my poor Russian, we manage to communicate somehow. I asked her about her European name.

"My father was a strong communist. He admired Clara Zetkin," she replied.

Zetkin, the German socialist-feminist, had inspired many of the early Bolshevik women; among them, Armand, Lenin's wife, and Kollontai, the radical revolutionary whose controversial writings on free love had greatly impressed me and my friends in the 1970s. In the 1920s, Zetkin had visited Baku, the intellectual and industrial centre of Muslim Russia at the time. She considered Muslim women the most oppressed of the Russian Empire's subjects, and campaigned vigorously for their liberation through education and unveiling. Hence many Claras in the Muslim republics. I had met a few already in Azerbaijan.

***

When my landlady came to visit me a second time, I found out she was not the owner. The flat used to belong to her parents, later inherited by her younger sister, Elmira, who died last year. On the day I moved in I met a middle-aged Kyrgyz man I took to be Clara's husband; he was helping her hang curtains in the lounge. Later in the afternoon, a teenage girl and a little boy turned up. She referred to them as her children. The boy was clinging to her, and the girl was quickly set to work, cleaning the bathroom. It turned out they were actually her niece and nephew. Clara seems to have completely stepped into her dead sister's shoes, acting as if in charge of the property, the husband and the children. But what about her own family? Women usually marry young in Central Asia and go on to have children very soon. A woman in her forties is often a grandmother. I can see that Clara must have been very good looking when young, before the onset of obesity. She would have had many suitors. But she does not mention anything about a husband.

Nina, daughter of the deceased owner, is sixteen, atypically tall and very slim. She greets me with a shy smile. This is her last year of school; she would love to enter our university next year. But the 2000 dollars yearly tuition fee may be beyond her family's means. To get a scholarship she would have to get top grades and improve her command of English. I have offered her an hour's conversation practise on Sundays. In our first session she told me she really missed living here, so close to her school. Her current home is in a newly built *microrayon* suburb, quite far from central Bishkek. It's a one hour journey, two bus-rides away. Her school friends mostly live in this neighbourhood, and her best friend, Irina, lives in one of the apartments facing this courtyard. When we stepped out onto the balcony, she pointed it out to me and said, "We homework together, Sundays. Now I no more see her." Her dark eyes were filled with sadness. Poverty had driven Nina from her home, and I was the new occupier. I felt like the usurper of her happiness. But what could I do? I needed a place and they needed the money.

"Would you like to go and see her when we finish?" I aked.

"No," she declined. She was due home to help her aunt with housework.

I went on to ask Nina about her siblings. She told me she had a twin brother who died six years ago, the day before her youngest brother, Aslan was born. She also had a fifteen year old stepbrother on her father's side, living with them since he was nine years old.

"But your step brother is younger than you," I puzzled. "Did your father leave your mother and go back to his first wife?"

"No, why? My father not divorce his wife before. She much older, have grandchildren."

Well, it didn't surprise me that her father had been a bigamist. Despite the Soviet laws banning polygamy, the custom had survived unofficially in Central Asia. My students often talked about it. But how did Nina's father, an older man, keep his relatively young wife happy and produce two children, with another wife tucked away?

Had he been rich, or high up in the party? I had come into their lives a decade after the Soviet breakup; I did not have the full picture. In the post-Soviet deluge, when factories closed down, savings lost their value, and the welfare system vanished, the malaise of new poverty gripped the nation like a plague. That was when Nina's father, an architect with 25 years service for the state lost his job; the construction business in the city was now dominated by Turkish companies. In the new era the knowledge and expertise of a Soviet trained man was considered obsolete. The redundant architect had to make do with a small income from handyman jobs for the wealthy in central Bishkek.

At the time, Nina's mother, an accountant, worked for the city authorities. With her salary rapidly diminishing in value, she took up domestic service to make ends meet. Like all Kyrgyz girls she had learnt to clean, cook and sew from a young age. The first family she worked for were Turkish diplomats. In the two years that she served them, she learnt the language and further developed her cooking skills, instructed by the accomplished wife of the diplomat. In particular she learnt to bake cakes and pastries. Eventually, she started her own small baking business at home, delivering her products to nearby shops. Most days there was little to do in the office; the city authorities were bankrupt.

Nina now began to tell me about her twin brother, with whom she shared the bedroom that is my study. One summer's day, six years ago, they had gone visiting a friend's house that was under construction. With the ground floor completed, the family had moved in, although the roof was not yet finished. Scaffolding stood outside the front. It was a hot day, and the children were playing in the yard. The family's two adolescent boys began to climb the metal structure. Nina's brother, not to be left behind, followed. Nina also wanted to join them, but they shouted at her, "You can't come. You are a girl." She felt disappointed and envious of her brother. The boys now stood on a plank of wood at the top of the scaffolding, waving their arms in a winglike motion. They boasted of seeing far into the distance like the eagles that flew overhead. Nina's brother had not quite reached them when all of a sudden a metal bar he was walking on came unhinged. He managed to hold onto one end as he fell, screaming with fear and calling for his mother. Nina then ran inside to tell her parents. The party were busy downing their vodkas, to toast the construction of the new house.

When everyone rushed to the scene, Nina's brother had already crashed onto the ground, head first, and lay in a pool of blood. Her mother, eight months pregnant, was kept away from the boy as her father carried him in his arms to a neighbour with a car, and onto the hospital. The boy died a day later, as his mother went into labour. Nina seemed still haunted by the memory of her brother's battered and bloodied face, distorted from the swelling of his brain. Later, in the years that followed, little Aslan had brought much joy and happiness to the family. Everyone said he carried his deceased brother's spirit. His smile seemed an exact copy, and he displayed a great fear of heights.

A month after Aslan was born Nina's father and his son from his first wife moved in with them for good. The boy's mother could no longer take care of him. She herself relied on her two married daughters for her livelihood. But Nina's growing happiness came to an abrupt end one day last year, when another tragedy struck. Her mother, a healthy, ambitious woman of thirty seven, suddenly fell ill after eating a plate of salad, and died the next day.

On that fatal day, Nina's mother had invited a number of friends for lunch. The previous day, she had gone to the Osh bazaar and bought a variety of salads to serve. This was a large open market on the western edge of the city, where everything from household goods to footwear, dresses and fresh food are laid out on stalls and bartered for. The meal had gone well, but early in the evening she had become very sick and was taken to a hospital. Her condition had deteriorated the next day.

"Was your mother allergic to anything?" I asked Nina, wondering how a plate-full of salad could kill a person. She did not know. But given the state of hospitals in this country, so many things could have gone wrong in the process of treating her. Fortunately for Nina, she had been out on that day and missed the lunch. She did not see her mother being taken away. The next day in the hospital, her mother seemed incapable of talking to her. She was gasping for breath, looking extremely pale. That was when aunt Clara came over from her home city of Tokmok to take care of her dying sister's family.

***

Later that afternoon, I meet a colleague, Reza, to go to our local fresh food market. It is a colourful place, an indoor square hall where stalls are laid out, covered with a variety of fruit, vegetables, herbs, dry fruit and nuts. The sellers are mostly Kyrgyz, but not the buyers. Prices here are higher than in Osh bazaar and other local markets. The cheap stuff is offered by a line of women on the street outside. They come dressed in rural fashion, long skirts and little headscarves tied at the back. They sit on a tiny plastic stool, offering their own produce from tin buckets.

Reza tells me, he finds the fresh produce here expensive, and only comes for the readymade salads. He points to a row of counters at the back of the hall and leads the way. There is an enticing display of neatly piled different beans, beetroot, cabbage, peas, and above all carrots. Grated carrot seems to be a national favourite in Kyrgyzstan. Every restaurant, café and canteen, including the one at our university, offers it, hot or cold. The Kyrgyz must have great eyesight

I stand by the counter, wondering what to chose, but the thought of the killer salad leaves me cold. I tell Reza about Nina's mother and my concerns. "Oh, no," he dismisses them. " Everything is clean and very fresh, he points out. "Maybe that woman ate a fish salad that had been left in the sun."

"I'll give it a miss for today," I tell him, and move on to buy a load of fruit and vegetables. The aubergines, in particular, look very appetising. They have ripened in the sunshine of Uzbekistan, as with the peaches and apricots that are exceptionally juicy and sweet. When we get back to my place, Reza carries most of my shopping up the stairs and I invite him in for Turkish coffee, his favourite. I get the stuff from the Turkish Beta Store, the only supermarket in town. In total I have only spent 400 Soms (eight dollars), on all the groceries. "Don't you find it very cheap living here?" I ask Reza.

"Yes, I guess ...," he confirms half heartedly, and adds that he has to save up for his trip home to Manchester at Christmas. His five year old son, Amin, just started school in September. "I should have been there for him, but this job came up ...." he shrugs with a guilty look on his face. He has mentioned being married, but never talks about his wife. Being estranged from her would be a good reason to come this far away. Here he can play the field; European and American men are keenly sought after by local women. Reza has the south Asian dark skin, which makes him less desirable in their eyes, though his British nationality more than makes up for it. He is slim, with a handsome face and an amicable persona, popular with the female staff. Not that I could be interested myself. God forbid! Being a Muslim man, twelve years my junior, he would never fancy me. Just as well, I am happy to have him as a friend and colleague.

Early that same evening, we go to the opera, accompanied by Gulnur, the office manageress in Reza's department, Julie, the American anthropologist, and a French couple, Marie and Gerard, both fellow-CACE teachers. Gulnur graduated from this university two years ago. She is half Uzbek, half Kyrgyz. I think she is having it off with Reza, on the quiet. She organised the tickets for everyone. It is a performance of Puccini's Madam Butterfly, one of my favourites. Every capital city in the former Soviet Union has an opera house built in the grand European style. Bishkek is no exception. Communist ideology considered access to high culture the right of the 'toiling masses'. Tickets are a dollar each, soon to go up to three dollars. A German woman in the audience tells me there is a Friends of the Opera Club formed recently to support local productions and help the artists stay in the country.

Tonight's performance actually has a soprano coming from Byelorussia, making it more popular than usual; the theatre is jam packed. The singer is great and the orchestra play well, but there is noise behind me; a couple of local women keep conversing. I turn around and give them a cross look; but they ignore me. I have noticed this kind of disregard for others in the audience in Baku's opera house. It makes the performances in Covent Garden worth every penny. I now try to ignore the noise behind me, and sink into the melancholic mood of the music; it's an evocation of the tragic-romantic story of Madam Butterfly and her doomed love affair. The sadness is made the more poignant for me, as I recall the real life story of Nina's family. It is hard to get it off my mind.

Not to wallow too much in unhappiness, I focus on the critical side of the operatic story, a tale of love, betrayal, humiliation and exploitation across alien cultures. American colonialism in the land of the rising sun follows the defeat of the Japanese in WWII, and a little geisha woman is caught up in a cycle of love and deceit with her American suitor, with tragic consequences for her and the child she conceives. Reflecting on the situation in Kyrgyzstan, I wonder, how many Kyrgyz Madam Butterflies will emerge now that the Americans have defeated their Soviet enemy.

***

After the opera we go to an Italian restaurant, offering a Kyrgyz adaptation of pastas and pizzas. Everyone is in a good mood. I participate in the banter and the laughter, but have a heavy sense of detachment; everything I utter feels like someone else's words. It is one of those occasional bouts of deep anxiety I cannot decipher, but why? My work at the university is going well and no worrisome news from home. I am finally distracted from myself, when the topic of bi-cultural identity comes up. Gerard was born in Paris to Greek parents and speaks three languages. Like me, he is tri-lingual. Reza was born in Pakistan and went to school in Manchester. He is of the opinion that growing up with two cultures gives you more of a birds-eye view of life. I agree with him and think that it can also make you someone hard to impress, but say nothing. Julie smiles broadly and says, "I never heard a word other than in English until I was twenty." She is from a strict Baptist family, born in a small town in Kansas; she goes to Mass every Sunday. Marie and Gerard often accompany her. I suspect more out of boredom with life in Bishkek.

***

Back home, I watch some TV before going to bed. I receive the BBC Prime channel on the cable. It shows old comedies and popular serials, the kind of programmes I don't normally watch. The exception is East Enders, that well-acted, gritty, unglamorous portrayal of life in London. My friends laugh at me, disappointed that a woman with a PhD can sit and watch trivia on a regular basis. But it is in the nature of soaps to be addictive. Their familiar, identifiable characters, a virtual social network concocted through the fantasy of a few professional writers. Gossip has an important function in human life, common to all cultures. Why else do millions make a ritual of watching them? Coming to Bishkek, I thought, a whole year without it would finally cure me of my habit. I could not imagine that soon the habit would turn into an addiction.

It was a few days after I arrived here that one night in my previous flat I turned the TV on and was amazed to see Pauline Fowler talking to her son Martin. What? East Enders in Kyrgyzstan? Oh boy! How reassuring that was. On weekdays at midnight, I could lie on my sofa for a half hour and completely forget I was in Bishkek. I was back home in London, close to everyone I loved, and none of the poverty, dilapidation, and the insecurity I had to witness here. Over there, I could nip out to my corner shop late at night, to do a last minute shopping, or if lonely, call Anna for a late night heart to heart, swapping notes on our sons and lovers. E-mailing is a monologue, too impersonal and unresponsive. I have only written to her once since I came here; this world is so far removed from hers, I don't know where to start.

Tonight my favourite soap is not shown; I switch to one of the Russian language channels. There is a Bruce Willis action film on with Russian voice over. This style of translating dialogue is very popular here; it is far cheaper than professional dubbing. If you are lucky, the voice over is done so badly that you catch most of the English dialogue in the delay. But after a while it stops being amusing. You just wish the robotic Russian voice would shut up and let the original dialogue come through. I stop watching and listen to music instead. Mein Herr is supposed to come to Bishkek next week. The weather is getting cold; the first snow is due before the end of the month. I will then need my winter coat and boots. Otherwise I don't miss him. The longer I stay here, the more I feel alienated from him and his ways: his taking the luxuries he lives with for granted and his naïve, good natured expectations of people. He cannot see the malice that surrounds the lives of so many people around the world. As long as he keeps his distance, going about his daily affairs in the safe confines of a highly developed country, he may keep his optimism about human nature and his trust in the power of human will. He can afford to laugh at the notion of *kismet*, the oriental concept of destiny.

"Wasn't that the title of a bad musical?" he once joked in response to me saying I believed in it. Brought up in the tradition of western individualism, he believes we are all masters of our own destiny, able to exercise control over the trajectory of our lives. Two hundred years of Adam Smith's "Rational Man" have been drummed into him through his studies of law and economics in Germany and the UK. "You make your own luck," he often says.

I wonder now, what he would say about young Nina's control over her destiny, and the tragic events that shaped her and her mother's life. What part did young Nina play in the breakup of the Soviet Union that led to deteriorating hygiene, health care and public services with dire consequences? What was bad by western standards, previously, had today become terrible. Nina's family, like millions of others in their region, had to reluctantly bear witness to Big Brother Russia washing its hands of its former colonies, telling them they were now free and had to fend for themselves. Unlike the Baltic republics with their independent history, these lands had only known modernity through Russia, later, the Soviet Union. They equated "progress" with being part of it. With independence, every republic had to survive in a climate of economic chaos. Their main trading partner, scientific centre, and master planner had vanished without notice.

And it was in such circumstances that the Central Asian republics, like abandoned orphans, began to squabble among themselves. Rivalries and inter-state tensions began to emerge over water resources, rights to mineral extraction, ownership of land, and trade tariffs. The ceremonious conferences have so far yielded few resolutions. Meanwhile, within the borders of each country, with the ensuing poverty and lawlessness, a musical chairs of wealth grabbing has begun. They call it the privatisation programme: state assets sold dirt cheap to those with connections to the former communist party hierarchy. In this imported game of neo-liberal market economy, a whole class of New Poor has arisen, not knowing which way to turn.

Nina's mother, growing up among the elite in her society, had once been assured a successful future as a civil engineer. The old piano she played over the years still stands in the corner of my sitting room. I am now the occupant of this woman's home, surrounded by the furnishings she has chosen. The place has her mark of identity, and I have not asked for any alterations. The family neither has the space to store my cast-offs, nor the means to acquire additional items. The only change I requested was to remove the very large machine made rug that hung above the sofa in the sitting room; a customary style of room decor in Central Asia. The walls had recently been painted in pastel green, and I wanted them clutter free. But when Nina came today she seemed disappointed.

"Why you no like the carpet?" she asked with a shy smile.

"I am used to seeing big rugs under my feet," I said.

She kept staring at the empty space on the wall, and with her mind's eye scanning the patterns and colours that evoked the bitter sweet memories of her life here. It was hard to ignore her sadness. But Nina is strong, resilient and ambitious, at least outwardly. She does her school work diligently and helps with housework. No doubt Clara's presence has been a great support to her and to little Aslan who seems a cheerful child.

***

On this night when I go to bed, my thoughts are with Nina's mother. I am sleeping in her bed, wondering what she was really like. I have not even seen a picture of her. Did she conceive those children on this bed? Was she lying here with pangs of pain on her last day before going to hospital? I feel wary of sleeping in a dead person's bed. A few days after I moved in I bought a new cotton mattress from the Osh bazaar to replace the lumpy old one that was here. Now I sense that I am in for a restless night of difficult sleep. I toss and turn for ages, before I finally doze off.

In my dream I am walking in the street outside the university. It is very dark and the place is deserted. As I get close to my building, I notice a figure approaching me slowly. It is a tall person in a black coat, wearing the tall Kyrgyz hat that men wear. The white felt stands very bright against the dark of the night. I lower my gaze, avoiding his face, and quicken my pace. I have the feeling that he is staring at me with menace. When I get close to my building, he gets closer. Now my pace slows down and I can't help but look up at him. How strange, it is not a male but a female with shoulder length hair. What is more, the stick-like figure she has her arm around is no object. It is a young girl, Nina.

Before they reach me, I have arrived at the arched entrance to my courtyard, and pass through very quickly, just avoiding them. I hasten my pace and almost run to my block. I scramble in my handbag for the keys. Seconds seem like minutes until I get hold of the key and turn it. But it's gone very stiff, won't open the door. I look sideways, and see the two figures are standing a few feet away. They have caught up with me.

"Help her. You have to," the dark figure yells, pushing the stick-like figure forward. Her words are emitted in blue electric waves against the dark of the night. But what help? I know that Nina badly wants to enter our university. If she could get a degree from there it would ensure her good job opportunities, and perhaps some prosperity for the family.

But I am in no position to secure such a prospect. I am not even sure that I will get my own son through university, let alone the daughter of some ghost. Then eventually, the door opens and I walk quickly up the stairs, which is thankfully lit. The figures have not managed to follow me. Once inside, I go straight to the kitchen and the balcony door, I look out from the unlit room to see if the ghostly figures have disappeared. There is no sign of them. The courtyard is silent and clear. I sigh with relief. A few seconds later, the voice is back, right behind me. I am terrified, yet ashamed of my fear. I turn round and head towards the kitchen door, hoping to escape this apparition. But as I dive into the hallway, I feel a massive impact, as if hit by lightning. The vibration is so strong; every fibre in my body is shaking. A shooting pain rises up through my chest to the crown of my head. I wake up drenched in sweat.

When I finally get up and leave the bed for the bathroom, I feel aching all over, my muscles stiff. I want to lie down again. Outside, the sky is a little lighter; dawn is breaking. There is the faint sound of a cockerel in the distance. I am glad it is a Monday, no classes to teach in the morning.

***

Later that day I am very busy at the university. The ethnology department has a meeting. Julie and I attend, along with the local staff, only one of whom, Gulzat, speaks a few words of English. The meeting drags on. I get the gist of what is being said. Julie who has to rely entirely on Gulzat's poor translation, nevertheless carries on with her nods and smiles, as if she follows it all. She has been timetabled to teach a four week staff development course in western teaching techniques. Attending a class taught by a white American is very prestigious here. But how is she going to communicate subtle ideas solely with charts and diagrams? When I raise this point with her, I get a stern look. "It is not a theory class," she scorns. Her glance then moves quickly onto the others and her smile reappears.   I try to ignore Julie's generally negative attitude towards me. Luckily, she can only manage the introductory courses, leaving me the theory classes. At least with the seniors I don't have to double up as a language tutor.

Chapter III

Tribulations of an absent mother

That evening, before going home, I pop into the staff computer room to check my e-mails. In my in-box there is one from Jamie sent earlier today. I am delighted; he has not written for some time.

Hi Mum, I had a lucky escape last night. A car hit me near Nottingham city centre, but I am OK. Just some bruise. Basically I went with my friends from university to a club in town. I left early because I was getting fed up with student social life and all these drunk dickheads. I was in the kebab shop getting something to eat and waiting for my friends to come out when this local gang came in they were taunting me. You know me I'm getting past all that bullshit but last night I was getting fed up with the whole nottingham scene and thought fuck this why should I take shit from these fake chiefs. I am not one of these country bumpkins here. When one of them pushed me I pushed him back hard. They were going to jump on me so I took off fast as I ran to the other side of the road a car hit me. I was lucky he did not hit me hard. They took me to hospital and gave me a few stitches in my head. They sent me home this morning. Dont worry about me Mum. I'm ok now.

The message sends a shiver down my back. I sit staring at the computer screen for awhile. A head injury is no trivial matter, how can I not worry?

Jamie's style is to resort to ample slang to cover up his sub-standard English and lazy writing; for years, a source of irritation for me, and regular arguments between us. But I don't care about any of that now; I am only concerned about how he is coping alone in that dormitory room, with no one to care for him. Is he telling me everything about his injuries? He is a proud boy, capable of taking a lot of pain, and concerned to be seen strong. In his last message a couple of weeks ago he had expressed unhappiness with his accommodation: all night noise of people coming and going, and frequent parties around him. He was not into binge drinking, or drugs, did not feel he fitted in culturally, and badly missed his friends in London. Still, he wanted to carry on, hoping he would adjust.

Now I feel guilty. I was the one who encouraged him to move out of London and live on campus, thinking he would be safer, able to focus on his studies. But expecting success at university from a dyslexic child is wishing for your number to come up at a prize draw. During his school years, I had so many PTA meetings, in which I was told he was at the bottom of the class. I would come away, feeling depressed, worrying about his future. After a year of haggling and hustling with the educational bosses, he was finally granted one hour a week of special tuition at what his class-mates called the "spastics unit". Jamie, as with the other boy in that unit, went along with a long face determined not to learn anything.

Land of Forty Tribes

Now I look back and blame myself most of all. If only I had been aware of his needs from the start, given him more attention and consistency, not had a change of career, life partners and residences. My Jamie had the instability of being the child of an anthropologist mother on the move, and a Peter Pan father. When I complain to my sister, Mina, she tells me off: "He is such a good boy, so charming. Forget about academic achievement." But how can I? I spend my time educating other people's children. When I tried to tutor him myself, it often deteriorated into episodes of stressful arguments and name calling. Eventually I gave up; I was no educational psychologist. And yet, he is a bright boy, a real lateral thinker. If only I had the money for a specialist private school, or if he had a more ambitious father. Steve was reluctant even to contribute to his private lessons, though he earned more than me. His excuse was, "I never had private tutors. I learnt everything at a state school."

In my frustration, I would fantasise about life in some pre-literate society. There, we would have no dealings with the written text. In the forests and by the lake shores, my son's creative streak would enhance his way with hunting animals, catching fish, and locate the precious hidden plants. His humour, good looks, and affectionate demeanour would impress his peers. He would grow up with great confidence, and I would experience motherhood as a life filled with pride and joy. This was a fantasy I entertained, living under the elitist, poorly funded British education system of the 1980s and 90s.

***

This evening after I log off the university computer, I have to rush to the internet café to call Jamie. It is not far from here, on Sovietskaya street, on the other side of the Oak Park. They offer satellite connected phones to call abroad, much cheaper than the landline. I can have a lengthy talk with my troubled son. The dusk has fallen and the streets are getting dark again. I have to cross the Oak Park in semi-darkness, avoiding all the potholes on the way. With careful rapid steps I proceed along a wide path lined with cypress trees. The moon shines dimly in the horizon, and there is silence all round, amplifying the sound of my footsteps. I try not to look far ahead; the silhouettes of the sculptured animals in the park have a ghostly appearance. But I am too anxious to be scared of the dark, or fear a mugger approaching. The thought of my boy, alone and injured in that dormitory room, is grinding my insides. All kinds of doom scenarios buzz around my head. He may be in a worse state than he is letting on. And here I am, six thousand miles away. What the hell am I doing in this bloody remote, underdeveloped country?

***

The internet café is a cramped place with three cubicles for the telephones, and half a dozen computer workstations in the narrow hall beyond them. There is a queue inside; I feel impatient and go outside to wait in the street. It's at the junction of a wide avenue, one of only a few in the city that is busy with traffic and well lit at night. Later there will be a bunch of young prostitutes, mostly Kyrgyz, huddled together on this corner, waiting to be approached by cars. I saw them for the first time a few days ago on my way back from a restaurant nearby. I was with my colleagues Reza and Jina.

"Do you want to interview them?" Jina had teased Reza.

"No. Thank you," Reza responded sharply.

The girls dressed in short skirts and little tops were shivering in the cold autumn air, only a few degrees above zero. Some of them, runaways from the rural regions had the fresh country look, with matching hairdos and cheap makeup. Winter seems to have suddenly descended on us. I wondered how the girls will fare in a few weeks time when we get the snow and ice.

Tonight, recalling the sight of those girls standing so close together for safety and comfort, I think of my own privileged position and that of my son. Whatever he has suffered, at least he is never exposed to the daily dangers and the degradation that these girls have to face. He lives in warm, comfortable surroundings, never has to hustle or labour hard to attain the basics in life. And like so many children of middle-class families in the West, he is neither aware, nor appreciative of his privileged life. In this consumption obsessed world view, prestige is established through wearing designer clothes and top Nike trainers, with action film macho men their heroes. This leaves little room for the notion of respect for parents and community elders. Sure enough, James Bond had no family ties or kin obligations. Similarly, Indiana Jones swept across a multitude of exotic locations; oblivious to intricacies of cultures he trampled on.

Jamie, emulating some of his London friends, often talks of *cotching,* their term for lazing about. This is in such contrast to the drive and motivation of the students here. But then these kids are socialised mainly through the extended family and the community. Western media is only just beginning to make inroads into their lives. Jamie and most of his friends, on the other hand, hardly know any family beyond the immediate members. It is the peer group who provide the close bonding and much of the legitimacy for their lifestyle, inspired by the media. What power could I have, a single parent, over such influences? I battled for years against those greater forces, sometimes with success, more often in failure. Finally, I took myself six thousand miles away, to the rooftop of Asia, and am nesting here. But the nest is empty and the scene has not left me. I am spared the daily grind, only to have to face major worries long distance.

***

After what seems like a very long wait, the queue has now diminished. I go in and enter one of the phone cubicles.

"Jamie? How are you love?"

"Hi, Mum. I am good, much better." He sounds cheerful.

There is a lot of background noise. He is at a shopping centre, he tells me.

"Should you be out and about so soon?"

"I am fine Mum. Stop worrying about me."

"You've got stitches in your head and you are wandering around a shopping centre," I shout into the tiny mouthpiece. The telephone connection is very poor, and I can hear the conversation from the adjoining booth. I press the headphones on my ears and listen intently. Jamie reassures me he is with a couple of friends and will soon return to the campus. I ask him about the events leading to his accident. He says he has put it all in the e-mail, and does not want to repeat. He tells me it is not convenient at this point to have a long conversation. But it never is with him. Chattiness is not his forte.

After I ring off I head home slowly, shivering from the chill in the air. In my absent-minded state, all I can do is pray for his safety and well-being. But I am an atheist, how can I pray? Then again, at moments of desperation I have turned to my early pillar of faith; the merciful Allah, or appealed to that force for goodness and creation that lies within each of us. I now wonder if my vague spirituality of the past will become a clear conviction in this harsh land, away from the comforts of my London home.

Along the route to my flat, the memory of the dream I had the night Jamie had his accident resurfaces and haunts me. The vision of Nina's ghostly mother dressed in black, clasping Nina's stick-like figure, is vivid once more. Jamie must have had his accident about the same time, around midnight, 5 a.m. Kyrgyz time. I feel a shiver run through me as I recall the memory of that dream impact and imagine Jamie's fear and pain on that night. I begin to walk very fast, almost running. Once again, I contemplate the return home to London. Not next summer or even at Christmas, but on the next flight, in three day time. I want to get away from these lonely, fearful dark nights. But alas, it is just not possible. I have to honour my commitment to my students and to CACE. What is more, there is a lot to explore about the country and the culture. I have barely begun. No, I have to stick it out, come what may.

My resolve brings a relief, though my spirits are low. I have now reached the entrance gate and begin to search in my bag for the keys to have them ready at hand. I like to minimise the nervous moments I stand alone in the dark at the entrance door of my block. Suddenly I hear a voice calling me from behind.

"Miss Omid?" I turn around. It is Jamila.

"What are you doing here?"

"We were about to go to Anna's place. She lives very near," Jamila points in the direction of Erkendik, going south. Her companion Anna, a Ukrainian, attends my anthropology class along with Jamila. She is in Bishkek on a scholarship from the International University;

her family live in Kiev. She has an intellectual interest in religion and is doing her senior thesis on the local Baptists proselytising among the Kyrgyz youth.

"Miss Omid, I came to the departmental office to see you today and waited for a while," Anna says in a disappointed tone. She has asked to be one of my tutees for her thesis. I tell her that since I don't have a personal office at this university there is no fixed place to trace me. We have to stick to an appointment system.

"Why don't you come into my apartment now and we have a chat." I offer, happy to have company.

"Is that okay?" Jamila asks. "I would love to see your apartment. Jildiz told me it was very nice."

Inside, the girls' presence radiates joyful warmth. I talk with Anna briefly about her work and give her an appointment for the following day. I offer them tea and biscuits; Jamila asks me if I miss home and my son. I tell them about his accident and my disturbing dream on that same night. I mention the death of Nina's mother and her ghostly appearance in my dream.

"You should listen to your dreams," Jamila responds, her eyes widening.

"In Kyrgyz culture we believe the ancestors give you messages in your dreams."

"But I am not Kyrgyz, I have no ancestors here."

"Now you live here, in that lady's home. Her spirit is not far from you."

She goes on to talk about her grandmother's dream last year.

"When I first told my mother about my plan to get engaged to Roger, she was not happy. When he came to visit us he was very nice to them, still they disapproved. She wanted me to marry a Kyrgyz man, not a foreigner. Then a few weeks later, my grandmother, who had been living with us since my grandfather died, had a dream. She was standing outside her old house in the village, waiting for her husband to return from his search for his horse. It was a beautiful horse he had been riding for many years and loved like a son. It was getting late and my grandmother was getting worried for her husband and his horse. Then she saw a rider galloping towards her with speed; she could not see the rider's face clearly, but recognised my grandfather's horse. When the man reached her, he dismounted and gave her the reigns. She suddenly recognised him. It was Roger. He greeted her in his foreign-accented Kyrgyz, as on that first day he had come to our apartment in Osh. After her dream, my grandmother began telling my mother that Roger was a good man and it would be the wish of our ancestors that he marries me."

"Maybe," I say in a sceptical tone, "your grandmother was really impressed that Roger had learnt Kyrgyz, but revealed it later."

"No, Miss. She really had that dream. It changed her mind."

I don't argue with her, even though I don't believe in the metaphysics of the dream world. My own disturbing dream of the other night when Jamie had his car accident has made me very uneasy and confused. "What is Roger's profession?" I change the subject.

"You have met him," she says with a grin.

"Have I?"

"Yes, at Julie's party. He was teaching here last year, now he works for an NGO in Osh."

I ponder for a moment and recall the American guy with a pony tail, in his forties. I remember the episode about the Tajik girlfriend and the morality police in Mashhad, when he was thrown out of Iran. I wonder if Jamila knows about it, but don't ask. He had most likely also promised marriage to that girl. Otherwise the family would not have allowed her to travel with him, even with her brother as a chaperone. The notion of a boyfriend does not exist among Central Asian Muslims. Even among the Russified elite, a girl may openly date a boy only if there is expectation of a marriage.

Now having fully pictured him, I say to Jamila, "He seemed much older than you."

"He is forty one, I think ..." Her tone tells me she is not comfortable with the 20 year age difference between them.

"He may look older but he is young at heart." Anna interjects. "I did a class with him last year. He used to invite students to his place and give advice. He is a kind man."

"Yes, his place is like a guest house," Jamila frowns. "In Osh, there are always young people coming and going." I notice Jamila feels quite insecure about her relationship with him, but at such a distance, how can she keep tabs on his dealings with the female students around?

After the girls leave, I sit down to review my notes for the following day's lecture. But my thoughts are on Jamila and her life. Earlier this evening, when I offered to prepare a brief meal for us, the girls were quick to take over preparations and setting the table. Afterwards, they cleared everything and washed up. Their domesticity and readiness to be of service reminds me of my own girlhood, 30 odd years ago. Such a contrast to the girls brought up in the West today. I think of my friend Soheila's eighteen year old daughter; she is in her last year of school in Berlin, where she was born. The girl is quite happy to lounge in her room, watching TV and phoning friends, whilst her mother labours in the kitchen, preparing a meal for the family. As for the state of her room, it always resembles the site of a burglary. Two years ago, when I visited them, she was in a state of war with her father, a university professor. He had been very unhappy with her poor school record, and every month running up huge telephone bills. After a particularly bitter argument, when she was very rude to him, he finally snapped and smacked her, after which, he had left the house, very distressed. She had then run to her mother and said she was going to call the social services and complain of child abuse. Later during my visit, when she repeated her allegation to me, I reminded her that she was no longer a child. "In Iran," I added, "girls your age may have to take care of a husband *and* children of their own." Her response was to shrug her shoulder and say "I don't care. I don't live in Iran."

Now I think of Jamila, the sweet girl, barely out of her teens, lying with that wrinkly Roger, having to worry about motherhood, a career and an income high enough to help her mother and brothers. Her mother's state salary is at subsistence level and her older brother's wages from a store in Osh do not go far either. Her younger brother is doing well at school and would like to come to Bishkek to attend university. Jamila is hoping that after graduating next year and marrying Roger she will be able to help fund his education. She told me tonight that Roger would like to have children sooner rather than later. That is understandable, given his stage in life. But couldn't he pick himself an older woman, better suited to his needs? No doubt he has the pick of the field in this country. I don't want to interfere in Jamila's private life, but she confides in me with such a sincere look, I feel involved.

As I entertain these thoughts, the phone rings. It is Gerhard.

"Hello Sima," he greets in his warm, manly voice, cheering me up from 6000 miles away. He is coming to Bishkek on Monday; I am to pick him up from the airport at 7 a.m. I am looking forward to receiving my laptop and the winter coat and boots I left behind, but not sure about his presence here. I am surrounded by young people; the colleagues I associate with are all under thirty five. I am struggling to fit in myself. How do I present a man with candy floss hair as my boyfriend? A husband may have been a different story; everyone would have imagined I have settled into a premature winter of my life. But I have not. I still have that dream scenario of meeting someone special to love and settle with.

Chapter IV

The Epic of Manas; story of a nation

The Kyrgyz are very fond of impromptu singing. I learnt this last week at our staff and students departmental meeting. On that occasion, after the introductions and discussion of the first year programme, there was a presentation of last summer's departmental expedition to an archaeological site in Eastern Kyrgyzstan. Following this, without much preamble, a number of students got up and began to sing folk songs. The staff members then joined in. We were all seated at long tables covered in embroidered cloth and laid out with quantities of fizzy drinks, fruit and pastries. Our American-Kyrgyz academic gathering soon turned into a jovial party. Meanwhile, I had to keep a straight face as I imagined a setting where my stuffy London university colleagues began to chorus an English folk song in the middle of a departmental meeting.

The Epic of Manas; story of a nation

A few days ago when I went into the office, I found Tinara, my Kyrgyz colleague, behind her desk, strumming away at her *komuz*, a guitar-like three string instrument. The only other person in the office was Aida, the departmental secretary. She was listening pensively to the haunting melody, as she filed her nails. Kyrgyz music, similar to the Kazak, has shades of Chinese, but easier on the western ear, and more melodic. Pity, so little of it is heard beyond Central Asia. Tinara then asked me if I would like to join her and a friend of hers for a walk in the mountains on the outskirts of Bishkek.

***

This is my first chance to get out of the city. We begin our outing by taking a *marshutka* (mini bus used as communal taxi) to a sanatorium in an outlying district of the city. It is a large, single storey, stone and brick building once used for leisure and convalescence. Today, however, the once beautiful gardens and the whole building are in the usual state of post-Soviet neglect, with the walls and paving chipped and cracked, and the vegetation dying. But as we distance ourselves from the decrepit building and take a walk through the natural habitat, the beauty of the landscape and the majesty of those distant snow-capped peaks imbue us with a sense of awe and humility. After yesterday's heavy rain, today has turned out to be warm and sunny, with only a gentle breeze. We are trekking unhurriedly, along a rough path towards high grounds that form a plateau with views of the whole valley and layers of mountains beyond.

Kyrgyzstan is truly a land of mountains. They cover over 90% of its landmass, nearly half of them above 3000 metre. A country the size of Britain, it is populated by under five million people, mostly living along the two major valleys, the Chui in the north, where Bishkek is situated, and the Fergana in the south, bordering Uzbekistan. The medicinal herbs that grow on these lush valleys and hillsides were well known and widely sold throughout the Soviet Union. Here, along our path, we come across a variety of plants I am not familiar with. There are delicate wild flowers with tiny yellow petals and thin stems. The trek is long. We take off our sweaters to cool during the uphill walk. I have no problem keeping pace with Tinara and her friend, Fatima, both in their thirties. Although much younger than me, they don't seem any fitter. Tinara has a heavy build and would be considered overweight by European standards. She has a broad face with a solemn expression. Her friend Fatima, on the other hand, has a warm and friendly demeanour. She is slim and shapely, wearing jeans and trainers. She is from Kazakhstan and works for an NGO in Bishkek; she speaks five languages.

Finally, we reach the plateau at the top. Nearby, there is a tall bush, under its shade we roll out our ground cover and have a little picnic. Tinara has brought fresh tomatoes, baby cucumbers, grapes and apples. We consume these with freshly baked bread we picked up from the local bazaar. Everyone eats with great relish the fruit and vegetables that are incredibly flavoursome. The small, perfectly shaped tomatoes, especially, taste like some heavenly fruit grown on another planet. Similarly with the baby cucumbers, so delicious no salt is needed. After we finish eating, we lounge on the ground, and Tinara begins a song. She has a melodic voice, gentle, and soothing. I ask her what the song is about. She explains, and Fatima translates. It is about a boy and a girl in love, on a summer's day. They come searching for each other in the mountains, and finally meet at the summit, never to return down below.

The Epic of Manas; story of a nation

In the quiet that follows our conversation, I look up and see a lonely falcon flying high above. I scan my eyes across the distance and I wonder where and how far he is going all by himself. The air is so clear I can see miles ahead. There are fir trees on the high hills to the east of us, ragged mountains in the far distance, and beyond them the snow-capped Tien Shan that runs along the edge of the horizon all the way to China. The tranquillity in the hills is only broken by the flutter of a white butterfly I can almost touch as it hovers over the blanket of mountain flowers that surround us. There are specks of pink, honey and sky blue on its stretched-out wings. There is such peace around me, I close my eyes and memorise the moment. I am in paradise, and like those lovers on the summit, never want to leave this piece of land beneath my feet. I have almost forgotten the weight of my body and the burden of my thoughts. I am like a *houri* in heaven. Not of the bashful virgin variety promised to the pious by the Koran, but the jaded, world weary sort, who has redeemed herself upon gaining entry into God's domain. In this blissful state of body and mind, I remain for some time, light as floating feathers. My companions have gone for a stroll nearby and I cherish my solitude and the high I have been feeling for the past hour, the kind of spiritual elevation only nature at its best bestows upon one.

On the way back, Fatima tells me they come to the mountains often from May to early October, when it is good weather. "We were lucky today," she says with a contented smile, "normally at this time, it is colder. But I think Tangri made a special concession for you as a guest here. He extended the summer by one more day."

"Tangri?" I ask

"The God of sky," she replies.

I look up. The sky is still a bright blue, though it is late in the afternoon and the sun is beginning to go down.

"Gok Tangri (blue sky) is very, very old Kyrgyz God, and for all Turks," Tinara says.

"It is our custom," Fatima adds, "people pray to Tangri and swear by it."

"I thought you were all Muslims," I mutter, but realise this is an example of Central Asian Islam syncretised with pre-Islamic indigenous beliefs. In fact the idea of a powerful sky appeals to me, irrational though it may be. A personal relationship with nature was something I had never conceived of. My life experience so far, has been totally urban. But I can see now, if I spent endless days under these skies, surrounded by those tall mountains, with my survival prey to nature's whims and outbursts, I may begin to feel different. Perhaps even pray to Tangri and fear its admonishment. This has been the way of the nomads here for the past thousand years.

On our way back, we come across a young man leading a small flock of black sheep across the rocky grounds and over rough stones. He is the sole person we have encountered in the hours since we started our walk in the hills. This is a country wonderfully unspoilt, its nature raw and pure. But my good mood does not last long once we get on the road we came from and wait for another *marshutka* to take us back to Bishkek. Soon a couple of Kyrgyz men join our queue and begin to approach us. One of them is very obviously drunk. He is a scruffy looking middle-aged man, with dishevelled hair and stubble; his shirt half way hangs out of his trousers. He babbles in Russian and staggers as he approaches us. The man with him, a younger Kyrgyz, looks embarrassed as he keeps pulling at the drunken man's arm to stop him from getting close to us. Luckily a minibus arrives soon. The driver and his assistant don't want to take the drunkard on board. An argument ensues, but eventually the guy is taken on. Tinara, Fatima and I quickly move to the back row to keep a safe distance. The guy goes on swearing and gesticulating his anger at an invisible foe. Fortunately he gets off before long, when we reach a row of bungalows by the side of the road. There is relief all round.

"Now you see why we have never been married," Fatima frowns.

"Alcoholism is a real problem here among our men." Tinara nods in agreement. But I know that there is much more to their remaining single than merely their men-folks' alcoholism. It is true that the post-Soviet economic hardships and insecurities have pushed up alcohol consumption in all the republics, especially in Kazakhstan and Kyrgyzstan, where there are large Russian communities. But more to the point for women like Tinara and Fatima, among Central Asians an ideal marriage partner is a virgin girl in her early-to-mid twenties. A thirty something female is considered well past it. This was intimated as much when Tinara said, "I had a suitor a few years ago, but my mother thought he would complicate my life, and I didn't fancy him, anyway. Now I don't think I'll ever find a suitable husband. I am getting old."

"How about you?" I asked Fatima.

"I had a boyfriend I liked very much, but he wanted me to give up work after we get married, and I love my job."

As it is, I wouldn't be surprised if Fatima and Tinara never get married. Sad outcomes, since in this culture a woman's social worth, as well as her own sense of achievement, rely mostly on motherhood.

Land of Forty Tribes

***

The day after my trip to the mountains, I had my meeting with Sabir, the Kyrgyz ethnographer who teaches part-time at the ethnology department. Aytan, my departmental colleague, had arranged the meeting and offered to translate for me. She is an Altay Turk, originally from Siberia, a sweet natured woman with a face the shape of the full moon and jet-black hair she ties into a bun. She moved to Bishkek after marrying a Kyrgyz man. Aytan has some knowledge of Turkish, after her two years in Ankara, but not enough to communicate complex ideas. So Russian and Kyrgyz words get thrown in and we end up with a linguistic soup of a discussion. It is a frustrating experience that makes me wonder how in the past so many western anthropologists set out to decipher and explain often obscure cultures through the use of interpreters. I am resolved to seriously learn Kyrgyz.

Sabir tells me, Kyrgyz culture is based on deep philosophical premises. As an example, he mentions the ancient belief that *Akil*, human wisdom, will bloom if fed with knowledge derived from myths given to us by the ancestors. The empty mind is barren, like an expanse of uncultivated land. He goes on to tell me, dualism is a fundamental principle in the culture; many root words have dual meanings. He mentions that Manichaeism has had a profound impact here, unbeknown to most people, but does not explain exactly what it is, beyond a simple dualism, common to Zoroastrian religion.

I tell him, Manichaeism itself grew out of this ancient religion of Iran, dating back three thousand years. The prophet Mani, a Babylonian by origin, had found favour in the court of Shahpur I, the Persian ruler of the Sassanid Empire in the fifth century AD. He preached a religion that synthesised Zoroastrianism with Judeo-Christian traditions, Gnosticism, and Buddhism. St. Augustine had been a Manichean before he became a Christian. Like the prophet Zoroaster, Mani claimed that the universe was based on the dual forces of good and evil, perpetually in battle with each other. According to Zoroaster, there was a sparkle of good in everyone; it needed to be cultivated to promote the victory of Ahura Mazda, the God of Goodness, over Ahriman, the evil lord. Mani's religion, on the other hand, considered most souls wicked and beyond saving. Reaching goodness was a tremendous struggle for humanity, demanding the renunciation of the material world, above all the pleasures, such as love, lust and procreation. When Mani fell out of favour with subsequent Sassanid rulers, he was executed and his followers fled Iran in search of safe havens in Central Asia, and beyond.

Recently, I have become aware of the great influence of Iranian civilisation on Central Asian traditions and languages. For instance, the Iranian new year festival of Novruz (new day), that celebrates the spring and renewal of life on earth, was, and still is, widely commemorated in all these countries. Zoroastrian temples and signs of fire worship have been discovered in parts of Southern Kyrgyzstan, as in many parts of Central Asia. The Sogdians, who spoke a language close to Persian (Farsi), had predated the Kyrgyz people as the inhabitants of this land, prior to Turkic tribes migrating here from Siberia. Today's Kyrgyz language is not only a Turkic language with some Mongolian words and recent Russian entries, it also contains many Farsi words. These include names of weekdays, albeit, different pronunciation. I mentioned these in class the next day; it amused my students. They seem ignorant of connections with Iranian culture, history and languages. As ethnology students, I reminded them, they should learn, above all, the historical roots of their own culture. This was something the Soviet authorities denied their parents' generation, in an attempt to distance the Muslim periphery from their non-communist neighbours.

***

After class today, I went for lunch to the university canteen with Jamila and Kasim. He is one of my two male students in the anthropology theory class. There are seven altogether in that class, seniors doing their final year of a bachelor degree. Kasim is the most able in that class. Outside the lessons, he hangs around with Jamila. He is a charming Kyrgyz boy with a handsome face, ever so polite. The other day, when I ran into him at my local minimarket on Sovietskaya street, he insisted on carrying my shopping all the way to my apartment. He has never been to the US, yet his English is at the level of those who have spent a year on an exchange programme. His analytical skills are also very good, one of my most intelligent students. His family, like the majority in the capital city are quite poor, but well educated. He has told me, his mother wants him to quit his part-time job after Christmas, to concentrate on his studies for the last semester. But with his father and brother both unemployed, Kasim is reluctant to give up work. The family badly need his income.

Jamila tells me, he owes 200 dollars, as part of his tuition fee for this academic year. He will have to pay soon, or drop out of his studies. "Doesn't the university have a hardship fund?" I ask. She is not sure. Kasim, meanwhile, keeps quiet. I can see he is embarrassed about it. I feel bad that I can't just give him the money myself; it's a whole month's salary for me. I have to find another sponsor.

The Epic of Manas; story of a nation

We move on to the subject of Kasim's senior thesis, a complex topic. He tells me he is fascinated with the subject of dream interpretation and the part it plays in Kyrgyz culture. He is especially interested in how dreams influence the *manaschi*, and his telling of the epic poem Manas. *Manaschis*, normally male, were story tellers, acting as focal figures in the community. Their recitals of Manas, an epic poem named after the eponymous Kyrgyz super hero, were an occasion for entertainment as well as enlightening the community. The epic of Manas is a trilogy of the life story of Manas, his son and grandson. It tells their attempt at uniting the disparate Kyrgyz tribes to defeat their enemies and establish themselves as independent people in the lands that are present day Kyrgyzstan. It reveals many of the myths and legends of the Kyrgyz, providing them with moral and spiritual guidance through the ages. A *manaschi* used to recite the epic in snippets to crowds at festivities. Being an oral tradition, improvisation was always part of the recital. He would weave in topical themes and characters to give it a flavour of the time.

I tell Kasim that studying the changing culture of *manaschi* could be a very interesting project. He could look at the way their role and function in today's Kyrgyz society has altered, which could illuminate many of the contemporary social changes. "Dreaming is an important part of the process," Kasim explains, "*Manaschis* are visited in their dreams in childhood by one or more of the Manas spirits and that is when they begin their recitation." I am very interested in how the dreams influence the stories they tell," he says.

"Don't go into the psychology of it." I advise Kasim to stick to an ethnographic account. He has little time to finish his project. He tells me that, Azamat, a teacher in our department, is also a *manaschi*.

"Have you interviewed him?" I recall an intense looking small Kyrgyz man.

"Oh, he is difficult", Kasim says with a stiff expression. "I have tried to discuss my work with him. But he won't talk about his own experience at all. If you insist, he gets angry. I have only heard him recite the Manas once, and that was in somebody's house. During his recital he became very emotional. He was tearful and shaking. Then afterwards, he went very quiet and didn't want to talk to anyone."

"It sounds like he is being possessed when reciting," I tell them.

"But sometimes he is kind and helpful," Jamila interjects. "I think he is just a very moody guy."

***

Later that day, I met Monica, a PhD student of anthropology from Cologne University, on a research visit. She told me, she knew a Dutch woman from her university, who came to Bishkek three years ago to research Kyrgyz culture, and was fascinated by the epic tale, and the way *manaschis* were inspired. She was fluent in Russian and also learnt Kyrgyz. She met Azamat that summer and they started a relationship.

"Are they still together?" I asked.

"I don't think so. It is such a long way to go for a visit." I told her I would be very interested to read any research material she may have published. Monica told me the woman had dropped out of university a few months after returning from Bishkek. "I think she had a mental breakdown and couldn't cope with studying any more. She went back to Holland soon afterwards. I met her one day last year when I visited Amsterdam. She was working in a health food store and was active with a Buddhist Order."

The Epic of Manas; story of a nation

What a pity to waste away her study and her findings, I thought. But it wouldn't be the first time a young student of anthropology with unresolved psychological issues is gripped with an identity crisis on a field trip, and subsequently goes mad, or goes native.

Later that evening, I begin to read an English translation of a shortened version of Manas. The original is in four volumes, greater in magnitude than the Indian Mahabharata, and the Greek Odyssey. Created by folk memories over a thousand years, it depicts the history of Kyrgyz people through accounts of their victories, tragedies and relations with neighbouring tribes. Manas is the superhero and the central character. He embodies great strength, bravery, and a sense of justice. He is a masterful horseman and skilled in martial arts. Some of the stories attributed to Manas may have originated later from the adventures of other military leaders. There is no way to know exactly with a purely oral tradition. Written accounts only go back to the middle of the 19th century. Kasim has told me that military leadership was very important in Kyrgyz society. The spirits of legendary soldiers, the *batirs*, used to be revered in the old days, and their names became emblems for the tribe.

***

In 840 AD, Kyrgyz tribal lords fought successfully against the Uigurs, the inhabitants of Xincan on the western edge of China. They were the most culturally advanced Turkic people of Central Asia with a unique script and a flourishing literature. In the vicious battles that followed, the Kyrgyz nomad armies sacked the Uigur capital of Beitin. Overcoming Uigur and Chinese domination, the Kyrgyz tribes moved south from their original habitat in the valleys surrounding Yenisei river in Siberia. The great hero instrumental in this victory was Manas, who managed to unite the forty disparate tribes, leading them to the Altai region, and eventually to the Alai mountains and the Fergana valley. Here some Kyrgyz leaders married daughters of local rulers creating lasting alliances that strengthened the Kyrgyz position against their rivals. The most notable was the marriage of Manas to Kanikei, the daughter of the khan of Bukhara. Manas's endeavours in forging the unity of the disparate tribes is seen as the root of Kyrgyz national identity, its name taken from the words *kirk iz*, forty tribes.

In 1995, with much pomp and ceremony, the millennium of Manas's birth was celebrated in Bishkek and in Talas -his assumed birth place in the north of Kyrgyzstan. The government set up a state board with a five-year mandate to publicise the epic of Manas in the media, the education system and among the public at large. Academic research and publications were commissioned, a major university, a high road, and a number of establishments were named after him, and the scene was set for the Manas mania that has since gripped the nation. It is as if the very word Manas defines the core of the Kyrgyz nation. The President, Askar Akayev, went so far as to declare that the seven principles encoded in the epic should guide the newly independent republic in asserting its independence and seeking prosperity. These were patriotism, national unity, humanism, cooperation among nations, hard work, and education; principles that Akayev deemed suitable for the purpose, based on his interpretation.

The epic trilogy tells the story of Manas, his life and heroic deeds, the life of his son, Semetei, who continues with the efforts to gain the Kyrgyz their independence and that of his grandson Seitek. In addition to stories of fearsome battles, the collection contains accounts of colourful feasts, races, and vivid dreams in which dragons, lions, falcons and hawks reveal good fortune. The birth of Manas himself follows such a dream. His father Jakib bey, son of Nagoi khan, has married the widow of his paternal uncle, Chiyirdi, and later a young wife, Bakdoolot. The epic begins with Jakib bey lamenting that he is already forty eight years old, and has no son to leave his fortune to. When he goes to the other world, the wealth he has amassed will tumble down like a fortress under siege. Regretting his vanity in not having children in his youth, he feels dismal in the day and is kept awake at night.

Seeing Jakib's anguish, his wives curse each other for not giving Jakib his due; they have remained infertile and "fruitless." Then one day, Chiyirdi, Jakib's first wife, already fifty years old, has a dream in which a grey beard, *ak sakkal*, approaches her, holding out a white apple as big as a dish and sweeter than honey. If she wishes for a son, she is to eat this and saddle a dragon. Upon eating the apple Chiyirdi bloats to an enormous size. Eventually, a dragon creeps out of her, its mighty hiss drawing half the world into his throat. Numbed and half-blind with fear the old wife wakes up and finds her husband in deep slumber. He has had a marvellous dream in which a bird with a strange cry, like no other, and gleaming from head to tail descends upon him; a hawk with a beak of steel, claws of gold and body of a white swan with gold feathers, washed in fragrant streams. Jakib feeds, grooms and trains the bird, seeing him grow mighty and strong, so much so, that all the earthly beasts scarcely dare to stir when he flies over.

Upon hearing of her husband's dream, Chiyirdi tells him this is a sign that God will send down to him the bluebird of happiness. But he must not reveal his dream to strangers, only to the nearest and dearest. She then urges him to call on his tribe to gather for a feast in which 40 mares are to be slain and fed to the guests. Jakib objects, considering it excessive and futile since there is no sign of a pregnancy yet. He cannot afford to spare so much of his herd, he claims. Then he goes to his second wife Bakdoolot's *yurt*, complaining about his first wife's demands. Bakdoolot now tells him of her own dream, in which his first wife, Chiyirdi, bears him the son he desires. She also urges him to slay 40 mares and hold a feast. When Jakib objects once more, she tells him, he has become a slave to his herds and his riches, not showing generosity to his folk. She calls him greedy and mean, and devoid of enough wisdom to rule over his people.

Reading this episode of Jakib's life, I am reminded of the custom of excessive generosity offered at feasts by tribal chiefs; it was a fundamental aspect of the culture of nomadic Turks through the ages. It marked the power and prestige of the khans and beys, as they sought to confirm alliances, win new friends, and keep in awe their enemies by displays of riches they could dispense with. The feasts also included an element of entertainment through staging competitions such as horse racing, wrestling, and shooting. The winners would then be rewarded handsomely. The example of this in Manas is the occasion when Jakib bey allocates large numbers of sheep, horses, camels and bags of gold coins for winners of races at a major feast; this was attended by Kyrgyz tribes, as well as Kazaks, Uzbeks, Kipchaks, and Tatars. The fame and glory of the event was carried far and wide across distant lands, even impacting their Chinese rivals in the West.

From what Jamila has told me, the extravagance at weddings, circumcision ceremonies and funerary feasts continues today among Central Asian people. Her uncle in Osh had saved up for 15 years to entertain 50 families in his neighbourhood, in addition to his extended family, friends and colleagues at a three day wedding feast. Such customs were often blamed by the Soviets for much of the economic underdevelopment of the region. They ignored the lack of investment opportunities under communism that motivated people to spend rather than save, and the role of this tradition in maintaining social relations within the community.

The question of bride price, *kalym*, another very old tradition in Central Asia was similarly viewed by outsiders as a sign of underdevelopment. In the case of Manas's marriage to the daughter of Atemir, the khan of Bukhara, for example, the khan, not happy with marrying his daughter to an outsider, and a fearsome nomadic warrior at that, sets a bride price so high he assumes Jakib bey cannot meet. But the old man has come a long way looking for a suitable wife for his son. Crossing high mountains, lakes, and valleys he has examined the beauties of Tashkent, Khiva, Samarkand and Bukhara. Manas, already thirty years old, is looking for a love marriage that will bring him the happiness he is lacking with his present wives, all of them captured as war booty. Sanirabiyga, the daughter of Atemir, is a most beautiful girl, beloved of the khan, attended by a whole host of maidens and servants in her own palace quarters. Jakib bey accepts the demand for the bride price, happy to finally get the khan's consent.

Manas then assembles the massive fortune requested for Sanirabiyga's hand and sets off for Bukhara, accompanied by his father and a large army. When he arrives there, Atemir, still not happy with the marriage, ignores his prospective son-in-law and instead, spends much time examining the wealth he has brought along.

These comprise a large number of herds of rare breed, and gold and silver. Feeling offended by his treatment, Manas, together with an aide, sneaks into Sanirabiyga's private chambers to introduce himself and win her heart. She recognises him and takes a liking to him, but pretends ignorance and rebukes him for taking such liberty as to push away the guards and her seven maidens to enter her chambers at night.

Manas introduces himself and tells her of the bride price he has brought along in order to take her as his wife. She is angry with his intrusion and responds by attacking him with a sword, injuring him lightly on the arm. Enraged by her audacity, he knocks her down and leaves the palace grounds. Atemir khan meanwhile has accepted the bride price and organises entertainment for his guests. There are 40 warrior lords, *bogatirs*, accompanying Manas. Each one is assigned a *yurt* with women servants. The women assigned to Manas's *yurt*, however, don't dare approach him. He is considered too awesome. He thus remains isolated with no food or drink for three days. On the fourth day, when his *bogatirs* (generals) come to visit him, he beats them and orders the sacking of Bukhara. The khan's daughter is alarmed by this turn of events and becomes repentant. She comes along with Jakib bey to intervene. She tells Manas that she had tried to test his character by her actions and he should not vent his anger on her folk, the Tajiks. They are not to blame. She asks him to calm his anger and take what he had come for. She will now submit to him and he will be her master. Convinced by her sincerity he revokes his orders and the Bukharans are spared from destruction by his troops. They now prepare for the wedding of Manas and his 40 warriors. Forty one *yurts* are assembled with a bride-to-be in each. The *bogatirs* ride their horses about. When a horse stops at a certain *yurt*, its rider marries the girl inside. As it happens, Manas's horse stops at Sanirabiyga's. The couple are then married and Manas takes his bride back to his land.

The Tajik princess, from then on known as Kanikei, takes on the role of wife and counsel to the Kyrgyz ruler. She helps him strengthen his alliances and consolidate his rule, overcoming his rivals: the Chinese, and other Turkic peoples of the region. Kanikei remains strong-willed and independent to the end. When, many years later, Manas is killed by his enemies, Kanikei refuses to obey the tradition of marrying his brother, Kobesh, who has succeeded him. Angry with her refusal, Kobesh sets a price on her head and that of her young son, Semetei. But Kanikei, along with her son, is helped by Manas's faithful friends to escape. Back in Bukhara she awaits Semetei's coming of age before he can resume the leadership of the Kyrgyz people.

The story of Manas and Kanikei reflects the culture clash between the invading nomads of Central Asia and its sedentary, refined societies, perhaps a major concern for the medieval urban dwellers of the region. But it is also the stuff of romance, literature and myth making in many cultures. Kanikei was no doubt saving her nation as well as her own neck by acquiescing to marry the conqueror of her land. Brought up with court etiquette and served by her maidens, she may have aspired to wed a spouse of her own ilk. But who is to say, she was not moved and impassioned by Manas's powerful presence in her private chambers in the night, announcing the great riches he had amassed to win her hand? The union of Manas and Kanikei is today idolised as a romantic tale and held in high esteem in Kyrgyzstan. But it is an account based on oral tradition, its truth hard to verify.

Land of Forty Tribes

***

The turn of the millennium, when Manas is reputed to have united the Kyrgyz people and led them to victory over their enemies was also the golden era of the civilisation of the settled peoples of Central Asia. The region they inhabited covered today's Tajikistan, Uzbekistan, and Southern Kyrgyzstan, all part of the ancient Iranian plateau. It gave rise to outstanding poets, philosophers, and scientists. The legendary Abu Ali Sina, known in the West as Avicenna, was born in Afshana, near Bukhara. A masterful horseman, poet, philosopher and one of the greatest physicians of the medieval times; his *Canons of Medicine* was still in use in Europe until the 17th century. As a schoolgirl in Tehran, I had been fascinated by his life story which I read with great interest. In my mind I would follow his journey south through the magical land of Turkistan, across deserts and valleys into the province of Khorasan, in north eastern Iran, and further west, to the ancient city of Hamadan, his final resting place. A romantic figure, galloping on his champion horse, he had gone through villages and towns, treating physical ailments and psychological disorders that had baffled other wise men.

The tenth century was also the time when Ferdowsi, the great Persian poet wrote his epic masterpiece, Shahnameh, the book of kings, based on oral history, as well as Zoroastrian priests' chronicles. Set in verse, it tells the history of ancient Iran and Turan, giving an account of their culture and cosmology. Prior to the migration of Turkic tribes to Central Asia, subsequently called Turkistan, the region was known as the land of Turan. The ancient wars of Iran and Turan compose major episodes in *Shahnameh*. The book covers stories of bravery, wars, romances, alliances and betrayals among people inhabiting the vast stretch of land that went from the river Oxus (Amu Darya in Uzbekistan and Turkmenistan) to the Euphrates (in Iraq and Syria). As with the epic Manas in Kyrgyzstan, Shahnameh is recited in Iran by story tellers called *naghal*. Traditionally, they would appear in a tea or coffee house reciting and improvising the stories to entertain and inform their audience of philosophical, political, and religious ideas. These would be contained in tales of immortality, justice, heroism, deceit, vengeance, the divine rule of kings, and stories with powerful female characters.

When I was at school, reading the *Shahnameh* we learnt that Iranians eventually defeated and subjugated the Turanians (ancestors of today's Tajiks). What we did not discuss was the fact that Turkic tribes ruled Iran for nearly a thousand years, beginning with the time of Sultan Mahmood of Ghazna, who commissioned Shahnameh, until the reign of Reza Shah in the 20th century. During this millennium, although Persian/Tajik remained the literary language of the peoples of Iran and Central Asia, Turkic languages were the ones spoken by the rulers of this vast region. Only in the 20th century, under the Pahlavi shahs, did the Turks become an oppressed minority in Iran, and Persian chauvinism dictated the academic discourse and language policies in the country.

***

Today I met my Kazak colleague, Askat, who runs the politics department. I had gone into their office to discuss one of the courses I teach for that department. It turned out I didn't have to worry too much about the details of my syllabus; this university, modelled on the American system, is more flexible than the British ones. Instead, we talked at length about the Soviet cities and Central Asian cultures. Askat has lived and studied in Turkey for two years. He is married, with two boys at primary school. He seems very appreciative of my knowledge and experience of the Middle East and this region, a sentiment not shared by others at this university. The majority of the foreign faculty express little interest or insight into Central Asia. Their choice of Kyrgyzstan is often based on lack of job opportunities back home, or in the case of academic oldies, such as Julie, a last ditch attempt at exotic travel and life experience in some far away land. The white Americans among the staff are considered by the locals to have the highest credentials. The head of ethnology, Svetlana, an ethnic Kyrgyz named after Stalin's daughter, certainly gives that impression. She does not display any particular interest in me or acknowledge what I have to offer her department. In contrast, she sucks up to Julie, who has the pretensions of a grand American professor. But of what and what is her background exactly? Nobody knows.

A few days ago, at an inter-departmental meeting, Julie was trying to please the provost and the heads of ethnology and sociology by denying that students in these departments had sub-standard English and poor academic skills. "My students are excellent," she said, referring to her group of freshmen in ethnology.

"Sure," I felt like saying, "they are excellent in singing Kyrgyz folk songs." But, I said nothing. I wondered if she is in any way aware of the shortcomings of school education in Central Asia, and the fact that it is only 11 years, sometimes even ten if a student skips a year to graduate early. But then, God knows what kind of educational standards Julie is accustomed to, clearly not that of Ivy League institutions. Last week after our meeting, Reza, harbouring his own grudge against her, did an internet search of her academic background.

He found out that her State University, down in the Bible belt, only offered anthropology as a minor to the undergraduates in the English department. So much for her claim of being an anthropology professor for the past 30 years in charge of a department.

As it happens, the top students in this university are at the politics department. There is a lot of demand for the subject, since politics is assumed to mean power, prestige and money. Widespread corruption of the state has meant enrichment through public positions. But this is also a subject that dominates the attention of western academia with regards to the region. The support that CACE has given to our university has focused on this department, building up its resources and staffing provisions. As a result, the politics department has been in a position to cream off the top applicants, most of whom gained fluency in English after a year of high school in the US. This is normally arranged through a student exchange programme funded by a US public body and the generosity of American host families in various states.

Alan Murphy, who was the head for the last three years, is still the guy running the show in that department. He has been very involved in its promotion and expansion. Previously teaching at a small East Coast college, he came to this university following the breakup of his third marriage and is now married to a local woman, 32 years his junior. He considers himself a Marxist, a child of the 60s who began with demonstrating for civil rights, then women's rights and human rights, and finally, Alan's rights. Anyone who disputes him is quickly cut to size. A big man, with an even bigger ego, his language is devoid of any subtlety or finesse.

Askat, on the other hand, is softly spoken and quiet, not a typical Kazak whom the Kyrgyz consider to be brash and aggressive. He grew up in Alma Ati, the largest city in Kazakhstan, only three hours drive, north of Bishkek. It is another modern Soviet city, like Bishkek and Tashkent, capital of Uzbekistan. I explained to him that I found the city centre here, with its broad avenues and wide pavements, soulless and alienating. It is as though the Soviet planners wanted to inhibit the city dwellers getting close together. So unlike many Middle Eastern, and some European cities, whose small centres have narrow streets, and are filled with people, shops and an air of conviviality. Here, the housing design similarly distances people. Windows of most apartments either face wide avenues or huge courtyards. When I said this to Askat, he responded, "I prefer our modern Soviet city. I found cities in Turkey, especially Istanbul, very noisy and claustrophobic."

Our discussion then continued with the subject of the Soviet's colonisation of Central Asia. Askat's view reflected the one-sided picture, often presented by today's Central Asian nationalists. It echoed the cold war era Sovietologists, "If Central Asians were left to their own devices, they would have developed far more. We have a lot of natural resources. But the planned economy of the Soviet Union worked in favour of the centre of power, which was Moscow, and generally Russia."

"You could have also ended up like Afghanistan," I told him. "You have a similar terrain with so many mountains and few natural resources."

Askat was not convinced. He had another gripe about the political domination of the region and the way Soviet authorities institutionalised ethnicity and emphasised ethnic differences. "That is why even the Kazaks here have not mixed much with the Kyrgyz, let alone other Muslim Soviets. Each community emphasised its own culture of music, language and customs. Diversity was encouraged, even exaggerated to dampen any idea of unity among Turkic people."

I told him that the Azerbaijani stallholder I met near my previous apartment had also complained about the isolation she felt as a member of a small minority, and that different communities hardly socialised with each other. Even within a community, Askat believed, it was the family relations that were the primary ones. Non-relatives were often ignored. "The irony for us," he said with a wry smile, "is that the Slavic people here united to maintain their power in the region. Marriages and close socialising among Russians, Ukrainians, Moldavians and other Slavs were much more common than among the Muslim Central Asians. Instead of us uniting to oppose them, they united to rule us."

Chapter V

Meine man in Kyrgyzstan

Here I am at Bishkek airport once more. I have been sitting at the arrivals hall since 7 a.m. glued to the TV monitors, waiting for his plane to arrive. It is now 8 a.m. and still no sign of it. The Turkish Airline's Istanbul-Bishkek flight simply displays, "delayed". Gerhard should be on that plane, having set off from Frankfurt yesterday afternoon. Feeling impatient I look around for a point of information. A couple of locals who were also waiting here have now disappeared. There is only the office for telephone taxis with an attendant. The dolled-up Russian girl behind the counter is busy flicking through a Russian edition of the Cosmopolitan; she sees me approaching but pretends not to. I ask about the incoming flight; she briefly looks up at me and says, "Go home, come after one. Maybe four hour waiting."

"How do you know?"

"Turkish office say."

"Why didn't they announce it on the monitors?"

"They told one hour ago." She continues flicking the pages.

I give up on her and begin to search the building for the Turkish Airline offices. There is something fishy going on and I am getting worried. At the far end of the ground floor I discover a broad set of stairs. I climb to the floor above where the departure lounge is located. There are a couple of cafes and on the other side of the hallway a number of unmanned check-in stands. There is no one around who speaks English. I only manage to get a response in Russian, "The flight will arrive later, perhaps after 1p.m."

Oh, damn it! I am teaching in the afternoon. What then?

Well, it's too bad. I certainly can't let that poor man arrive here and fend for himself. He will get snapped up by one of those cowboy drivers who suddenly appear the moment a foreign plane lands. Once the guy grabs hold of your suitcase you have no choice but to follow him or your luggage is gone. Gerhard has never been further than East of Istanbul, or south of Malaga for that matter. The desperation and cunning of the locals here will be beyond him. And if he is mugged on the way to town, he will lose everything including my laptop. He may end up in the middle of nowhere, lost with no money. What a welcome to the country! No, I can't risk it. I have to hang around till he arrives. But first, I have to find an information point for the Airline.

I go downstairs, looking for one, then back up the stairs, along the long corridor. Finally, I decide to enter the café I have located, to have tea and perhaps a change of luck. Inside, among the crowd I see a woman's familiar face. It is Aytan, my Altay colleague from the department. I notice she is sitting with a group of foreigners at a table.

"*Marhaba*," I greet her in Turkish and ask her what she is doing here.

She tells me she is seeing off a group of Austrian academics returning home after a research trip to Central Asia. Aytan speaks some German and has been hosting the group for the past few days. This morning they are to catch the flight to Istanbul and onto Vienna. It would be the same plane I am waiting for. Now they just have to sit and wait for information.

I tell Aytan about my German friend's anticipated arrival and my class this afternoon. She says she will help me locate the Turkish Airline office. We set off looking and find it tucked away behind a wall at the end of the corridor. I am relieved to deal with Turkish officials, with whom I can communicate properly. At first, there is only a young Kyrgyz woman attending the office. She tells me politely in fluent Turkish what I already heard in English and Russian.

"Tell me something new," I plead with her.

"There is some trouble with the planes, but we don't know what. You have to wait until the boss arrives. He knows more."

"What trouble?" Aytan and I say in unison. She looks as alarmed as I am.

"I don't know. You have to wait," the girl repeats.

Another half hour goes by, as we speculate with trepidation what may be the problem. Perhaps the plane developed a technical problem and could not take off from Istanbul airport. It is normally a five hour direct flight. Aytan cannot leave the airport until her guests have safely boarded the outward plane. Meanwhile, we sit impatiently in this office. She is now looking forward to meeting my guest from Germany. She welcomes the opportunity to practise her German with him.

"If you are busy during the week, I can take him out one day to visit the city," she offers.

"Inshallah. But let him get here first."

We have a few minutes of silence, then a Caucasian looking man in a smart suit, with a dark moustache, walks into the office.

"I think that is the manager," Aytan says. I approach the man and enquire about our flight.

"We've had a problem," he replies. "I have to make a call. I will let you know soon."

Before I respond, the man is off to another section of the office behind a closed door.

"Bloody hell," I curse quietly and return to my seat.

A few minutes later, the guy is back.

"The plane you are expecting from Istanbul has been diverted to Almati. We don't know when it will be here. But we will let you know as soon as we have more information."

"Why Almati?" I ask, "The city is north of here, beyond our plane's flight route."

Before the guy replies, the phone on a nearby desk rings. He turns away, picks up the phone and starts another conversation in a quiet voice. He is clearly hiding something from us; I listen intently.

"In the afternoon," I hear him say, "the crash? ... Yes, we are dealing with it. Yes, it was early this morning."

My God! I gasp. Has Gerhard's plane crashed on arrival? I know his flight from Istanbul was the only passenger plane due to arrive early this morning. No, it can't be true. I tense up with fear and worry and turn to Aytan.

"Did you hear that? There has been a plane crash here at the time our plane was to arrive."

"It can't be," she says in disbelief. "We would have heard the noise, or something."

"It must have arrived before we got to this building," I say in desperation, thinking the worst, but hoping that it was another flight. What a terrible thought, to wish this on others. But the idea of my dear Gerhard coming half way across the world to see me and ending up in the wreckage of a plane is just too distressing. And there I was, worrying about him losing his wallet and my laptop.

The darkest thoughts run through my head as I fidget on my feet, waiting for the manager to finish his call. When he finally puts the phone down he dashes to the other room to answer another call. A few more minutes pass by until he comes back in. I almost jump at him, yelling,

"For God's sake, tell us what is going on. Who has crashed? What are you trying to hide?"

"*Bayan* (Lady)," the man cuts in, trying to calm me. "Your plane is safe and has landed in Almati. It will be here this afternoon as soon as we get the go ahead."

"Then what is this talk of a crash, which plane?"

"Well, it is not quite clear yet ..."

I can see the guy is hesitant to reveal his information. Is the bastard resorting to the old Soviet dictum of "lie first, explain later? I grit my teeth.

"Look," I say in a firm voice. "I know that flight TK 474 from Istanbul was the only passenger plane due to land at 7 a.m. this morning. What plane has actually crashed here at that time?"

The guy looks at me for a moment then at Aytan and back again. Finally he says, "It was a Russian cargo plane coming in from Moscow."

"Have there been any casualties?" Aytan asks.

"We hope that nobody died. Ambulances were here on the scene very quickly." Well, it is sort of a relief. But what about the poor crew on that plane? "The runway has been closed for the moment," he continues. "I suggest you ladies go and have lunch. Come back after 2 p.m. Your plane will definitely be on its way this afternoon."

"Let's go out and get some fresh air," I suggest to Aytan.

***

On the ground floor, we discover another café, situated outside the main building in a courtyard. There are plastic tables and chairs, a few pot plants and quite a few customers enjoying the mild autumn sunshine. Among them are the stranded passengers waiting for the plane that is now on the tarmac at Almati airport. We have been to the café upstairs and told the Austrian group about their flight's delay. Earlier, when I was looking for a place to have some tea, I had discovered another small eating place on that floor, a kind of hamburger joint catering for the American taste. A couple of GIs in uniform were sitting there munching away. There are a few of them also in this outdoor café, where we decide to have our lunch. Part of the airport doubles-up as an air base for the American forces. This place is on-route to Afghanistan, hence the prominence of Kyrgyzstan since 9/11 for refueling planes and providing services.

"I am not sure about American food," Aytan says, having surveyed the menu.

"They also serve spaghetti Bolognaise. That is a bit like your *lahman*."

Aytan is embarrassed to admit she can't afford to eat at a foreign restaurant. But I know better, so I insist she orders something and tell her she is my guest. There is a Russian and a Kyrgyz waitress serving, both of whom speak some English, which is just as well; the customers who normally eat here are mostly Americans. At a table nearby, a group of five soldiers are laughing and talking loudly. The Russian waitress has been at their table for some time, taking orders in between flirting with a good looking Texan guy. One of the other soldiers then calls over the Kyrgyz waitress whose attention I had just managed to attract. She ignores my call and goes over, embarking on an animated chat. I wonder how long it will be before we get served; with no breakfast this morning, my stomach is sending distress signals.

"I don't like seeing so many of them here," Aytan says, pointing with her head in the direction of the noisy Americans. They have sunk into their chairs, legs wide apart, as if lounging in the privacy of their bedroom.

"Their culture is so different from ours," she says in a disapproving tone.

"Don't judge all Americans by the standards of these men. Soldiers are a rough bunch everywhere."

"I know," she agrees. "I have seen some nice Americans at the university." Aytan goes on to complain about the American soldiers you see in bars and cafes across the city. "They can throw their money around and buy our girls cheaply." She goes on to say that last year, when the air base was leased to the Americans, there was opposition in the local media and discussion of how it was going to corrupt the morals of local people. She believes the government didn't care, "After all it is not the daughters of those in power who are poor and may be tempted."

"Do you see prostitution a big problem here?"

"Ugh, don't ask," Aytan rolls her eyes in disgust. "They say Bishkek has become the prostitution capital of Central Asia. We even export them in their thousands every year, to Dubai, Istanbul, Russia, and other parts of Central Asia."

After we finish our meal, Aytan goes back upstairs to see to her Austrians. I remain at our table, and order another tea. I am enjoying my enforced break in the sunshine. Most of the other customers have now left, and the place is peaceful. I take out an article I had brought along in case of a delay and begin to read about the impact of kinship on the structure of markets in an African town. As with so many current academic articles, it is full of jargon, its basic premises unnecessarily abstracted. I scan over a few pages with little interest. I have a struggle to fix my mind on African cultures and economic principles. My thoughts keep reverting back to the earlier events of the day, leaving me anxious. What if something terrible was to happen to him? No, I couldn't face that. I still love the guy.

So many memories of our life together come back to me, the trips we took around Germany, France and Switzerland. Gerhard loved quaint, old churches, and I began to appreciate and even pray in them. For him what mattered were the history and the aesthetics of the place. For me, it was the peace and serenity within those walls. My Muslim background did not stand in the way of me appreciating the spirituality of the environment. Then there are my memories of our time together in his house, that beautiful art deco building in Bad

Land of Forty Tribes

Godesburg, suburb of Bonn, by the River Rhine. I recall my first day there, exploring the neighbourhood, impressed with the giant trees and the lush vegetation. Like Alice in Wonderland, I felt dwarfed by my surrounding, half expecting magic.

I spent part of every summer and many weekends and Christmases there. I would cook turkey, the English way, for our main meal of the festivities, and Iranian dishes on other days. Jamie was often with us, along with at least two of his three children. It felt like one big happy family sitting around that huge mahogany table he had inherited from his mother in Berlin. On Christmas Eve, he would light the two dozen tiny candles that decorated the large tree, giving the room a far more romantic feel than the glittery paper decoration we use in the UK. Then there would be the ritual pre-dinner walk along the river bank. A good meal always required a good walk, he thought.

Now coming up to his 69th birthday, he is beginning to slow down. How many more years of an active life can he expect? What does the future hold for us? When he is off on that final journey, I will be the grieving girlfriend. All his assets and his generous pension will go to another woman, the nominal wife he parted from years before he met me. When we first met I had just given up a well paid but dull job in local government for a long course of study in anthropology that would earn me a PhD, and give me more time to spend with my son. I chose the path of study, thinking I could have the joys of motherhood, intellectual fulfilment, a satisfying career, and eventually meet someone special to marry. What a pity my life was not a Hollywood script or I could have had it all!

***

Upstairs in the departures lounge, Aytan is saying goodbye to her Austrian friends, now checking in. The Turkish Airline flight has finally landed. We go down to the arrivals hall and wait for the passengers. A while later they file out, but no sign of Gerhard.

"I am sure he came on this flight," I tell Aytan. "He phoned me yesterday from Germany and said he was about to board the plane.

She approaches one of the officials and questions him.

"There is a VIP lounge round the corner; he may be there." The man leads the way. When we get there, I see a small bar at one end, where Gerhard is seated with another man. They are talking and drinking beer.

"Hi," I throw my arms around him, giving him a big hug and a kiss.

"How did you end up in this corner? We've been waiting for you for ages in the main arrivals."

"This is David," he introduces the man sitting with him. "We've been keeping company since Istanbul. David suggested we wait here for his driver to collect our luggage. He will give us a ride into town afterwards."

"I have already hired a driver to take us," I inform them.

As we wait for Gerhard's suitcase to arrive, David offers me and Aytan a drink from the bar. The two men seem to have struck a friendship during their long wait together. David is a bulky, middle-aged English man with bushy ginger hair. He works for an oil company with a subsidiary in Bishkek and is quite familiar with the city. He will be staying on for a week, and wants us to join him for dinner one evening.

***

Friday is the day Big Clara comes round to do the cleaning. This morning when she came in, I introduced her to Gerhard before I left for work. The two of them have no common language, but seem to manage to communicate somehow. Gerhard told me he went for a walk in the city in the morning, returning in the afternoon with a big box of cakes. He then treated Clara, and Nina, who had dropped in after school, to cakes and freshly brewed coffee. Sampling the coffee he had brought from Germany was a touch of luxury for Clara. He had also taken photographs of her and Nina, promising to give them copies. Clara, of course, was totally enchanted by this "*ochin kharasho*" (very nice) friend of mine. She smiled broadly every time she referred to him. When I told her he was leaving the following week, she immediately asked when he was coming back. Not for a while, I said.

Gerhard has begun to like Bishkek. He is good at orienteering, and after a couple of days of being shown the streets and shops around the centre, he goes out by himself every day. He is familiar with the post-communist state of disrepair from his visits to East Berlin and other Eastern European cities. He is not phased out by the potholes on pavements, or the crumbling plaster and peeling paint on the buildings. Typical of him, he already discovered an art gallery in Oak Park on the way to the university, which I didn't know about. The Russian woman running the gallery speaks a few words of English, enough for Gerhard to buy a number of paintings from her, and discover that she is a single mother, living with her eleven year old son in Bishkek.

He had also bought me a beautiful broach crafted by a local artist and a couple of necklaces for his daughter and daughter-in law. "In

Germany you would pay four times as much for such handmade jewelry," he commented afterwards. I popped in there this morning, curious to see Kyrgyzstani paintings. As in most other former Soviet republics, a tradition of classical European art was established here, producing accomplished local painters and musicians trained by Russian masters. This gallery is owned by an artists' collective, most of them living on the edge of poverty. The main room of the gallery is packed with water colours and oil paintings stacked in untidy piles. There is poor lighting and almost no heating; a sad environment for the beautiful artwork that lies here.

When I returned home later that day I found a couple of large and one small oil painting in my sitting room. "How are you going to carry all this back?" I asked.

"You have a lot of bare walls in this apartment," he replied. "Wouldn't you like to hang some of them?"

"Well, …" I surveyed the paintings again. They were mostly landscapes painted in the European classical style by Kyrgyz painters; none to my taste exactly. But as I kept looking, a couple of them grew on me. Even so, I warned him, "I may not be able to bring them back. I'll have a lot of luggage myself."

"That is all right," he said, smiling. "I can pick them up during my next visit in the spring."

Next visit? Christ! He is taking so much for granted. Am I going to remain unattached until next spring? Oh no, I don't want to think about it.

Later that evening, we were invited by David for dinner at the American Club. It is a bar and restaurant in an old barn type building with American décor. The flag on the wall above the bar, the memorabilia, and the blues music set the scene for a menu of ribs, burgers and beer. There are only a few foreign diners at the place, no uniformed Americans among them. David offers us cocktails to start with, followed by the best wine on the list, a Georgian import, and insists we order a three course meal. I guess it is all on company expenses. Later on, he quizzes Gerhard regarding his contacts in a German petrochemical company. I can't figure out exactly what our ginger host does; I imagine he is one of those international wheeler dealers, freelancing his social skills along with his technical knowledge. He has been involved with Russia since the early 1990s and travels frequently to Kazakhstan.

"How do you get on with the government bureaucracy here?" Gerhard asks.

David says corruption is the big problem. Every major deal has to include a payoff to the Akayev family, after which you have to satisfy others down the line of authority. "This is a very poor country," he adds. "90% live on less than 30 dollars per month, and there is the 1% super rich." I point out the regional disparity, with the south a lot poorer and less industrialised.

"Yes, there has been a lot of unrest in the south," he says, shaking his head. "Akayev's clan is closely associated with the north, and ..., God knows how long he is going to last."

Our conversation soon moves to personal matters. The television screen above the bar is switched to the fashion channel. An endless stream of young women, some in their teens, parade up and down the aisle, wiggling their skinny behinds. We are thankfully spared the background music. David points to one of the young women with a pretty face and says: "There is my wife's double again." He has set up his young Russian wife in a newly built grand apartment in a suburb of Moscow. He lives part of the time with her and their three year old son. The woman has an older boy by a previous relationship, also living with them. David appears familiar with the fashion channel and tells us it is one that his wife and her friends often watch when they get together.

"Don't they get bored? All these repetitious images" I comment. David tells us, they make fun of the girls.

I turn my glance to Gerhard; he seems to be watching the channel with quiet interest. No doubt the beauty of the woman resembling David's wife did not escape his attention. What a contrast to the physically unattractive husband. In the dim lighting of the bar room, David's reddish complexion and rough features look particularly unappealing. In comparison my man appears so much more handsome, even if old. I feel content I am not compromising as much as that Russian woman.

Back in my flat we have some tea and chat about our impressions of the evening. Gerhard seems to be in a lively mood and in no hurry to go to bed. I tell him I am too tired and tomorrow we have a long day ahead of us. We'll be setting off for the Issyk Kul lake resort. When I say "good night" he gives me a suggestive look and asks, "Are you going to let me share your bed one of these nights?" I tell him, "Yes, tomorrow." and go straight to my bedroom. He's been sleeping in my study since he arrived in Bishkek. I've had no desire for him. Have I lost all interest in sex, or am I just feeling cool towards him? We'll see. Tomorrow is another day.

Chapter VI

The lovely Lake Issyk Kul

Issyk Kul (hot lake) is the second largest lake in the world; it stands at an altitude of over 1600 metres. An inland sea of sky-blue water and sandy beaches, it is an expanse of over 6000 square kilometres of water set on the edge of the Chui valley, east of Bishkek. High mountain ranges are visible all around the lake shore, the tallest being the Tien Shan, over 4000 metres high. It stretches along its southern coast. Mystery and legend surrounds the lake. At its eastern tip, ruins of an ancient city is thought to have been submerged under water. The western edge of the lake is a two hour drive from Bishkek and another hour to its eastern edge. The resort we are heading for today, Aurora hotel, is a former Soviet sanatoria located on its northern shore. It was a major holiday resort and a convalescence centre for communist dignitaries from all over the USSR. The pride of Kyrgyzstan and the jewel of Central Asia, the lake carries a variety of minerals that give it curative properties and a distinctive light blue colour.

On the northern shore, breathtaking views of Tien Shan can be seen along the edge of the horizon on the other side of the water. Here, green meadows, fertile valleys and relatively prosperous villages abound. Privatised tourism is gradually developing in the area. Super rich Kazaks have already built a number of plush villas; their oil economy easily dwarfs that of the poorly resourced Kyrgyzstan. With a direct road under construction from Almati to the beautiful resort of Cholpan Ata, no doubt mass tourism by Kazaks and Russians north of the border will eventually overwhelm the region.

I got a glimpse of the rich villas a few weeks ago on the way to a weekend workshop at the Aurora, organised by CACE. The trip was a treat for the sponsored faculty in various countries of Central Asia. On the way there I also noticed this remarkable looking, large cemetery. Today in our privately hired car, I had the chance to ask the driver to stop by so I can get a good look at this highly picturesque place and take photos. The cemetery is set off from the road by a white wall, over a metre high. On the other side snow–capped mountains line up along the edge of the horizon. I had never seen such ornate gravestones and decorative structures. One in particular, roughly three metres high and four metres wide, had little columns at the top and a number of colourful paintings across. Others though smaller, had the facade of little domed buildings. It was as if the deceased were each given an individual shrine.

Such ostentatious eternal resting places mark the Kyrgyz's high regard for their deceased kin. This veneration of ancestors, referred to as the cult of ancestors in ethnographic literature is in fact common to all Turkic people. But among the Kyrgyz and the Kazaks it is particularly heightened. The last time, when we went past this cemetery, a couple of my Kyrgyz colleagues sitting near me murmured words of prayer and ran their right hand over their face, in a Muslim sign of respect for the dead. I asked one of them if he had any relatives buried here. He replied "No. But we always show respect when we pass a cemetery." In a discussion I had recently with Jamila about religion she told me, it was not only *Guda* (God) that she feared, but also the spirit of her grandmother and whether she would approve of her conduct. "The *arbak* (spirit of the ancestors) are very important for us. If you don't respect them, your place will be in hell forever," she said. She added that every year on the anniversary of the death of her grandparents they go to their graveside and bring food and pray there.

***

It was early afternoon when we arrived at the Aurora resort. The huge complex is a three storey elephantine hotel of very long corridors, an indoor swimming pool, large dining rooms, numerous therapy rooms on its ground floor and beautifully landscaped large gardens that run into a woodland by the lake. The rooms are clean and comfortable, furnished old-fashioned style. We could have gone to a smaller, more modern hotel I was recommended. But I fell in love with the gardens in this place when I was here before and knew Gerhard would also like it better. What is more, there is a lovely sandy beach close by where you can watch glorious sunsets in the evening.

When we arrived at the hotel foyer, there was a noisy group of guests waiting for attention. Being the first weekend in November, the low-season, I had not expected to queue in the reception. The group of 20 men and women seemed mostly local Russians, with a few Kyrgyz among them. A big, burly Russian man, with greying blonde hair, was leaning on the reception desk. He was flanked by a couple of middle-aged Russian women. The guy was clearly frustrated with the lack of attention from the hotel staff. The rest of their group, chattering away, waited on the side. I moved forward behind the Russian man, hoping the wait would not be too long. The man was now shouting and banging his fist on the desk.

"Bloody drunk," I said to Gerhard, "I wonder how long before *we* get seen to." Gerhard stood patiently and did not react. Then finally a young woman appeared behind the reception desk, quickly uttering some words I didn't quite understand. The man ahead of us then turned round, smiled, and made a sign for us to move forward, saying, Pazhalsta (please).

"Thank you, we can wait," I replied in Russian and smiled back.

"No, you are guests here. Please go ahead," he insisted. His companion, a smartly dressed middle-aged woman said in English with heavy Russian accent, "We are big group, we'll wait."

As we began to register for our room, the guy introduced himself as Sergey, and shook hands with us. He was a businessman from Bishkek. His company was celebrating its tenth anniversary this weekend. He had offered his staff the trip to Aurora as a bonus. His wife Elena, accompanying him, taught English at the state university. When Sergey found out that Gerhard was German he gave him a pat on the back and said he was of German Jewish origin. His parents had been deported to Kyrgyzstan during World War II and settled in Bishkek where he was born. His wife was also a Russian German whose parents had been exiled here. Finding out about Germans living in Kyrgyzstan was no surprise to Gerhard. He had read about it in a book on the Rusland-Deutche and informed me of it. Most Germans, mainly farmers, had migrated to Russia in the 18th century, following the accession to the Russian throne by the German Catherin the Great. In the late 19th century, when Russia invaded Central Asia, Germans from Ukraine and the Crimea were offered land in today's northern Kyrgyzstan. The final wave of Germans arrived in Kyrgyzstan, and Kazakhstan, exiled by Stalin during WWII; he suspected them to be Nazi sympathisers.

"My family have all left," Sergey told us. "They emigrated to Germany a few years ago. My son is now studying in Wuppertal University."

"Didn't you want to also move there?" I asked.

"No. We have a good business here. If we moved over there we would be unemployed, living on little money."

Gerhard was skeptical of those gaining entry to Germany through their claim to German or Jewish descent. I had heard him say, "We have high unemployment in Germany and still, Jews from the East can just come in, get permanent visas, and immediately go onto welfare." But Sergey clearly didn't fit into that category. As we picked up our bags to go to our suite, he told us, "This evening we are having a celebration dinner in the main dining room. I am inviting you to join us."

I was very happy with this invitation. I did not fancy a boring evening together in that huge, half empty dining hall, eating the unappetising food I remembered from my previous visit. As it turned out, at Sergey's party they served a decent range of Russian salads, beef and pork dishes, puddings and at midnight, a beautiful birthday cake. In addition, there was plenty of Russian champagne and vodka on offer which was consumed in between frequent Soviet style toasting. Glasses were also raised in our honour, the special guests from Germany, which we reciprocated, wishing the company many more years of success. When the meal was over, a band came onto the small makeshift stage and began playing western pop and Russian dance music. Everyone was up dancing, most of all Sergey himself.

Gerhard was not a keen dancer; instead he took out his camera and busied himself documenting our night of fun. He took many photos of the company employees, the waiters, the musicians, and most of all, a woman in the group, a Russian buxom blonde in a bright red dress and matching lipstick. I had begun the evening quite self-conscious of my casual clothes: a shirt and jeans, in anticipation of a sporty weekend. But after a few glasses of champagne, I was ready to have a go at Middle Eastern dancing; the band was now playing Uzbek pop, similar to contemporary Iranian music.

"You are good dancer," Elena commented when I took a break.

"Oh, I am getting too old for this," I muttered, my heart pounding fast.

As I looked across the room I caught Gerhard's admiring gaze. He smiled appreciatively. Suddenly I had a sense of déjà vu. It was another party, in another big hotel, on the shores of the Bosporus. I had just met my German prince, and he had been wooing me all evening.

***

Gerhard Von Stein, the grandson of a wealthy German landowner had grown up in a noble household from Berlin. Notions of honour and duty, fundamentals of Prussian masculinity, and a strong desire to maintain tradition were ingrained in him as a boy. In such a universe the need to gratify oneself, to seek profit or pleasure was secondary to the call of duty. When Gerhard, after 20 years of marriage, could no longer live with his wife, divorce was not a ready option. The mother of his children had to remain his spouse in the eyes of the law, as she remained so forever, in the eyes of his family. No one in his family had ever sought a divorce, he claimed. Beside which, the nobility were inclined to marry within their own class. A common foreigner was no marriage material.

Did all this make him a mean or dispassionate lover? Not at all. Gerhard's cool and calculating demeanor concealed a caring and considerate friend, lover and companion. For a decade now, he had afforded me a life-style beyond my own means. When we were together we somehow found so many things to do, to see, and to discuss, despite the culture gap and the generation divide between us. He was my History Man, and my tutor in German politics, though we often argued. But what I learnt most from him was the love and knowledge of classical European art and music. In the past, Gerhard had spent a year doing a Master's degree at Cambridge and loved coming to visit England. We met as frequently as our busy lives would permit, in one or other of our two home countries and holidays elsewhere in Europe. But soon it would be time for him to leave, or for me to return home. The love yo-yo that went on for a decade in all this coming and going began to wear me down emotionally, though I grew more and more attached to him. How the hell was I ever going to break the chain?

The lovely Lake Issyk Kul

***

Now this morning in our hotel room, when I woke up next to him, feeling the warmth of his body and his amorous touch, I was once more united with him in our lovemaking. Then afterwards lying in his embrace, I was reminded of the transience of our union. He will be back in Bonn next weekend and in the meantime I am too busy with work to take any time off. When I came to Kyrgyzstan I had promised myself this was not to happen; I would end my relationship with him. My love affair had turned into a union of convenience, tinged with frustration and heartache.

But then he arrived here, lending me his listening ear as I poured out my concerns about my work, Jamie, and my career. He always listened patiently, at times giving me advice and offering support, though I am never sure how much of it he takes in. Beneath the skin, on that handsome face of flesh and blood, there is a mask of inhibition that conceals much inner thought. Still, I loved him all these years, and I still do. But now he has many worries of his own. The latest episode of family trouble has been brewing up for some time. His younger son, Thomas, has become involved in a fraudulent business deal that threatens to send him to jail. The devoted father believes it is all down to the bad influence of his son's friends, and his eagerness to prove himself a success in business. Gerhard's children could never be really at fault, not as far as he is prepared to admit. Still, the man has been in real pains about the turn of events, and I feel sorry for him.

When I got back from work a few days ago I heard him shouting over the phone in German, "Nein, nein... ." telling his son he should wait and do nothing until his return to Germany. They will then go together to see his lawyer. Afterwards he kept pacing around the lounge, scratching his head, then went out to buy some bread we didn't need. I had a vague idea of the trouble from what he had told me the day after his arrival. But as usual, I had to question him at length and read between the lines to get to the crux of his problem. His son's misdeed was his dishonour, hard for him to face. After some debating, it transpired that prison was a far shot. It was more a case of large fines, most of which *fati* would have to cover. This became clearer to him after our long discussion into the night. Then exhausted as I was, I had to stay up past midnight to finish marking essays. Gerhard himself was not a big talker. Every now and then, when my natural exuberance got too much for him, he would retort, "silence is golden."

Indeed, meine man was not one to blurt out his feelings, readily complain, or moan. He had great capacity to endure hardship and pain in silence. He had been born into a Prussian culture of rolling back tears and biting lips, made the more severe by the sacrifices that the War demanded of his generation. In surviving the ruin of his hometown, the great city of Berlin, he had learnt the passive resistance to pain, how to keep it under wraps. But in the Middle Eastern way I grew up, emotional expression was not only condoned but expected. For urban dwellers in Iran, noise and speech were signifiers of human life, reflecting the glow of energy at its core. Persian culture, famed for its love of poetry, its "roses and nightingales" was one in which utterances superseded corresponding actions. One made love, fought battles, found one's rank in life, and confirmed relationships, much through words. For the literate man and woman the experience of life was poetry in motion. Silence was certainly *not* golden.

The lovely Lake Issyk Kul

***

On our second day in Issyk Kul, we embark on a walk in the hills surrounding the Aurora sanatorium. Trekking through rough grounds covered in bushels we climb to the high point of the nearest hill where one can see a clear view of the vast lake shimmering in the bright midday sun. A few modern buildings, three or four storeys high, are dotted among the greenery of numerous gardens with a variety of trees. On the other side of the hill lies a village with an assortment of small, mostly tin roofed, wood and mud brick houses. On the main street, dusty and unpaved, there are a few small, ramshackle houses, a rough border of bushes and trees, and no shops to be seen. As we proceed on this road, a group of middle aged Kyrgyz women come past dressed in long skirts and colourful headscarves. The four women occupy the width of the narrow street as they stroll by, arms linked, chatting. A little later, a horseback rider gently gallops towards us. He is a Kyrgyz man with a long moustache. Alongside him an adolescent boy rides a pony, its reins held by the man. The father and son are wearing the *kalpak*, a tall white felt hat with black embroidery.

Soon we are by the edge of an open field and another interesting image presents itself. There is a house nearby with no fence skirting its garden. There are a couple of eagles perched on wooden stands, their paws tied down with ropes. A young Kyrgyz woman comes out of the house, smiles, and noticing that we are foreigners, greets us in Russian. She invites us to take pictures. But one of the eagles has now stepped down onto the ground. The woman approaches the bird, egging it on to get back up the stand for a good pose. No luck.

"He doesn't want to," she says in a disappointed tone, as if dealing with an unruly child. "The two of them help my husband catch pheasants," she explains. The domestication of wild birds is quite common around here, I am told.

We take our pictures regardless of the unruly eagle, and follow with snaps of the five foot high pyramids of mud bricks drying in the sun. Then the woman's four year old girl with an angelic cute face comes running to us. She is wearing a short red skirt with a denim jacket, and has shiny black hair cut short above her ears, very modern in contrast to her mother's traditional look. She poses with no inhibition and I take a picture of her before she disappears, giggling. Further down the path, we come across an orchard where a couple of yurts have been erected on its grounds, home to a number of families. Away from the yurts there are a number of rugs spread on the ground in between the trees. Today is Sunday, a day of rest and festivity. Groups of men, wearing *kalpak* hats are sitting cross legged on the rugs in the shade of the fruit trees, chatting. A number of women and a boy are busy going in and out of a yurt carrying trays of tea they serve to the men. We move onto the main asphalted road that eventually brings us back to the entrance gate leading to Aurora's grounds.

Later in the afternoon we take a walk to the lakeside. Its shore is a stretch of soft sand that loops at the far eastern end of the lake. Behind us are trees and bushes and around us none of the signs of a commercialised beach. On the western side the soft sand stretches forever. In the horizon is the snow covered Tien Shan range that runs into China. An eternity of mountains tower over the tranquil waters, their white peaks piercing the bright blue sky. I feel as if I am standing by a sea on the rooftop of the world; I am in the presence of nature at its most divine; it is awe inspiring. Was this how the nomads of Siberia felt when they first came upon these shores; the shores of the holy lake Issyk Kul, enshrined in legend and mystery?

Gerhard is duly impressed and wishes that we could swim in that beautiful clear water. But we are wearing woolen sweaters, would have to wait until June for the opportunity. After a stroll on the beach we head back towards the meadows beyond the landscaped grounds. There is a stunning view of contrasting colours in the foreground. An abundance of birch trees with white barks and golden leaves surround the meadow, interspersed with dark evergreen of massive pines. In the background are rows of green hills, behind them stony, brown mountains, and beyond those lie the massive Tien Shan range.

"This reminds me of Switzerland," Gerhard says, delighted with the view.

"Oh, wait till I show you my favourite spot," I enthuse, as I lead him by the hand along a shingled path, flanked by tall poplars, and through the gardens.

Finally, we reach the pond on the other side of the hotel, on the edge of the gardens. There is a disused café at one end, open only in high season. There is not a soul in sight. A feeling of solitude and eternal peace hangs over this place. We sit on a bench by the pond, facing the picturesque mountains in the far distance, its image reflected in the crystal clear water. All round the pond there is a panorama of autumnal colours: yellow, gold, orange and the mellowing green of weeping willows. The tips of the willow branches almost stroke the surface of the pond, as if reaching out to drown their sorrow. The still pool of water facing us is turned into a gigantic mirror, reflecting the colourful panorama and doubling our delightful view. It's a heavenly picture postcard image we imprint in our minds, as we sit in silence, gazing ahead.

I feel elated and exhilarated in this most romantic corner of the world. I am holding the hand of a man I have loved for a long time. I turn round looking into his eyes and say: "Gerhard? ..." but I can't finish my sentence, and look away. Is there any point in bringing up *that* subject again? I am acting on an impulse. What I really want to say is:

"Let's get off this impasse in our relationship. Let's just get married and start planning a proper life together for however long we've got left. I will look after you in your old age if you give me the next few years, when you are still strong."

But it is not that simple. He will have to first divorce Erica, and that he won't do. Is his unwillingness a way of avoiding a second marriage? I can never be sure.

"Yes, Frau Professor?" he says, "Gerhard your obedient servant."
I take a deep breath, sigh, and just say:
"Did you miss me since I've been here?"
"Yes, I missed you very much ..." There is a loving, sincere look in his eyes. "But I know it was important for you to come here."

Oh, for fuck's sake, I feel like saying. Always appearing considerate and correct, and not facing facts. My love life is equally important to me. I wish to be settled, live in one home, one country, and have a man by my side that I can rely on. Basically, I wish to be married. But the truth is his life is full without me; he is hardly ever lonely. Marriage does not offer him any of the benefits it offers me. On the contrary, it compromises his freedom with dispensing his wealth and the obsession with his family. Four years ago when he retired, he made a financial settlement with Erica. But he has left it at that. If

I question him about his reluctance to get a formal divorce so we can get married I will hit a wall of silence, as it happened before. Or, I may get a dumb answer such as, "But we are of different religions". I snapped back: "When was the last time you went to church, or I went to a mosque?" No answer. Since then, I have resolved not to ask again. I will not demean myself.

Now I take a final look at this enchanting corner of the world, before we leave to return to our hotel room and get ready to depart. The sun is going down and shadows are building up all around us, reminding me of life's imperfections. If only I could stop my mind reverting to that damned subject, I could be happy with him, cherish the time we have together, and accept this as my fate. Is happiness submission to one's destiny, one's *kismat*? Who knows? Fatalism certainly makes it easier to bear the irresolvable.

***

Today is a Saturday, the start of my weekend. With Gerhard gone, I have the place to myself and feel a sense of luxury with all that space around me, though I also miss him. It is mid November and the weather has turned very cold suddenly. The nights are long with freezing grounds as we head towards Christmas. But inside my apartment, it is the summer. The heating, regulated by city authorities, is on full blast, yet the sun shines brightly through the windows. I have to leave one open to cool my sitting room. I play one of my jazz CDs loud and jive about, moving from room to room. This morning Hussein called and invited me to the opera. He is going with Gulnara, his unacknowledged girlfriend. Gerard and Caroline will also be there. We'll go for a meal afterwards.

Land of Forty Tribes

Gerhard departed early yesterday morning. I came home in the evening, reclaiming my study. I was back to my nightly round of entering the apartment, checking all the windows were firmly shut and putting on the double lock on the front door, not to be opened again until the next morning. The routine has the feel of: my home my prison. For indoor entertainment, I only have the English language news channels, a round the clock coverage of world disasters, wars, and economic upheavals. When I thought about the weekend ahead, again all alone, I got depressed. I always hated it after he left. I would get attached during our time together, then spend days trying to readjust and be content with my own company.

The night before he left, Gerhard invited me to the Hyatt Regency for dinner. It is the only five-star hotel in town. It has a modern décor in the style of luxury European hotels with a touch of Kyrgyz arts and crafts. We had to walk through the casino to get to the restaurant. Kyrgyz bunny girls in black bowties and hot pants stood idly around the empty room holding out their serving trays and smiling into space; a sad sight. In the corner, visible from the restaurant tables, a four man band played traditional jazz. A Russian musician was blowing into his saxophone with gusto, inspiring a hall full of imagined music lovers. The few people occupying the tables near us kept on chattering among themselves. At one table there were a couple of American GIs with two local girls. At the other table there was a couple, a tall mature looking western man and a much younger blonde female. We seemed to be the only diners; the others were just having drinks. Half way through our meal a group of foreign men in suits came along and occupied a table near the couple. I turned round and looked at them, curious as to whom they may be. As I looked closer, beyond the group, I recognised the attractive looking man of fifty-something. He was leaning towards his female companion, a faint smile of content on his face as he gently stroked her back.

Gosh! I know that man. He is the president of our university, Andrew Bailey. But the young woman didn't look like she could be his wife. I heard they had a grown up son living on the West Coast. My colleague Elmira told me she had come to live with him over here in the first year of his appointment. She didn't like it much and spent most of the following year back home. Well, I wondered, how can a marriage survive the challenges of a western man let loose in Central Asia? Those guys here, young and old, really have the field to themselves. Simply being a western male enables them to pick the best of the bunch among the thousands of pretty, young and well educated females; many of them with knowledge of English, desperate to find a way out of the hardships of life here.

When I told Gerhard about all this, he took a discrete look at the couple and asked, "Is she a student at your university?"

"I don't know. I have never seen her before. She looks like a local Russian."

"Well, the guy is going to have an expensive divorce on his hands if he carries on with her."

"Or he could keep her a mistress forever," I said, not hiding the sarcasm in my voice.

The band had now stopped playing; we finished our meal in silence. Gerhard ordered some coffee, then asked, "Where would you like to spend Christmas?"

I could see he had already moved on mentally. I had to follow suit, not to spoil our last evening together. "At home," I said, "I want to see Jamie. Besides, I have to go to my university and pick up some more reading material for my students for next semester. The only problem is …"

"What is the problem?"

"Well, if we take over the flat for a couple of weeks when my tenants go on holiday, they won't pay the rent for that period."

"That is alright, I shall cover it for you," he said in a matter of fact way.

"There is also the problem with the roof," I added. "You said the tenants phoned and complained just before you left for Bishkek?"

"Oh, yes. You have to get the guttering sorted out. And get a proper builder this time." He paused for a moment, then said sharply, "I don't understand why you don't employ an agent to manage the property for you."

"I don't understand why *you* don't understand that I have to economise to pay off the mortgage on the Brighton flat." We had bought the place a couple of years ago, two thirds in cash that he put in. The rest was a mortgage in my name. I aimed to finish payments next summer.

"As you wish," he replied, looking away. He then asked how long I would be staying in London. I told him, two weeks. He offered to stay on until my return and take me to the airport, as I would have a lot of luggage.

"Thank you, that will be great," I said, and leaned over to give him a kiss on the cheek. His help was always invaluable to me.

Chapter VII

The American professors

Today we had our student talent show at the Bishkek Opera building. The place has a grand auditorium with highly ornate ceiling, a huge chandelier, and red velvet seats. A Soviet house of culture, its salubrious environment echoes Russia of the 18th century. The audience, however, was very much the contemporary Bishkek: mainly staff and students from our university, plus a number of government ministers, and President Akayev's daughter. The whole show was written and directed by the students, venting their frustration with certain members of staff. At one point, Alan Murphy, the head of politics department, had a towel on his head, running around the stage, chased by disgruntled students. The comedy sketches were then followed by a number of songs performed on the stage. A blousy Russian teacher at the university sang an aria by Puccini, followed by a pretty Ukrainian girl from the psychology department. Her Celine

Dion number was a performance worthy of first prize in one of the TV talent shows I have seen back home. Another student, a Kyrgyz girl from the American Studies Department, complimented a Madonna song with her smooth voice and seductive dance movements.

The show finished early evening. Afterwards I took a walk to the underground shopping arcade built underneath the cross-section of Sovietskaya and Moskovskaya streets. The location doubles as an underpass for pedestrians crossing those busy broad streets. The passageway is lined with little shops and stalls selling very cheap personal items from socks and underwear to toiletries, stationery, music and film videos and posters. In the afternoons, there are often young people sitting on the entrance staircase, playing the guitar and singing Russian folk songs.

Half way through the underpass, I came across Alan. He was carrying a small bag of shopping in addition to his briefcase. "That was a good show today," I told him. "I really enjoyed it."

He nodded in agreement and asked if I would like to join him to go to the Fat Boy to have something to eat. "Yes, I would love to." I followed, glad for company and the chance to get to know a senior colleague.

Fat Boy was a casual type of café restaurant frequented by people from our university. It had wooden chairs and plastic tablecloths. The walls were livened up with a number of water colour paintings and there was a bookshelf in the corner of the room displaying English language novels for loan. There was a bar on the lower ground floor with a dartboard on one wall used by the ex-pat community. This evening only a couple of tables on the ground floor were occupied.

We took our seats and ordered food and beer. Alan was quick to down his half a litre of light beer and ordered one more before the meal arrived.

"How do you like living in Bishkek? Have you got used to it?" he asked.

"Yes, it's quite a laid-back place."

"I love it here," Alan said with a broad smile. "You can live very cheaply, and the students are great to work with. Wouldn't you agree?"

"Yes, I find them very motivated and full of respect for the teachers. But we are very short of resources, and there is little effective management of the place, especially in my department."

"Your department is all run by local staff and they haven't got a clue. If you stayed a couple more years, you could run the place and get it into shape."

I thought for a moment, letting the idea sink in, then said: "That may be, but I have commitments back home, and besides, I miss London. … Don't you miss home?"

"Not really," Alan said calmly and continued to take large mouthfuls of his pasta dish. After a pause he added: "I do miss my son sometimes. He came here last summer and had a good time. He got on well with Alex."

Alexandra was Alan's wife. I had met her recently at a university function, when we had an interesting discussion about President Putin and his handling of the Russian oligarchs.. She was a Ukranian, teaching in the psychology department, a rather plain-looking, mousy young woman. She was a graduate of St. Petersburg University; had returned home to work at a university in Alma Ati, where her parents lived, before coming to Bishkek.

"She seems quite young," I commented to Alan.

"Alex is almost 30 years younger than me. It took me a year to woo her." He grinned.

"Oh," I said and left it at that. No doubt his US citizenship, not to mention his position at the university were seductive factors. But I was not going to risk the wrath of Big Alan by raising my doubts.

"What are your plans for next year?" he then asked. "Will you stay on at the university?"

"Probably not," I said, and meant "most definitely not."

"You should think about keeping your position here for a few more years. You could build up the discipline of anthropology at the university, have your own department and do a real service to our students."

"Yes, it all sounds great, but ..." I hesitated for a moment. "This country is a male haven, and I am a woman living on my own."

"Yes, yes, I see that," he said knowingly. "Well ... Alex had already been married and divorced in St. Petersburg. She had lived there for a year before she returned home. She told me quite frankly that in Central Asia her prospects for a decent husband were very bleak. Fuck! I am not surprised. Men here are arseholes. They are misogynous, lazy and irresponsible."

Good God! What language for a university professor. I was taken aback with his sweeping generalisation and felt like saying, "How lucky for you that local men are so hopeless". I now wondered for how long his young wife was going to tolerate his boozing, the foul language and his looming old age. I recalled the scene at the Hotel Pinar foyer when we had attended a university function, earlier in the year. Poor Alexandra had become really embarrassed by her husband making a scene. He had begun denouncing the imperialist American government and its agents, just as a group of US air force officers in uniform came past. She was afraid that if one of the airmen responded, a fight would break out. Alan had been knocking back a great deal of the free wine we were offered at the reception that afternoon.

Now as we nearly finished our meal, a middle-aged Caucasian looking man walked into the cafe and sat at a table by the window. "There is David Thompson." Alan waved to the guy to join us. "He used to be the president of our university before Andrew."

David was a stocky man with a paunch and thinning grey hair. He had a pleasant demeanor and spoke with a quiet voice. When he found out about my familiarity with Turkey and the Turkic world, he said he had lived and taught for many years in that country. He claimed to be fluent in Turkish and have a knowledge of Kyrgyz language. His social science first and second degrees had been from Yale and he had taught at Boston University for a few years. I gathered he was around Alan's age, in his early sixty's. After a brief conversation, our talk inevitably moved on to the topic of men and women over here.

"I am encouraging Sima to forget about London and stay on to build anthropology for us," Alan said laughing. "But she doesn't like the men here. She can't wait to get back to her Brits."

'That is not true," I protested.

Our former president gave me a direct look and said: "Let me tell you something, lady. If you are looking for a partner, this ain't the place for you."

"No thank you, I already have one," I retorted. "I just don't like the privileges foreign men have over here."

"Oh, the women here like older men," David Thompson

responded with an air of confidence.

"In the States young people are very keen to stick to their own age group. But here it is different. It is even better than in Turkey. Over there young women wouldn't feel free to mix with men, there is a moral restriction."

Clearly Turkey, especially the western region, was more developed than Kyrgyzstan. Any poverty that existed was not the new poverty of the post-Soviet kind. The society had its own tradition and history of accommodating inequality and deprivation. Women did not sell themselves so readily as they did over here. These guys, no doubt, knew all this in their heart but would not admit it.

"Don't you think," I asked, "it is the natural way that a person would prefer to mate with someone of similar age?"

"Not necessarily." David shook his head.

"I mean," I continued, "if it was not for economic reasons, and putting aside moral pressure from the elders, a young woman would prefer a young man."

"In nature," David went on, "the female seeks out the strong male to protect the offspring and ensure continuation of the species. In our human society a man with means, economic or otherwise, is the strong male."

"Let's put it this way," I pointed to the three young women at a nearby table, "If these women had a free choice between a young man and someone your age, wouldn't she choose the youth?"

"Oh, I can compete very well with the boys out there," David said with a self-satisfied expression. I looked at him closely. Which bit of you? I felt like saying; your greying bald head, or your pouch? But I didn't. Instead, I suggested we change the subject, and asked why he had given up his job as our president.

"I didn't get on with the governors," he said with knotted eyebrows. "I had my way of doing things. They wanted something different. At the end it became too stressful and I quit. I now have an easy job, none of the hassle of running that university. I have time to enjoy myself."

We moved on to talk about the new student intake. David and Alan both agreed that girls here performed much better than the boys.

"I run the entrance tests for the Student Exchange Programme, selecting local school graduates for their one year study at high schools across the US," Alan said. "If we didn't introduce quotas for the boys, we would end up with 90% girls."

"But even in the West, girls do better at languages and humanities," I said.

"That may be true. But women here are so much more capable and hard working than the men. You'll find the NGOs and foreign organisations are keener to employ women than men."

"Yes. I have noticed this in shops and bazaars also."

"My theory is," David informed, "The boys here have very bad role models. Since Stalin's time men have internalised the idea of keeping one's head down and not showing initiative. On top of that, you have the unemployment since the breakup of the Soviet Union. It has hit the men harder. There have been massive redundancies in industry and engineering. In many locations they have totally shut down. These are the male dominated sectors. Men are really lost. There is in fact a crisis of masculinity here."

"I like that," Alan said with a wry smile, "the crisis of masculinity. That pretty well sums it up." But this was no news to me. I had read about men in the former Soviet Union having great difficulty coping with the challenges of post-Soviet unemployment and loss of identity; they looked for comfort in alcohol and drugs. The women were often too busy trying to keep the family together, and having to make up for the loss of welfare provisions for the children, the sick, and the elderly. They coped, utilising the multi-tasking skills they had acquired as Soviet women. In those days they were expected to do most of the housework, have careers and be socially active.

But whatever this crisis of masculinity was, and however it played itself out in public life, for the educated young men here it did not help watching their female cohort elevate themselves through their sexuality. Kasim commented on this one day, when he said, "The girls here have it easy. Look at Jamila, she is taken care of by Roger, and Botagoz, another class-mate, has a Lithuanian boyfriend who works for a foreign bank."

Chapter VIII

Bride kidnapping

Today, I heard a shocking story of the kidnapping of a female student. I was on my way back from a morning class on the second floor. When I got down to the first floor landing I came across Jildiz and another Kyrgyz student standing beside her, both looking glum.

"What's up Jildiz? You alright?" I enquired.

"I am alright, but my friend, Baktigul here, just came back from burying her sister."

"I am so sorry. Why did she die?"

"She drowned in the river a few days ago."

"What was she doing there?"

Baktigul looked at Jildiz for a moment then turned to me with downcast eyes, "She … she was kidnapped for marriage."

"What …? What actually happened?" I was shocked and asked her to explain.

A few days ago a former roommate at the dormitory where she shared a room with her sister, Nazgul, had invited them to a dinner party that evening. Two other friends who lived nearby were also invited. Baktigul did not go, but her sister went along, accompanied by the other two girls. Those girls lived in an apartment with a relative and invited her sister to stay the night with them. The next day Nazgul did not turn up. Baktigul, now getting really worried, contacted the two girls she thought her sister had stayed with. They told her that at the party there were three young men, friends of their former roommate's husband, who insisted on giving the girls a lift back to their apartment. Then in the car, they told them their intention was to *ala kachuu* (bride kidnap) Nazgul. The girls had protested, but could not convince the boys to bring her back. The one who wanted to marry her was from Naryn, the same as the guy who had invited them to dinner. Naryn province is in the far eastern corner of Kyrgyzstan, bordering China. It is a seven hour drive from Bishkek. Despite the long distance, the boys were planning to drive Nazgul there that night to the kidnapper's family home for a marriage ceremony.

"Why didn't those girls go to the police immediately?"

"The police wouldn't have helped."

"Why not?" I asked, surprised.

"Because …" Baktigul responded in a depressed voice, "*ala kachuu* is considered our tradition and people don't like to interfere if they think a girl is kidnapped for marriage. Nobody goes to the police to complain."

"But how did your sister die?"

"I don't know exactly …" Baktigul paused, then wiped her eyes and continued, "I heard that those boys dropped the other two girls and drove off to Naryn with my sister who was crying and protesting. On the way, she had asked them to stop to let her go for a pee. I think she wanted to run away."

Baktigul began crying quietly. Seeing her friend's distress, Jildiz put her arm around her, comforting her, then turned to me and said, "Miss. Nazgul was going to finish her degree in fine art this year, and wanted to be an artist. She was very good painter."

Baktigul remained quiet for a while, wiping her eyes, then continued, "She had her high heel shoes on ... difficult to walk on rough ground. The weather was very cold that night and they were near a big river. Maybe she lost her way, and then fell into the river. They found her body two days later."

"Did they catch those boys?"

"They have gone into hiding. They had phoned their friend the next day and told him about my sister running away. This is how we found out about it. The police have arrested the one who had arranged the party. He knew about the kidnapping plan."

"Are you now pursuing the case to get the kidnappers arrested?"

"We can't do much about it. We have left it in the hands of the police."

"You have to push the police. You can't let the bastards get away with it," I said, my voice brittle with anger .

"Bride kidnapping is in our culture, what can we do?" Baktigul said with disdain.

"Miss Omid. *Ala kachuu* is part of our culture," Jildiz confirmed in an equally resigned voice.

"For God's sake!" I protested, "Killing young women can't be in your culture. You have to stand up to this abuse."

Jildiz responded with an ironic smile, as if to say, "Don't waste your breath; we've heard it all before."

Baktigul just stared into the distance, her grief etched onto her face.

Later that day I looked out for Jildiz, but could not find her. I was very upset that such a terrible thing should happen to a student at our university, and disturbed by the passivity of these two girls in the face of a serious crime. I wanted to learn more about the custom. What was this culture of wife grabbing all about? Did Kyrgyz men really feel entitled to snatch a girl from wherever and force her into marriage? Did they easily get away with it?

Recently, I had heard about the custom from Zarina, my student in the politics department, whose best friend was kidnapped for marriage. Zarina was doing her final year thesis on women and leadership in Kyrgyzstan, supervised by me. In our bi-weekly meetings we sometimes discussed personal, as well as, theoretical issues involved in gender and politics in the country. Only five foot high, slender, and softly spoken, Zarina possessed steely determination. I could always hear her approaching the tutorial room from the stomping sound of her high-heeled shoes. There was an air of confidence about her, shared by many of our students, considered the elite of the education sector in the country. I could not imagine any man coercing our proud Zarina into marriage. If faced with kidnappers, I hoped she would resist and find a way out. But what if she was raped? I don't know how she would cope with the shame of it, and not capitulate.

***

Zarina's family lived in Naryn city, the centre of the province. She went to school before coming to our university. The year in between, she had spent in Texas as part of a Student Exchange Programme. Her host family were a lawyer with his wife and two teenage children; they welcomed their exotic guest from Kigistan, as they pronounced it. Living with them, she had learnt to be a little more assertive and not shy away from expressing her opinion. Zarina had returned, determined to study law and politics, subjects considered male domains in this very patriarchal society. Her parents, though, did not take her choice of subjects seriously at first. After all, it was the degree from the International University and fluency in English that was important. Their ultimate concern was the kind of husband she could attract, rather than her career prospects.

Then within a couple of weeks of her return from the US, all kinds of arguments had ensued. She objected to having to do all the housework along with her mother, whilst her father and two older brothers did nothing but leave dirty dishes and clothes about the place, watch TV, and entertain friends and relatives. Another point of contention was the role and function of the town *ak saqqal* (grey beards). Nobody had elected this council of elders, yet they mediated with government in running the affairs of the town. They were the body with strong moral authority over the residents. An uncle of Zarina, a prominent trader in the city, was among the group. Nonetheless, she dared to denounce the council as undemocratic, a vestige of the past, and declared that after she graduated with a law degree she would campaign to oppose their authority. Her father was very angry with her and told her he had no money to fund her education in Bishkek. She would have to remain in Naryn and find herself a job or a husband, neither of which remotely appealed to her. Zarina's expectations had been raised well beyond what the poverty stricken Naryn could offer.

"Maybe a young man will soon snatch you," her mother snapped one day, "let's hope he has enough money to provide a life for you and your children."

Zarina had sobbed for days. The hope of returning to that dream world of American suburbia, where luxuries on offer included gender equality, was now fast diminishing. Her host parents had promised they would assist her return to Texas to do a post-graduate course, if she did well in her bachelor's degree in Bishkek. She was sure she could do it, once she got into the International University. Then one night, after a week of sulking in despair, she had a very vivid dream. She was standing at the back of their house where there was a patch of rough ground stretching to the foothills of the mountain that surrounded the city. It was dusk, and still no stars above. Suddenly a vision appeared to her. A giant white horse, its body covered in shimmering gold dust was galloping down the steep slope towards her. Atop was Kanikey, Manas's wife, fully bejewelled, wearing her tall white hat, and an embroidered gown with golden tassels. Once by her side, the great lady made a sign for her to climb on behind her. This she did as if picked up by a magical force, and they rode together to Issyk Kul. Once they had reached the shore of the lake, another horse appeared, silently waiting for its rider. Zarina mounted this horse and let it take its course as it followed Kanikey in the direction of Bishkek.

The next day Zarina woke up in a cheerful mood, offering to do the housework with no complaints. That evening she told her parents about her dream in detail, adding that she knew this was a sign she was destined to go to the International University. If her parents didn't help her, she would run away to Bishkek and look for a job, any job, to pay for her fees. "You will end up abused and maybe dead," her father had yelled at her. "I will not allow it." A week later, her mother woke up one day saying she also had a strange dream. Zarina's grandmother was on a bus going to Bishkek, but the vehicle just would not move. A number of strong men had come to push the vehicle, but they could not shift it. Then Zarina had got on to say goodbye to her granny, at which point the bus had suddenly started to move. But after Zarina got off the vehicle once more stalled. This happened again and again, until Zarina finally took a seat on the bus to accompany her grandmother. Her mother now concluded that she was meant to go to the International University. The following month Zarina was in Bishkek enrolling for her degree course. Her father had to borrow 200 dollars to pay towards her fees. The other 1500 came from the scholarship she had already won the year before.

***

A couple of days after I heard Baktigul's story I met Jildiz in class and arranged to meet her afterwards for tea. The cafeteria was quiet in the afternoon. We could sit and chat. Two of my female students, Botagoz, from Kazakhstan, and Zarina, were also there, just finishing their tea as we arrived. I sat with them to talk about bride snatching.

"Does it happen much where you come from?" I asked Zarina.

"Oh, yes," she said. "Two of my friends from school were kidnapped last year and forced to marry. Their parents knew of the intention of the guy but didn't stop it. In one case, the girl was very unhappy about it. But she gave in."

"What made her?"

"Once a girl enters the man's house and spends a night there, it would be very shameful for her to return to her parents. Most men would avoid marrying her."

"But what if the girl loves someone else, or just doesn't fancy the man? Can she get out of it?"

"She can," Jildiz commented, "if she is really smart and knows how to argue her way out."

"Yes, this happened recently," Zarina began to describe the case. One of the first year students, who had been on the Exchange Programme the year before, had gone back home to Osh city in the summer. A boy from a small town nearby was working in Osh and fancied this girl. He arranged with his friends to borrow a car to kidnap her, and told his family he was bringing her over. His family then threw a party for their arrival, and invited their relatives to celebrate. But when the girl was brought in, she kept arguing and would not let them place the wedding scarf on her head. She told them, she had three more years at the International University. If she married their son, they would have to pay her tuition fee of two thousand dollars a year and rent an apartment for them in Bishkek. Otherwise, she insisted, her parents would not agree to the marriage. They had invested a lot in her education and wanted her to finish her studies. The boy's family could not afford any of this and decided to return her home before the morning. "I think they realised she would never become an obedient wife," Zarina concluded.

"I could not imagine you either," I looked at Zarina. She chuckled.

"But seriously, you girls must feel very insecure walking the streets of Bishkek, thinking any young man around may grab you, drive you away, and force you to marry him."

"Educated men from Bishkek wouldn't do that" Botagoz said. "It is men from the countryside who do such things."

Bride kidnapping

"How about in your country?" I asked her.

"Over there this custom is also coming back, but in most cases the girl already knows about it and wants to marry the boy. This way they avoid an expensive wedding and the man doesn't pay the *kalym* (bride price)."

"We always hope," Zarina interjected, "if we are kidnapped, it is the right man who does it." They all laughed.

"What about the *kalym* for a bride kidnapped here?" I queried.

"The boy's family still have to pay it," Zarina replied. "But they pay less. They may give a sheep instead of a horse or a few hundred dollars cash. It could even be a few bottles of vodka."

Jildiz gave her a skeptical look and said, "In Bishkek no family would accept less than 2000 or 3000 dollars."

We then moved on to talk about the tragic case of Baktagul's sister. Zarina and Botagoz had already heard about it and could not understand why that girl had taken such great risk, in attempting to run away under those difficult conditions. After they left for their next class, Jildiz said to me, "You know, Miss. I didn't want to say it in front of them. But my suspicion is that Nazgul was raped and they threw her body in the river to cover up."

"That is horrible. Why do you think that?"

"Because when her body was found they discovered her nose was broken, and she had many bruises on her body. How could that happen if she had just fallen into the river?"

"That is a sickening thought ... Did the police do a forensic investigation? You said she was buried a day after she was found."

"Forget about the police." Jildiz said with a frown. "You can even buy your way out of prison if you pay the bribes. They say, it costs 5000 dollars per year of prison sentence, or if you have connections at the top you get less years. Sometimes they just let prisoners out after a period, because prisons are full."

"Has anyone in your family been kidnapped for marriage?"

"Yes, my cousin Samira. Two years ago when my sister came here to study, we shared an apartment with my cousin, her husband and their baby. It was very bad marriage. He used to get drunk and beat her on the head. We were afraid that she was going to have brain injury."

"Why didn't she leave him?"

"She would have had to go back to her parents' home, which was crowded and she hated the aunt who lived with them. That aunt had helped her husband kidnap her."

I asked how he had kidnapped her, and she told me the story.

Samira's husband, Oktay, was from a village in Jalal Abad, in the south. He had come to Bishkek a few years ago to work. He was a handsome man, but not well educated, a bit rough. He worked in a shop near where Samira lived and always chatted her up when she came in to buy things. She was a pretty girl, had just finished doing a course in hairdressing, and was hoping to get a job in one of those expensive salons in the centre of Bishkek. He had asked her out a couple of times, but she turned him down, knowing that her parents wouldn't approve. Then one day, he told her he was moving back to Jalal Abad and asked her if she would see him off at the train station since he may not be back for a very long time. She agreed.

Then at the station after the whistle blew and they said goodbye, he suddenly grabbed her and pulled her inside the train. He wanted her to accompany him to his village, to get married. Samira was not strong enough to overcome him and remained on the train. He told her, his family were expecting them the next day and had organised a party to greet them. He had already told her aunt in Bishkek about his intention and she was in agreement. She would tell her parents later. Samira was very unhappy and pleaded with him. But he kept telling her how much he loved her and if she stopped the train and went back, he would kill himself; he couldn't live without her. In truth he was ashamed of not finding a wife after three years in Bishkek; his mother had told him not to come back without one.

Samira told him that she was in no way prepared to live in Jalal Abad. "We'll come back soon and live in Bishkek', he promised.

Still, she did not want to marry him, but after spending two days with him on that train, she was very concerned about returning home and facing her parents. Meanwhile, her father's brother, who lived in the adjoining village found out about the event and phoned her parents. He then went with his wife to see her after she arrived. He had asked his wife to discuss with Samira how she felt about this man, and if she wanted to go back. He could not have this kind of intimate talk with his young niece. But his wife didn't really care much and did not encourage the girl to leave. She basically sided with her husband's family, especially her mother-in-law who had always resented Samira's mother for keeping her son so far away in Bishkek.

Hearing her story I said to Jildiz, "I take it you don't live with your cousin and her husband anymore,"

"No. She is back with her parents, and her husband is on the run."

"Why? What did he do?"

"He tried to rape my sister one night. We reported him to the police, and now Samira and my aunt are angry; they won't speak to us."

"That's awful. But why blame you?"

"Oh, that is another story ... Do you want to hear it?"

"Yes, go on."

"It was two years ago. I was invited one night to a party near my aunt's home. It finished late, so I decided to stay the night at her place. When I got there I found Samira was there with her baby. She had had a fight with Oktay, and left him. Then the following morning, quite early, there was a knock on the door. My sister was standing outside, tearful and shaking. She had a black eye and bruises on her arm. She told me that Oktay had gone out drinking heavily after the fight with his wife, then come back home and insisted on my sister having a drink with him. When she refused, he began to hit her. She struggled to get away, once through the front door, and the second time through a bathroom window. Both times he managed to drag her back inside. Meanwhile, an old neighbour had come out onto her balcony and seeing what was going on, assumed it was a domestic fight, and did not want to interfere. Then in the morning, Oktay told my sister to come with him to the bazaar; he was going to buy her a new dress to replace the one he had torn. She went with him to the bazaar but managed to lose him and took a *marshutka* (minibus) to my aunt's place."

"Did you then tell your cousin what had happened?"

"Oh, I was mad. I wanted to go to the police immediately; that man had to be stopped. But we had to inform my cousin first. So we went back inside to tell her."

"What was her reaction?"

144

Bride kidnapping

"She became very angry and even blamed my sister for having a soft spot for him. My aunt then suggested that we stay at her place and wait a few days for her son and husband to return from a trip outside of Bishkek, to teach him a lesson. They didn't want us to go to the police. But I disagreed. In a few days the bruises on my sister's face and body were going to fade and we'd have no proof."

"So did you finally go to the police?"

"Yes, and they tried to arrest him. But he went on the run, and we never heard from him again for a long time. Then, a few months ago, we heard that he was in jail. He had raped the daughter of an influential man, and this time the police had got hold of him. He was given a five year jail sentence. But now, a year later, he may be released. They say the jails are very full. The government can't afford to house and feed all the criminals."

"Will your cousin finally get a divorce?"

"No. She says she doesn't want to end up alone, and have to take care of her child by herself. Now she blames me and my sister for reporting the incident. My aunt and uncle also take her side. They all blame us for causing that man to go on the run. My cousin thinks that whatever finally sent him to jail may not have happened, if he did not have to run away in the first place."

"Well, it sounds like your cousin may soon have him back," I said with concern.

"Yes, I think so too. I just hope he doesn't kill her the next time."

Hearing Jildiz and Baktagul's stories, I felt really sad and angry. Had violence against women gone up in the post-Soviet era? Given the rise in poverty and criminality, I suspected it to be the case. Harking back to patriarchal traditions in the name of nationalism certainly didn't help. Bride kidnapping had many social, cultural and economic facets. I wondered how many cases were entangled in family politics. Had it increased in the post-Soviet era? I was really curious to find out more. I should include it in my research agenda for the coming months.

***

This afternoon, we had a big ceremony in the university theatre, celebrating a decade of achievements. The board of governors, members of staff, and selected students filled the hall. I found myself sitting next to David Thompson, the sexist professor. He looked smart, dressed in a suit and tie, his potbelly out of view and had a neat hair cut. He gave me a friendly smile; if I did not know him better, I may have found him appealing. As we sat waiting for the ceremony, he told me about his idea for a research project on bride kidnapping and asked if I would be interested in conducting a survey among my students. He thinks the tradition is much rifer in rural areas, and that it was never abandoned in Soviet times. He believes that in Kyrgyzstan women are much more accepting of forced sexual relations, and ultimately rape, than they are in the West.

"They think the man must really want it and need it, so they resign themselves to it," he said in a matter of fact way.

Bullshit! I thought. Central Asian women may be among the most subservient in the world, but I could not go along with such misogynous assumptions. There are many studies done around the world that indicate rape to be not just a violation of the victim but also a power play and a form of punishment. David may consider himself a post-modernist, and not want to judge local cultures. But as I see it, forced sexual relations and marriage are deplorable, whether in one of the Stans, or elsewhere. Giving it the benefit of the doubt through notions of cultural relativity is to forego humanist principles.

The highlight of the ceremony this afternoon was the presence of His Excellency, President Askar Akayev. He arrived with his entourage, walked up to the front row amid enthusiastic applause and took his seat a few rows ahead of me. I was able to have a good look at him as he went past. The man really is a gift to the cartoonists: head, the shape of a cantaloupe, with a large bald patch, slanted eyes and thick black eyebrows. Not that over here anyone would dare mock him in print. I am bemused, however, when I think of the Persian equivalent of his name, Asghar Agha (without the Russified 'yev' ending). It's a common, working-class name in Iran; not one you would associate with the president of a country.

But actually, the guy is far from common. He has the dignified look, befitting his position. I have seen him on TV, speaking a refined, fluent Russian in the manner of an academician. He was the president of Kyrgyzstan Academy of Sciences in 1989. Perhaps if he had stuck to his "optics and precision engineering", not venturing into the convoluted world of Central Asian politics, he could have still carried the respect of his nation. And there is the gossip about his drinking habit, whilst his wife is the strong man running the affairs of the state. Akayev's regime may be the most liberal of the Central Asian dictatorships, however, there is much public talk of corruption in his government, and his family amassing a fortune.

Emil, my Kyrgyz colleague from the politics department, told me, when he was first elected in 1990 he was a highly popular leader, expected to take the Kyrgyz nation through the post-Soviet phase of democracy and development. But before long, his rule descended into the old Soviet pattern of behind the scenes bargaining with regional clans, and doling out favours for loyalty. He never tried to promote a multi-party system of politics, or even establish his own party structure. He co-opted those who went along with his government; anyone disagreeing was left in the cold, or punished.

Akayev began his speech, praising and thanking international donors for assisting the university and bringing western education to Kyrgyzstan. Behind him, on the flanking walls of the stage were large portraits of the great ideologues of the revolution: Marx, Engles and Lenin. Their ghosts watched over the demise of socialism. Old communists, turned fervent nationalists, now governed the region, saluting the material gains of their former enemies. Today, it was viva private enterprise, and long live education as commodity. The Soviet education system no doubt had many serious flaws. But it did inculcate discipline and give the students knowledge of the classical world in a way that would be the envy of many state schools in the UK and the US. Clara, my landlady, who trained as a chemist in the 1970s, is certainly a product of that system. She seems familiar, not only with Tolstoy and Gorky, but also with Homer and Charles Dickens. Little Mira, on the other hand, has learnt about Madonna, hip hop and rap, but she could not locate where Greece is on the world map, let alone, ancient Troy. Books that Clara received for free at school are offered for sale at prices beyond the family budget. Not that Mira would have much interest in reading history or literature. There are no jobs around that pay a living wage for such knowledge.

President Akayev, of course, made no mention of the shambles that the local education system was, or the brain drain in the teaching profession, especially of the ethnic Russians. Neither did he talk about the corruption: students purchasing grades in place of books. Education in this country has been starved of funding for a decade. It cannot self-generate income, since the population is too poor, and entrepreneurs are not queuing up to invest in it. Our establishment, however, partly political in its foundation, and partly relying on the pockets of the elite, is above such concerns. To keep face, any hint of corruption among the staff is hushed up. The management of the university frowns upon discussing such matters.

So far, luckily, none of us foreign professors had the occasion to face this. That is, until Reza's recent experience. He told us about it last night when we met with our colleague, Gerard, for a drink in the evening at the little candle lit café on Sovietskaya street. Reza ordered a double cognac, in place of his usual single, and quickly began to talk about the attempt by one of his students to bribe him.

"Imagine the cheek of that brat," he began. "He has hardly attended any classes this semester and comes to me on Monday, pleading that I waive the attendance requirement for him to take the exam next week. He insists I give him a one hour private lesson before then, expecting that I would reveal some of the questions. What would be my fee? I asked. I wondered how far he would go. He grinned and said 'You name your price, my father can afford it'. The little bastard thinks just because I have Pakistani origin I can be easily bribed."

"But you know the students here are used to paying the professors to get through exams," Gerard commented. He had taught for a year at a national university in Tashkent in the late 90s.

"I don't fucking care," Reza almost yelled, "I didn't come here, half way across the world, to tarnish my professional career for the sake of a few hundred dollars."

He then went on to tell us that he had immediately raised the issue with his head of department, Tatiana, a local Russian, who subsequently referred the matter to the provost, Arslan Nazimbayev. A former deputy minister, Nazimbayev was the most senior Kyrgyz at our university. He had called a meeting to discuss the issue. But the student had denied everything and claimed the reason for his poor attendance was the way Reza taught his class: the lectures were incomprehensible and the course reading material too difficult. The fact that Reza's very slight stutter got worse under pressure at this meeting, didn't help his case. He was kept back by the provost and quizzed at length about his past teaching experience. The student, however, was simply told he could take an alternative course taught by a local teacher, even though it was well past course withdrawal date.

"That Nazimbayev is a bit of a snake," Reza fumed as we were about to leave the café. "He puts on this air of sympathetic, westernised professional with us, but I am sure he is on the take, him and that Tatiana. Have you seen the Mercedes he drives? And she has already been on two trips to the US this year."

Reza, I thought, was justified in his anger with his student's attempt to bribe him and the official cover up, but the sad fact was that local people had to supplement their earnings to survive. A few had the startup capital to engage in entrepreneurial activity, or found second jobs that paid a living wage. More often the staff at educational establishments resorted to bribery. In our university the practice was an exception. Generally across the country and beyond in the former Soviet republics, monetary success seemed to preoccupy everyone above all else. The post-communist world had become the ultimate materialist society, where money was the arbiter of almost all human relations. It had turned into the opposite of what was promised by the great communist ideologues, their portraits still hanging on the stage at our university theatre. Was this a price for the failed socialist experiment that was the first of its kind?

Chapter IX

Arab missionaries and Kyrgyz girls

The world of Islam in Bishkek is tucked away in a newly refurbished building, courtesy of the Saudi mission to Islamise Central Asia. The Hazreti Umar Institute (named after the second khalif, ruler of the Muslim world) is an Islamic college with 400 students drawn from all over Kyrgyzstan. The building is also the site of the city's main mosque. In the Soviet era, Bishkek, as with other major cities in Central Asia, was mostly populated by non-Muslim Slavs. In Kyrgyzstan even the ethnic Muslim population had little regard for observing Islamic practices. With religion highly restricted by the authorities, much of the religious knowledge was lost. Very few people performed the daily prayers, *namaz*, or kept fast during Ramadan, and rarely anyone could obtain the permission for *hajj*, pilgrimage to Mecca. Being a Muslim became far more a cultural identity, than a religious affiliation; a situation that persists today.

This afternoon I accompanied Jamila to meet imam Abdalim

Bakiyev, who acts as the deputy mufti (religious leader) of the country. To enter the mosque, we took a short walk in the courtyard and waited by the entrance door of the inner hall for the permission to go to the imam's office. This featureless building with its white-washed walls seemed a far cry from the beautifully tiled, turquoise domes and minarets of the Muslim places of worship in Uzbekistan and Iran. Standing at the doorway, I took a look at the plain, empty interior, but did not enter. Central Asian mosques are very much a male space, not welcoming women. Jamila certainly had no experience of worship in one and stood back. Female piety in these societies was always confined to the domestic arena, with the exception of visiting shrines that was particularly popular among women.

After a long wait, we were called to a small room on the first floor. A stocky man in his forties greeted us with a warm smile. He was of Tatar origin, he told us, which explained his light skin and hazel eyes. The Tatars, originating from the Volga region of Russia, had come to Central Asia in the 19th century as teachers and preachers, spreading an enlightened version of Islam. Our liberal imam began by apologising for being difficult to get hold of, and for cancelling our previous meeting. He had only just come back from a trip to America. Then as soon as I put a question to him, his mobile rang, followed by the land line, and then, his second mobile. He had only given us a half hour for the interview. At this rate, I worried, most of my questions would remain unanswered. But this being Central Asia, time was rather elastic, perhaps no one would kick us out on the dot.

Bakiyev began by talking about the increase in religious following after the erosion of communism. At that time there were only around

30 mosques across Kyrgyzstan, he told us, today there are 1600, plus seven Islamic colleges and 35 madrasas (Islamic schools), six of them in Bishkek. They train religious teachers for schools and imams and *moldos* (village mullahs). "We have real shortage of funds," he told me, shaking his head, "the government does not provide us with a budget and we have no income from religious endowment or Islamic taxes." He went on to express his hope that the madrasas and religious education at schools would make young people aware of the need for a religious establishment and their own obligations towards it. Meanwhile, he complained, the imams and the *moldos* have to sell goods in the bazaar, or find a second job to earn a living.

"Ask him which countries are their biggest donors?" I said to Jamila.

"Those with highest wealth, like Saudi Arabia."

"What about Iran?"

Seeing him hesitate, I added: "The government of the Islamic Republic has a mission to promote Islam around the world. But they are Shii and you are Sunni."

"Oh, we don't distinguish between Shiis and Sunnis," he waved his hand. "We try to keep friendship with all Muslim countries. We were separated from them for 70 years; we don't like to emphasise these differences."

"But some groups like Hizb-Ut Tahrir are very adamant about the distinction," I said.

"Wahhabis, Hizb-Ut Tahrir, Ahmediyye, Akramiyye, these are not well-known groups over here," he said. "They originate from abroad. Ahmediyye and Hizb come from England."

Jamila had told me about the Hizb recently. She had secretly met some members when visiting her fiancé, Roger in Osh. They were a radical Islamist group, strong in the south of the country with an international constituency, and headquarters in London. As for the Wahhabis, a highly puritanical sect originating in 19th century Saudi Arabia, they have been active in Central Asia since the region opened up to outsiders. But the other two groups? I have never heard of them. Since there are no more legal barriers to religious activity in Kyrgyzstan, Bishkek is flooded with many brands of missionaries: Baptists, Bahais, Jehovas Witnesses, the Hare Krishna, all actively proselytise here. The city has become a religious *bazaar*, promising salvation, robed in colours of different creeds. Only the extremist Islamist groups have not made much of an inroad among the relatively Russified, multi-ethnic population here.

When we got to the end of my questions, the imam informed us of a seminar session for women this afternoon. "Why don't you attend?"

"But I have no scarf to cover my hair, neither does Jamila."

"The seminar is open to the public as well as girls from Islamic colleges. You can go as you are."

Then, just as we got up to leave his office, he looked at me with a shy smile and said to Jamila, "I have a question for your teacher."

"Pazhalsta," (please), I said and sat down again.

"My daughter is finishing school next year. She is very interested in studying medicine in America. I want to find her a scholarship. Do you know of organisations that would help?"

I paused, thinking that perhaps he should contact the CIA. They have plenty of money for good establishment Muslims like him. But he seemed such a nice man, so I just smiled and suggested his daughter should come and see me at the university. I could then guide her through the relevant literature.

Outside in the corridor, I said to Jamila "Does he really think, once his daughter gets through a medical school in the US, she will want to come back here and live by his rules?"

"No," she said flatly, "but he and his family could go there."

Gosh! I had now met a mullah who is keen on America, the Great Satan.

As we began to ascend the stairs to get to the seminar room, Jamila turned to me with a twinkle in her eyes and said:

"Miss. Don't you think the Imam was hot? Lovely eyes …"

"Jamila … Behave yourself," I said. You are in a holy place."

She giggled away.

***

The seminar on women and Islam is held in a classroom on the upper floor of this two storey building. It has already started when we arrive. The room is filled with rows of dark plastic chairs. There are around 200 young women seated, not all of them with *hijab*. It's a relief. At the front, with his back to a white board, stands an Iraqi visiting religious teacher, speaking in Arabic. He has the mandatory three day stubble of Islamist men wishing to look modern. Next to him, a young Kyrgyz male in a white cap and a goatee listens intently, waiting for his turn to translate. Both men are dressed in open neck shirts and cheap suits.

I can only catch the Arabic words that have entered Farsi; Jamila whispers the translation. There is little emotion in the Iraqi preacher's voice and gestures. I wonder if he has repeated this same lecture too many times. His aide, on the other hand, gives a highly animated Kyrgyz interpretation in the sing song voice of a *manaschi*, and the emotive tone of an evangelist. His young audience seems captivated with his message, "Religion is all that matters in life, more than the air we breathe and the food we eat. In the West and among the non-believers here, women reveal their bodies and are treated like sex objects. But a woman should be treated like a gem, a pearl to be discovered in the mouth of a shell. A man may give up his life, diving into the deep sea to fetch her. But these immorally revealed women are like the honey that draws the bee to itself. What the bee cannot see is the poison in the honey."

Oh boy! What girl could resist being fetched by a gallant diver and taken away from the dark seabed, into the world of sunlight and fresh air? To be rescued by this aquatic prince charming, is that not worth hiding behind any number of veils? From what I know, Islam considers sexuality a major threat to social harmony, unless harnessed and regulated by religious authority. The agent of this potentially destructive force is the female body, its public exposure a source of temptation and social mischief, the *fitna*. In this way of thinking, the man, as with a beast or a child, possesses little inner control. The onus is on the woman to cover up, to keep temptation out of his way. The two and a half hours of the Iraqi preacher's lecture finally is at an end, with no question and answer. When everyone gets up to leave, they form a queue in front of the large table ahead. They have to sign the daily attendance register to receive their stipend of 250 Soms (five US dollars) at the end of the two weeks. In addition, they are offered a warm meal every evening to break the fast (*iftar*).

Among the women queuing to register, three of them are clad in black, head to foot. The only visible colour is the embroidered hem of their large scarves and the skin around their eyes. They look as if dressed for the streets of Jeddah, or Sana.

"They must be Wahhabis," the girl sitting next to Jamila says. "They are dressed like this because their husbands insist."

When the three come past, talking and laughing in hushed voices, I look close; there is a youthful shine to those dark, almond-shaped eyes. Though I am very curious, I don't approach them with questions. Fundamentalist Islam in Central Asia is a very sensitive subject, not to be broached with strangers.

Jamila asks the girl beside her, a first year student at this Institute, why she has chosen this Institute.

"I wanted to strengthen my religion as insurance for the next life."

I enquire who covers her expenses. She tells us, the college provides accommodation and pocket money during their study. She is from a small town in Issyk Kul. Her parents had encouraged her to take up the opportunity. They were both unemployed and could not support her. Her father had been going to the mosque for the last couple of years, where he heard about this Institute and its provisions for the students. She now hopes that when she finishes, she can get a job teaching religion at a school, or, if she is lucky, as an Arabic language translator.

Finally, we are out of the lecture room. The corridor outside is crowded. Some of the girls have already been to the prayer room; others are waiting to go in to perform their *namaz*. In another ten minutes it is time for *iftar*. The girls are all fasting; you imagine them starving by now. But I remember from the days when I used to fast and go to school, that by the time of *iftar*, the hunger was gone, replaced by a lightheaded feeling. Then just as we start to make our way towards the main exit, I hear female voices talking in Farsi. How strange! Are there Iranian girls among this bunch? Maybe they are related to the embassy staff. A few weeks ago on the Erkendik Boulevard I came across a man who resembled an Iranian embassy official. He wore a dark suit with an open neck white shirt, no tie, and a three day stubble. His woman, wrapped in her black chador, trailed a few steps behind him. The embassy here is in fact very small, so is the resident Iranian community. Recently I met a few of them through one of our students. They were runaways from the Islamic Republic, claiming to be Baptist converts. They had managed to get on the waiting list for the US emigration.

When the Farsi speaking girls approach us, I notice they have typically Kyrgyz features, framed by large scarves.

"Are you Iranian?" I ask in Farsi.

"No, we are from Kyrgyzstan. What about you?" Their eyes widen with curiosity.

When I tell them I am Iranian, their faces light up. They are eager to practise their Farsi, spoken with a cute Kyrgyz intonation. They have learnt it as part of their degree in Islamic studies, supported by an Iranian programme. Unfortunately, this was terminated recently, leaving them short of funds. What they would really like is to learn English, but they can't afford to pay for language tuition.

"You know," Jamila tells them with a straight face. "There are Christian charities that provide free English language tuition. But you have to practise reading the Bible."

The girls are not amused.

Soon it is time to break the fast and everyone heads for downstairs where the *iftar* meal is laid out. Jamila and I are invited to join.

"But neither of us were fasting today," I tell the girls.

"It doesn't matter. Please come and eat with us," they insist.

In the corridor, on the ground floor, there is a very long line of table cloths laid out on the floor, in the way of *sofreh* in Iran (ritual meal offered on religious occasions). Most of the seminar attendees are here, sitting cross-legged on the floor around the *sofreh*. There are soft drinks, bread, a plate and a spoon laid out for each diner. We sit waiting for the *plov* to be served. This is a common Central Asian rice dish cooked with carrots and mutton. Soon there is a murmur among the girls that rises to a chorus of melodic Kyrgyz song.

This much I had expected of a gathering of Kyrgyz girls with their love of impromptu singing. But as I listen more carefully, I am suddenly aware of the words being in Arabic. "What are they singing?" I ask one of the Farsi speakers.

"They are reciting pre-*iftar* prayers," she responds.

I listen some more. But I don't hear the guttural sound of Arabic in which Muslim prayers are normally recited. Instead, there are tender voices uttering prayers as if a melodic love song. They are performing a hybrid of Muslim Middle Eastern worship and Central Asian love of nomadic music. It sounds delightful; I want to find out more about the ways local Islam has adapted to Kyrgyz life and culture. Once we finish with the meal, the girls ask with genuine interest, "When are you coming again?"

"*Inshallah*, one day next week," I tell them.

When we come out of the building, it is already nightfall. The street outside is very dark. We walk carefully, taking small, slow steps along the rough surface of the road. The air is cold and crisp. There is little light or sound from the low rise buildings in the distance. We could be in the countryside for all I can see in the dark. I look up ahead at the sky; there is the thin crescent of a radiant moon facing us.

"Of course today is the first day of Ramadan, and the new moon," I say to Jamila.

"Oh!" she exclaims, looking up at the sky intently. She then bends her head, bowing to some invisible deity and repeats the gesture twice more.

"What are you doing?"

"I am greeting the new moon."

"Why?"

"Because it brings good luck for the rest of the month. You should try it, Miss," she says in earnest.

"I don't think the moon will accept my reverence. I am not a believer."

She gives me a disappointed glance in the dark and walks ahead. As we come onto the main road there is the sound of a car approaching. It has the lit up sign of a taxi on its roof. She quickens her pace and hails the vehicle. It is a very calm, quiet night. I look up again, and marvel at the stunning view, the silver crescent, amid a canopy of glittering stars, is etched onto a dark velvet sky. I feel so miniscule, yet not alone. I can feel the sense of connection to this beautiful vast space. I stop for a moment and gently bend my head three times, then proceed towards the waiting cab.

***

Islam as a religion was a relative newcomer to northern Kyrgyzstan and much of Kazakhstan. Beginning with the 17th century, Uzbek Sufi missionaries, traders and soldiers of the Kokand khanate (principality) had ascended the high hills and mountains separating the Fergana Valley from its northern neighbours. At first it was the local lords and tribal chiefs (*manaaps* and *beiis*) who took up the call, along with their slaves captured in tribal wars. Slavery in fact was not abolished in Central Asia until the 20th century. The rest of the population followed the new religion sporadically. However, what emerged was not the orthodox religion of the Arabs or Iranians but their own local version that accommodated many of the beliefs and practices of the nomadic tribes of the region. That was based on a cult of nature; worshipping the sky, the moon, the stars, water, trees, rocks and mountains. They were all holy elements, to be respected and prayed to at times of hardship and difficulty.

The holiest of the elements was the great God of sky, *Tangri*, worshipped by the ancient Turks. Even today in the Kyrgyz common parlance its name is invoked to curse or to bless: *Tangri jalkasin/ ursun* (may *Tangri* protect/punish). Then there is the ancient Turkic Goddess *Umay Ene*, still today invoked to protect women, children, and family life. Recently I found out that the word *Umay* (meaning womb/vagina) among the Mongols and the Volga Tatars, was the root of the name Homa, a magical bird of the Persians, and a popular female name in Iran. Another element of folklore, common with Iran, is the belief in the evil power of *Jinn*, other-worldly creature inhabiting the depths of the earth. It can appear in different forms to the unsuspecting victim, bringing illness or death. In the Iran of my childhood, and still in the rural areas today, a sick person may consult a clairvoyant called *dua nevis* (prayer writer, in Persian). He dispels the *jinn* from the sick person's body through providing the prayer notes that act like magic spells.

Among the Kyrgyz, the shamans, called *bakshis*, or *bubus* are called upon to cure the sick and dispel the bad spirit, the *jinn*. In addition, they may act as clairvoyants, expected to solve all kinds of problems from personal to financial. And this is not only among the rural folk of remote regions, but also consulted by Bishkek businessmen, university teachers, and all kinds of people in the country. My colleague, Aytan, recently told me about the widespread belief among the Kyrgyz of the power of the bakshi. She also told me she knew a very good one, whom she consulted when her daughter had fallen ill and the doctors couldn't sort it out. "I can take you to see her one day. You can consult any problems you have," she offered. I knew little about the subject, assuming it the domain of those studying American Indians and Africans. Now I have discovered it was one of the strongest beliefs among ancient Turks, still prevalent here. But how does all this regard for supernatural sit with Islam, a strictly monotheistic, rational religion? Besides, what happened to 70 years of atheism and being governed by principles of scientific socialism?

There is an idea that Islam among the nomadic people of Central Asia was a veneer over the pre-Islamic beliefs and customs. But perhaps atheism was an even thinner veneer over their deeply held belief in God, whatever its name: Allah, Guda, or Tangri. Under decades of communism much of the population in Central Asia maintained its belief in the Almighty, and upheld its faith in the form of localised Islam. They did this through sacrificing animals, reciting Koranic prayers and mass visits to shrines. The Soviet state could only ban religion and weaken its authority in the official domain, not in people's hearts and minds.

When we discussed the subject in the class one day, a student from Jalal Abad in the south stood up to tell us about his parents experience in the 1960s. Their village had been suffering a drought for many months; the animals were dying and the crops were mainly destroyed. Finally one day, the village elders got together and asked each yurt to donate a sheep and seven loaves of bread. This, they took along with many spoons and a *kazan* (large cooking pot) to the fount of their local river which had dried up. There, the sheep were sacrificed and their blood let flow into the riverbed. A number of young men and boys, including my student's father, then stood up facing Mecca and prayed for the rain. Afterwards the meat from the sheep was cut up, boiled, and fed to the gathering party. The remainder was taken back to the village and distributed among the needy.

***

It is a week since our visit to the Islamic Institute. Jamila and I plan to go there once more this afternoon. I wait for her in the tutorial office. We are to meet at 1 p.m. to discuss her research proposal. She was to give me its outline a couple of days ago; I am still waiting. At three we are to be at the Islamic women's seminar. It is nearly 2 p.m. still no sign of her. The girl is so bloody unreliable. But it is no good getting angry with her; she always has some great excuse delivered in her reticent voice and downcast eyes. The fact is she lacks the skills for writing a thesis. What is more, like most of our students, English is her third language. I only agreed to supervise her because of my own interest in researching women and radical Islam here. But this jolly Jamila thinks she can get away with skipping the hard work, by charming others to get her through. I should drop her really, but I don't have the heart to.

Finally, I go looking for her. There is no news of her at our departmental office, so I aim for the first floor food counter, where students congregate to buy drinks and snacks. And there I see her. She has just arrived in the building, looking very off colour, with watery eyes and sniffling. She has a woolen scarf wrapped around her head.

"I am sorry Miss. I got a bad cold since yesterday." she says in a coarse voice.

She claims she has called the office and left a message for me. I doubt it, but don't waste time arguing. Communication in this department is more a case of the blind leading the blind, even without the language barrier.

"Let's get some tea and go back to the tutorial room," I tell her. "You are in no state to go and sit in those cold rooms in the mosque. Have you taken any medicine?"

She ignores my concern and goes on in an excited voice: "Miss. I have some interesting stuff to tell you. … Do you remember the girl who was sitting near me last week at the Islamic Institute seminar? The one who took insurance on her next life?"

"Yes, the girl called Fatima."

"She told me, sometimes she went with the other girls from her Institute to visit street prostitutes to advise them against their bad work and help them find a way out. I asked if I could go along next time."

"Why?"

"Because last year I wrote a paper on prostitution in Bishkek. I wanted to find out more … ." Jamila was interrupted by a sneeze. "Anyway, we met last night and went to Sovietskaya street. We found a group of prostitutes hanging around there. But it was freezing. I think that is how I got this cold."

"Were you wearing this?" I point to her light anorak.

"This is my winter jacket, Miss. I always wear it. It is O.K."

When we go back upstairs and sit down, Jamila unwraps her woollen scarf. I notice she has a bruise on one side of her face.

"How did you get that?" I ask.

"Oh, I …," she hesitates, as her fingers run up the side of her face stopping just beneath the ear where her smooth skin looks bruised.

"Does it hurt?"

"No, only if I touch it," she says with knotted eyebrows. "That Mama Rosa was a big fat bitch."

She then gives me a run down on the events of the night before.

"At first there were only three girls on the street corner. We tried talking to them for a while, but they didn't want to discuss with us. I think they didn't trust us. Their Mama kept interfering. She even asked me if I was interested in working for her. I told her I was a university student. She said: 'So what? You wouldn't be the first. But if you want I can take you to a better location where nobody will know you'.

I was angry with her, but didn't say anything. It was bad luck that Fatima's friend couldn't come, so there was only two of us. We decided to leave then but two more girls came. One of them was someone Fatima knew from her hometown. They started talking, and that girl began crying. I think she was worried about her family back home. She wanted to earn some money to send them. She begged Fatima not to tell anyone she had met her."

"Didn't Mama Rosa object to you talking to one of her girls?"

"No. She was busy arguing with a group of men who had stopped their car close by. They wanted to take two of the girls away. There were maybe three men in that car. They shouted and argued for ages. Finally they took just one of the girls. A man also appeared from nowhere. I think he was Mama's boss. He looked in our direction and said some things to her. She then came to us and told us to get lost. We said, 'We are about to leave, just give us a minute to finish our conversation'. But the fat bitch started pushing Fatima, then pushed me. I pushed her back and told her to fuck off. Suddenly she punched me in the face. I fell on the ground and she was about to kick me, when Fatima pulled me away and we ran. The man came after us but he fell over, so we managed to get away. It was dark, and the road was bumpy. My heart was thumping so fast, I thought it would jump out of my body. I prayed to Tangri, and all my *arbaks* [ancestor spirits]."

Jamila begins coughing, her face looking taut, as if re-living the trauma of the night before. There is a silence between us as I try to digest her disturbing story. After a while she looks at me with anxious eyes and says:

"Miss …Please, don't say anything to anybody about what happened. If Roger finds out, he'll kill me."

"I won't," I reassure her, but tell her she really can't go chasing after prostitutes in the freezing night. It is too dangerous. Try interviewing them during the day, I suggest. "What is your fascination with this subject, anyway?"

"During the day they dress normal. It is difficult to get hold of them." She then lowers her gaze and adds, "We have so many sex workers now in Bishkek. People say we are the sex capital of Central Asia. If you go out alone at night cars stop to pick you up. Even when you carry books they think maybe you are pretending. I hate it."

I give her a sympathetic look and say, "Go home and keep warm. We'll tackle piety in Bishkek another day."

***

It is now over a week since our last attendance at the women's seminar at the Islamic college. Today once more, we tiptoed our way into the seminar room, with everyone staring at us. I recognised a few of the faces. But this time there were no uncovered heads. All those without a scarf last time must have conformed. Even Jamila soon pulled out a tiny scarf from her bag and partially covered her head. She looked like one of those Kyrgyz country women. Later on, when the lecture was over, a group of girls near us asked Jamila why I was not wearing a scarf. I told them I never did, unless I was inside the prayer room of a mosque.

"Do you do the *namaz*?" asked another girl, looking at me directly.

As I hesitated for an answer, yet another one asked if I was fasting. I had no ready answer for these intruding questions. It was hard for me to just lie outright and say "yes"; neither could I simply reply in the negative and risk losing their respect. So I ended up explaining that I could not fast whilst working, since my blood sugar dropped after a few hours, leaving me weak and lethargic.

The Arab speaker today had the same jovial Kyrgyz interpreter by his side as at our last attendance. He spoke of the Five Pillars of Islam, and went on to emphasise the need for morality and charity. But most of all he talked about the Day of Judgment. According to the Prophet Mohamed, he told us, it would come when the world was turned upside down; when the laws of nature were broken and the young had lost respect for their elders. An example of this was when girls with higher education became arrogant and disrespectful towards their mother. They would then look down at her and tell her to be quiet because she did not know anything. This would be the end of the world.

As I went on listening to the Arab preacher, I began to think, it sure was the end of one world and the beginning of another. The old world of Soviet certainties cocooned in isolation, had come to an end a decade ago. The youth here in Bishkek, like in every other major city in Central Asia, now had to cope with the confusion of values and identities that have emerged in this new era. The internet, cable and satellite TV, and contact with foreigners are transforming their world and presenting them with a range of ideas, information, and attitudes unknown to their parents. But this mainly impacts the new elite here. The majority, as with most of the girls in this assembly room, lack the resources, financial or linguistic, to have much access to western media's output. They remain naïve and receptive to puritanical ideas that relate to their ethnic and religious background.

When the preacher finally finished his talk, he proposed a prayer to those assembled. It was a prayer in honour of our mothers, and to commemorate those who had passed. The girls began to chorus in their soft, melodic Arabic and I found myself joining in, though more in sentiment. The atmosphere had become very evocative; I had a vision of my mother as I recalled her on my last visit to Tehran, six years ago. She had been diagnosed with cancer, with only a few months to live. I didn't remember her being particularly religious; but on that visit I noticed her performing the *namaz* and reciting mystical poetry. I imagined now, how touched she would have been to hear these Kyrgyz girls recite a verse of the Koran in this corner of the world, and to see me joining in. The sense of sorrow that had overwhelmed me then, was suddenly upon me now. I discreetly wiped my eyes, and kept my head down.

Later on, Jamila and I attended the *iftar* dinner with the girls, sitting cross-legged on the floor. The food was the same as before: oily *pilov*. I just ate a little, out of courtesy to the girls. The Farsi speaking girls were sitting with us, joined by a girl I had not met before. Her name was Raziyeh, an Uzbek-Kyrgyz girl from Jalal Abad, in the south. Initially, she had come to Bishkek to enter the State University to study economics, but was not accepted. Subsequently she had applied to the Rasul Akram Islamic University that provided free tuition and accommodation. Last year the Iranian sponsors had withdrawn funding from the programme, leaving the students in serious difficulty.

"Can't your parents help you out?" I asked her.

"They both work for the government and don't earn much," she replied. "But even if they could they are not happy that I am at this university, because they don't want me to wear the *hijab*. When I first came to Bishkek I used to wear short skirts and tight jeans. No one in my family wears the *hijab*. But after my first year at the Rasul Akram, I began to develop my *iman* (faith). I wanted to become a pure person and clean inside, a real Muslim, and learn to read the Koran."

"How do you support yourself?"

"One of my cousins who moved to Bishkek last year has let me share her room for now, and I teach one day a week religious studies at a school here. I had hoped to study English language at university and then get a job as an interpreter. But they don't teach English language at Rasul Akram."

I then asked the three Farsi speaking girls how they viewed their job prospects once they finished their studies.

"Our best chance is teaching," the tall girl replied. "Schools are always looking for teachers of religion."

"But you won't be able to live in Bishkek on a teacher's salary," I said.

"Maybe we find a husband and he helps us." The girls giggled.

"If they don't find a husband here," Jamila commented to me in English, "they'll have to go back home to the south where their families live."

"But how are they to find husbands, anyway? I asked. "They only socialise with other females."

"Sometimes they meet boys in public places," Jamila continued. "If they fancied each other, the boy would approach the girl's family to ask for her hand. But if they were far away, he may come and see her teacher at the university to ask for her hand. The teacher would then tell the girl she should assess the boy's degree of faith and see if he is a real believer."

Outside the mosque building, on our way home, Jamila went on to tell me that some of these girls may be kidnapped for marriage. "It is less hassle for the boy and probably cost the family less in bride money."

"But kidnapping for marriage is not allowed in Islam," I responded.

"Boys who get a wife in this way are not religious," she replied. "They just follow the tradition and their families encourage them."

Yes, come to think of it, last week during our interview with the imam he had mentioned the Institute losing a fair number of its female students each year following marriage. I wondered how many of them were kidnapped.

Later that evening, reflecting on what I had heard and seen at the Islamic college, I was filled with a sense of irony at the turns of women's history in this region. For centuries, highly patriarchal cultures, tribal wars, and practice of slavery had reigned over Central Asian societies. Whether they were nature loving nomads of the north, or the literate urban dwellers of the south, wealth, age and gender were the important markers of an individual's status. At the bottom of the social hierarchy was the young woman, *gelin*; she was expected to obey her husband and serve his whole family. If her husband died whilst she was still young, it was expected of her to marry his brother, or another close kin. If she refused, her family had to return the bride price. Those living in the cities were very much restricted in their outdoor movements due to sexual segregation and code of honour, *namus*. They had to wear the all engulfing *paranja* (burqa), though rural and nomadic women were less restricted.

With the dawn of the 20th century, news of modernising movements among Azerbaijanis and the Ottomans had begun to infiltrate the East, enlightening the small elite society of the Bukharan Khanate (principality). Then in 1917, with the Bolshevik takeover of power in Russia, commissars, revolutionary agents and Red army brigades began to sweep across Central Asia, turning the small trickle of calls for social reform among the elite into a torrent of revolutionary demands for the majority. The Bolsheviks decided that in the absence of a local working class, they should look to the female population as surrogate proletariat, potential allies in liberating Central Asia. Since women's subordination was justified in Islam, they hoped attacking the religion would undermine the power and authority of Muslim clerics and religious institutions. But the various anti-religious campaigns in the early 1920s were not successful. Hence, by 1927 the new strategy of accelerated campaign for the emancipation of women was launched. They called it *hujum* (onslaught). It focused on unveiling of women, and promoting their literacy and legal rights.

At the height of the campaign, burning the *paranja* ceremonies were organised at public rallies; women were urged to take off their veils and throw them onto huge bonfires. Those who took up the call had to return home in shame, having participated in this public act of undressing. Many were punished, some even murdered by irate husbands and fathers. A lot of women then put the burqa back on, waiting for their daughters' generation to finally dispense with this cloth cage that was so at odds with the new state's doctrine of gender equality. The tragic stories of the time did not only involve the indigenous women. The activists working on projects to liberate women included Russian pioneers, idealistic female Bolsheviks who had trekked a thousand miles or more, sometimes leaving husbands and children behind. From education, to unveiling, employment, and awareness raising, a series of innovative programmes were devised in an attempt to promote women's emancipation in the East. Some of these Russian women also faced harassment, assaults, and even murder. Could any of them ever imagine the great granddaughters of those they had fought to liberate would one day turn full circle, donning the veil?

Chapter X

An interlude in London

What a joy it was to be back in the capital of the world. My two weeks had passed me by like a high speed train; on the tracks one minute, gone the next. Even the grey skies and days of drizzle did not bother me much. I had left behind gloomy days and lonely nights in frozen Bishkek, coming back to a mild winter in London. On my first evening home, I went down the high street to my local supermarket, filled with a sense of luxury and a lightness of being. I could keep my head up and let my mind drift as I walked down the road; every step did not have to be watched closely to avoid stumbling into a pothole, broken paving, or an unmarked cellar-opening. The shops were filled with brand new shiny goods of all kinds, and sellers eager to serve. This was middle-class London, a world of material comfort and lawful living. The police kept the peace without demanding tips, and medical care was free for all. No wonder so much of the third world wanted to flock here. And some did, by hook or crook, creating so many ethnic niches that the English could no longer claim the city their own. Their numbers dwindled as more and more retreated to the nearby small towns and the countryside. In my neighbourhood today, most faces were either dark-skinned, or spoke with an Eastern European accent.

But my greatest joy was to see the sweet face of my little Jamie. Of course he is no longer little or sweet, except in my maternal mind. As if I needed a reminder of this, much of Christmas morning was spent trying to get him out of bed; the night before he'd been clubbing with his London friends. Most of the cooking, as per usual, was done by me, with Gerhard preparing his favourite vegetable, potatoes. On this day, I always kept to the British tradition of stuffed turkey, which meant an early start. In the earlier years, before Gerhard's children branched off, they would be with us in Bonn for the occasion. I then got some help from Daniela, his daughter, and Thomas, his younger son. Now on this Christmas Day, Gerhard was quite agitated and began to complain, "At my parents' home we had to be up for breakfast at 8 o'clock. No matter what time we went to bed."

"You grew up in a barracks," I snapped.

He ignored my remark and went on: "You really spoil that boy. You enforce no discipline on him."

"That is not true," I retorted. The fact was, I had tried hard but had little success battling on my own against the tide of London's youth culture. Gerhard was two generations behind, and in any case, had never wanted to be a stepdad to Jamie. Now I had enough of him recalling his disciplined German childhood. He would not admit that he could not enforce those standards on his own children, yet he demanded it of my son. The hypocrite!

That evening after Mina called me from Canada my mood really lifted. My beloved sister was coming to stay with me for a few days over the New Year. She would be on her way to join her family for a holiday in Iran. I let Gerhard assume that she was coming with her husband and her two sons to stay with me. He then decided he would return home a few days after Christmas and spend the Silvester Eve with his sister in Hamburg. I had gone along on a number of occasions, but was more than happy to give it a miss this year. Anna had invited me to a friend of hers for a party and I would be taking Mina along. We hoped to be dancing the night away. This was one night when I did not want to feel mumsy or past it. Gerhard was well aware of my family's disapproval of us not being married. If I had said my brother-in-law was not coming, he would have been happy to stay and come with us to Anna's friend. I know that he likes mingling with my friends and joining in their joviality. They in turn, like him a lot, just as my family would, if they got to know him.

When Mina came over, we began in our customary way discussing relationships and family grievances. I was never happy about our brother, Mahmood's, attitude to me. He always complained to the family that I had become too westernised and lost my roots; I had compromised myself with this conjugal relationship out of wedlock. A few years ago when he visited London he avoided coming to my place, telling Mina "I am not going there if that German is around." This big brother of mine has lived in the US for over 30 years and still thinks that whatever the little sisters do rubs on his *namus* (sexual honour). I told Mina, our father was never a dictator like him. She, as ever the peacemaker, reassured "Oh, come on Sima jun. Mahmood is only worried that you are wasting your time with this man. His concern is out of love for you." I told her that for men like our big brother love only implies possession and control.

"You are not being fair. Iranian men may be possessive and not so well mannered with their women; but they stick with their families. Not like that English husband of yours, ready to take off the moment life gets tough."

"Well, who drove me into Steve's arms?" I was hinting at Mahmood's relationship with me in the first couple of years I lived under his supervision in the States. He was four years my senior, at the time living and studying in Michigan. My parents thought that he could keep an eye on me, a young virgin, just out of school.

This was the end of the 1960s, when we walked barefoot in the park with flowers in our hair and idealism in our heart. When I met Steve, the groovy English guy at our university, I was fascinated with his anarcho-syndicalist ideas and denunciations of the authoritarian family. He had come over for a year's study, and appeared to offer an escape from the clutches of my brother. In my second year at the university, even though I had moved to a student dormitory, Mahmood kept an eye on my every move. That was the year I met Steve and decided to move to London to continue my studies. My brother was angry, warning me of all the possible dangers facing me, on my own in a foreign metropolis. But I managed to convince my parents that London offered me a better educational venue; they were happy for me to be in a location half the distance Michigan was from Tehran. Of course I made no mention of Steve until a couple of years later when we were about to get married. They were expecting me to return to Iran, the day I received my degree, and get married to one of the many suitors who had approached them for my hand.

Chapter XI

Partying with the ex-pats in Bishkek

On the plane back from London, I met Steven, an Oxford graduate, with a dry sense of humour and caring attitude. He was a social worker on his way to oversee the operation of his NGO in Kyrgyzstan. A couple of weeks later, on the first of February, he invited me to a Robert Burns night. Far from an evening of poetry reading, it turned out to be an ex-pats night of eating, drinking, and Scottish knees-up. The venue was the Fat Boy; rows of tables and chairs had been packed onto a small stage in the basement. Around 60 people turned up. I sat with Steven and four other people including a couple of local women, an American, and a Russian male, both forty something. The American, a rather fidgety, balding guy, told us he worked with the coalition forces at the airport. He kept getting off his seat to answer calls on his mobile. He spoke fluent Russian and seemed to be friends with the Russian guy, Boris, who did not speak a word of English. I took the American to be a CIA man; according to Boris, they had both been in Afghanistan over a decade ago. Boris was blonde and stocky, with a warm smile and a friendly demeanour. He had been a professional soldier, and was now working with the Special Forces in Kyrgyzstan. When I told him that I taught at the International University, he gave me a warm smile and said, "I am pleased to share this table with a beautiful lady like you. I would have loved to be one of your students."

I smiled back, thinking; it had to be a Russian man flirting with an older woman. Still, it was an ego boost, the likes of which I had rarely received since coming to Bishkek.

One of the two women at our table, a Russo-Tatar, spoke quite good English and helped me with my Russian. At one point, when the American at our table went out, I told Boris I found it interesting the two men were now buddies. Just over a decade ago they had both been in Afghanistan: Boris with the Soviet army, the American aiding the Mujahedin. Now they were allies in a new, ambiguous war without frontiers. Boris shook his head, giving me an ironic smile and said nothing. I guessed that after the war the two men could form comradeship as professional soldiers. They were not the ones designating the enemy.

The following Friday, I saw the American once more. This time, he was at the bar of the Hyatt Regency hotel having a drink with a group of western men. I was there with Carolyn, and three other colleagues. When we arrived in the bar/restaurant area we noticed Andrew Bailey, our president, sitting with a young woman at one of the tables. It was the Russian girl I had seen him with, when Gerhard and I had a meal here one evening. Andrew now invited us to join them. There was a four man Kyrgyz jazz band in the corner, dressed in black, playing like professionals. I wondered where they could have been trained. After we had ordered some beer, I told my colleagues about the American at the bar, whom I had met at the Scottish dance night and pointed out the irony of his current friendship with the Russian Boris, his enemy in Afghanistan. How the world goes round in circles, if you wait long enough, I said. Andrew commented, "Who knows, in ten years time we may be allies with Iraqis against Turkey." But I could not see this coming. America was just gearing up to embark on a disastrous war with Iraq, the outcome of which was unclear.

The three local teachers at our table were young Kyrgyz men with Master's degrees, strongly influenced by the US education system. In their enthusiasm for everything American, they dismissed much that was Kyrgyz or Russian. All this, of course, pleased Andrew's ears, and the other Americans at the university. What they especially liked hearing was that Russian was on its way out in Central Asia, and English was rapidly taking its place. When I said, I see Turkish language here spreading faster than English, they all looked at me with blank faces. This language was in fact taught at a number of schools, colleges, the Manas University (larger than ours), and to the employees of Turkish restaurants and stores in the city. For the Kyrgyz it was a far easier language to learn than a European language. True enough, in the 20th century Russian had been the lingua franca of all Soviet citizens, facilitating exchange of ideas and contact with modern and classical Europe. Higher education everywhere was conducted in Russian. But in the century before that, Persian had been the common literary language, linking the region with Iran, the Caucasus and the Ottomans. Much of this, however, was lost to the generations growing up in the 20th century.

Partying with the ex-pats in Bishkek

When we finished our drinks, Andrew asked the waiter for the bill, then did a quick calculation of each person's share. We all paid promptly, but I couldn't help thinking how miserly it was of him to ask the poorly paid local employees to contribute. I could not imagine it of a Middle Eastern or Central Asian man in his position. But then he sat with us socialising as equals. As for the girl with him, she sat in silence throughout, whilst everyone else spoke and expressed opinions. She must have been bored stiff with our company, though he tried to reassure her every now and then, running his fingers up and down her back. She may be a nice girl, very intelligent, sexually pleasing, and all that. But she is a local Russian in her twenties, last year's graduate with a bachelor's degree from our university. He is, on the other hand, my age, or older, with many years of management experience, a PhD. and a grown up family. What could they have in common? Not much, I guess, except her desire for material gain, and his for sexual gratification. Oh, what the hell! Let them be happy. We all live a temporary reality of sorts over here.

***

Steven is still in town. I am grateful for having him around and sorry that he will leave in a couple of weeks. He has energised my social life, inviting me to a number of restaurant outings with his associates. But that is as far as it goes. He is a lot younger than me and there is no sparkle between us. This weekend he invited me to another get together of the ex-pats, mostly NGO workers at the Euroasia Club. The venue was a large dining hall recently renovated with modern decor and low lights. A number of tables were lined together to accommodate our group of 20. Most of the other customers seemed to be Kyrgyz, with a few Slavs among them. A small stage on the side had been allocated for dancing. Soon after we arrived a local band started playing variations of disco and pop music.

As in other modern restaurants and cafes, you don't see any middle-aged local customers. Those who can afford to frequent these places are usually young people in their twenties and thirties. They are very often employees of western organisations and NGOs. This is a big sector in Bishkek. You wonder what is happening to the over forties generation. All the knowledge, skills, and experience they accumulated over many years are now considered obsolete, remnants of the Soviet legacy to be unlearnt. The exceptions are the communist officials who grabbed much of the state assets in the early days, turning them into their own private fortune. Whether in the government, the parliament, or among the business Mafiosi, it is their children who have access to all the luxuries, leisure, and the education that ensures their place among the future elite.

This evening I sat with Alice, an American teacher at the International School and Jimmy, a kind looking, bearded and bulky Australian. He worked for a foreign company in Bishkek. Alice, a petite woman in her thirties, had given up her job with a travel agency in Seattle to come to the wonderland of Central Asia. This was her second year of living in Bishkek. She lived with her eight year old son, Nicholas, in an apartment in the centre. Tonight the boy had come along with his mother, well equipped for a night of boredom with adults. He had a quiz book, sheets of paper, coloured pencils, and a little HE-Man doll. Now and then, when he tired of his artistic endeavours, he would finger wrestle with his plastic muscle man. Nicholas reminded me a lot of my Jamie at that age, a lonely child having to amuse himself in the company of grownups. But I could never imagine taking Jamie to a night club late in the evening, and even less, moving him to a country as far away and as alien as this.

After we had been chatting for a while, Alice told me about her difficult life back home. "Last year was the worst year of my life." she said, moving closer to me out of her son's earshot. "It was worse than the divorce ... Nicholas is my pupil at the school and my companion at home. He fights with me over everything he has to learn: math, Russian language, music lessons, you name it ..." I felt sorry for the boy, but also for his mother not realising how intense the one-to-one mother-child relationship could be in the absence of an extended family. Could the divorce have been that bad to warrant an escape to Central Asia? My sympathies for the boy grew as he began complaining about the smoke in his eyes and took off his glasses to wipe them. His mother had just gone off to the bathroom. I asked if he wanted to go to the bathroom to wash his eyes. He said "No," and quickly put his glasses back on. I tried to cheer him up, but he was not very talkative. Then suddenly he turned to me with a triumphant look, and said "Yesterday, I became an uncle."

"Oh, how is that? You are so young."

"I have a sister much, much older than me."

When Alice returned I offered to sit with her son, whilst she went for a dance. Nicholas wanted to talk about his friends and family back home; I let him go on. I had become his new friend.

Close to midnight I was ready to leave. Steven, myself and a couple at our table had decided to share a taxi home. I said goodbye to Alice, Nicholas and Jimmy and went to the lobby of the club to get my coat. Just then we heard a loud noise of shattering glass from the dining hall. We all ran back in to see what was up. Little Nicholas was standing by our table, looking pale and shocked, his spectacles taken off. There was a trickle of blood round the side of his head and a cut above his eyebrow. His mother was frantically searching his head and his clothes for broken glass. Jimmy stood nearby; there was blood on his cheek, and on the back of his hand. A couple of women hovered around Nicholas and Alice, trying to comfort them. The dancing and the music had stopped. All you could hear was the sound of shouting and swearing coming from the far corner of the hall.

It appeared that a group of men arguing minutes earlier had got into a fight, smashing bottles and glasses, but were stopped by the staff and other customers. Back in the lobby, as we paid the bills and were collecting our coats, the Kyrgyz manager approached, apologising in Russian. He offered us another table to sit at and have a drink. But no one wanted to take up his offer. Before leaving, I went over to Nicholas and shook hands with him. "You are a very brave boy," I told him. "Now you have a big story to tell your sister." He nodded and gave me a faint smile.

Chapter XII

Changing family lives in the new era

The following morning, my first class was the year four, gender and politics course. The students are an ethnic mix, almost a microcosm of Kyrgyzstani society; four Kyrgyz, including a half Uzbek girl from the south, three Russians, and a couple of Koreans whose families fled here in the Korean war of the 1950s. This was an elective subject and attracted only female students, except for one token male. He stopped attending after three weeks. Apparently, he had only signed up for it out of curiosity, but found the discussions "irrelevant" according to what he told Yulia, one of the Russian girls. I would not be surprised if all that talk of gender equality and women's empowerment alienated him. He always sat right at the back, never participating in the discussions. Yulia, on the other hand, would sit in the front, next to her friend, Valentina. They looked and acted like twins; both of them tall, blonde and pretty.

Land of Forty Tribes

A couple of weeks ago I had set the class an assignment requiring them to write about gender relations and the division of labour in their own family and community. Some interesting stories emerged. Among them, Valentina and Yulia's accounts seemed to be in line with the changes I have read about in the academic literature. Valentina's family story was as follows.

I live with my parents and my four year old daughter in a microrayon (suburb) of Bishkek. My mother, forty six years old, is a doctor, and my father, fifty one, used to work as a coal miner. He is now a pensioner. I lived most of my life, until I finished school in a small town, Kizil Kiya, in the south. The breakup of the Soviet Union has completely changed people's lives in my community. A lot of industry closed down soon after independence. Most of the men in the town and some of the women became unemployed. Then the money started to devalue fast. People lost all their savings in the bank. My family had saved up enough to build a house, but after the devaluation our money could only buy a bottle of samogon (home-made vodka). People were in despair. They had lost everything necessary for a good life; money, jobs. So they began drinking, especially the men. The situation affected the men much more. They had lost their power, because they had little or no income, and they had nothing to do all day. At least women had housework and taking care of the family. My mother and I used to do all the cleaning, laundry, cooking, even the shopping. When my father worked in the mines, he used to go out at 5 a.m. and come home around 6 p.m. He was exhausted, so he never did anything around the house, even at weekends when he did not go to work. My mother always excused him, saying: "he has a difficult job, he needs rest."

Changing family lives in the new era

When we had guests, my father wanted to pretend he was the boss; he would give orders and not lift a finger to help. But in reality it was mostly my mum who decided things and he couldn't go against her. Sometimes, he got angry that she was going out too much, but he couldn't stop her. In Soviet times my parents earned about the same. But my father gave most of his income to my mother, because she was in charge of buying everything for the home. He just kept three Soms to buy himself cigarettes. Now, it is me and my mother who are the income earners in our family. My father has learnt to do the cleaning, laundry and sometimes even cooking. In the past women had a lot of power in our community and in my family because they were better educated than the men. Most Russian women in my family and our neighbourhood had university education, whereas our men only had a high school diploma, or technical education. The women used to work in healthcare and education, but most men worked in factories and in mines. My mother had spent many years studying to become a doctor. But my father didn't even finish high school.

Yulia's story was equally revealing but a little unusual in her mother's multiple marriages.

I am twenty one; I have lived in Bishkek all my life. My mother is an engineer, unemployed since 1991 when Soviet Union broke up. Her first husband was a childhood friend. They used to play together and she would rough him up. Later they went to university together and decided to get married. Each had a stipend that was enough to live on, and even support a family. They shared all the chores and child care after my brother was born, but my mother took care of their money. Later her husband started a small business and also bought a very large aquarium with lots of beautiful fish. She would take care of them and loved them a lot. But now and then he took some out, sold them in the bazaar and kept

187

the money, even though *spekulant* (trading) *was considered immoral. He even bought himself a motorbike. So one day my mother got mad and sold the aquarium with all the fish in it. When they broke up he took much of the furniture even some things that she had bought.*

Her second marriage was to my father. He used to do most of the cooking in our home, but only because he liked to cook. My mother, as before, managed their salaries, and when they divorced he left everything they had acquired during their marriage to her and the children. After their divorce she married her third husband. This turned out the hardest and unhappiest marriage of my mother. He ran a small business, and my mother was unemployed at the time, but he only gave her money for food and clothing. Everything else, such as the car, furniture and television, he bought it himself. Most of his money, in fact, went into expanding his business. This man was very dominant, telling my mother who she could go out with, or invite to our home. He even tried to control me.

Nowadays, my mother lives with her fourth husband. They have been together for seven years and she is the dominant one. He had a job for a while and supported her financially. Now he is unemployed, so they both work in our datcha, (summer house), *growing vegetables. There is some equality of labour between them. My mother washes clothes and cleans; her husband does the dishes, most of the shopping and cooks. But most of the women I know in my community are housewives; their husbands earn the money and are the head of the family. It is prestigious among the young to stay at home with kids while the husband is doing some kind of business. But older women whose husbands are away or unemployed they do trading activities to survive. I know many such doctors and engineers who go to Russia with bags of goods to sell over there.*

Changing family lives in the new era

During the seminar session when the students discussed the theoretical relevance of their family stories, both Yulia and Valentina were echoing strong sentiments against the breakup of the Soviet Union. This was despite the new opportunities available to the young. Yulia was especially keen to emphasise that in a referendum of 1991 most people in Kyrgyzstan had voted against the dissolution of the Soviet Union. The lack of enthusiasm for independence among Central Asian republics was in contrast to the Baltic republics. In those societies a sense of nationhood had been firmly in place before the Soviet invasion that followed World War II. The tribal societies of Central Asia, on the other hand, only realised their nation state once the Soviet regime took over from the tsarist colonial administration. Following independence the Russian communities in Central Asia, who for over a century had led a privileged colonial life, lost their special status. Their situation was a little better in Kyrgyzstan, and especially in Kazakhstan where nearly half the ethnic population were Russian. In these republics, Russian was designated an official language, along with Kyrgyz or Kazak. Hence they did not have to learn the local languages, and with Russian being the inter-Union language, they had a head start in education and economic activities.

***

Tonight I went with Nazira, my Kyrgyz colleague from the politics department to visit her sister's family. We have become good friends and I wanted to get to know a Kyrgyz family. Nazira teaches political science to our freshmen students. She graduated from this university three years ago, following which she got a scholarship to study for a Master's degree at the Central European University in Budapest. She is a very bright young woman, culturally sophisticated, but rather plain looking. As such, she is not well placed to find a suitable husband in this part of the world. Her 27th birthday is approaching soon, and she has no one on the horizon. Last semester she began dating Fuad, a visiting teacher at our university. But after only a few dates and one weekend together, he dumped her for another young woman in their department. I told Nazira she was being unrealistic in her expectations of him. But I felt sorry for her, considering the great significance of marriage and motherhood for a woman over here. A childless female past marriage age is considered a failure, a flower that has never bloomed.

And yet, Nazira has so much to offer her family and her society. She is by far the most educated among them, and the only one with a professional job. Her parents live in southern Kyrgyzstan; she regularly sends them money and funds her brother's higher education in Osh. Nazira's sister, Zamira, whom we visited tonight is two years older than her, already married with a couple of toddlers in tow. She had studied dentistry, but is now a housewife, good at making pickles and jams, which she sells at a local market. Her husband is a pharmacist, earning a monthly salary of 140 dollars. The family live in a one bedroom flat in central Bishkek. It is one of the apartment blocks built in the 1960s, already quite run down. A curtain in the way of a door separates the small kitchen from the entrance hall. In the sitting room an old dining table and six chairs are crammed in between a shabby sofa and a matching arm chair. Zamira has already set the table in anticipation of our arrival, and cooked us *lahman*. I have brought along two boxes of chocolate and two kilos of fresh fruit. She thanks me repeatedly, saying it is too much, I could take some back, which I decline. She then gives me one of her home-made jam jars and apologises for running out of the pickles.

When Zamira's husband arrives, he is quick to take the older child onto his lap and keep him amused whilst his wife gets on with serving the food. Nazira informs me that her brother-in-law is good with the children and does help around the house. "My sister is lucky. She has found herself a good husband."

"He looks like the educated, genteel type," I tell her. I continue to have a conversation with the couple in a mixture of Kyrgyz and Russian, at times aided by Nazira. The young man is curious about my age and asks bluntly how old I am. I ask him to guess. He ponders a little and says "thirty seven may be thirty eight?" When I tell them I am fifty, he can't believe it. "Do you have any grandchildren?" is the next question.

"People here ask very personal questions." Nazira says in English, "I hope you don't mind."

"I am used to it." I tell her. "It is the same thing, from the Middle East, all the way to China; people often express their interest in strangers as candid curiosity. It is a way of being hospitable."

In the taxi home, Nazira and I begin discussing male-female relations here. She tells me, her brother-in-law is from an educated family in Bishkek. She says, Kyrgyz men from the north are a little more egalitarian with their women than those from the south. "I think in the south there is Uzbek and Tajik influence; they are more oppressive to women."

"But isn't it also that the south is poorer and less developed?"

"That is true as well." she says, and adds, "You know, last summer when I went home to Osh for a month, my brothers kept complaining that I didn't cook and take care of them when our mother was not around. 'You are not a real woman' they would say. I got angry and said, 'I am the one working and sending you money. You want me to do all the housework as well? In future I won't send you any money."

"And did you?"

"I have to. My parents are poor; they need help. But I have had many arguments with my mother, and told her she had spoilt the boys. I think now finally, they are beginning to change. On my last visit the boys were helping to cook and washed up afterwards."

***

Last week I called Kasim into the office to have a word with him about his recent lack of class attendance. He is a bright boy, normally very studious. I was concerned. It turned out he had taken on an additional part-time job to pay off the outstanding 200 dollars of his final tuition fee. I told him it would be a great shame to mess up his degree because of the money, he should drop the job. I will try to find him a sponsor. The next day I enquired once more about the student hardship fund; there was none available to him. Damn it, I thought, I can't let the boy fail. Maybe I should just pay it myself, though it will be my month's salary. Then in the afternoon at the university canteen I came across Sam, a retired politics professor from Indiana on a short visit. We had tea together and a long chat about the politics and social situation in Kyrgyzstan. I told him about the financial problems our students faced and mentioned Kasim's predicament. Here was a young man, very capable, aspiring to do a PhD, but faced expulsion this semester if he didn't come up with his outstanding fee. Sam sympathised, but did not say much more. The next day I happened to see him again over lunch. He told me he had been thinking about my student. "I would like to help him." he said. "Can I ... give you the 200 dollars for his fees?"

What a kind soul, I thought. His generosity really touched me; I felt like getting off my chair to give him a hug and a kiss. But that may have embarrassed him, so I just thanked him and said, "I will ask Kasim to see you. You can give it to him directly." Later that afternoon, I got hold of Kasim and told him about the offer. He was so overjoyed; he threw his arms around me and kissed me. "I don't know how to thank you Miss Omid."

"Thank Professor Engelton. But don't miss any more classes."

"I promise." He went off with a beaming smile. A couple of days later, he came to see me with the news that the university had in fact reduced his remaining fee to one hundred dollars. "Shall I return the rest of the money?" he asked.

"No. Keep it," I told him. A hundred dollars would not make a big dent in Professor Engleton's pocket; he had already written it off. Kasim, on the other hand, with both parents unemployed, had a hundred and one need for that money.

At the weekend, Kasim, accompanied by Jamila come to visit me at home. They are more than just students; they have become my young friends. I admire them for their commitment to their families, and their respect for knowledge and experience that makes them look up to their elders. Seeing them turn up unannounced is a nice surprise. Jamila is carrying a small bunch of roses. She says they are from Kasim, to thank me for helping him with his tuition fee and for the reference I gave him for a scholarship application to a Swedish university. He has just passed their first stage tests. After I offer them tea and biscuits I ask Kasim about his plans for next year. He tells me if he gets the scholarship, he will go to Sweden to do the Master's degree, then return to Kyrgyzstan to teach at our university. He has a lot of good ideas about rearranging the ethnology department, and raising the standards for the students. After teaching here for a couple of years, he hopes to get a scholarship to do a PhD in the US.

"What do your parents say about it?" I ask.

"My mother wants me to continue with my education. She says if I go abroad, she will go back to the job she had with the railways. But I don't want her to do that. It was very hard work and it made her sick. If she can't get some other work, I will stay here and try to get a job with an NGO or a foreign organisation to help my family."

I turn to Jamila and ask her about her plans for the next academic year. She has been quiet, looking subdued. She says Roger has been negotiating with her mother for them to get married in August. In a glum voice she says, "I would like to contribute to the wedding expenses." At present she has a part-time job, teaching English four hours a week at a secondary school. It pays her 80 dollars per month; considered good money over here. She sends part of it to her mother, whose monthly salary as a school teacher is only ten Som (less than three dollars). Jamila's rent for the small apartment she shares with a fellow-student is paid by Roger. To save up for the wedding, she will need an additional casual job.

"What about *kalym*? Is Roger going to pay it?" I ask.

"Yes, of course. He was talking about buying an apartment in Bishkek, so my brother could come here to study. My mother would come to join him."

"Could he afford it? I have heard even a small apartment here will cost around 10000 dollars."

"His parents are rich. I have been to their house in Connecticut. It's huge."

"What do they say about his marriage to you?"

"I think they liked me," she says with a shy smile.

I am sceptical about the whole proposition. Roger is forty already, and keen to have children soon, she told me recently. "Do you think you are ready for motherhood?" I challenge her. "I thought you wanted to further your studies,"

"Yes Miss. I want to be like you." She looks at me bright eyed. "I want to have a son and one day get a PhD."

As Jamila and I keep talking, I can see Kasim is looking a little impatient. I don't think he appreciates hearing about Jamila's marriage. After he goes out to buy some milk to have with our coffee, Jamila tells me she has some doubts about marrying Roger. On her last trip to Osh she found a couple of the young women working in his office hovering around him. One of them sounded like she was intimate with him. Jamila felt very insecure about her relationship and wondered if he was going to marry her after all. She came back to Bishkek, crying for days and wanted to break it off with him. David Thompson, whom she knew from attending his class last year, was going to start a new job with an American organisation in Alma Ati. Last week he invited her to come over after her graduation in June and promised to find her a job there.

"I can still take up Mr. Thompson's offer and go to work in Alma Ati." Jamila says as she walks over to the kitchen and begins to wash the breakfast dishes I have left in the sink.

"Please, don't touch anything." I tell her. "I don't want you to do housework around here." But she is so fast; there is no time to argue.

"What do you think I should do next year Miss?" she asks, as she dries her hands.

"I think you should stay away from that old lecher. You know he has a reputation with female students."

"Yes," she says with a look of mischief, "But I can take care of myself."

"Maybe. But you are still very young. A lot to see and experience."

"Do you think I should marry Roger?"

"You've asked me before. Do you really want to?"

"I am not sure. I want to get a Green Card. But, ... I think I also love him. He is good to me."

"Just don't let yourself get pregnant soon, whatever you do," I advise her.

Once Kasim returns, we stop talking about Jamila. When they are ready to leave, he picks up her heavy backpack and carries it. I notice the affectionate glances they exchange as she thanks him. They are soon out in the courtyard. I watch them through my kitchen window, walk away side by side, Kasim's hand on her shoulder. I begin to wonder: can those two afford to get too close to each other? She needs Roger, and he needs his freedom to fulfil his academic ambitions. Yet they are so well suited to each other; same age, same culture, both of them young and sweet, a good looking pair.

Chapter XIII

The magnificent Samarkand

On the plane to Tashkent I found myself next to Jane, a forty-something red haired lawyer from Mississippi. With her designer top and carefully manicured nails, she radiated a sense of glamour. We got chatting straight away. She was on a two-year assignment to democratise Kyrgyzstan, commissioned by the American Bar Association. This was the end of her first year, spent mostly in meetings with representatives of local authorities, organising awareness training for the judiciary and the police. In her broad southern accent she talked about her frustration in communicating with the Kyrgyz officials. "Language is not the problem," she said, tapping on her seat's arm rest, "I have a very good interpreter; he comes with me on every trip. It's their mentality that sucks ...; trapped in Soviet and Central Asian mindsets."

I asked her what they discussed at their workshops. "Basic human rights issues and differences in Kyrgyz and American legal systems," she replied. "We ask the participants how one could rectify injustice in Kyrgyzstan."

"What is the response like?"

"I can never be sure ..." she stopped and looked straight at me. "But to be frank, I think a lot of them come along for the free lunch and the time off."

"Are you really surprised?" I asked. "If a policeman takes bribes so he can feed his family ..."

"Oh I know, I know," she interrupted, "corruption is endemic here, and there is a lot of poverty, but one has to start somewhere."

"Well, I don't think your starting point is the right place," I suggested.

"What would you recommend?" she asked in a weary tone of voice.

"I would begin by doing something about his wages, before discussing the merits of the American legal system."

"Maybe," she shrugged. "But we can't prop up the economies of all the corrupt countries in the world. Anyways, the richer countries in the neighbourhood are no better."

"Then maybe you are better off back home, without all the stresses here."

"I can't do that," she said sharply. "I have a big mortgage and need the money from working overseas."

Seeing the lines of stress on Jane's forehead I went on to ask her, "Are you now off on holiday?"

"Yep," she said with a glint in her eyes. "I am off to Rome for a week to meet a friend of mine who is flying in from Atlanta. I am hoping we will meet some hot Italian men."

"I wish you good luck," I said with a tinge of envy.

"I deserve it." She laughed. Earlier we had exchanged notes on the frustrations of being a single female in Bishkek, and the unfair advantage western men enjoyed. In the silence that followed, I wondered how long it would be before I got a lucky break. It sure wasn't going to happen in this part of the world.

***

At Tashkent airport the formalities of getting through are surprisingly swift. The whole place is fairly quiet. I am to be picked up by a local colleague, Suleiman. I keep wondering what to do if he doesn't turn up. I have no other contact in the city. He has promised to drive me straight to Samarkand, where I will stay for a couple of days at the house of Spanish colleagues, Alfonso and Rosita. Suleiman is an Uzbek national, similarly sponsored by CACE; he teaches at the State University in Tashkent. He completed a Master's degree at Indiana University three years ago, and speaks excellent English. We all met at the CACE convention in Issyk Kul, at the end of October. On the coach trip back to Bishkek, Suleiman and I had long discussions about Uzbek people, and the history and literature they shared with Iranians. He seemed to be very interested in my Iranian background and keen to converse with me, though generally he appeared rather reserved.

When I mentioned my interest in visiting Uzbekistan he offered to arrange a trip for me. He had friends in Tashkent, a young couple who would accommodate me for a week or more. I told him that Aynur, a Turkish sociologist colleague at my university in London had discouraged me doing research in the country. She had been on many field trips there and considered it her domain of expertise. When she heard that I was planning to apply for a grant to conduct anthropological research in Uzbekistan, she warned me of the difficulty of penetrating Uzbek culture. "They are introverted people, very aloof," she said in her usual emphatic manner.

When I reflected on her remarks during my discussions with Suleiman, his response was, "Nonsense! You come and see for yourself. We are very sociable people."

It seemed that in the scholarly scramble for Central Asia, Aynur had her own agenda, keeping me off my academic interest in the region.

Finally Suleiman arrives; I recognise him straight away. Relatively tall and well built, he has typically Uzbek features: high cheekbones and black hair and eyes. His slightly receding hairline gives him a more mature look than a man in his mid-thirties. "Welcome to our country," he says with a smile and we shake hands. He apologises for being late and leads me to his car. We set off for Samarkand straight away. "It will take us around three hours to get there," he informs. "I will stay the night and come back in the morning. I am not teaching till the afternoon."

I thank him for his kind offer. It is a relief not to have to make my own way there. I tell him that many years ago I owned a Lada in London.

"You mean the English buy Russian cars? They are crap." He chuckles.

"It was a good student car, very cheap," I say.

He asks about the types of cars people drive in the UK and says that the elite here drive top German cars. Ordinary people can only afford Russian cars, if that.

We drive along some of Tashkent's wide avenues, hemmed in by low rise modern Soviet buildings. Soon we have reached the highway out of town. The airport is actually quite close to the city centre. The road condition is good, no potholes. It's a pity about the weather; it's quite cold, and the sky is overcast with drizzling rain. "Is this the usual weather in March?" I ask. He gives me a playful look and says, "You brought the English weather with you."

A few minutes later we have reached the edge of the city and are stopped at a police checkpoint. I pull out my British passport, but they ignore me. He has told them I am an academic guest. Once we are through, he tells me there may be six more, but not to worry, he has all his documents at hand. "What is this, a police state?" I bemuse. He gives me a wry smile and says nothing. I ask him what he thinks of the long arm of the Uzbek state and the terrible torture going on in the prisons here. "I read in one report they boil prisoners."

"We are not cannibals," he retorts.

"Are you telling me they don't severely torture political prisoners?"

"I don't know. I am not involved in politics."

I gather from his tone of voice that he does not want to discuss the subject. I am disappointed; I want to find out more. From the news reports I have read the regime seems obsessed with the Islamist threat, and plays to the post-September 11 anxieties of the US to prop up its rule. Perhaps he just doesn't want to voice criticism in front of someone he doesn't know very well. I shouldn't blame him if there are eyes and ears everywhere.

In any case, I rely on his hospitality; better not enter a political argument. Instead, I revert to the safe subject of talking about Uzbek language and literature. He agrees that we have a common literary heritage spanning a thousand years from the time of Ferdowsi's Shahnameh, the Book of Kings. He tells me, he has read some of it in its Russian translation, but would love to learn Farsi to read it in the original. "You know that for many centuries, Persian was the literary language for all the Turkic people, as well as, the Iranians" he says.

"Yes, of course. We read the poetry of Nizami and Molavi in our school books in Iran," I reply and add that, Nizami, the Azerbaijani poet from Ganja in the Caucasus, has been compared to Shakespeare, his love story, Leili and Majnoon, a classic tale of tragic love, well known in many countries from Turkey to Central Asia. Similarly, the great Sufi philosopher poet, Molavi, known as Mevlana by the Turks, wrote virtually everything in Farsi. He was actually born in today's southern Uzbekistan.

"I would love to visit Neishahpoor, Isfahan and Shiraz," he says with enthusiasm. "I think Iranian civilisation is one of the greatest."

"If you like, I still have relatives in Tehran. I can help you arrange a trip there."

"Inshallah." He smiles.

I go on to ask him about the Uzbek language, which I will need some knowledge of on this trip. He explains some of the basics of the grammar and vocabulary. I believe although the grammar is Turkish, more than 60% of the vocabulary derives from Farsi, including Arabic words that have entered it. I tell him that if I lived here for a couple of months, I think I could pick up the language quickly.

"Yes, with your knowledge of Farsi and Turkish it will be very easy."

After about an hour's drive we come across a colourful sight. The countryside has so far looked quite dull on this cold and grey day. There is a low mountain range in the distance and rows of plane trees dotted around. Nearby, lined up along the road, appear a dozen local women in multi-coloured long skirts and peasant scarves. They each stand behind a bright red or yellow display, presumably items for sale to the passing cars. When we go past the first lot of women, some of them wave for us to stop. The women have rectangular wooden boxes the size of a child's coffin standing upright in front of them. On closer inspection, I notice they are shallow boxes lined with apples, some bright red, others golden yellow. At a table nearby, homemade jams and pickles in large glass jars are also on offer. The men selling them are seated on little stools, unlike the women who are shuffling from foot to foot to keep warm, as they wait for the odd customer to come by.

Suleiman stops the car to buy some. I also get out to take pictures. A tall Uzbek man approaches us and asks Suleiman something I don't understand. He has an imposing appearance in his knee-high black leather boots and dark blue silk coat. Suleiman speaks briefly with the man, then goes over to the fruit sellers. He barters with a few of the women for the apples and finally buys five kilos to take back to his family in Tashkent. He is from a large family with five siblings; two of them still live at home with his parents. He is the only one living away from home, and still single, rather unusual for an Uzbek man in his thirties. I wonder what lies in his past: a failed love affair with a Russian; or does he have an Uzbek woman tucked away somewhere. But I am not going to ask any personal questions, in case he gets the wrong idea. He is going to be my host on and off for the next ten days. Formality in our relations will maintain his respect for me. As it is, he is quite a courteous man and I am beginning to warm up to him. He has definite masculine charm, though I felt immune to it during our meeting in Issyk Kul.

***

It is dusk when we reach Samarkand. The streets are very quiet, with little traffic. I am not going to see much of this great ancient city tonight. As we drive through the dimly lit streets I observe rows and rows of tall trees and one or two storey buildings. We are now in the Siyob district, east of the city. It is an old quarter with winding alleyways, and traditional brick-built houses secluded within high walls. This is where our friends, Alfonso and Rosita live; they are both CACE sponsored teachers at the Samarkand State University. The last e-mail message from Rosita had asked me to go to Kogon street and look for the Zarafshan café. I should phone her from there and she will come to pick me up. "You won't find the place on your own," she warned. Suleiman had received a similar message. But finding Kogon street proves to be no easy task. There aren't any road signs and we have no map to go by. The few passersby we approach give conflicting directions.

"Why don't they just admit they don't know the area?" I am agitated, though aware that accuracy and time are highly elastic concepts in this part of the world.

"They just want to help," Suleiman says in his calm manner.

"Some help ..." I mutter and lean back in my seat.

When we finally locate Kogon street and the Zarafshan cafe, we sit in Suleiman's car, whilst he dials our friends' mobile and landline numbers repeatedly. But alas, nobody picks up either of the phones. Where on earth are they? They knew we would be arriving at this time. It is getting very cold and I am really hungry.

"Let's go inside the cafe to warm up," I suggest.

The place is a small diner with wooden benches and tables.

There is a Slavic looking young couple at one table, and two Central Asian males at another. The best thing about the place is the warmth generated by a large kerosene stove near the counter. I order a *shorba* (mutton stew) and go over to stand near the heater for a minute.

An hour goes by and we still haven't got hold of Rosita and Alfonso. The food and tea have warmed us up; we are ready to venture out. Suleiman manages to get directions for the house. We leave the car on the road and walk through a number of the alleyways, then past a courtyard and into another walkway. Finally we locate the small two-storey house with white-washed walls and iron gates. We knock and knock, pressing the bell intermittently. There is no answer. An Uzbek woman then comes over from the neighbouring house to tell us she has seen them leave earlier this afternoon, but does not know where they are. "Damn it. Let's go back to the café," Suleiman says and mutters a curse in Uzbek. We set off again, back through the winding alleys, too tired and disappointed to talk.

Back in the café we order some more tea and Suleiman calls again. Still no answer. "So what shall we do now?" he asks.

I am rather baffled and don't know what to suggest. After a silence, he says, "Shall we try a hotel? It may be too late to go back to Tashkent."

I hesitate to reply, not happy with the idea.

Noticing my reluctance, he offers to drive us back to Tashkent, for me to stay at his friends' place.

"Oh, no," I decline. "We can't land on your friends in the middle of the night."

"Then let me think …" He ponders for a moment and says, "I used to know someone who owned a small hotel in Samarkand. He always invited me to visit. I see if I find his number. He will give us a discount. It will be much cheaper than those big tourist hotels."

Well, it won't be cheap for me, I am thinking, I should pay for two rooms. But that is not the worst of it.

As Suleiman flicks through the pages of an old address book, I glance at the few customers who have come in since we were last here. There is a Russian couple sitting close to us, and further away, a group of three local men. I catch some of what they say, which is in Tajik, a language very close to Farsi. They seem curious about me and my companion, speaking in English. I look like a Tajik myself, except that I am dressed western style in close fitting jeans and a sweater. Over here only teenagers dress this way.

Now as I think about our options, I feel distinctly uncomfortable. Not that I am worried about him bothering me in any way, only that it won't look good, too many possible implications. I can just imagine what his friends may think about it; and I have to face them in Tashkent. Am I exaggerating? The greater part of me says, yes. I am a mature, liberated woman; going with a male colleague to a hotel for the night to stay in separate rooms. So what? But this is the heart of Asia, the continent I grew up in, and not the emancipated, liberal Europe. I can well imagine the gossip: a woman travelling alone with an unrelated young man; staying with him in a dingy, little hotel. Middle-aged professor, or not, how shameless she must be.

I try to dispel these thoughts, when Suleiman finally manages to get hold of the hotel owner after a number of calls. We are certainly not spending the night in that decrepit Lada, I tell myself, even if the bloody Spaniards don't turn up. I just hope they do. I have now become aware of signs of attraction between us that is putting me on my guard. Previously I had assumed that Central Asian men, being highly male chauvinist, only fancied younger women. As for myself, I hate such men; they never respect the women they sleep with. Am I thinking in stereotypes? Earlier, when we had a meal here, he insisted on paying the bill. When I offered to share, he adamantly refused, saying: "In my country guests don't pay."

I responded in a teasing voice, "But I am much older than you. I should be treating you." He looked me up and down and said, "You certainly don't look it." His appreciative, lingering gaze went right through me. I could feel the heat of a blush on my cheeks and looked away. There was no mistaking the look of desire in those ebony eyes.

Suleiman has just finished talking to the hotel owner. He turns to me and says, "My friend's hotel is not far from here. Shall we go there?"

"Let's try the house one more time" I suggest. "They may be back by now."

***

When we get to our friends' house, there are lights in the upstairs windows.

"They are in. Yes, they are in." I am jubilant.

Alfonso opens the door. "I am so sorry man ..." He gives Suleiman a big hug, then turns to me; we kiss on both cheeks.

"We got back 15 minutes ago, must have just missed you. But I was about to come looking for you."

Then Rosita appears in the small tiled courtyard. "Sima," she calls out in her high pitch voice, "how nice to see you."

She apologises and reels off a list of mishaps: problems with both their mobile phones, and the ceremony this afternoon that had gone on longer than expected.

Never mind me, I am thinking. I did not consider myself entitled to any great hospitality. But what about this good friend, who was also invited to their house for the night? On the way here, he told me Alfonso had called on him on a number of occasions in Tashkent and stayed overnight. Suleiman, in return, was invited many times and had never come. But despite our let down tonight, he seems reluctant to criticise our inconsiderate friends. I can see the man is not a moaner.

Once inside, we are given a tour of the house; it's in the style of a small modern villa, with three bedrooms on the first floor. On the ground floor there is a new kitchen and bathroom next to a large rectangular room that has two sets of French doors opening onto a raised patio area. The room has parquet flooring and tall ceilings; its cream walls illuminated by a crystal chandelier. There is a piano, a leftover from the Soviet days, a large dark sofa and an armchair at one end. A dining table and four chairs are placed at the other end.

"The owners built this house four years ago," Alfonso informs, "but they never lived here. I think they are keeping it for their children."

"You mean their son," Rosita interrupts. "Daughters will move in with the husband's family, once they get married."

"But traditions are changing. Aren't they?" I comment.

"Slowly," says Suleiman.

When we get ready to go to bed, Rosita asks me where I would like to sleep.

"Somewhere warm," I say.

The magnificent Samarkand

"The warmest place in the house is the sitting room; the heater is very good, but there is no bed."

I tell her I don't mind sleeping on a mattress on the floor. In Central Asia, as in Iran, every household has at least one or more cotton or wool mattress to offer the guests. This house is no exception. Rosita and I manage to pull out a thick cotton mattress from under a pile of books and boxes in one of the spare bedrooms upstairs. The main bedroom where our friends sleep is bright, warm and tidy. The other two rooms, on the other hand, are cold, dark and dingy. In the smaller one, where Alfonso and Suleiman are sitting by an old desk, a three-bar electric heater has just been turned on. The two men are peering over Alfonso's laptop, discussing their subject, international relations, and sipping vodka. I think this is where Suleiman is going to sleep; tucked inside a sleeping bag Rosita has just dug out for him.

When I get to lie down at long last, I wrap Rosita's duvet around me, feeling comfortable, warm and cozy. I am among new friends, in an environment reminiscent of my childhood. Here is similarly, a neighborhood of brick built houses with partially paved gardens, interspersed with flowerbeds. Each house is secluded within tall walls with iron gates opening onto winding alleyways. An odd feeling of nostalgia sweeps over me; I am displaced in time and space. The fresh, earthy smell in the yard and the silence of the night take me back to the old Tehran of my early years. But that city has long vanished. In its place, there is an abundance of high rise buildings, highway driving, and over-polluted living. Now here, in the stillness of this tranquil city, I lie peacefully, thinking I could sleep a whole week and not wake up. But in a few hours I will have to. Everyone is leaving the house at 8 a.m. I shall also get up to say goodbye to Suleiman before he leaves for Tashkent and get ready for the day's sightseeing.

The poor man. How is he managing to get to sleep, crumpled in a rough sleeping bag in that cold room? But he is young and strong, he should be alright. In my mind, I take a journey back to that warm, sunny afternoon in October, when the two of us took a brief walk in the gardens of Hotel Aurora, by lake Issyk Kul. I remember his tanned look and the muscular body in that short-sleeved amber T-shirt; an attractive, unassuming guy, I thought. At the time, we were having a heated debate about America and Europe's relations with the Middle East. In our disagreement, I felt immune to his masculine charm. But this afternoon, during our ride together, I began to warm up to him, appreciating his kindness and his interest in Iran. With his body so close to mine, I could no longer ignore the manly charm he radiated. Again later, sitting across the table at the Zarafshan café, there was that look of desire that sent electric waves through me. The mutual attraction was undeniable. Now tonight in my fluid imagination, I lie in his embrace, underneath this duvet, and make tender love to him. There are no barriers or awkwardness between us, and I have no fear of him losing respect for me. A life lived in one's imagination can be wonderful in its perfection.

***

In my early youth, I had only vaguely heard of Samarkand, the fairy tale city that lay beyond the edge of the modern world. Like a jealously guarded captive wife, she was secluded in the confines of her master's domain, the communist Russia, for decades cut off from her brethren folk across Iran and Afghanistan. Samarkand and Bukhara were legendary cities in Iranian literature. Hafiz, the great mystic poet of the 13th century, would grant them to the Turkish beauty from his native Shiraz, if only she would return his love. As with most

Iranians, I thought of western Central Asia (Uzbekistan, Tajikstan and southern Kyrgyzstan), as historically part of Greater Iran. The region was referred to as Turan in Ferdowsi's epic Shahnameh (Book of Kings). It was the site of many mythic battles between Iranians and Turanians. The related sagas and their heroic characters appear in Shahnameh. The region had formed part of the Persian Empire founded by Cyrus the Great in the fifth century BC. Its inhabitants, Sogdians, the descendents of the mythical Turanians, spoke a language in the Iranian family of languages. Ancient Samarkand, referred to as Afrosiab in the Shahnameh, was totally destroyed by Alexander and his Greek army. Its ruins lay on a hilltop north of modern Samarkand.

Later, beginning in the sixth century AD, as Turkic tribes migrated westwards from Siberia, the Sogdians of Samarkand settled into an uneasy alliance with the nomadic tribes that surrounded them. In centuries to come the fusion of Turko-Iranian cultures diversified as the Turkic people spread west and south. Then from the 10th till the 20th century various Turkic tribes governed Central Asia and Iran. The only interruption was the century long rule of the Mongols who, as with the invading Turks before them, converted to Islam and adopted a settled way of life.

Before the Mongol invasion, Samarkand and Bukhara had been the great Islamic centres of learning in science, art and architecture, as well as hubs of international trade. The various routes on the Silk Road, where goods were carried, cultural exchanges took place and religions spread passed through these great metropolises. They linked Europe with Near and Middle East, through to Central Asia and China. The wealth generated by the traders, greatly enriched and enlightened these cities, making them the envy of the medieval world.

The intellectual giant of the 11th century, Ibn Sina, was tutored at the madrasas of Bukhara; Islamic schools that trained men in sciences and religious matters. They produced teachers and prayer leaders as well as judges and administrators.

Then in the 13th century, divine Bukhara was laid to ruins. Its palaces and fortification, mosques and madrasas, all destroyed by the advancing Mongol armies, led by Timujin, known as Chingiz Khan (the Great Khan). He was, ostensibly, avenging the murder of his trade delegation by a local governor. But in reality, Chingiz Khan and his band of tribal chiefs had greater goals in sight in subjugating the territories of the Khorazmian kings. They were ultimately to take full control of trade along the Silk Road. This imperial ambition eventually brought them to Iran, where they devastated many of Khorasan's great cities, and onto Eastern Europe and Russia, then finally to China, conquering half the globe. The city of Samarkand, however, swiftly submitted to the will of the human hurricane that was the Mongol invasion. The foresight and diplomacy of its citizens had saved it from major destruction.

Situated in a fertile valley by the river Zarafshan (radiating gold) old Samarkand was famed for the delight of its gardens, as well as the greatness of its mosques and madrasas. A century after the Mongol invasion, Timur, the son of a local Turco-Mongol chieftain rose to power with the ambition to surpass Chingiz Khan in conquering the world. He almost managed it in the second half of the 14th century, when he conquered Iran, Turkey, Baghdad and Damascus, then advanced into Russia and Eastern Europe, in addition to much of India. It was finally at the start of the 15th century, as he amassed his troops to face the Chinese, that pneumonia put an end to his world devouring ambitions. The great city that Timur had designated as his imperial capital was further developed by his successors, utilising the labour of artisans captured from around the world. It reached its zenith of prosperity, art, and architecture in the 15th and 16th centuries.

Today, I visited this Timurid city, restored by the Russians. In the morning, Rosita and I set off for the university, located in one of the Russian built 19th century districts of Samarkand. Leaving the narrow alleyways of the old town we walked onto a wide, leafy street, and hailed a taxi. Rosita gave the directions in Russian and we had a short ride to the University Road, a wide avenue flanked by huge plane trees. Modern Samarkand is a very green city with numerous public parks and an abundance of red and white mulberry, and cherry trees. There are low rise buildings, and little traffic on the roads. It circles the medieval city dating back to the time of Rome and Babylon. At its centre is the medieval square, Registan (land of sand), a major tourist site; that houses Timur's mosques and palaces.

At the university Rosita introduced me to her teaching assistant, Feridun, a native of Samarkand. He was an ethnic Tajik with a strikingly handsome face with Caucasian features, light skin and dark green eyes. He suggested we first go to the university cafeteria which was located in the vicinity of Registan. The place was a huge dining room; quite empty at the time. The food, a wide variety of Central Asian dishes, Russian salads, and soups looked colourful and very cheap, at least for the dollars in my pocket. When I insisted on paying, he seemed embarrassed, but finally agreed, when I said, "Please imagine you are my son."

Feridun had a Master's degree from the Middle East Technical University and was fluent in English, though sometimes we switched to Tajik, He told me that the current population of Samarkand and Bukhara were 80% Tajik. Under Stalin, borders of Central Asia, as with the Caucasus, were drawn such that a great ethnic mix was created in each republic. This minimised nationalist demands forming alongside ethnic solidarity. Thus the borders of Tajikistan had bypassed the most historically important Tajik cities, Samarkand and Bukhara. In a similar way, the landmass known as Turkistan was broken into segmented republics, sometimes arbitrarily. The consequence in the post-Soviet era was the inter-ethnic rivalry, conflict, and political upheaval across the region.

I asked Feridun why there was not much ethnic tension in these Tajik areas, governed by an Uzbek regime. "Our President is also a Tajik. He keeps the Uzbek mafia around him under check. But once he goes …" he raised his eyebrows.

"I've heard that he is a brutal dictator."

"We've always had dictators as rulers. Do you think the next guy would be different?"

"But wouldn't you like to see it change one day? We now live in the 21st century."

"*You* are. You live in England."

My young guide then began to tell me about his time in London last summer when he spent two months on a course sponsored by an NGO he worked for. He had found the city impossibly expensive, but still had a great time; there being so much to do and to see. He was especially impressed with the grand buildings in central London and wanted to know more about their origin.

The magnificent Samarkand

"Those majestic buildings you saw around Hyde Park, Trafalgar Square, and many others," I told him, "are leftovers of the British Empire. For two centuries the city had received the wealth British colonisers gathered from Asia, Africa and the Americas." But more than the history, it was the contemporary scene in London that interested Feridun. He was impressed by the sense of freedom that prevailed over there. It seemed to him that people could do and say whatever they liked and no one censored them, especially regarding sexual matters.

"I saw a boy and a girl kiss very sexy in a bus stop and nobody look at them. They don't feel shame?"

"Over there, people just look the other way. It is considered rude to stare."

"*They* were the rude people to kiss like that on the street. Here, even prostitutes take you inside somewhere." He grinned with a tinge of disgust. It occurred to me that he was reacting in the way I have seen Middle Eastern visitors do when faced with similar scenes in London.

Feridun then told me about his accident two days before he left London. He had tried to get off a bus on the busy Oxford Street as it had just begun to move, and landed on his wrist, fracturing it. Soon someone had called an ambulance and he was taken to a nearby hospital. He spent the day there, receiving free treatment. "You know," he said, wide eyed, "they did x-ray. They gave me dinner and medicine, and I paid nothing." Then added wistfully, "You are very lucky you live in England, so great country."

Leaving the cafeteria it was only a few minutes' walk to reach Registan. This was Timur's blue city, known as such, because of its magnificent blue tiled buildings, built in the two centuries following

215

his death. Lord Curzon, the Victorian explorer, had referred to it as 'the noblest public square in the world'. It was indeed a very impressive, large square, open on one side and flanked on three sides by monumental mosques and madrasas. They formed a trio of buildings with glittering ceramic facades dominated by giant hundred foot portals and crowned by dazzling domes, with blue tiled tall columns in each corner. In the centre of the square lay a large rectangular pond. Its water would have been used in the past for ablution prior to the *namaz*. Monumental buildings arranged around an open square were, in fact, typical of Timurid town planning, although they often displayed the work of Iranian artists and craftsmen.

For me, the distinct feeling as I viewed this spectacular sight was one of déjà vu. I was at once reminded of the Naghshe-e Jahan Square in Isfahan with its beautiful turquoise domed mosques and exquisitely tiled buildings, built by Shah Abbas in the 17th century. However, there was a difference. The madrasas and mosques of Isfahan had their facades covered with neat, pretty tiles, harmoniously patterned, and modest in scale. Registan, on the other hand, was grand and majestic. It dwarfed you as imperial buildings often do. There was a profusion of colours, and varying geometric patterns overlaid with calligraphy. The glazed and ceramic tiles on the exterior walls, the minarets and the domes were in every possible shade of blue, from the lightest sky to the deepest navy, interspersed with green and gold, a dazzling sight.

The largest and the oldest of the buildings in the square were a two storey madrasa housing 100 live-in students, and an adjoining mosque. They were built by Ulugh Beg, Timur's grandson, in the early 15th century. He was a scholar and an astronomer, built the observatory near Samarkand, and discovered 200 stars. He also devised the world's most accurate calendar for centuries to come. He had succeeded his grandfather only a few years after his death and turned his capital into an intellectual meeting point for astronomers, poets, theologians and architects. Ulugh Beg himself taught mathematics at this madrasa and was keen to promote the teaching of science. But this most cultured, rational man eventually fell victim to the influence of the clergy and the power struggle within his own family. In a palace coup in 1449 he was beheaded on the orders of his own son, Abdul Latif. Following his death, the observatory was razed to the ground, later excavated in the early 20th century by Russian archaeologists.

The madrasa on the opposite side to Ulugh Beg's, the Sherdor (Lion Gate), is so called due to the pair of lions depicted on the tiling across the top. Each lion carries an image of the sun on its back. This image of lion and sun, I remember from my childhood. It was adopted under the Shah as Iran's national symbol and the marker of its imperial past. It appeared on our national flag, official documents, and school textbooks. After the revolution all traces of it were eradicated; replaced by a stylistic representation of the word Allah in Arabic.

The third madrasa, Tilakari (Golden), situated between the other two, had its interior walls and the ceiling ornamented with dazzling splashes of gold. The small chambers opening onto the courtyards of these madrasas were formerly student rooms. Nowadays, they catered for tourists, offering handicrafts, silk scarves, and miniature paintings. But today there was no sign of them. The courtyard outside was a paved garden with rose bushes, trees and the odd bench. I suggested to Feridun that we sit down for a while to rest our legs. The sun was shining bright and the air, pleasantly warm. I felt distinctly nostalgic, breathing the sweet scent of roses in this serene environment. I said to Feridun, "Thank you for bringing me here. I never imagined it to be so beautiful and so large."

"I knew you would like it." He said cheerfully, his emerald eyes shining bright.

"And that Ulugh Beg, what a remarkable man."

"We had another great astronomer, Tusi. Have you heard of him ?"

"Yes, of course."

"How about Ibn Sina? He was great scientist, philosopher."

"Have I heard of Ibn Sina? He used to be one of my heroes. He is one of Iran's greatest national figures."

"No, they were Tajiks."

"O.K. let's not get into that debate," I said in a good humoured way. I did not want to challenge 70 years of Soviet rule that had inculcated a 'Tajik' identity, distanced from the Persian speakers.

***

After visiting Registan, Feridun took me to a research centre, partly sponsored by UNESCO. It was housed modestly in two rooms and had a collection of French and English language books and journals. The whole place had the newly renovated look of an organisation funded with western money. Among the collection on display, I found a book on Samarkand and Bukhara with chapters on Timurid history. I asked if I could borrow the book for the night. "No, you can't," the girl in charge said flatly. Whilst I was arguing with her, a man walked in. Hearing that I was from London University, he came over and introduced himself: Kamran Asadov, a Tajik archaeologist at Samarkand University. When he heard of my Iranian origin, he gave me a big smile and said, "It's my dream to visit Isfahan and Shiraz". He then offered to get me the book I wanted to borrow. Feridun had to leave at this point, but I stayed longer to chat to the Tajik archaeologist.

Kamran Asadov had wanted to be a historian, initially. But the Soviet authorities imposed censorship and too many restrictions on the study of history, so he settled for archaeology instead. At the same time, he pursued his interest, specialising on the Timurid era. Kamran invited me to join him in the next door office to have tea. As we sipped our drink, I mentioned that I was aware of Amir Timur's image over here as the great heroic leader and a just and benevolent ruler. But in Iran, he is known as a vicious conqueror, partially crippled, who ransacked and destroyed some of our greatest cities. In Persian literature he is scornfully referred to as Teymur-e Lang (Lame Timur).

"Iranians may hate him, but Amir Timur was the most remarkable man," Kamran said with admiration. "Even though he had a leg injury and was lame in one arm he conquered half the world and commissioned the most beautiful buildings in Central Asia."

He went on to talk about Timur's exceptional ability to organise and plan strategically. He had ranked and administered his army in a complex way, ensuring discipline and just rewards. He acquired their weaponry not only through the war booties and taxes on conquered lands, but also through the wealth that came via trade in the region. Samarkand had become very rich by developing its bazaars, and caravanserais.

"You know more than me about his achievements and great skills," I said, "but I can tell you that to invade and rule Iran, he resorted to unparalleled use of terror, surpassing even the Mongol army. In Khorasan, they say, he built mountains of skulls and minarets of eyeballs."

Kamran laughed. "Here he is considered very differently. Karimov and the government go on about the glorious days of the Uzbek nation and eulogise him as our superhero; they are not interested in his dark side."

"Yes, I know about this", I said, and told him about an interview I had read in a current issue of the *Central Asian Times*. In that, Karimov talked about his recent state visit to Spain. On his first night there, he claimed he had an inspiring dream of Amir Timur; he called the greatest leader, unsurpassed in his statesmanship.

"What a role model for your leaders," I said to Kamran. "When do you think you will do away with the legacy of khans and emirs?"

"Never!" he said laughingly. "It is part of our heritage. But today the world is changing; so I guess we will too."

I now wondered if this glorification of Timur in the new era was another attempt at nation building through cultural authenticity. I have been told that in recent years the Uzbek media have been busy telling people how to celebrate Novruz (a spring festival) in the proper way, and TV programmes frequently debate notions of an ideal marriage, including the duties of a good daughter-in-law.

***

Timur, an illiterate war-mongering megalomaniac, was in fact one of the greatest patrons of art and architecture in the medieval world. He commissioned some of the Islamic world's most beautiful buildings, his legacy perfected by his descendents, culminating in the Indian Mogul dynasty. A masterful chess player and grand strategist, he was nevertheless a nomad at heart. His tent, his harem and his aides were all taken on military expeditions, along with the cooks, the butchers, the bakers, and mobile Turkish baths for the refreshment of his warriors. What anchored him in his globetrotting was the desire to build his capital, Samarkand, so majestic that it would elevate him above his legendary ancestor, Gengiz Khan. But even more than the Great Khan, his skill in imposing discipline over his troops and winning their loyalty were matched by his savagery in battle. After the sacking of each city even the cats and dogs were slaughtered, though their master architects and artisans were spared. From Isfahan, Shiraz, Azerbaijan, Turkey and beyond all manner of craftsmen and builders were transported to Samarkand to work on his grand palaces, mosques, and madrasas.

Gonzales de Clavijo, the Spanish ambassador to Timur's court in his final year of reign, reported the city life in Samarkand to be the envy of all Europe; there was ample supply of food, security, comfort and leisure for its 150000 inhabitants. The city life stretched as far beyond the enclosing walls as it did within, where great numbers of houses, orchards and vineyards were demarcated by streets and open squares. Timur took personal interest in the construction of major buildings. When the grand mosque of Bibi Khanum, for instance, was completed, dissatisfied with the result, he had it rebuilt under his own supervision. Getting old and weak at this point, de Clavijo reports, he was carried in a litter to the building site, where he would throw cooked meat and coins at the masons whose work specially pleased him.

In the new city, Persians, Arabs, Turks, Moors, Greeks and Armenians, mingled freely with their Mongol and Turkic masters. Among them, the Sayyids (descendents of the prophet Mohamed) had a special place of honour, respected by Timur himself. In general, he spared the lives of the *ulema* (Muslim clergy) during his invasions, and kept them on his side, though he limited their authority, allowing free consumption of wine. De Clavijo mentions an interesting episode that sticks in my mind.

Samarkand is at the height of its development and Timur has ordered the demolition of a group of houses to pave the way for the construction of a broad street lined with shops and storage facilities. The new bazaar is built hastily in 20 days and nights of constant labour. The home owners, however, are left with no compensation, and do not dare approach the mighty Amir; instead they ask certain Sayyids for help. These men, equally scared, have to wait for an opportune moment. Timur is a keen chess player, and during one such game the holy men cautiously raise the issue with him.

"All the land in Samarkand is my private property," he bellows. "I have paid for it with my own money."

"But your eminence ..." a squinty Sayyid begins.

Timur rises from his cushion, eyes bulging with anger, and pulls out his sword. "I have the title deeds in my possession," he screams at the man. "Who are you to question me?"

The Sayyid, shaking with fear, bows and quickly leaves, happy to save his head. There is silence all round and the subject is dropped.

To dispel images of war and brutality, I try to focus my mind on de Clavijo's detailed description of the royal feast that concluded a month-long celebration of the wedding of Timur's grandsons. It was said to be the greatest Central Asia had known. All the ambassadors at Timur's court, his extended family, and those of the Samarkand nobles are there. The venue is the royal camp, with a cluster of thousands of tents pitched on the bank of the river Zarafshan. The most magnificent among the royal enclosures is the pavilion. It is the height of a two storey building with a domed ceiling, and outer walls of quilted silk woven in bands of yellow, white and black. There are windows all round and a large entrance with beautifully crafted wood and cloth doors, shaded by a large, embroidered awning. A masterpiece of nomadic engineering and aesthetics, it has the look of a castle from afar. Inside, massive poles in blue and gold, aided by multi-coloured ropes hold up the huge structure. The domed ceiling and the inner walls are lined with crimson silk tapestry embroidered with gold thread and embellished with jewels. Walls of looped silk hanging from the ceiling form parting archways within the great hall and silver eagles at four corners gaze down at the company below.

Among the guests at the feast is Timur's favorite wife, reputedly a Chinese princess. She arrives accompanied by 300 of her ladies-in-waiting, 15 of whom carry the hem of her red silk robe embroidered with gold thread. When she sits three ladies hold her tall headdress, heavy with pearls, rubies and emeralds, and surmounted with a plume of long feathers. Her face is painted white and her jet black hair hangs loose over her shoulders. Timur, old now, wears a white silk cloak and a tall white hat glittering with precious stones, set off by a large ruby at its crown. He makes it clear that in spite of his frailty, he is still in command. The other seven wives of Timur, some of them, grandmothers of the grooms are also in attendance. How did they feel, I wonder, being displaced in the old tyrant's heart by a young Chinese princess?

Land of Forty Tribes

***

Today, rich or poor, Central Asian marriages are celebrated in the most lavish manner a family can afford. Their prestige in the community depends on this. The tradition was maintained, and even reinforced in the Soviet era. For decades under that system, lack of opportunities to invest in property or expensive goods oriented investment in other directions. Accumulating jewelry, expensive gifts, extravagant weddings and circumcision parties, and bribes, all became channels for dispensing wealth. These were in fact investments in social relations, necessary for gaining access to scarce goods and services. In an economy with shortages in most things; to jump queues one needed friends in all walks of life.

This morning I heard an account of such a wedding from Farhad, a male student of Rosita. He was married last year, aged twenty. At his wedding, he told me, a thousand guests had been fed during three days of celebrations. A tent had been set up on a side street nearby, lined with tables and chairs to accommodate the flow of guests. Farhad's father ran a modest fruit export business.

"How could your dad afford it?" I asked.

"He was saving up for years for this occasion," he replied in a proud voice.

"Wouldn't it have been better if he had given you the money instead, you could have bought yourself a car?"

"No. He wouldn't do that. It would be shameful. Everybody expected a big wedding; all my father's contacts, friends, and the *mahalla* would have been disappointed." *Mahallahs* are neighbourhood committees chaired by a community elder and regulated by the government. They are seen as the bearers of Uzbek morality; in practice, controlling the population.

The magnificent Samarkand

After the wedding the couple had to carry on living in the young man's room at his parents' apartment. They were clearly not a rich family.

***

This morning I met Feridun once more to look around another major historic site, the Shah-i Zinda (Living King). A royal cemetery, it is assumed to be the burial site of Qusam Ibn Abbas, a cousin of the prophet Mohamed, who is reputed to have brought Islam to Central Asia. A place of pilgrimage since the 11th century, Timur rebuilt it for his family and other distinguished locals. To enter it you had to go up 36 large stone steps built into the ancient city walls. The stairs took us to a narrow street of mausoleums, flanked on both sides by tombs and mortuary chapels with luminescent blue tiles. At the entrance there was a small area of worship open on two sides, with a highly decorated tall wooden ceiling. Normally, an imam, seated on a large square bench would be reciting prayers. But today it was very quiet and there were no worshippers present.

We walked slowly down the winding alleyway, stopping by each mausoleum to take a close look. Their facades, their portals and inner chambers were all inlaid with a magnificent collection of mosaic and majolica tiles in calligraphic and geometric patterns. The sea of blues was indeed overwhelming; every shade, from the palest sky to the darkest ocean had been worked at. This was no ordinary tourist site. There was a distinct feeling of spirituality in the air; an awareness of eternity enlivened with high aesthetics, as if these royals were never meant to die. They were surrounded by one of the greatest artistic collections in history created by artisans and architects assembled from around the world. Among them was Ustad Yusuf of Shiraz, a Persian, who unusually had left his name and the date, 807 (1404-1405 AD) on a wooden door carved with exquisite delicacy.

Interestingly, the two most beautiful mausoleums in the complex were that of Timur's sister, Shirin Bika and his niece. It was not clear to me if these had been powerful women. Generally, in societies dominated by war and conquest, neither the women nor the feminine values have played a major role. Nonetheless, in the courts of Timurid dynasty, who ruled Central Asia from the 15th to the 17th centuries, there were some powerful women participating in the affairs of the state. Perhaps the best known of them was the wife of Shahrukh, Timur's successor. She took an active part in governing the empire and was able to overrule Shahrukh's choice of a successor to the throne.

When we finally exited the Shah-i Zinda, I mentioned all this to Feridun. He turned to me with a challenging grin and said: "So you are a feminist."

"Yes, I am," I said firmly. "Do you know what that means?"

"They are against men."

"No, you are wrong." I went on to explain that feminism was a term with negative connotations in the political history of the Soviet Union. It was denounced by the Bolshevik ideologues and activists as a bourgeois ideology that divided the proletariat movement. That is what gave it a bad name. I mentioned that feminism was a struggle for women's rights, which I believed was badly needed in the strongly male-biased societies of Central Asia. Feridun had gone quiet, digesting what I'd told him. After a while he turned to me and said, "Of course I agree with women's rights, but some women today expect too much from men."

The magnificent Samarkand

"Like what?"

"Like, I tell you, I have a girlfriend, a Russian from Samarkand. She is nice girl, but ..." he hesitated, looking away.

"But what?"

"She always press me to earn more money and spend more. But this is not all ..." he lowered his voice, and added, "she want me always satisfy her in sex. I mean, ... she think she should climax every time we, ... you know ... and if she don't, it is my fault."

I had to restrain myself not to laugh. I could see this young man had a lot to learn about women's sexuality, but I was not going to be his tutor. So I just brushed off the subject and told him it was time for me to set off to meet Alfonso and Rosita for lunch.

After I had said goodbye to my hosts in Samarkand, Feridun came promptly to take me to the communal taxi rank for Tashkent. An old Volga was waiting in line for a fourth passenger to fill up the car, before it set off. As we said goodbye, Feridun gave me a big hug. I kissed him on the cheek and told him I hoped to see him in London one day. "Give me a call if you come. I'll take you out.

"Inshallah," he said, delighted.

As the car speeded away, I turned round and saw him wave goodbye, gazing at me with affection. What a sweet, young man, I thought. That Russian girl should go easy on him.

Chapter XIV

Tashkent; the greatest city in Central Asia

I am sitting in the back of a communal taxi, a 1970s black Volga, heading for Tashkent. There are two Uzbek guys next to me, squeezing me into the corner; the one in the middle is twice my size. He is dressed in a neat suit, holding a briefcase on his lap, talking numbers on the mobile. I understand all the numbers he is referring to, since they are the same as in Turkish. I also catch some of the spoken words. He is bartering with someone over the sale of a Mercedes car.

After only one hour the fat businessman gets off at a village en route. What a relief! But no sooner do we set off, than the car stalls and the driver gets out inspecting the engine. Within a minute of moving, it stalls again. The driver turns the ignition switch several times, calling out to Allah and powers beyond for assistance. The passenger in the front, a smartly dressed woman in her fifties, complains; her husband is anxiously waiting for her at the drop off point. She goes on to talk about the problems they had with their Volga; its details I don't understand. In my rudimentary Uzbek I tell them I also hope we won't be late; a friend is to pick me up at the stop. The woman, upon hearing me talk, turns round and stares at me. "Are you a foreigner?" she asks.

"Yes. I am from Iran."

"Welcome. We don't see many Iranians here. Were you a tourist in Samarkand?"

"I was visiting some friends."

There is an inquisitive look on her face. "How come your hair is not covered? All the women in Iran have to cover up."

"Yes. But this is not Iran."

I can see she is not convinced. I add, "Not even my mother covered her hair before the mullahs came to power. Only my grandmother did."

She does not comment further, and soon turns her attention to the driver.

But I am not listening to their conversation. My mind has drifted; I begin to ponder my trip to Samarkand and the time I spent with Suleiman. The memory of that afternoon and evening together runs through my head like a movie shot in slow motion. I recall his words of interest, the smell of his after shave, and his gaze of desire at me as we sat in the café. Yesterday morning, when we said goodbye, he gave me a hug, then kissed my hand, not letting it go, and simply said, "I will pick you up at the drop off point in Tashkent." Our eyes were locked and I found myself lost for words. With our friends watching, all I could manage was a shy "Thank you." Now as each scene is replayed in my mind, I am, once more, caught in the thrill of attraction that had engulfed me at those moments. I wonder how my situation with him will turn out over the next few days. I believe he is separated from his wife and shares an apartment with another man. He has arranged for me to stay with friends of his, a young Uzbek couple. I now imagine a scenario in which his friend is away and he invites me to stay with him for the night. Would I go? And what about facing my hosts afterwards? Being a respectable older woman and an academic at that leaves no room for a night of unlicensed passion. No, I simply can't afford to lose their respect.

Another couple of hours go by, and at last we arrive at Tashkent's bus and taxi terminal. It is in a large parking lot where taxis ferry people all over Uzbekistan. I am really excited at the prospect of seeing him again. The woman passenger gets off and waits next to me on the pavement. A few minutes later a black Volga pulls up and she departs. Despite the nightfall there is still busy traffic on the highway and a stream of cars drive in and out. I am grateful for the light provided by the headlights of these vehicles. As in Bishkek, most street lamps here are broken. In the fluctuating light I can see the outline of bushes and trees that fence the open space we are at. It is ten minutes since I have arrived, and still no sign of him. What if he doesn't come? I don't know a soul in this city.

Another few minutes pass by. Then finally, I spot a white Lada parking nearby. I recognise the driver, but not the passenger.

"Hello," I wave to Suleiman as he approaches. He has a serious look on his face and only briefly shakes hands with me. "This is Rufat, my friend," he introduces. "You will be staying with him and his wife, Fereshteh."

Rufat is smaller and shorter than Suleiman and looks younger.

He has a cute, clean-shaven face, with Uzbek features.

"We have heard so much about you," he says in good English. "My wife is very excited to meet you."

***

It is my second day in Tashkent. The apartment I am staying at is a typical three-room late Soviet construction on the third floor of a five-storey building. There is no lift in the building, and the stone stairs are chipped and worn on the edges. There is a shower room, a tiny kitchen that opens onto a dining room, a sitting room and a bedroom, all very small in size with low ceilings. When I arrived here last night the couple offered me the sofa bed in their sitting room. The room faced a major busy road, very noisy and too warm. I feared a sleepless night, so I asked if I could sleep on the velour mats on the floor of their dining room.

"No. It is no good if you sleep on the floor," Rufat objected. "Please let us prepare the sofa bed for you. It's very comfortable."

I knew the offer was out of respect for me, but I did not trust the thin mattress and the springs in that cheap sofa bed, so I turned down the offer. The couple themselves slept on a cotton mattress on the floor of their bedroom.

Rufat told me he has a Master's degree from the US and currently works for an American NGO in Tashkent. Previously, he worked in the Kazak capital, Alma Ati, and has been on work trips to Iran and Turkey. A smart, ambitious young man, he would love to get an executive position with the Ministry of Education, but lacks the necessary patronage. He complained that not much had changed since the Soviet times. "Too many regulations and staff meetings, but at the end it is the rector who makes all the decisions."

"I know about these problems from Kyrgyzstan," I responded. "The rector is the Emir of the Universitystan."

He laughed and said, "We have some very old teachers at my university. There was an eighty year old economics professor. He could hardly stand on his feet. All he could talk about was the Marxist theory of surplus labour and capitalist exploitation. He basically came to collect his wages and the bribe money."

"Didn't he get a pension?"

"Pensions here are so low; you can't live on them," he said, shaking his head, "teachers rely on bribes. As a student you have a choice: either study hard, or pay the teacher. The rich kids of course don't do much study."

"What about you?" I asked.

"I paid for one of my classes in the second year, because I missed a lot. My father became ill that year and I had to stay at home in Andijan to help his business."

***

Rufat's hometown of Andijan in the Fergana valley is a ten-hour car ride north east of Tashkent, close to the Kyrgyz border. It is a historic city, with a traditional and religious outlook, not as cosmopolitan as Tashkent. It is also the centre of the country's small oil producing industry. Rufat's wife, Fereshteh, also from this town, came to Tashkent last year after marrying him. She is eighteen, ten years his junior; a slim girl, with gazelle-like brown eyes, flowing dark hair and a charming smile. Her name, Angel in Farsi/Tajik, befits this very congenial, sweet girl. In the morning she offered to be my guide around the city. I could see she was keen to practise her English. I asked her where she got her knowledge of Tashkent and its history from.

"I learn it from my husband," she replied in a proud voice. "A few years ago he work as a tourist guide. He has much knowledge."

"Was your marriage arranged?"

"I was thinking it was chance, we meet in my university. He came there, ask if I want to be in a discussion group he organise for language students. We meet a few times, and one day he took me to lunch. I really liked him, I thought he was very clever. After he went back he phone me many times. Two months later he come back to Tashkent and ask me to marry, but I wasn't sure. I had a few *sowchi* (suitors) that year. I told my mother before, I want finish my studies, then get married. Then when I told her about Rufat, she said 'yes, we know, he tell *vaseteh* (go-between) to ask us, and we agreed'. Afterward, I hear Rufat come to Andijan a few months before, look for a wife. Mother of a girl in my class work like *vaseteh* for many people. She arrange our meeting. I was angry with him: why he not tell me the truth. But I was in love with him."

This evening when Rufat returned home I could see the young love between them was still in bloom; they kept hugging each other, in between her serving him like a maid. Upon entering the flat, he had tossed the bag of shopping and a file of papers he was carrying onto the floor, expecting her to pick them up. She did this promptly, and fetched him the drink he asked for. Soon he'd positioned himself comfortably on the sofa and began flicking through the TV channels.

"You want to watch CNN or BBC?" he called out to me.

"Either one, you chose." I was helping set the large coffee table they used for dining. The food was almost ready. Angel had already prepared it in the brief hour we were back from our outing in the city.

I had offered to help, but she declined, saying, "You rest. I am used to make dinner." Watching the speed with which she diced the carrots, I could see she was already an experienced cook.

"When did you learn to cook?" I asked.
"When I was six years old."
"That young?"
"When I was eight I make dinner for my family."
"But at eight you would have been too small to cook. Could you even reach the worktops?"
"No problem," she shrugged. "I could stand on a stool and do work."
"Did you also have to do housework then?"
"When I was ten I had to sweep the street outside our house. That is a girl's job. It was good because my mother have a busy job in an office; she needed help in the house. My sister got married that year and I have two older brothers. I was the only girl."

After we had almost finished eating I asked Rufat what time Suleiman was going to drop in to see us.
"He is not coming."
"I thought last night he said he would." I kept my voice casual to disguise my disappointment. I had been looking forward to seeing him this evening. Last night he had left very quickly once he dropped us off at Rufat's apartment. He seemed distracted and distant. I had a feeling something was up.
"He is a bit busy at the moment," Rufat went on. "His wife came to see him a couple of days ago. He is taking her back to Syrdarya, early tomorrow morning."
What! Suleiman's wife is around? And all this time he'd been

seducing me. True enough, on our way to Samarkand he did vaguely mention being married, but gave the impression he had parted with her long ago. At the time, it seemed inappropriate to show interest in his marital life; I was keeping my distance. "Do they have any children?" I finally asked after a silence, bracing myself for more bad news.

"They have two girls."

"That is strange! He never told me he had children."

"Well ... ." Rufat gave a meaningful smile. "Suleiman doesn't like talking about his wife and children in front of everyone."

The bastard! A wife and two little girls and he had the cheek to make a pass at me. I was filled with anger and disappointment, wanting to shout and curse aloud. Instead, I just stared at my plate, and shoved the last bit of the noodles into my mouth. I had to pretend I did not care.

***

The next day I was off again with Fereshteh, visiting the city. Some of the streets and buildings we passed by reminded me of Spain. There were wide tree-lined avenues, and public buildings with neo-classical European architecture. The oriental touch was evident in the Uzbek motifs on the facades of many concrete apartment blocks. The city had a very spacious feel, with lots of green spaces. Huge plane trees, tall poplars and oaks, lined most streets, offering welcome shade in the blistering summer heat. On the whole, modern Tashkent, like Bishkek, was planned as a model of a new Soviet city; regular, systematic and spacious.

Land of Forty Tribes

Poverty seemed less visible here, and there was a much greater presence of uniformed police on the streets. In Bishkek, I hardly ever saw a policeman on the beat. As a foreigner I could feel safer here, not so wary of vagrants and potential muggers. But at what cost was the apparent security? This was a police state riddled with corruption, and run by former communists turned staunch nationalists. The present leadership sought to enforce its legitimacy through reclaiming history. It depicted a proud past in which the person of Amir Timur, his rule, and his conquests were highly idealised.

A showcase for this was the recently built Amir Timur museum, a two storey white circular building, with a green dome roof. From afar, it resembled a giant crown such as those worn by the emirs. Fereshteh was keen to show me this major tourist site, proud of the era when "Uzbeks ruled the world." Praising Amir Timur was not allowed in Soviet times, she said. Inside, this grand, ostentatious building had gleaming white walls, a massive marble staircase and a huge crystal chandelier. The place had the shine of new money. But I was disappointed to find little in the way of artefacts or historical information. The large portrait paintings of the past emirs were mostly drawn from imagination; real life drawings were prohibited in Islamic art. What was telling about this museum and its post-Soviet raison d'être was a plaque with large writing hung on the upstairs gallery. It quoted Islam Karimov, the President: "If somebody wants to understand who the Uzbeks are, all the power, might, justice, and unlimited abilities of the Uzbek people, their contribution to the global development, ... he should recall the image of Amir Timur." But which image? I wondered. Surely not the one I grew up with in Iran. No, the one offered a few steps away on the same floor. Here a plaque with words attributed to Amir Timur addressed his "mighty descendants, the conquerors of kingdoms". It urged them to observe order, discipline, equality and justice in running the empire, and show compassion to the lower ranks of people and the distressed, in all the provinces.

Wow! What a benevolent, merciful ruler! What would the people of Isfahan in 1388 have thought of such claims? That is, the handful who escaped the total massacre of the city, where over 50000 skulls were left in neat piles around its periphery. This was to be a lesson to the other captured cities, in case they planned resistance or rebellion. Inevitably, the terror tactic worked well with the people of Shiraz, next on the route to the shores of the Persian Gulf. They submitted readily to Timur's savage army, paying whatever ransom was demanded. In any case, they had little possibility for concealing their wealth. Information regarding the citizens' wealth: money, livestock, and other valuables, would be gathered through informants prior to the arrival of the army. With the city gates sealed off, the tax collectors then set to work, accompanied by torturers who enforced compliance.

After visiting the museum, we walked on a short distance before entering a luscious park named after the great leader. This was a large public space with delightful gardens and fountains, bordered with shiny brown marble and a beautifully crafted cast iron fence. In the centre of the park, there was a large marble base, above which stood a life-size statue of Timur on horseback, majestically pointing to the horizon. In the past there used to be a massive bust of Karl Marx standing in this location. After independence it was taken out and replaced by the present statue. What a changeover, I thought. The 19th century philosopher of human condition and the guru of a great many liberation movements, East and West, was now replaced by a ruthless conqueror.

Which way was this country heading? I very much hoped not in the direction of the Shah's Iran in the 1970s. The Shah-anshah (king of kings) had invested huge expense, pomp and ceremony in celebrating the 2,500 year foundation of the Persian Empire. But six years later, despite having the mightiest army in the Middle East, he was toppled from his peacock throne by a bunch of mullahs. Over the years, the arrests, torture and execution of his "terrorist" dissidents, somehow did not impede the revolution against him.

***

Tashkent, 'city of stone' (in Turkish/Uzbek), is in fact two cities in one: the old town, *eski shahar*, dating back to the first millennium, and the modern city built by the Russians in the late 19th century. Much of historic Tashkent was destroyed in a massive 1966 earthquake, leaving only a couple of mausoleums and a major mosque and madrasa. The ancient city was an important crossing point for trade caravans by the time of Arab invasion in the eighth century. After its devastation by Mongol invaders in the 13th century, the city once more began to grow and prosper under the rule of Ulugh-bek, Timur's highly cultured grandson. Its good fortunes continued through the 15th and 16th centuries under the Shayban Shahs, in spite of the decline of other Central Asian cities on the silk route. Many of the present day architectural monuments, mosques, madrasas and mausoleums date from that era. When the Russian invaders arrived in 1865, they found a city well secured within strong walls and numerous entry gates. It had been the seat of rivalry between the khan of Kokand and the emir of Bukhara, who ruled the region. Although the Russian troops were far outnumbered by the khan's soldiers, they had the superior firepower to overcome the defending forces and take over the city.

They then set to build a neighbouring town across the Bozsu canal from the old town and made it a base for their advance into the rest of Central Asia. The newly built city soon began to fill with Russian settlers: landless peasants, merchants, adventurers, and pioneers of all kind. The late 19th century Tashkent, a divided EuroAsian city, then became the capital of Tsarist Turkistan. It also functioned as a centre for Russian espionage in Asia. This was the era of the Great Game, a game of intrigue and rivalry between the British and the Russian empires. In the last decade of the 19th century, the development of the city took on a new significance with the arrival of the Trans-Caspian Railways. The newly arrived industrial workers now formed the small band of revolutionary proletariat who were to support the import of the Bolshevik revolution into Central Asia. Following the October revolution in Russia, the city became a battleground between the communists, the opposing White Russians, and the Muslim insurgents. In the ensuing civil war the Bolsheviks finally won over their opponents and in the 1920s established a Soviet regime in the Land of the Turks. For the devout Central Asian Muslims, this eventuality meant being governed, not only by an alien race, but also by the alien dogma of *Allahsizlik* (Godlessness).

And so it was that the indigenous population responded by retracting its faith into the realm of private life. At home, generations of children were taught to fear Allah, pay regular alms, visit shrines, and worship communally in secret make-shift mosques, whilst at school atheism was top of the agenda. In time, a profound private-official duality governed the minds and deeds of every Muslim Soviet man and woman. In the decades that followed, large cities were dominated by Russians and other Slavs, who composed the majority of the industrial workforce. Local Muslims only slowly began to integrate into urban life. Russian language became the *lingua franca*, and western high art, along with Russian translations of western classics, were brought to the intelligentsia and the workers alike.

A poignant example of this was the establishment of an opera and ballet theatre, the beacon of high art, in the capital of every republic. Following independence, the one in Tashkent was renamed Alishir Navoi, after the great Uzbek poet. I visited it this morning with Fereshteh. The exterior had the same sort of grand, neoclassical European architecture as the one in Bishkek. It was, however, a lot larger, over three storeys, with grand marble staircases, and many rooms, in addition to its main performance hall. The side rooms were all in pastel green, their walls ornamented with elaborate Uzbek motifs in white. The ticket price, nonetheless, was only one US dollar, as in Bishkek.

***

Later, that evening, I went along to a restaurant where the ambience, décor, and music was very much Russian, with a multinational mix of clients and cuisine. It was another reminder of the city's cosmopolitan past, dominated by Russian culture. I was invited there by Eleanora who manages the affairs of CACE in Uzbekistan. I first met her last October at the convention in Issyk Kul. She was an Uzbek-Tatar, in her early thirties, and very independent. A few years ago she had left her husband and two young children behind for a year of study to obtain a Master's degree from the Central European University in Budapest. When Eleanora heard of my presence in Tashkent, she invited me to visit her in her office this afternoon.

I took Fereshteh along with me. She had become my guide to the city. Not long after we arrived, Michael also dropped in for a chat. He was a young Irish man from Dublin on a year's contract to teach at the State University in Tashkent. Michael had spent the previous two years teaching at a university in Ukraine where his girl-friend lived. He found his job here frustrating; his students had poor English, and lacked the ability for independent study.

"They want to be spoon fed everything," he complained.

He was meant to teach sociology to Master's degree students, but found himself covering first year undergraduate work.

"I have given up on the syllabus I had prepared. I just improvise from week to week."

Fereshteh, silent so far, commented, "We don't learn good English in school. In university students have to learn everything teacher say. We don't have many books for study."

"But your English is very good. Where did you learn it?" Michael complimented her in an eager tone. He had not taken his eyes off her since his arrival in the office. Fereshteh explained that she was learning English at university. Before that, at her final year of school, she had a very good teacher, an American Peace Corp volunteer called Sharon. In the summer, before her return to America, she had organised a summer camp for the girls in Andijan. She called it 'girls lead the world'. Here they received English lessons, played games, did art work, and engaged in debate. At night they would listen to music, and sing. "That was the best week in my life," Fereshteh concluded with a big smile. Her youthful sincerity was captivating. We all smiled back.

"I love that. Central Asia led by girls." Michael grimaced. "They could certainly do with a dose of American feminism here."

"How come your parents let you join this camp?" I asked.

"You forget," Eleanora interjected, "her parents were from the Soviet generation. They grew up with mixed Pioneer and holiday camps. They were common all over the USSR."

Later that afternoon I sent Fereshteh home in a taxi. Eleanora had invited me to a restaurant to welcome me to Uzbekistan. I could see that my young friend would have loved to stay on in our company. She had been listening intently to the debate between Eleanora and Michael on Uzbek politics and gender relations. But I was not going to make Rufat jealous by keeping her away for the evening.

Later on, Eleanora drove me to the restaurant she had mentioned earlier. Michael had already arrived with a friend of his who was visiting from Russia. Inside, we entered a large dining area, dimly lit, filled with the smell of tobacco. On a small stage at the far end a number of musical instruments were set up, ready for a later performance. The place was packed with diners, half of them Slavic looking. After waiting for some minutes, a young blonde waitress approached us, and led the way to an adjoining dining area with vacant tables.

"So, we are not going to hear all that lovely Russian dance music," Michael said with a note of sarcasm. The heavily synthesised Russian pop was often played at such venues at high volume. We could still hear it.

Soon after we sat down, a group of four Central Asian men arrived at the table next to us. The waitress came quickly to serve them, and returned with large plates of shashlik, and a litre bottle of vodka. The music had also become upbeat, our corner no longer a quiet haven in this busy restaurant. We ordered our meals and began a lively conversation. I was having shashlik, served with rice and salad, accompanied with local champagne ordered by Eleanora. I felt relaxed, really enjoying the food and the company. The Irish guys were cracking jokes as they reminisced their experiences of the past year. A while later, Eleanora's cell phone rang. She quickly picked it up and responded in Russian. After she finished talking, she turned to me and Michael and said in a cheerful voice, "That was Suleiman. He is nearby. He will join us soon."

My heart sank; I did not expect to see him this evening, and had no wish to. Why did he have to turn up suddenly, and spoil my evening?

When Suleiman arrived he shook hands with Eleanora, Michael, and his friend, then came over to me. I remained seated and did not make a move. I just nodded and gave him a frosty smile, hoping he would sit at the other end of our table. Instead, he picked a chair from a nearby table and sat right next to me. After a few moments I got up and pretended I needed the bathroom. I would have preferred to leave the restaurant altogether, but I had not finished eating, and expected a lift back with Eleanora.

Luckily the bathroom was the European type and clean; I could sit and think in comfort. Fereshteh had told me this morning that Suleiman did not get on with his wife, and for the past two years lived mostly away from her. I could see there were a lot of complications surrounding him; I should ignore the trip to Samarkand, and just consider him a kind, and appreciative colleague. He was too young for me anyway. When I returned to our table, Suleiman leaned towards me and asked softly, "How do you like staying with Rufat and Fereshteh? She has really taken to you."

I tried not to look at him directly. He had his gaze fixed on me; that contemplative look with a hint of a smile.

"She is a nice girl, I like her very much," I replied with a blank expression.

But in that brief moment when our eyes met, I felt the sexual buzz that had gripped me in Samarkand. I looked away quickly and pretended I was listening to Michael talking to the other two.

"I am sorry," he went on. "I have been very busy these last two days. I couldn't come and show you the city."

"You were visiting your wife's family, I heard," I said aloud, so others could hear.

Michael and Eleanora, both turned their heads. They obviously didn't know he was married.

"Ex-wife," Suleiman said sharply.

I went back to conversing with the others. Soon the bill was brought to our table. Eleanora picked it up promptly, refusing contributions, and said, "This goes into the annual entertainment budget of CACE."

Once we got onto the street I confirmed with Eleanora that she was giving me a ride back. Suleiman, watching me closely, stepped forward, saying: "I will take Sima back to her place. I am going that way."

"Are you sure?" Eleanora asked.

"Yes. I was going to call on Rufat this evening, anyway."

I felt obliged to comply; it would have seemed very odd, otherwise.

During the drive Suleiman did a little guided tour, telling me about the buildings and the major avenues we were going past. He seemed to be in a cheerful mood. But I was not listening. I kept silent, staring at the road ahead. Finally I said, "Are you sure we are going the right way? We have been on the road for 20 minutes, and we are nowhere near Rufat's apartment."

"Are you counting the minutes till you get rid of me?" He laughed.

"No, I am just tired. I want to get back soon." I kept my gaze on the road.

"Okay. We will go straight there. But can I take you out tomorrow to show you something of Tashkent at night?"

"I am going to be busy tomorrow night. I have to give a talk at the university the next day."

"What about the day after tomorrow?"

"I don't know. I may be busy again."

"You are angry with me," he reproached. "Why?"

Suleiman had now turned to me, his eyes off the road. A car coming in the opposite direction got very close and he had to swerve sharp to avoid an impact.

"Keep your eyes on the road," I said, agitated.

He slowed down and took a turn into a quiet side road, then stopped the car and faced me, "Look Sima, I think you are angry with me, and I don't know exactly why. But you must let me explain some things."

"There is nothing to explain," I said with a shrug. "You and your friends have been very hospitable to me. I just ..."

"Then why are you angry with me?"

"I am not," I said with a raised voice.

"Then why are you shouting at me?"

"I am sorry." I continued to look past him at the road ahead.

"God damn it. I know when a woman is angry with me." He frowned. The cheery mood had now deserted him. There was an awkward silence between us. "You see, ..." he began in a solemn voice, "I have a complicated situation. I don't really have a marriage, only responsibilities."

The genuine unhappiness on his face made me curious; I wanted to know more and asked him to explain.

He told me he had got married 12 years ago to a second cousin. Their mothers, first cousins, had arranged their engagement when they were at primary school, to be married once they finished with their education. A couple of years after their wedding a baby girl was born. But their conjugal union was not going well. Suleiman had just completed a Master's degree at Tashkent University, and wanted to go abroad to further his studies. He was keen to travel and see the world. She, a pretty girl, with only consumerist ambitions had done teacher training and enjoyed working with children. Then five years ago, he got a scholarship to do a Master's degree at Indiana University. In his second year he met an American woman with whom he had an affair. She invited him to move in with her and her young son, offering to marry him so he could get a green card. He loved it in Bloomington and hoped to do a PhD and settle in America. But first he had to come back and divorce his wife.

"Then how come, when you came back instead of separating, you produced another child?"

Suleiman ignored my sceptical tone, and continued, "I was the first person in my extended family to study in the West. When I came back, all the *ak saqqal* (the elders) in our family, even some people from the *mahalla* came to see me. My daughter was six at the time. I had not seen her for over two years and I missed her."

"What about your wife?"

"She was very excited at first, showering me with affection. I felt confused and duty bound. She had been living with her parents in Syrdarya, near Tashkent, and teaching in a local school. I had the impression that she was now more independent, would not cling to me like she used to."

"So what went wrong?"

"I hit reality after a few weeks. I could not forget my life in America, the way most people behaved in an open and honest way. Here everyone seemed to have a hidden agenda, especially my wife. She was always gossiping about the relatives, no interest in the world outside. Even her manners and the way she fussed over me, irritated me. I was missing Lizzy, my girlfriend in Indiana. Finally after a few months, I brought up the question of divorce. But she got mad at me and started to cry and say she was pregnant. I told her she should have an abortion. I didn't want to bring another child to share our misery. She became hysterical and claimed that I had deceived her into thinking I still loved her and wanted another child. But that was such a lie; I wasn't even in love with her at the beginning, how could I love her now, after America." Suleiman's features had hardened in an expression of anger.

"But if she loved you, she would have been very disappointed with your attitude. You should have made up your mind before you got the poor woman pregnant."

"Oh, Dilora knew how to get things her way. She could always put on an act. She told her mother all kinds of stories about us and got her to complain to my mother and sisters. After that they all ganged up against me. I was the bastard; I did not respect our traditions and care for my family ... it was horrible ..."

"So how did you resolve it finally?"

"I got a job with a western NGO and travelled around the country; it paid me more than the university teaching. I owed money to my brother, Mukhtar; he had been looking after my wife and daughter while I was in the States. Then I sent her and the kids back to live near her family in Syrdarya. It's only an hour's drive from here."

"And she went along, just like that?"

"No. Not just like that. We had massive arguments. She was always jealous, pestering me about where I was, and whom I was with. Once she even threatened to poison me. Finally it got so bad; I lost my temper one day and almost killed her."

Oh, my God! Suleiman battering his wife was not something I wanted to hear.

"It was an accident," he went on, "I didn't want to hurt her. She threw a crystal vase at me. I dodged, it hit the wall and smashed to pieces. I then got mad and gave her a slap. She slipped and fell to the floor right next to a big piece of broken glass sticking up. It had missed her throat by a few centimetres. I realised then we had to part, no matter what."

"It sounds awful ... ."

" Yep ... It was." He gave a wry smile. "You probably think it is all my fault. You couldn't imagine how manipulative women here can be."

"Why not?" I replied sympathetically. "I come from a culture not so different from yours. Cousin marriages used to be very common in Iran, and still are in the rural areas. I know how people can get trapped in an unhappy marriage, but Muslim men usually have more exit routes."

"Not always." He said tersely, then turned the ignition on and began to drive.

A few minutes later we had reached the entrance to Rufat and Fereshteh's apartment block. Suleiman switched off the engine and turned round to me. He seemed to have regained his friendly demeanour. But I remained sceptical and wary of him. "Can we talk about these exit routes next time we meet?" he said in a jokey voice.

"I don't know…," I muttered. "We all make decisions we have to live by. I have enough complications of my own to figure out."

"I would like to hear about some of yours. You heard all about mine."

"I don't think you would understand or agree with all the choices I have made."

"Why? Because I am a Central Asian male chauvinist?"

"I never said that," I protested, wondering if I had been too hard on him. I had no solid reason to doubt his story. He sat looking dejected for a while, then said calmly, "I told you things I have never told anyone. But if you don't want to see me again, I won't bother you. Rufat can take you to the airport when you leave."

Oh, dear. I could see I had offended him, and felt bad; he'd been so nice to me all this time. "I am sorry Suleiman." I put my hand on his arm. "You've misunderstood me. Let's have another chat soon."

He did not respond. So I leaned over and gave him a brief kiss on the cheek before I got out. Following this he stepped out of the car and said, "So are you free day after tomorrow? Can I take you out then?"

"Yes. But give me a call, maybe we can even meet tomorrow evening."

***

The old town, *eski* shahar, separated from the new town by a canal, is an Uzbek enclave with narrow dirt roads and single storey mud brick houses. It is within walking distance of where I am staying. I visited it this morning, guided by Fereshteh, who seemed familiar with the maze of alleyways. Some of the buildings looked quite derelict with the outer walls peeling off. In one such building we came across an open brick oven, where a young Uzbek man was taking out round loaves of bread from the oven and piling them on a wooden counter. I bought one from the elderly man sitting behind the counter; we began eating the delicious hot bread as we strolled.

Soon we came across an old house that belonged to Rufat's aunt. "Let's go in and say hello," Fereshteh suggested. The entrance door to the courtyard was left open, we could just step in. The house was built in an L shape around a square yard with fruit trees and rose bushes. It had pretty, ornate wooden doors and window frames. When we knocked on the front door, a plump woman in her fifties appeared. She was dressed in an *Atlas*, the traditional rainbow coloured silk dress, with a little scarf tied at the back of her head. Seeing Fereshteh, her face lit up. "Marhamat, Kiring," (please come in) she said in polite Uzbek.

"This is Farzanah *opah*," Fereshteh introduced her. I couldn't see much resemblance to Rufat in her broad face. Only when she smiled there was the same welcoming expression.

Inside, we were warmly greeted by Rufat's cousin, a teenage boy, and a girl, Farzanah's daughter-in-law, both dressed in jeans and T-shirts. After we had sat down around the low table in the centre of the room, the girl passed the baby boy she was holding to her mother-in-law and went out to fetch tea for us. She returned with a loaf of fresh bread, nuts, dry fruit and cookies. Next, she brought in a large pot of green tea with small serving bowls. After a half hour of conversing in Uzbek, in part translated by Fereshteh, I made an excuse for us to leave and declined the offer of lunch; we had dropped in unannounced, and I was not hungry at all. But despite my lack of appetite, I had to eat a big chunk of bread they offered. "It is polite to accept the bread when you visit," Fereshteh urged me in English.

Leaving the old town, we then headed for the Charsu bazaar, just outside the exit point. This was a huge open space, a sort of Central Asian farmers' market. There was a crowd of about a thousand people, mostly dressed in traditional clothes of the countryside. Anything from pottery, plastic crockery, carpets, clothes, and shoes, to belts, batteries, and bicycle parts were offered by individual sellers. In between, there were many stalls selling cooked and raw food, and a section where fresh fruit and vegetables were on display. A number of *chaikhana* (tea houses) served *shorba*, the standard mutton soup, and green and black tea. The colourful hustle and bustle and the chaotic organisation here was a world away from the orderly, modern metropolis that surrounded it. The place was in sharp contrast to the city's clean wide avenues with few pedestrians and expensive shops. Here one could feel the human warmth that enriched many Asian cities far and wide.

***

After our return from the bazaar this afternoon Fereshteh began preparing the national rice dish, *plov*. She told me I had to taste the home made variety. I told her I was expecting a call from Suleiman and we may go out this evening. "Then you eat it tomorrow," she insisted. I was giving a talk at the university the next day, so I sat in the sitting room and began to work on my paper. But my mind kept wandering off, dwelling on what Suleiman had told me. Could I really believe everything he said? No doubt he was telling me *his* version of the truth. I wondered what her story would be. Did she realise, letting him go on that long journey would ultimately put him beyond her reach? And what about the fight? Did he have a violent side underneath that calm exterior? Hard to know.

I had recently read a report by an American legal NGO on domestic violence in Uzbekistan. It indicated that, in line with other Central Asian republics, the phenomenon was widespread and growing in recent years. It was reinforced by a potent mix of male supremacy in the culture, new poverty, and disinterest by the authorities. Another contributing factor was the dominant culture of honour and shame. It was considered shameful to complain of abuse in the home to people outside the family. But did any of this apply to the man I have fancied so much? Today when I tried subtly to quiz Fereshteh about Suleiman's temper, all she would say was: "He is really nice man. He never very angry." I had to leave it at that; I did not want to appear too interested. And what about this woman in America? I could well imagine him attracting women with the way he walks and talks. Did he love her and leave her?

***

It is now 11 p.m. Fereshteh and I are getting ready to go to bed. I can see she is a little anxious; her husband has not returned yet.

"Does he often come home so late?" I ask.

"Sometimes," she says. "I am lonely when he is not here." "I miss him."

She seems to be mostly dependent on him for company. He doesn't allow her to socialise with young people from the university, or in the neighbourhood. She can only go out accompanied by her husband or brother, and is instructed to come home as soon as her classes finish.

Finally, we hear the front door open and Rufat arrives. He looks lively with flushed cheeks. He has been celebrating with visiting guests from abroad. His NGO has now successfully completed the phase one of their project. A little later, Rufat goes to the kitchen and picks up a bottle of vodka along with two small glasses.

"Please join me," he hands me a glass. "Let us drink to your stay in Uzbekistan and our project's second phase."

"What about Fereshteh ?" I ask.

"She doesn't drink alcohol," he answers.

I look at her. "No thank you," she confirms demurely. I wonder how much of her reluctance is due to my presence, the aunty figure. Traditionally in Central Asia, and many Muslim countries, young people did not drink or smoke in the presence of their elders. Young women generally refrained from both. Today of course, everything is changing. In some of the expensive restaurants in Bishkek and Tashkent, you can see some fashionably dressed women exhaling puffs of smoke.

After we go into the little sitting room with our drinks, Rufat tells his wife to fetch some snacks for us to accompany our drink. When we finish the brief toasting, he looks at me with sleepy eyes and says: "You know Miss Sima, those clothes really suit you."

I glance at my outfit: black jeans and a fitted top, and wonder what he is on about. Rufat then with his hands in the air makes the sign of a female figure and says: "If only my wife could have a body like you at your age ..."

I laugh and say: "She may do, if you look after her."

Fereshteh comes into the room at this point. He pulls her towards him and says: "I always do." Then gives her a kiss on the cheek and adds: "Don't you think I look after you well?"

"Yes, very much," she replies, then turns to me and rolls her eyes.

Earlier this evening, Fereshteh was in tears. Her mother-in-law had phoned to say, Rufat had not called them for some time; it was her duty to remind him. "Do you want him to forget us?" Fereshteh now worried that the woman will talk badly about her to her family. "But even I don't see my husband much," she lamented. "He is always busy and not listen to me."

Good God! What could I say? In this society, young daughters-in-law were often the most exploited in the family, but I couldn't tell her that.

"Maybe you speak with him." she pleaded. "He respect you."

"Oh, if only!" I mumbled, knowing that Rufat would not appreciate me interfering in his family affairs. So I just said some words of encouragement to console her. She cheered up a bit and said,

"You know, Sima *opah* ... I like to have a job when I finish university. But my mother and mother-in-law talk with Rufat and decide I should have a child in last year of university. I don't think he want me working even after I finish. But I like to have my own money and travel to other countries."

I put my arm around her and said, "I am sure you can do it if you are really determined." She smiled and gave me a thank you kiss.

***

It is my last day in Tashkent, and I woke up with aching limbs. These nights on the floor have finally taken their toll on me. I am glad to be leaving tomorrow and get back to my own bed in Bishkek. Then soon after my shower, the phone rang. It was Suleiman. He apologised for not calling me yesterday. He had been tied up with a job for his brother. He would come to my talk at the university, and take me out afterwards. "Why don't we just meet after I finish," I suggested, thinking that all that talk of women's rights may alienate him. Most men over here felt threatened by it.

"But I don't want to miss your talk. It's an occasion to hear a British Iranian scholar speak."

After I put the phone down, the excitement of seeing him again, kept me afloat as I dressed and made up, more attentively than usual. Finally, I put on my matching silver and amber earrings, a gift from Gerhard long ago. That man had such good taste. Looking at them, I was reminded of our time in Paris, and the little antique shop near the Seine, where we bought them. It felt like a century ago. So far on this trip I had not thought about him once.

"You look very pretty, Sima *opa*," Fereshteh complimented me as we were ready to leave. She was coming along to my talk.

***

At the university, we were met by Raziyeh, the woman who had organised the session for me. She was another local CACE teacher with a Master's degree in political science from the Central European University. As with Eleanora, she seemed aware of the many subtle, and not so subtle, ways in which an Uzbek woman was marginalised in public life. Michael and Eleanora had also turned up. My talk was held at a large old style classroom that could fit in around a hundred people. Most of the young attendees were girls. Three male and one woman teacher also came, and sat right at the front. Suleiman arrived some minutes after I had begun. The room was almost full; he had to take a seat at the back, barely visible from where I was standing. As I went ahead with my talk I looked around at the audience, wondering how much of it they comprehended. I was trying hard to pick simple words to explain not so simple ideas. I knew that there would be some students whose English was good enough, and then there were my CACE colleagues, including Suleiman. His fluency was excellent, though his first languages were Uzbek and Russian.

During the talk I informed my audience of how the position of women under the Islamic regime had actually progressed in some spheres. There were more girls than boys entering university, and we had more women managers, government executives, artists and movie directors than previously, under the Shah's regime. The streets of Tehran nowadays were full of women drivers, some even driving buses and taxis. In the former Soviet republics, I reminded them, women had only recently begun to drive cars. But paradoxically, the laws in Iran, in line with the *sharia*, were much more discriminating to women, particularly the family law. Here in Central Asia, on the other hand, the laws were most progressive, a Soviet legacy of gender equality. However, ethnic and religious traditions kept them subservient to men, with little personal autonomy. Central Asia was another case of women's contradictory position in society.

After I finished speaking there was a question and answer session in which a male student got up and said, "My sisters are free to travel, study, do what they like. One of them went to Turkey to work and got married there. Why do you think they not free?"

Hearing this, Raziyeh got up and said, "My husband did not want me to learn to drive for many years. Then last year when he got a job abroad, I had to learn to drive so I could take the children to school. Even then, his parents were objecting. Women in our culture are really restricted where they can go and what they can do. But most people don't think about it, because they don't know any different; they haven't seen how women live in Europe and America." After the session ended, Raziyeh came over to me and said in an ironic tone, "You know, after I got my licence, my mother-in-law kept phoning, asking me to take her here and there, like it was my duty."

It was now time for lunch and the five of us, CACE teachers, were invited by Raziyeh to dine at the university canteen. It was a self-service standard Uzbek menu of chorba, plov, and manty (meat dumplings). After we'd sat down Raziyeh thanked me, and asked if I could come over again to give further talks on the subject of Islam and women.

"There is so much ignorance here about the Koran ... ."

"But I am no scholar of Islam," I pointed out, "I have only done some studies."

"It doesn't matter," she said in a reassuring tone. "You grew up in Iran, you know more about religion." She went on to say that people here had lost their knowledge of Islam during the Soviet period and attributed all kinds of practices to it. What is more, Wahhabis were coming to the country with a mission to convert the locals, and women who went to Mecca came back telling all kinds of things about what Islam required of women.

"They are re-Islamising our society in a bad way." She said anxiously.

I told her that if she could raise funds for another trip, I will try. I still had so much of the country to see. I was especially interested in visiting Bukhara with its divine mosques and madrasas, not to mention the Emir's winter and summer palaces. A middle-aged Iranian businessman I met in Bishkek had told me about his recent visit there with his wife. "The streets, the buildings, the whole ambiance of the place reminded us of old Iran, we felt like children again." he said wistfully. "There were these white mulberry trees on the street, full of fruit. My wife and I kept jumping up and grabbing the branches to pick the fruit." He went on to say, "Now you are in Central Asia, you should definitely pay a visit there."

As we continued chatting, I noticed Suleiman was not participating much in the banter. Now and then, when our eyes met, he would acknowledge me with a little smile. Finally, when we had all finished and were out on the street, he approached me and led me by the arm, whispering, "For the rest of today, you are mine."

"Am I?" I gave him a look that said, "Cheeky."

"Yes please, professor."

"Alright."

Suleiman then went to fetch his car. I said goodbye to everyone and told them he would be taking me to another appointment.

***

Tashkent; the greatest city in Central Asia

On a sunny spring day, Tashkent is a delightful place to visit. A beautiful city at any time of the year, this is when it's at its best, with the blistering mid summer heat still months away. There are luscious parks, wide avenues with orderly traffic, and clean streets shaded by tall trees. My favourite place was the Japanese garden, a pretty little haven of peace, neatly landscaped with miniature trees and plants, bordering a large park. Then there are the grandiose squares, with massive fountain displays and ostentatious government buildings that reveal the wealth the regime splashes on itself. What it's like in the poor peripheries of the city, I have not found out. But I wouldn't be surprised if the dilapidation and neglect of these areas is in sharp contrast to the lavish attention given to the city centre. I observed this in Baku, where the regime is equally concerned to impress the foreigners, most of whom congregate in the centre.

Today, Suleiman took me to the Sailgokh street, popularly known as the Broadway. It is the lively hub of the city, full of young people, with modern shops, bars and cafes. Part of the street is pedestrians only, allocated to the artists. Rows and rows of oil and watercolour paintings were on display at very low prices. Some very good works were among the many done by amateurs. There were also a number of local artists offering to draw portraits. I could just imagine Gerhard loving the place and spending a long time browsing through. But this was no time to think of him and stir up guilty feelings. Who knows in whose company the man was enjoying himself at this present moment. For sure, being lonely was not a major problem for him, at least not in the way I endured it most evenings in Bishkek.

When we had finally sat down on a bench in the surrounding gardens, I said to Suleiman "Why didn't you call me yesterday? Did you forget about me?"

"Forget about you? Never." He gazed at me with eager eyes and paused. "Since I came back from Samarkand, I have been thinking about you all the time. I've missed you so much. ..."

I smiled and looked away. We were in this very public place, where a display of passion would have been improper. After a silence, I made a move to resume our walk, and tried to divert from personal feelings.

"So what do you think of women's situation here?" I asked.

"Awful ..." he paused briefly. I wondered if he was weighing up his answer to suit me. "A lot of it," he went on, "is due to under-development and our isolation from the rest of the world. You see ... we did not have an oil wealth, or the opportunities of interacting with the West, like you did in Iran. Whatever we had, like our cotton industry, was shared with the rest of the USSR."

"But wealth by itself doesn't promote gender equality. Look at Saudi Arabia".

"Yes, of course. But we did have a background of liberal ideas with the *Jadidist* thinkers at the start of the 20th century. Their progressive position got buried under a pile of Soviet propaganda."

History had been one of Suleiman's majors during his first degree, though it was taught with a lot of Soviet biases. After the independence, when new publications emerged, he was keen to uncover his nation's lost history. The *Jadidists*, he discovered, had called for reform in all areas of life, from observing public hygiene and economic planning, to democratic governance, and education for women. The word *jadid* (new) referred to advocating a modern education system that rejected the *maktabs* (traditional Islamic schools) where only the scriptures were taught by mullahs. *Jadidists* saw no conflict between modernity and Islam. They thought that a good Muslim should be knowledgeable, modern, and up-to-date with the times.

"*Jadidists*' ideas of Islam were so different from the puritanical crap you hear today," Suleiman said, frowning.

"Who do you think influenced them?" I asked.

"Enlightenment ideas had come from Europe to the Ottomans and Russia, then to the Caucasus and to us. Have you heard of Fitrat?"

"Yes. I once translated some of his writing from Farsi to English."

"Well, he wrote both in Uzbek and Tajik, which you call Farsi. He had studied in Istanbul just before the First World War, and was influenced by Ottoman intellectuals. He wrote a lot about the corruption of government officials and how the mullahs kept the population in a state of ignorance and superstition."

As we walked and talked some more, I could see that Suleiman was very knowledgeable about Central Asian history and literature and was pleased with him being familiar with Persian literature. His recent academic studies, however, had focused on the foreign relations of the US with Asian countries. And it was on the question of Iran and the US that we had our biggest disagreement, coming to it from different knowledge bases. But I was not going to let that theoretical issue cloud our feelings today. It would take many hours of debate and discussion to familiarise him with what I knew.

We had now gone back to the edge of the Broadway. It was getting dark, with the area becoming very lively. "Do you like Indian food?" he asked. "Yes, I do. Especially if it is in a quiet place." We held hands for the first time as we walked over to his car; I felt wrapped in the warm glow of his affection.

***

The restaurant he takes me to is dimly lit, with mellow Indian music in the background. I am happy we have avoided the popular big venues with their ear piercing live bands. After we order some curry dishes, our talk returns to the Bukharan intellectual, Fitrat and his writings. Most of these were written in Farsi, the literary language of the region at the time. Suleiman tells me, he would love to read them in the original, but more so, to read Hafiz and his *ghazal* (verses). He knows they are masterpieces of Persian poetry; he suspects the translations he has read did not quite convey their depth and elegance. We go on to discuss Molavi, considered by some the greatest Sufi poet. He was born in Balkh, south of today's Uzbekistan, spent part of his life in Iran and settled in Turkey, where he is referred to as Mevlana. His shrine in the town of Konia, in central Turkey is a major site of pilgrimage. Although a Turk, he wrote virtually all his poems in Farsi. But tonight we don't argue about his nationality; there are too many contenders for this. I tell him that my favourite verse is the one about the *ney* (reed) and its lamentation. It begins:

"Listen to the *ney*, and its cry of separation.

Whence taken from the *neystan* (reed bed) ;

My tune has sung tales of sorrows;

Hence tears of men and women that follows.

"This is too sad ..." He says, looking me in the eye. He then takes my hand in both hands and asks, "Are you unhappy about your love life?" I sigh and say nothing. "Are you?" He repeats, stroking my hand.

"Well ..." I tell him a little about Gerhard and that I have a complicated situation with him. He loves me but cannot fully commit himself. So we live in different countries, and have separate lives. I am not happy with it, but feel stuck.

"Do you love him?"

"I don't know any more ... I used to."

"He must be a fool not to want to marry you," he says, holding my gaze.

I tell him that my own situation with my son and my career had also got in the way. It sounds better than admitting he did not love me enough to compromise with his other commitments.

"You are such an attractive woman in every way. Why do you go with these western men? They could never see the passion in your heart. You should stay with your own kind."

I want to tell him that I don't know what my kind is any more. But I stay silent, trying not to blink, in case tears drop onto my cheek. He has touched something deep within me, yet he is the wrong man, I tell myself. I must change the subject and deflect my thoughts. He orders some tea to finish our meal, and I ask about his plans for the future. He says he has had it with this country. There is so much corruption and nepotism, he wants to get out. "To get a good job in this country", he says with a wry smile, "You have to either have a lot of money, or be related to someone high up. I am a little guy with no connections."

He goes on to tell me that he is applying to get onto a PhD programme in the US. If not, he can renew his contract with CACE for one more year and try again the following year. We go on to talk about the next CACE convention in May, which will also take place in Issyk Kul. We will no doubt meet there again. He asks if I will be coming back to Tashkent to visit and give more talks. I tell him it is very doubtful, as I have a full schedule of teaching until May and a commitment to go to Osh in April. I will be giving a set of lectures over there and conduct some research.

"It would be lovely to have you here again soon," he says, smiling. "You said you'd love to visit Bukhara. I could take you there."

Our drive back to Rufat and Fereshteh's apartment is a short one. On the way we are mostly silent, we've already said so much, and got so close to each other. After he stops and turns off the engine, I face him and say "Suleiman, I would really like to thank you for arranging this trip for me and your hospitality. I have had such a wonderful time."

"I thank *you* for coming, and letting me enjoy your company and share your ideas."

As I lean forward to give him a good night kiss on the cheek, he moves closer and brings his lips to mine. First it is a hesitant kiss. But then he puts his arms around me and pulls me close. In his embrace, I let go, and we kiss with open mouths and the passion that has engulfed us for days. It's a long kiss that unites the life force of a man and a woman in those ardent moments, tying in their Yin and Yang.

"Oh, Sima *janim* ..." he whispers in my ear, "You have stolen my heart, and now you are going away ... Can't you stay a few more days?"

I sigh deeply and say, "I wish I could." But we both know it is not possible. Tomorrow, a Sunday, I have my return flight; classes start the following day. We kiss again with full passion and say goodnight. He walks me to the entrance door of the block and departs.

I begin mounting the steps but I am too excited to go straight back inside. I need some air. So I go up to the top floor, then descend down again and take a walk round the block. Oh God! What am I getting myself into? I know all the signs of love descending, the deluge that sweeps you away. But there is still time to quash it. I just have to concentrate on the negatives: my scepticism of what he's told me, our age difference, and the culture gap. Face it woman, I urge myself, it is just lust, plain and simple. But something tells me it is more than that, and alarm bells ring loud and clear. Am I making a fool of myself? As I mull over these thoughts, pacing the dark street, I suddenly notice the figure of a drunk male approaching. He stumbles into a lamp post, its light bulb long burnt out, and mumbles words I don't understand. Yes, being a fool is exactly what I am, strolling by myself late at night in this strange city. I quicken my pace, almost running, to get away from that man and head for the entrance door of the block.

Chapter XV

Polygamy in Kyrgyzstan

Today was the twenty first of March, the first day of Novruz spring festival. It is a time for renewal of nature and remembrance of people, celebrated most extensively in Iran, where the tradition originated from. It marks the start of Iranian New Year, set at the precise moment of the equinox. Friends and family members dressed in new outfits visit each other, offering money and gifts to children and youngsters. There is a public holiday lasting several days and everywhere the air is filled with felicity and joy. Houses, shops and offices are cleaned thoroughly and decorated with greenery to welcome the good spirits; they will occupy the premises for 13 days. Yesterday I was thinking, there is no Novruz for me this year. In London, I would celebrate it with my Iranian friends, but here in this remote part of Central Asia, who has heard of it.

Polygamy in Kyrgyzstan

But boy, was I wrong! Today turned out to be a public holiday, and a colourful day of festivities in central Bishkek. In the morning I was invited to attend a celebratory ceremony at the Manas University, where I teach a class. The university is one of the largest and best equipped in Kyrgyzstan, funded mostly by Turkey. Students here all learn Turkish and English; some hope to get scholarships for higher degrees in Turkey. As a special guest at this outdoor student show I was seated in the front row, alongside the rector and the senior staff. A large stage was set up, above it at the back a yurt facing us.

The ceremony began with a fire dance on a patch of rough ground next to the stage. A group of a dozen boys and girls in ethnic costume circled around a bonfire, swaying and singing in Turkish. I was reminded of the fire jumping rituals in Iran on the last Wednesday before Novruz. Fire as a purifier is considered sacred by Zoroastrians. With the expansion of the Persian Empire in the fifth century BC, the religion had spread to this part of the world. Celebrating Novruz had later been established all over Central Asia, especially among the settled people of the south. Then when the Soviets took over, they wrongly associated it with Islam and banned its public commemoration. But what has all this got to do with the Turks? I had never heard of Novruz being celebrated in Turkey, except among the Kurds. This must be a new trend, affirming their ties with Central Asia.

In the afternoon when I returned home, I found major festivities in the vicinity of Erkendik. Ala Too square had been decorated with colourful flags and ribbons. On the adjoining Chuy Prospect scores of stalls were selling food, soft drinks, knick-knacks, and toys and balloons for the children. Masses of white plastic tables and chairs had been placed around the stalls to accommodate the participants.

Land of Forty Tribes

There was the sound of music coming from different directions. When I took a walk in the nearby park, I came across a number of horses specially dressed for the occasion. Dark pink, embroidered felt had been placed over their saddles, as if they were about to attend a party. Among the large crowd of men, women and children there were some older people in ethnic costumes: embroidered gowns, long coats and tall white hats. It was a warm, sunny day with the joyous feel of a festival in the air, a happy occasion for Kyrgyz families.

During my walkabout I met my student, Jildiz. She was out with her baby and her sister. The half Afro-American baby looked so cute with his Kyrgyz eyes, fuzzy brown hair and the little embroidered cap. Rather heavy, he was carried alternatively by his mother and his aunt. Nobody here seems to use a buggy or a pram to transport young children, only the human arms. Later that evening, Mina called to wish me happy Novruz. I told her I had called Mahmood this evening, to give him my greetings, but couldn't get through.

"Mahmood is worried about you living there, all alone," she said. "He thinks you should come and live near one of us."

My Big Brother had never approved of my change of career. He considered me foolish giving up a secure local government job with reasonable pay to enter the academia, and an uncertain field such as anthropology. For my thesis I had chosen to do fieldwork in Iran, and I lived partly in my parents' home. My family's only concern for me at the time was my single status; everyone was on the lookout to get me married again. Now that my parents are deceased, my brother considers himself the head of the family. With all the news and views on terrorism, he is baffled why I have chosen this poor, backward corner of the world to work in. "Mina jan," I said to my sister, "For years I wanted to come to Central Asia to do research and discover the region. Can't *you* explain it to Mahmood?"

"I think your work is interesting, and it should help your career," she reassured me. "Just be very careful. Don't go out by yourself in the dark."

I had already told Mina about the situation here and the problems with personal safety.

"How was Uzbekistan?" she then asked.

"Amazing. ..." I began telling her about the sites I had visited, the glorious Samarkand, and some of the things that reminded me of Iran. But I did not mention anything about a romance in the air. I did not feel like delving into that subject just yet. Since my return I have only spoken to Suleiman once, and that was on my first evening back. I thanked him again for everything, and he said he missed me already. He promised to call me soon, but he hasn't yet. It is ten days since we parted. I still remember the intensity of passion we both felt on that last evening together and when we kissed goodbye the next morning just before he dropped me off at the airport.

Meanwhile, Gerhard has called me twice. He knew I was due back on that Sunday evening and phoned very promptly. I was not very talkative, just told him I was tired from the trip and needed to go to bed soon. He understood. Yesterday evening he called again to wish me happy Novruz and we had a long chat. He told me he is thinking of coming to visit me in April during the Easter vacation. I told him I will be going to Osh to give seminars at the university.

"Then I can come beginning of May, if you like."

"May is no good for me, either. It's exam time and I'll be too busy then."

There was no response. I could sense his disappointment in the long silence.

"You know that I am coming back in June," I said reassuringly. We'll then see each other in London, or I'll come to Bonn."

"You don't want to see me till June?"

"I never said that ... I am just letting you know that I don't have time."

Gerhard was obviously missing me. Last month he had his 69th birthday. He was suffering from flu on that day and had to cancel the celebratory meal with his children and his friends. He called me to say how miserable he felt; I tried to cheer him up, long distance. He kept asking me what my plans were for our summer holiday. I told him it depended on my job applications in the UK and the US. He then suggested that if I moved out of London, he could fully retire and come to live with me part of the year. Oh really, how adventurous of you, I felt like saying. The guy just doesn't get it. If I move to a new environment, with the possibility of starting a new life, why would I take him along?

Now tonight, with the Novruz over, I have to wrestle with that damned grant application. Such tedious business; you have to second guess the assessment board's preferences, and their published "guidelines." One may as well buy a lottery ticket to raise funds. Meanwhile, at fifty my chances of a full-time teaching job are rapidly diminishing. I don't have the right constituency of support, or the academic patronage to boost my application. I just did not do enough networking in key universities, or hang around conference halls, chatting up the bigwigs in my field. Mothering Jamie, and trips to Germany took up too much time and energy.

Polygamy in Kyrgyzstan

***

Today is a Sunday, the last one in March. Mira came to visit me for her weekly English language practice. Her family can't afford to pay for private lessons. So I've given her a good dictionary and some reading material that I help her with during our meetings. Like most young people over here, she is quite keen to learn. In return, she helps me shop at the local fruit and vegetable market and carries the stuff home.

Later in the afternoon, Mira and I watched the news on the BBC World Service. For a third day I was gripped with disbelief and anger as I watched American planes savagely bomb Baghdad. The bully Bush's "shock and awe" is meant to bring Saddam and his army to their knees, but what of the children, the old, and the sick in that city? They must be shaking with fear and the children crying ceaselessly, as they hide in darkened basements, hoping to escape the clutches of the monster. But the monster is a highly trained American pilot feeding on a staple of disinformation by his government. The immorality of mass killings is then neutralised with terms such as "collateral damage". And to think that our born again Christian Blair is a party to this madness. I wish I was in London and could join my friends who marched along with two million others against this war. Over here there were hardly any dissenting voices. Only Alan Murphy and a hundred of his students went out to Chui Prospect to demonstrate. People here see America as the consumerist utopia with unbounded personal and political freedom. They are reluctant to criticise the US government and its ventures around the world. Besides which, the Arab Middle East seems far away.

Mira, as I expected, knew nothing about world politics, or why America was bombing Iraq, though she was curious. I told her a little about the geo-politics of the region, why oil was such an important commodity, and the role it played in shaping much of the 20th century politics of countries such as Iran, Iraq, and the Gulf states. We had been talking, with the World Service news channel in the background, when my eye suddenly caught the sight of a young woman I knew from London. She was on the campus of the American University in Cairo, commenting on the impact of the war among the Arab youth.

"Oh, I know that girl," I looked closer at the TV screen. She was one of my students last year. I heard that she was moving to Cairo where her parents lived. A little dynamo, she was an incessant talker in the seminar sessions, frustrating everyone.

"What a small world!" I said to Mira. "Here I am in Bishkek watching my student from London appear in front of the camera in Cairo to comment on a war between the Americans and Iraqis."

***

Last night I had a little escape from all the doom and gloom of current news and world politics. I went along to a party at the Manchester Club. This was a bar/restaurant done up to resemble a British pub favoured by Manchester United fan club. There are club emblems hanging above the bar area and the memorabilia, including a club shirt, displayed on the walls. The pine tables, chairs and benches give the place a young, sporty feel. When I arrived, there was loud music, the disco beat, and the hall was packed. Most of the crowd were Americans, among them a few young Kyrgyz and Russian women. On the dance floor, it was mostly women dancing together. I got myself a drink and went over to talk to Louise, a woman from Oregon in her forties, who runs the Peace Corp in Kyrgyzstan. She told me, they had 50 volunteers in the regions, teaching English at local schools and a few involved in rural development projects. I told her I admired the Peace Corp institution and the generosity it displayed abroad. The same with the student exchange programme that is funded partly by the US government and partly by the hospitality of host families. Teenagers from recipient countries attend a high school in the US for one year, learning about the American way of life. What better way of gaining future allies and partners than by impressing their young at an early age. I told Louise I wished the British government had more foresight and offered similar programmes.

As we were chatting, I caught sight of a red haired woman on the dance floor. It was Jane, the lawyer with the mission to democratise Kyrgyzstan. I had met her on the plane to Tashkent. She was dancing energetically opposite a large man with a reddish white complexion. He seemed to have difficulty keeping pace with her, as she gyrated, swinging her ample hair with the rhythm of the disco beat. The guy was sweating profusely. His dark hairpiece had shifted, revealing a bald patch. A few minutes later, with the change in music, Jane stopped dancing and came over to the bar to pick up her drink. The wide collar of her crimson top had slipped down one shoulder, giving her a seductive look.

"You look like someone from Gone With the Wind," I told her.

"Oh, Ye," she laughed. "Just call me Scarlet."

"How was your holiday in Rome?" I asked.

"Fantastic," she smiled broadly. "I picked up a man the second day I was there, and we spent the whole week together. The weather was wonderful. I didn't wanna come back."

I remembered Jane telling me on the plane, how much she looked forward to meeting an Italian man. She had been here for more than a year, and still no sexual partner.

"So, you did get yourself a charming Italian."

"No, he was an American," she said with an ironic smile.

"Are you going to see him again?"

"I don't think so. He was married."

Later that evening, Jane introduced me to Diana, a young lawyer in her twenties, a Jewish New Yorker, who also worked for the American Bar Association. She had arrived in the country only three weeks ago and was still digesting her inter-continental culture shift.

"I never knew this country was so poor," she said with a sorry expression. "It is really sad when you see the beggars and those children on the street."

Hearing this, I relayed to her a recent conversation I had with a local policeman. He was an Azerbaijani, married to a Russian, and lived in Bishkek since 1972. He'd been working for the police force for over 20 years. After the Soviet breakup, he began importing wood from Russia to make a living. Kyrgyzstan, he told me, was the purest of communist republics. There was little corruption here, nothing like in Azerbaijan, or the rest of the Caucasus. People believed in the principles of socialism. There weren't any super rich and those who were high up in the party, enjoying privileges, had to hide their wealth. Crime was dealt with swiftly, and criminality was not a way of life in those days.

When Diana heard all this, she said, "the disparity you see over here we also have back home in the US. That was what prompted me to leave New York and come to Bishkek. I made my final decision one day, when I was on a subway train, reading the New York Times. In the "style" pages I came across an article about the latest fashion fads in the city. It mentioned a designer shower curtain that had become a must have for the rich; it cost $5,000. As I was reading this, I looked around me, on that same train, there were homeless people travelling back and forth all day, to keep warm."

***

Today I am getting ready for my trip in a couple of days to Osh city in the south east of Kyrgyzstan. It is a 16 hour journey by car, so I will fly there. It is the second largest city, with a population of 250000, considered the capital of the south. They say the south is like a different country, its culture and politics distanced from the north by massive mountain ranges that zigzag all the way there. Whilst the north has a larger Russian population and cultural influence, the south has a multi-ethnic mix of Central Asian Muslims, with large Uzbek and Tajik minorities. The two southern provinces, Jalal-Abad and Osh are located in the Fergana Valley, a region divided up between Kyrgyzstan, Uzbekistan, and Tajikistan. The Valley is hemmed in by two gigantic mountain ranges, the Tien Shan, bordering China in the east, and the Pamir, bordering Tajikistan in the south. It is an agriculturally rich land, the home of ancient civilisations, dating back three thousand years. The wealthy Davan kingdom with its many cities had flourished here centuries before Christ. It was known for the magnificence of its horses, the swift Davansky, immortalised on rock drawings near the city of Osh. At various periods, since the fifth century B.C. the region had entered the domain of the Persian Empire.

From the seventh century, Turkic tribes began to descend from the northern Steppes, displacing and assimilating the Iranian tribal nomads in the region. Later, at the beginning of the 16th century the Fergana Valley was once more dominated by Iran when Shah Ismail, the founder of the Safavid dynasty, conquered much of Central Asia. With the demise of the Safavids, the Kokand khans began to rule Fergana until their defeat in 1876 at the hands of invading Russians. The Tsar's army, inspired by the example of European colonisers, assumed a "civilising mission" in its conquest of Central Asia. The region began serious decline since the 15th century, when European advances in navigation led to diversion of East-West trade to South Asia, away from the towns on the Silk Road. Central Asia, henceforth, was in a state of social and cultural stagnation.

***

My trip to Osh is funded by CACE, as part of a series of outreach educational activities to benefit the south, which is highly under-resourced. Each one of us CACE teachers at the International University, are to make a trip south to give at least a couple of lectures. I am booked for two sessions, after which I will have a couple of days to explore the city. I would have loved to also visit the neighbouring province of Jalal-Abad; it's reputed to have great natural beauty, with many lakes, rivers, waterfalls, and Alpine covered hills. It was a holiday resort in the Soviet era, with children's pioneer camps and guesthouses. The region has agricultural riches such as massive fruit and nut forests, including ancient walnut groves. It also has the largest hydroelectric station in Kyrgyzstan, coal mining, gas and oil extraction, and petrochemical industries. Yet, it has the highest rate of illiteracy and most of its population have little access to safe drinking water. Jalal-Abad, the most socially backward region in Kyrgyzstan, is in fact a good example of the way under the Soviet administration in Central Asia, industrialisation co-existed with much under-development.

The issue came up in one of my classes a few days ago. We were discussing polygamy in Kyrgyzstan. The practice was banned under Soviet laws, and greatly diminished due to the communist party's vigilance. But in recent years it has resurfaced. Although still banned, it is sanctified through Muslim marriage contract, the *nikoh*. When I asked the class if any of them knew personally of cases of polygamous marriages, two of them raised their hands. In one case, a student told us about his uncle having married a second wife through *nikoh*. That man lived in a village near Osh and spent most of his time with his second wife who was a nurse in Osh city. Another male student mentioned a family friend who was known to have a second wife. After some debate about the rights and wrongs of these cases, a female student, normally a very quiet girl, raised her hand and informed the class of a case in her home town of Jalal-Abad. "We have a neighbour," she began, "they say he have four wives. He is rich man. He own many orchards and businesses. He want to be deputy in next elections. Of course only first wife is official, but she is old. Second one he marry with *nikoh* a long time ago and he has two children with her."

"And the other two?" I asked, echoing everyone's curiosity.

"The third one live in Osh, and work for one of his businesses. The fourth one ... I am not sure, but I heard she also live in Osh."

Wow! Everyone was impressed. At the end of the class, I told them that I would love to interview a woman in a polygamous marriage. When everyone left, Nazgul, a female student from Issyk Kul approached me and said "I know of someone like that. I can ask her to come and see you tomorrow. She is in Bishkek now."

"Do you know her well?" I enquired.

"Yes. She is a relative." was her brief answer.

The next day, I met her and her relative, Gulnara. For our chat, I took them to a little café in the park, just outside the university building. After we sat down Gulnara asked if Nazgul was a good student.

"Yes. She is very studious and never misses a class." There was a look of relief on the woman's face and a beaming smile on Nazgul. "But her English is poor," I added. "She needs to really improve." Looking somewhat concerned, the woman asked what could be done about it. Were there any affordable language classes I knew of? If not, what else could she do? "How come your relative is so concerned about your education?" I asked Nazgul.

"Mmm ... Miss. ..." Nazgul was blushing, "She my mother."

"Oh, I see." I did not push the point further, realising that the girl had been embarrassed to reveal her mother's polygamous marriage.

Gulnara, a slender woman in her forties worked as a midwife in the local hospital in Karakul, a small town in the Issyk Kul region. She earned barely enough to support her family. Her son had just finished high school and as yet had no job. She had married Nazgul's father in 1979, and divorced eight years later. Soon afterwards she had sent her children to live with her parents in their village. She had to take a second job to earn enough money to build a small house with two rooms. When it was completed she brought her children and her mother over to live with her. Her relationship with her current partner, a lawyer, had begun a few years ago. He came to visit her regularly and stayed overnight. He was married with two grown up children. His daughter was already married, with children of her own, and his son still lived with their mother. She had become mentally ill a few years ago and needed personal care. Gulnara's partner felt that he could not divorce his wife, though he wanted to marry Gulnara. For the past few years he had gradually become the man of her household, providing practical and financial support. His plan was to have the religious marriage, *nikoh*, as soon as his son was married. The daughter-in-law would then take care of his wife and he would be free.

"But what does *nikoh* offer you?" I asked Gulnara.

"He will be accepted by my family and the neighbourhood", she looked in Nazgul's direction. "They will consider him my husband and a father to my children, and he will participate in our ceremonies."

"But how do you feel sharing him with another woman?"

Gulnara sighed, "Of course, I feel jealous when he visits his other wife. Every woman would like to have her own husband." Nazgul was watching her mother anxiously. I wondered how often this delicate issue had come up for discussion. In Central Asian cultures parents often had great authority over their children, their personal decisions not open to debate.

"But it is not only the money," Gulnara continued. "It is also to have company and to have someone do a man's job around the house, and outside. He is a lawyer. He has good contacts." She went on to tell me that although she had two brothers living in her town, they were not close to her and neither helped her out. So much for the strong kinship system in Central Asia, I thought. Or maybe they were the exceptions to the rule.

Earlier this semester, in one of my ethnography classes, I had given the students an exercise on assessing kinship relations among the Kyrgyz. They were to draw up a list of all the terms used in the language to designate family members. They came up with a list of over 45 different terms of reference. This vast vocabulary located a family member precisely in terms of their line of descent, gender and generation. For instance, the term used by a woman referring to her sister or brother-in-law varied from that used by a man. This was in turn different for the older and younger in-law referred to. Such a complex system of naming kin members could be indicative of strong kinship relations.

But the current economic situation and general insecurity had fractured many families. As for Gulnara's cool relations with her brothers, I did not query further, to save her embarrassment. I only asked if she knew of any other woman in a conjugal relationship with a married man. She knew of seven or eight such cases, but only two of them had entered a *nikoh* marriage.

"I think it is normal to be a second wife when you are alone," she said in a matter of fact way, and added, "There are not many single men close to my age. Here, married men take it for granted they can have a relationship with another woman. You hear of so many deputies and other men in high positions who have a mistress or a second wife, especially if they are rich."

"What about in Soviet times?"

"I did not know of anyone in a second marriage in those days. Long time ago, before the Soviet government, some men had two wives. They used to live altogether, both wives in the same house. The older wife was called *baybiche*. The younger wife, they called *tokol.* She had to serve the older wife as well as her husband.

Polygamy in Kyrgyzstan

The situation with polygamy that Gulnara described echoed what I had heard from a women's Non Governmental Organisation (NGO) in Bishkek. I had visited this organisation back in November in the company of one of my students, a Ukrainian girl; she had worked with them, and came along for translation. Similar to most NGOs here they worked on a shoestring budget, relying on a few employees and volunteers, and constantly hustling for grants from western donors. They provided legal and psychological counselling to women. Many of their clients had been abandoned by their husband following his newly acquired wealth through business. The other frequent calls came from women suffering domestic violence. The legal system and the police offered little help. The victims often did not refer to them for the fear of shaming the family and losing their breadwinner. I could not find any statistics on the subject. But going by the client calls this group received, and anecdotal evidence, the new poverty and the growing wealth gap were promoting a return to polygamous marriages.

The Kyrgyz woman who headed this NGO, Svetlana, was a fifty year old former scientist. She had a friendly demeanour and welcomed us warmly. When she found out I was originally from Iran, she gave me a big smile, and said, "I went to Mashad for *ziyaret* (pilgrimage) three years ago, and loved it. It is a great city. Imam Reza's shrine is so magnificent, I went round it many times to do my prayers.

"Are you Shii?" I asked.

"No. But it doesn't matter. We are all Muslims."

When I asked Svetlana about the specific difficulties women faced since independence, she replied: "Everything. ... Today women have a lot more insecurities, emotionally and financially." She went on to say that violence against women and ideas of polygamy had deep roots in the culture. But in Soviet times if a man beat up his wife or openly took a mistress, his wife could take it up with the local Zhensoviet (Communist Party Women's Committee), and it would have serious consequences for him. Powerful men always had mistresses, but extra-marital relations were conducted in secret. Neighbours and colleagues could report misbehaviour to the party branch. "But today there is no one to go to," she shook her head. "Money decides everything, and most of it is in the hands of men."

***

Tomorrow morning I am off to Osh, the real hinterland of Central Asia, where I expect the city's architecture and material culture to resemble far more the region's past than the Russified modernity of Bishkek. I am both apprehensive and excited about this trip. All the unknowns are awaiting me: the plane journey with the Kyrgyz airline (with the worst safety record in the world), the mad taxi rides to nearby towns, and surviving the local food and hygiene. But to say I know Kyrgyzstan, I need to visit the Fergana Valley and see the other face of this nation. I first heard about the Fergana from Persian literature. This highly rich, fertile land, endowed with great rivers, lakes, and abundant minerals has sustained civilisations and diverse cultures for thousands of years. The beautiful Alai mountains, and the emerald green Alai valley at its foot, are just south of Osh city.

This is also the region, where a most remarkable female Kyrgyz leader, Kurmanjan Datka, lived and ruled for many decades in the 19th century. Her picture adorns the face of a 50 Som banknote in recognition of her statesmanship at a difficult period of Kyrgyzstan's history. I had heard a lot about her from my student Zarina who was doing her final year thesis on women leaders in Kyrgyzstan. She was always going on about her being an exemplary woman leader, commanding the loyalty of an army of 10000, despite the patriarchal traditions. I told Zarina, I knew that among nomads women often played a major role. Moving herds and households on regular basis required close cooperation between the sexes. But leadership of the tribes and commanding their warriors; wasn't that a bit farfetched?

"No, Miss," she replied with some certainty. "Kurmanjan was given the title of Datka (General), because at the time, she commanded the Kyrgyz tribes and their forces in the south."

Jamila had also mentioned her a number of times as an example of women's powerful position in Kyrgyz society in the past. She took special pride in being from the Mongush clan, the same as Kurmanjan Datka, and claimed to be related to her. She referred me to a recently published biography of her. "Please read it, Miss," she urged me. The book sketched out a life of heroic and tragic turns reflecting the fortunes of Central Asia in the 19th century; an era of Russian expansionism and colonial rule.

Kurmanjan Datka, also known as the Queen of Alai, the region she came from, was born in 1811 to a simple nomad family. When she was eighteen years old, she was made to marry a man she had never met before. But on her wedding day, upon seeing him, she took a dislike to the man and refused the marriage. She then fled to China to escape the anger and resentment caused by her break with tradition. Later on, she returned to live in her father's yurt, and three years later married Alimbek Datka, the ruler of the Kyrgyz of Alai. She bore him many children and participated in governing the people under his rule. Then in 1862, following Alimbek's murder by his political rivals, Kurmanjan gathered her husband's faithful commanders around her, and established her own rule over the Alai region. Her leadership was subsequently recognised by the Khan of Bukhara and the Emir of Kokand, and she was given the title of *datka* (general) by her subjects. During her rule, Kurmanjan married one of her *batyrs* (local commander) and was able to maintain the devotion of her people; they considered her a wise and just ruler. But the winds of change were already blowing across the mountains and valleys of Central Asia; the Tsar's army had begun its conquest of the region.

Initially, the Kyrgyz of Alai were successful in their resistance to the Russian advances. But by 1876 the futility of battling against the superior Russian forces were becoming apparent, and the region submitted to Russian rule. Kurmanjan's statesmanship came to its own, as she maintained her rule over her subjects in coexistence with Russian colonial rulers. But there was unrest, as local people resisted Russian rule. Soon tragedy hit Kurmanjan's family when two of her sons and two grandsons were arrested and sentenced to death on charges of smuggling guns and killing a customs official. Some of her followers urged her to stage a rescue attempt but she refused, saying she would not let her personal interest cause further suffering for her people. Russian retribution for such an outcome would have been severe. In a final cruel twist she was obliged to attend the hanging ceremony of her sons and grandsons at the main square in Osh city. Following these events, the broken-hearted queen of the south gave away all her properties and took up life as a recluse in a village in Osh until her death in 1907.

Polygamy in Kyrgyzstan

***

Tonight, contemplating the tragic fate of Kurmanjan Datka, I am filled with sadness and admiration for this remarkable woman. But thinking about mothers and sons, brings me back to my Jamie. I have not talked to him for some time. His e-mail correspondence is very brief, and my maternal advice is no doubt dismissed as electronic nag. What if he has another accident, or gets beaten up?

As I ponder these dark thoughts, sitting in my lonely flat, the phone rings, its impact amplified in the silence of the night. I am not expecting anyone to call me at this hour. Gerhard has already phoned the previous evening. Who could this be? "Hello. Miss Sima?" a masculine voice greets me warmly.

"Hello ..." I respond with a little hesitation.

"Don't you recognise me, your Uzbek admirer?"

"Oh, Suleiman. ... This is a surprise."

I have not heard from him for the past three weeks. The passionate feelings I brought back from Tashkent, have become distant memory. Early on, after my return, I had tried calling him a number of times, but either I could not get hold of him, or the line was bad and we only had a brief conversation. Tonight, however, the line is remarkably clear; I can almost feel his physical presence. He apologises for not being in touch earlier, telling me he had a lot to deal with: his brother's business, his work at the university, a brief illness, and so on. It seems that the list is long, and his excuses impeccable. I tell him that I am actually off to Osh the next day and will be away until the following week.

"When you are in Osh, can I come and see you at the weekend?," he says finally.

"But it is a long way from Tashkent."

"I may be going to Andijan with Rufat this Friday, I can come to you on the Saturday, if you like."

"Well, I don't know. My timetable is not clear yet. I have a couple of teaching engagements and some travelling to do around Osh. I think I am going to be quite busy."

"I can come late Saturday afternoon," he insists, "after you have finished whatever you are doing. Please, let's make time, Sima janim," he pleads in a tender voice. "I have missed you so much ... "

"Let's see."

I am rather sceptical. If he had really missed me, how come he did not call except on that first day after my return? What does this man want with me, I ask myself. Yesterday, I gave in to Gerhard and agreed that he would come to Bishkek to visit me in ten days' time. He is good company as a friend. What with my work schedule, worries about Jamie dropping out of university, and Gerhard's steadfast loyalty, Suleiman seemed like the fantasy man I should leave behind in historic Samarkand. And now in this eleventh hour, he phones, just before I am out of his reach for days. What timing!

We continue talking. Suleiman is in no hurry to cut our conversation short. He tells me about Rosy and Alfonso's job offers from a university in Spain. He then asks with interest about my students, my social life in Bishkek, and my son. As we reminisce about our journey to Samarkand and my last day in Tashkent, I feel nostalgia and a tinge of excitement rising in me. The phone line stays clear throughout, and we chat for a full half hour. It must be costing him a lot. We finish our conversation with the agreement to meet on Saturday, around midday. He will come and pick me up from wherever I am staying at. I don't have a mobile phone, which makes things more complicated. But he is confident he will find me on Saturday, and offers to drive me around Osh.

Afterwards, as I get my papers together and pack my briefcase, I glance quickly at my calendar. Today is a Monday. There are four more days to go before Saturday. Don't get excited, I tell myself. Gerhard will be landing in Bishkek, the week following my return. Suleiman will just remain a colleague, and we'll have a friendly meeting in Osh. I am not up for any more emotional turmoil, I remind myself. In a couple of months, I'll be back to my routine life in London, picking up where I left off. I shall be chasing after lectureships, looking to publish my articles, making ends meet, coping with Jamie, and no doubt, seeing Gerhard on and off. There will be no room for long distance romance.

Chapter XVI

Osh; an ancient crossing on the Silk Road

Here I am, finally arrived in Osh aboard a decrepit little Russian Tupolov. It is a 12 seater archaic flying machine with a propeller engine, the kind I have only seen in World War II movies. Inside, the seats looked ancient, and on the floor there was a stretch of worn carpet, its little holes glaring at me. I was the only woman on the flight, apart from a Russian stewardess, who offered us a tasteless fizzy drink in plastic cups. Just before the take off she took her seat, staring out of her window for the rest of the journey. The passengers, engrossed in noisy conversation, appeared to be Kyrgyz officials on a mission. I sat stiff with anxiety, attempting to read a copy of the Central Asia Times. Each time there was a turbulence I looked out of my window, all I could see was the sharp peaks of a mountain range that stretched to eternity. Emergency landing on this terrain could only mean certain death.

Finally after 50 minutes of sweaty palms and fidgeting in my seat, we were on the ground. I stepped onto the tarmac and took a deep breath; the sun was shining, the air was mountain fresh, and the temperature pleasantly warm. I was happy to be alive. Michael, my American fellow CACE teacher, and Yilmaz, one of his students, were waiting for me in the small airport lounge. They had a taxi waiting to take me to my apartment in town.

As we drove through the dusty streets, I could only see low-rise buildings, mostly Soviet built blocks, a couple of mosques, and a few small shops. There was not the abundance of tall trees and the greenery as in Bishkek or Tashkent. At any rate, the city was a lot smaller.

What was prominent was the view of Suleiman Too, the holy mountain that dominated the city's landscape and history. A monument had been built at the top and a large park lay at its base. The place was the main point of attraction for a great number of visiting Central Asian pilgrims. The apartment block I was to stay at was located on a main road facing the south side of the mountain. It was a three storey building in the usual state of dilapidation. There was peeling paint on the walls of the staircases, with many stairs worn at the edges, and cracks on window frames and entrance doors. But inside, the flat was not too bad. There was a bedroom with a double bed and dressing table, a sitting room with the standard tacky old sofa that turned into an uncomfortable bed, a small basic kitchen, and a bathroom with a shower and toilet.

When we arrived at the building, Michael kept the taxi waiting and came in briefly to check everything was alright. He then told me he had invited a few friends for dinner that evening and could come to pick me up later to join them. This was good news; I looked forward to meeting new people. But my cheery mood did not last long. After he'd gone, I went into the bathroom to test the shower, and found the bloody thing didn't work. There was only a trickle of water you could hardly wash your hands with. No hot water in the kitchen, either. Once again I was reminded of how primitive the material conditions were over here. How the hell was I going to have a shower in the morning? I began searching the kitchen cupboards for a large pot to boil water in. But the largest one was only a half litre capacity. Oh, damn it! I should have checked the water system whilst Michael was here. He was in charge of arranging accommodation for visiting teachers. Why didn't he ensure that everything was in order before committing me to this place?

To relax a bit, I went back to the kitchen and looked for a kettle and teapot to make tea. I had brought some tea bags and coffee from Bishkek. Waiting for the water to boil, I stood by the kitchen window, scanning the scenery. Here I had the best view of the mountain that lay on the other side of the broad avenue facing my block. Suleiman Too was a jagged rocky mountain, oddly shaped, with no clear peak. Looking at it from this distance, it resembled a reclining pregnant woman. There was the hump in the middle, and at one end, it had the shape of a large head. I had heard that its strange shape was the reason the mountain was considered sacred. Large numbers of Central Asians, including infertile couples and women wishing for pregnancy, came to visit it regularly.

***

Michael's flat was a few streets away with a structure similar to mine, except that he had a balcony enclosed within glass walls. It had been turned into a dining area with a low table and cushions on the carpeted floor. At the back there were open grounds with trees and shrubs. Tonight there were seven of us eating here, including Yilmaz and two of Michael's female students. The girls had prepared the food that afternoon. They served, and later cleared and washed up. Bermet, the prettier one of the two, was one of Michael's third year students; she seemed intimate with him. He was helping her write a paper for a student competition that could win her a trip to Bishkek. Conveniently, her family lived in a small town outside of Osh. It gave her a lot of freedom.

"Hi, Sima. Nice to see you again," Roger greeted me when he arrived. I had not seen him for some months. He had cut his long hair short, looking balder and younger than I remembered him. There was a tall and slender, white-haired woman with him. She looked like she could be his mother.

"This is Elizabeth," he introduced her. "She is from the Peace Corp, here to teach English."

I was really surprised to see an old woman, a Peace Corp volunteer. Normally they were young graduates off to explore the world, before they settled into careers and families. They had the idealism and the stamina of their youth to rough it in third world conditions. This lady looked like she could be their grandmother. As we chatted, she seemed equally curious about me and invited me to her apartment for a drink the following evening.

Meanwhile, I noticed Roger being very friendly with Bermet's friend, teasing the girl about the writing on her T-shirt. Poor Jamila, I thought. No wonder she gets so jealous about the girls around her fiancé. Jamila is certainly a lot more charming than this girl. But she is far away on the other side of the mountains, whereas this one lives round the corner.

"Jamila sends you her love," I said aloud.

"Yah, I talked to her a couple of days ago," he replied, showing no reaction.

"Is she coming here to join you at the end of the semester?"

Roger looked at me as if to say, mind your own business.

Well, as far as I was concerned, the guy was more than welcome to all the local girls he could lay his hands on. In fact the sooner one of them snatched him off Jamila, the better for her. It would relieve her of the prospect of a bad marriage. But I knew that if he dumped her, she would be very hurt, and it would ruin her plans for a life in America. I did not wish that.

***

This morning I was taken to the Osh Technological University to give the first of two talks on women and Islam in Iran and Central Asia. The audience, a couple of hundred students and a few teachers sat all ears, but I wondered how much of it they could understand. Then at question time, a small Kyrgyz girl with plaited hair stood up promptly and asked: "Are you a Muslim yourself?" I took this to mean: are you a practising Muslim? The answer to which was a firm 'No'. But such an admission would have undermined my authority in their eyes, yet I didn't want to lie. So I waffled a bit, feeling uneasy all along. Now thinking about it, I should have just said, 'Yes,' and moved on. Over here, religious identity, as with ethnic identity is assumed fixed, it's what you are born with, rather than what you currently believe in.

After the talk finished Michael took me to lunch and then to my apartment. When I arrived I found the landlady, two workmen and Yilmaz waiting by my front door. "We fix shower now," Yilmaz announced. This was followed by a half hour of noisy discussion before they all left, no explanation. Finally at 5 p.m. the four of them returned, equipped with a small tool box. I told Yilmaz that I was expected at Elizabeth's at 7.

"You go. When they finish, I close doors," he said in a reassuring tone.

"No, thank you. I'll stay."

Finally at 8 o'clock, I could dash off to my appointment, but no gift in hand. Luckily on the main road I did find a shop selling a variety of groceries. I looked through; there was nothing particularly appetising. So I just picked up some dry cookies, a bottle of vodka and a bottle of water. As I was leaving, I noticed a little refrigerator counter at the far end. In there, I could see a variety of sausages and an amazingly fresh looking block of Gouda cheese. Had this come all the way from Holland? The Russian shopkeeper said, "No. It's from the Baltic countries," and offered me a piece to try. Indeed it tasted like the genuine stuff, if a little sweeter. I had now found something to please my host; I hoped she would appreciate my rare finding. She was probably as bored with the local diet as I was.

Elizabeth's one-bedroom apartment was in a block similar to mine, though in a better condition. Soon after I arrived the electricity went off. She told me this happened often, but not to worry; she always kept a set of candles handy. Outside there was still the fading light of the day, so I went onto her balcony to view the surroundings. It overlooked a large square in the middle of which stood a very tall statue. It was of a Kyrgyz woman in ethnic costume with the pot-shaped hat traditionally worn by married women. I guessed that it was a monument to the legendary commander, Kurmanjan Datka. I asked Elizabeth and she confirmed. "When it's sunny and warm," she said, "I put a chair out here and read a book. I love the view."

"Don't the neighbours come out to look at you?"

"No, they are very discreet. But they must wonder what this old foreign woman is doing here by herself. One day one of my male students asked if I worked for the CIA."

We both laughed at the thought of Elizabeth a spy. She was an elegant old lady, with a full head of grey hair and a cool demeanour. A few years ago, soon after retiring from her job as a librarian at California State University, her husband had died. That was when she began to look for a new direction in life. Finally last year, aged seventy three, she enrolled as a volunteer with the Peace Corp to serve in Central Asia. "You are a brave woman," I told her.

"Ah, there is even an eighty year old woman working with the Peace Corp in Mexico."

Gosh! By that scale I have decades of adventurous life ahead of me.

"You see ..." she went on, "Coming here had been a bit of a fantasy for me. I had never been anywhere beyond Europe."

As we chatted, I looked around the room; there was a collection of beautiful handicraft my new friend had assembled. They were mostly wall hangings; some were embroideries on silk, others, colourful images made of felt. One in particular reminded me of a Matisse painting. On a mantel piece by the window, there was a collection of very cute Kyrgyz dolls also made of felt. From what I had already seen in a couple of galleries in Bishkek, the Kyrgyz seemed masters at working with this material.

Soon it was time to have our dinner. Elizabeth served a vegetarian dish she had prepared for us. We began to eat in the cosy atmosphere of soft candle lights, sitting on floor cushions around a low table. She was very pleased with the cheese, but didn't want to drink the vodka. "I have very little alcohol these days," she said. I also abstained to keep her company, no need for alcohol. Soon the subject of Roger and Jamila came up. Being part of a handful of Americans in the city, Elizabeth saw a lot of Roger and Michael. When I told her about my reservations regarding Jamila's relationship with Roger, she responded, "He loves her a lot, and takes good care of her. He could be a good husband to her."

"But she is so young and he is twenty years older. Besides ...." I stopped myself talking about his philandering, in case it got back to him.

"You know, age is not everything," she said in a motherly voice. "There are other things in a relationship just as important."

"Yes, I know," I sighed.

Elizabeth gave me an inquisitive look, and I could see she wanted to know more about me. I told her briefly about Gerhard, that he was an upper-class German, a lot older than me, very cultured and a real gentleman. We had been together for ten years. I said it all in the past tense, implying our relationship was over.

"Interesting man ..." she said approvingly. "It must have been good if it lasted that long."

A thought then occurred to me. Someone like her could have been a much more suitable partner for him: similar age, Germanic descent, interest in the arts, not too passionate. But would he ever look twice at a woman her age? He only had an eye for good looking, younger women, though he would never admit it. Of course I was not going to reveal that side of him. Let her imagine I have been having a long affair with a very desirable man. But where did all this leave me? Any less of a hypocrite? I had not said anything about a Suleiman character on the horizon, either. Well, let him stay among the clouds. Who knows if he is going to make it here this weekend? My life will be a lot simpler if he doesn't. But I so wish he does!

***

On my second day here Michael took me to the Osh Theological Institute. This was a small college, housed in a recently built modern building, funded by *vagf* (religious endowment) from Turkey. It offered courses on Islamic studies, philosophy, English, and Turkish. After two years here, students could get a grant to study for another two years at the Theological Institute in Ankara. The principal and his deputy, both Turkish nationals, greeted me warmly and offered me tea. When they found out that I wanted to interview some of their students, they quickly gathered half a dozen of first and second year students in a classroom to meet me. The girls looked like they were from low-income families. A few of them wore the *hijab*. Raziyeh, an Uzbek girl of twenty three in her final year had already done the two years in the Ankara Institute and was fluent in Turkish. She agreed to translate for me. I asked why some had adopted the Islamic dress. She explained it through her own example,

"At school we were taught that the *hijab* was a sign of backwardness and women's oppression. But when I was in Turkey I learnt otherwise. Now I find that on the streets men are more respectful of me. They even slow down their cars to let me pass."

At this point one of the other girls raised her hand and gave an account of her cousin's experience. Like most of the students at this college, her parents had encouraged her to enrol in the hope of advancing her job prospects. But when she returned from Turkey wearing the *hijab* they were not happy and wanted her to continue at another university. She then enrolled at the Osh State University, studying economics. Here there was too much pressure to veil.

It seemed that the Saudis were not the only ones bent on re-Islamising Kyrgyzstan. The Turks, or at least the Islamist forces over there, played their subtle part. Southern Kyrgyzstan with its mix of poverty and stronger Islamic tradition was not only receptive to the outsiders' missionary attempts, but a fertile ground for radical Islam. Come to think of it, I have noticed more veiled women in Osh than in Bishkek, though they vary greatly in appearance. Some are in jeans, barely covering their hair, whilst others wear full-length robes and scarves that hug their faces.

Chapter XVII

The Wahhabi women of the south

My second talk today was at a college in Kizil Kiya, a small town south
west of Osh. For my trip there I took a taxi, accompanied by Samira,
a flatmate of Michael's girlfriend, Bermet. She is a fourth year student
at the same university, and has reasonable command of English. She
came dressed in jeans and a T-shirt, and has a boyfriend studying at
her university. Her parents, liberal minded Kyrgyz father and Tatar
mother live out of town. They would like her to go to Europe to
continue her studies, if she can find sponsorship. Samira kept asking
me about England and what life is like for students over there. I told
her studying is harder in a city like London with many distractions
and everything so expensive. She looked very disappointed.

Our journey took just under two hours. The route went through
rolling green hills and farm land. Along the road there were poplar
trees and flowering bushes. Every so often one could see on the

distant hilltop a solitary rider galloping along. When we arrived at Kizil Kiya, a rundown small town, we took a dirt road to an old two storey building, its white-washed façade discoloured and chipped with age. We then entered a courtyard through large iron gates, its blue paint coming off with the rust. Inside, there was cracked paving everywhere. I was to give a talk at the faculty of English language and humanities. Here the students were taking English language classes as part of their degree course. Anticipating their English to be at very low standard, I had tried to tailor my speech. But using simple words to convey complex ideas was no easy task; my academic training certainly did not encourage it. On the contrary, journals and textbooks were filled with articles in which the author's lack of insight and imagination were camouflaged with a mass of technical jargon.

The office of the dean of the faculty was a small one-room cottage facing the main building. The dean, a grey-haired Kyrgyz man in a cheap suit came out to greet us, offering me a bouquet of flowers. He smiled broadly and said, "We not have much foreign teacher come. It is honour for us." We were then invited into his office and offered refreshment. A small table had been laid out with cookies, fruit, and a tea set. The dean was keen to try his rudimentary English on me. I, in turn, wanted to have a go with my equally basic Kyrgyz. Since Christmas I had been taking language classes. We now had a go at communicating through a mishmash of languages. After a while, the faculty head teacher came in to join us. She was a squat, Kyrgyz woman with thick glasses, in a long skirt. "Welcome Professor Omid," she said. "Students very happy you come."

This was amply demonstrated later in the lecture room, where an audience of 50 students and a few teachers were waiting for me. When I entered the room everyone stood up and clapped. Their enthusiasm, given the poverty, both humbled and saddened me. I wished I could do more to advance their education. But for now, I could only hope that my brief talk was not all lost on them. I was comparing the situation of women here with that in Iran. They needed to broaden their awareness of women's status in Muslim countries. Throughout my talk, however, everyone sat still, watching me with blank faces. A decade ago, when Russian was the language of the ruling power, people all over Soviet Union had regular contact with it through books and the local media. Even in the far corners of the Union, such as in the Fergana Valley, it was taught at school. Today, on the other hand, they needed wealth and privilege to come to grips with the new ruling language, English. And my audience here had very little of either.

After my talk finished, I did receive a couple of questions from the front row, where a few of the teachers and the dean were seated. I assumed not all was lost on my audience. When we came out of the room the head teacher invited me, Samira and two other female teachers to her office. As we proceeded along the corridor I noticed a couple of veiled girls among the students. Their head-to-foot *hijab* stood out among the otherwise unveiled students. I asked Samira if I could interview them. The girls seemed hesitant at first, but my celebrity status must have convinced one of them. She was a petite Kyrgyz girl with a pretty face, framed tightly in a crème scarf, wearing a matching ankle-length coat dress. When we entered the head teacher's office a male teacher got up and offered me his seat. We were now a crowd of six facing the young student. A bit intimidating, I thought. I told the male teacher we were going to discuss some feminine matters, and he offered to leave.

Zahra was a second year English major with very poor command of the language; Samira had to translate. She had been living in Siberia for three years with her parents before returning to Kizil Kiya with her sister. They now lived at an aunt's house. At school in Siberia she had developed a general interest in religion, though not particularly in Islam. Then moving back to Kizil Kiya she became very influenced by her aunts and their form of fundamentalist Islam. This diverged markedly from the traditional folk Islam they previously practised. They now rejected the veneration of saints and shrines, and relied solely on a literal interpretation of the Koran by a religious teacher they met once a week. The woman had been on the *hajj* pilgrimage to Mecca three years ago, and was tutored in Wahhabi Islam. Zahra's group included 20 women, mostly young, all unemployed, some with children at home. Zahra was the only university student among them.

"What do you think is the purpose of this way of dressing?" I asked her.

"It discourages temptation in men," she replied with an air of confidence. "It makes women feel virtuous. It's good for society."

There was a look of disapproval on the teachers' faces. They began whispering among themselves.

"And how do you, yourself, feel about it?"

Zahra glanced at the teachers, then looked at me and said, "I am happy wearing the *hijab*. It makes me feel that I have washed away all the pollution in me, all my sins."

What sins! I wanted to say. It wasn't as if she was part of the ruling elite, or the business Mafiosi in the south.

It soon became clear that Zahra had been brainwashed with fundamentalist ideas concerning women and gender relations. She believed in strict gender segregation and primacy of male authority.

And that women should only work as teachers, doctors, or nurses. "If a woman wants to get a job or travel beyond 80 kilometres," she said in earnest. "She should get her husband, or father's permission."

"Why 80 kilometres?" I asked, bemused.

"That is what our religious teacher told us."

"Nonsense," said the head teacher in Russian, giving her a pitiful look.

Next, I asked how she would feel, if her husband married a second wife.

She raised her head and said softly, "One's first love should be for Allah. The husband takes a second place." Seeing the sceptical look on everyone's face, she added, "I would respect my husband's wishes and obey him. It would not be a problem."

"But you will be jealous. You won't like it," the head teacher told her.

"No, I won't," she insisted.

Outside in the corridor, I took Zahra aside to have a quick chat out of the others earshot. "You can tell me now," I lowered my voice. "Are you a member of the Hizb-ut Tahrir?"

"Yes. I am," she said in English and gave me a coy smile. "I not tell near teacher. But you are foreigner."

Later on our way back to Osh, Samira said with a tinge of envy, "That girl looked so virtuous. I wish I could know more about her beliefs." Her reaction surprised me. I had assumed her to be firmly westernised. But I could see that Zahra's fundamentalist model of femininity offered freedom from the pressures the post-Soviet modernity imposed on young women. They did not have to follow the dictates of western fashion or the urge to consume the goods and services the majority could ill afford. Zahra offered an alternative model of contentment, even if based on female submission.

The Wahhabi women of the south

In recent years, the Fergana Valley with its stronger Muslim tradition has become the hotbed of radical Islamism. But unlike the Uzbek government that represses all forms of dissent, Kyrgyz authorities have a more lenient approach. The southern region of Kyrgyzstan, being poorer than the rest has become fertile ground for the propagandist work of fundamentalist Islamic groups. The major one among them is the Hizb-ut Tahrir, its headquarters based in the UK. It targets the young and calls for the establishment of *khalifat* (just Islamic state), that would eliminate corruption and the gross inequalities in the country. On the question of women, the group's constitution stipulates strict segregation and obedience to the husband.

***

There are two more days left before I return to Bishkek. This morning I was woken up by a phone call from Suleiman. It came as a real surprise.

"Hello, Sima *janim*. How is Osh?"

"Interesting ... But how did you get this number?"

"Aah ... I have my ways, sweet lady." he chuckled. "I am going to drive Rufat to Andijan this morning. I should get there in the evening. I will come to see you tomorrow."

"Are you sure? I mean ..."

"Why? ..." he interrupted me. "I miss you ... Don't you want to see me?"

"Yes, of course, I would love to see you. But you are coming a long way; will you be able to get back in time?" I knew that the border would be closed at night.

"If it gets late, I'll find somewhere to stay for the night, or sleep in the car."

All this, just to see me for a few hours? He really was trying to charm me. But he didn't need to. I had already fallen for him in Tashkent; though I didn't show it. Now my mind began to race ahead with excitement. So it was happening; a day from now he could be at my door. And where is he going to spend the night if it gets late to return? A hotel will be expensive for him, and it will be unkind to let him sleep in a car all night. I will then have to offer him that uncomfortable sofa bed in my sitting room. But how will that work out with the two of us alone in this apartment? Surely the temptation will be too strong. And if I give in to the passion, he is not someone I can have a one night stand with. I already feel too involved. With these thoughts crowding my head, I began to pace about the apartment, habitually tidying in anticipation of receiving a guest. I then went to the bathroom to look at myself in the rusty old mirror there. Oh, God! My skin looked dry and sallow and I could detect dark circles under my eyes. For the past few weeks I had been overloaded with work, neglecting myself. Fortunately, my toiletry bag still contained the facial scrub and mask, and the expensive moisturiser I had brought from London. I could now put them to use.

But ironically, today was a day when I wanted to look very plain. I would dress in an ankle length skirt, a dull T-shirt, and no makeup. I was happy to look my worst; I was meeting a bunch of fundamentalist Muslim women. The introduction had come via Aliyeh, a Tatar woman whose son, Izzat, was one of Michael's students at the Osh Technological University. I had met them both at Michael's place. Izzat was seventeen, a very bright boy, spoke English fluently, though he had never been abroad. Aliyeh suggested that

The Wahhabi women of the south

Izzat could bring me to the Islamic women's centre and stay with me to help with translation. The native language in Osh is a dialect of Kyrgyz with Uzbek influences, barely comprehensible to me. Aliyeh herself was to attend a little later. She told me she went to the weekly meetings to gain spiritual solace and overcome her worsening anxieties. She worked as a nurse at the local state hospital. Her husband had become disabled years ago, and since then, she had a real struggle bringing up Izzat and his younger sister on her very low income.

***

The Imanli Gadinlar (Devout Women) Centre was located in a single storey building recently renovated with white-washed walls inside and out, and minimal furnishings. It used to be a former state-owned store, bought by its current wealthy owner during the first wave of privatisation in the early 1990s. Two years ago after his return from *hajj*, he had donated it to this group to promote knowledge of Islam among women and girls. Izzat and I met mid-morning to go there. When we stepped into the hallway I noticed the door to one of the rooms open and around a dozen young girls, probably aged 8 to 12, all with *hijab* come out. The woman who had opened the front door appeared in an ankle length dress and a large headscarf. Izzat introduced us and asked if we could speak to the teacher there. The woman took us into one of the rooms off the hallway and pointed to the floor cushions where we could sit and wait. Some minutes later she returned with another woman, similarly dressed, and introduced her as the owner's wife. Behind them a third woman stepped in; she wore a dark robe dress, black headscarf, and a black *nikab* (face veil). She was introduced as the teacher. I sat with my bare head and short sleeves, feeling practically naked.

305

I told them I was a teacher at a university in Bishkek, doing independent research, and had nothing to do with the government, or the media. The teacher gave me a stare then mumbled something to the owner's wife. After some hesitation, she told us there were around one thousand women attending the centre once a week; an exaggeration, I thought. They learnt Arabic and studied the Koran and the Hadith (the sayings of the Prophet). Sessions were held twice a day, three hours each. There were also a number of girls aged fifteen and older. No mention of the younger girls that I had seen when I came into the building. I then asked if I could record our conversation for my own future reference. "No," the owner's wife responded promptly. The teacher looked at her, then turned to me and said, "But you can take notes if you want." I began to scribble quickly.

In the conversation that followed, the heavily veiled teacher was echoing the fundamentalist line on women with some folklore thrown in.

"If your hair is uncovered" she warned, "angels who sit on your shoulders will leave you. The angel on the right notes down everything you do right, and the one on the left, everything wrong."

Great! I was now free of 007 angels perched on my shoulders.

"But why do you cover your face?" I asked. "This is not stipulated in the Koran."

"If a woman is beautiful she must cover her face." The teacher informed us in a confident tone.

Well, if this applied to her, I could not see any evidence of it.

"In Iran," I told them, "the progressive mullahs say that a woman may wear the *hijab* inside, by being modest and chaste."

"Oh, no," the veiled beauty shook her head, waving a finger at me as she got up and fetched a copy of the Koran from a shelf on the wall. She proceeded to read me the verse, 'Nur'. This passage instructed Mohamed to tell his wives and those of other Muslims to cover their head, neck and bosom, lest harm came their way from the unbelievers. This verse has long been open to interpretation among Muslim scholars and theologians. But the woman insisted it was a command from God to all Muslim women, and asked, "Are you Shii?"

"Yes. Most people in Iran are."

She stared at me through the slit in her *nikab*, then turned to the other two women and said, "Shii *bizim doshmen* (Shiites are our enemy)."

"What bloody *doshman*," I muttered. So it seemed that Wahhabi prejudices and Saudi ambition to dominate the Muslim world had penetrated all the way here.

A little later when the session started in the larger assembly room, around 60 women had gathered. They were mostly dressed in shabby, cheap clothing of the poor, some, the newcomers, wore short sleeves, others were fully covered up. I was offered a chair in the front row and sat looking conspicuously foreign. In my defiance I did not wear the scarf I was carrying in my handbag. Soon the teacher emerged through a back door and stood by the blackboard. I hardly recognised her with a dress and the little scarf that revealed her square jaw and strong features. If she considered herself a beauty, she must have a very supportive husband!

For the first hour of the meeting we listened to the teacher's sermon on righteous behaviour. "Thou must avoid sin and prepare for *ghiyamet* (day of judgement). There are the unscrupulous businessmen and officials who seek their own pleasure at the expense of the poor.

They shall meet their comeuppance on that day. And those who disobey the commands of Allah in the words of his messenger will have to account for their deeds." She declared this, waving a finger at her impoverished audience. As I looked around I noticed a few of the older women sighing and wiping their eyes. Izzat's mother was also there, sitting at the back.

In the second part of the session, the teacher picked up a piece of chalk and began to slowly explain the Arabic alphabet. A few of the women took notes. The Saudis had supplied Central Asia with large numbers of the Koran soon after the breakup of the Soviet Union. They were now busy training official clerics and lay preachers such as this woman. Last year she had attended a course in Medina and was now using the book of *hadith* she had been given to prepare her talks. The fundamentalist brand of Islam she was promoting among women and girls in Osh made little accommodation with the requirements of the 20th century, let alone the 21st. When earlier I said to her: "You all want aeroplanes, modern medicine, and computers, but reject where all this comes from."

She looked at me with a bold expression, and said: "You can fly in an aeroplane, wearing the *hijab.*"

Sure you can, I thought. But such a gender-segregated society could only be a consumer of modern life, not its producer. The Gulf States, with their immense oil wealth, may easily under-utilise their womanpower, but could a poor country such as Kyrgyzstan afford that?

Last November, after what I had seen in Bishkek at the Islamic seminar for women, I had a discussion with my colleague, Mukhtar, about the re-Islamisation of Kyrgyzstan. "What these preachers are promoting," I told him, "is more a case of Arabisation." He agreed and went on to say that propagating re-invented traditions, inspired by desert dwellers of Arabia, would only impede his country's development. Their history and environment was markedly different. Arabs living in the desert had to avoid the burning sun and let the moon guide them in the cool of the night. Hence, they adopted a lunar calendar. The Kyrgyz and the Kazaks, on the other hand, were people of the mountains and the steppes; they were sun seekers. "These Islamists come here," Mukhtar complained, "and tell our people that in Islam, praying at the shrines is sacrilegious; they should only gather to worship inside a mosque. But *mazars* have been our holy places for many centuries. If Islam is a universal religion, why should we be subject to *Arab* history and tradition?"

***

This afternoon, after I left the Devout Women, I went to the street of *chaikhanas* (traditional tea houses) in the centre of town. These are practically restaurants serving *shashlik*, and *lakhman*. They are in a row of low terraces along a quiet, dusty street. Each has a number of carpet-covered wide wooden benches you can sit on and lean on cushions. Food and drinks are served on a low table atop the bench. Walking past them, I could smell the barbequed mutton and see the waft of smoke coming out of the open kitchens. The mostly male clientele inside were a mix of Central Asian ethnic groups: Uzbeks, Kazaks, Kyrgyz, Uyghurs and Tajiks. Here I had the feeling that I was in the heart of old Asia, sampling the sights and sounds of the Silk Road. Along this route, stretching from the Bosporus to China, the Turko-Persian peoples have mixed and mingled for centuries, unhurried by the passage of time.

Land of Forty Tribes

The *chaikhana* I chose to eat at was the busiest; a good sign. I sat at the only unoccupied bench and ordered a dish of *lakhman* and tea. Soon a woman approached and asked to share my bench. She was an Uyghur, a Muslim Turkic group, based in Xingjian province of China, neighbouring Kyrgyzstan. Their language is close to Turkish, so we could communicate. Until last year she had been a nurse earning ten dollars a month. She now worked with her husband, buying imported Chinese clothes from the Dordogne bazaar in Bishkek, the largest in the country, and sold them locally. This earned them around a hundred dollars a month, enough for her family of five to live on. She told me she had never heard of the *Imanli Gadinlar* group. But over the past few years, she and her family had begun to fast during Ramadan, though they did not know how to do the *namaz*. "We pray in our heart," she said.

After finishing her meal, the Uyghur woman wanted to consult a local *bubu* (shaman) nearby. These women were reputed to have healing and clairvoyant powers. Would I like to join her, she asked. I said 'Yes'. I was curious. We left the *chaikhana* and proceeded along the road towards the bazaar. Before long I noticed Samira and Bermet were coming in our direction. They were off shopping, they told me. I mentioned my intention to visit the *bubu* nearby.

"Those women are dirty and ignorant. Don't believe anything they say," Bermet said with disdain. Samira was less dismissive and agreed to accompany me to assist with translation. The *bubu* was an old Kyrgyz woman with dark, leathery skin and half-rotten teeth in a long, shabby dress. She sat by the wall in a shaded spot, close to the entrance of the bazaar, with a couple of plastic stools next to her. She told us she received 30 to 40 clients per day, mostly women seeking cure for various physical and psychological problems. The men often came with business dilemmas and wanted to know about the future. She had first realised her healing powers 20 years ago after a bout of serious illness. Her father and grandfather had acted as shamans. Recently it turned out, her son had also inherited this gift.

I asked the *bubu* to diagnose my ailments. I had a condition that had bothered me for years. She gave me a piercing look and mumbled something I didn't understand. After a long pause she took out a string of rosary beads from her side pocket and began turning them over as she uttered a prayer in Arabic. Next she fetched a palm size metal box from under her chair and took out a piece of shiny brown stone. She placed this over my head, before rubbing it on my back. Finally, she took my left hand and pulled at each finger, then took my pulse and gave her verdict.

"You have a problem with your heart and kidneys.

"What is she on about?" I said to Samira.

"Don't worry," she explained, "most people in Kyrgyzstan have kidney trouble."

Following her generic diagnosis, the *bubu* offered me a head and neck massage with healing effect. I looked at her coarse hands and dirty finger nails and said, "No, thank you".

"Why?" She gave me a disappointed look and added, "You were poisoned as a child. That is your problem."

"What?" I puzzled.

"Drink *kumis* (mare's milk) first thing in the morning and eat lots of carrots, cabbage and fruit," she recommended.

"Where am I going to find *kumis* in London?"

"Ignore her. She is false," Samira shrugged.

Land of Forty Tribes

After concluding our session the woman asked for 5 *Som* (10 cent) as her fee. I paid her 20. She smiled broadly, revealing a whole set of stained, broken teeth. She then motioned a man standing nearby to take my seat. The guy, holding a smart briefcase, had been waiting patiently for his turn. Once we left, Samira told me that her mother knew a *bubu* she consulted whenever she had to make a difficult decision, or if one of her children were ill. She added, "That woman is real clean, not like this woman. Why did you pay her extra?"

A thought then occurred to me. As a child I had caught an infectious disease which according to some medical theory may have contributed to my condition. Could that be considered a form of poisoning?

***

Early that same evening Samira came with me to visit Suleiman Too, also known as Solomon's Throne. According to local legend the Prophet Mohamed and Alexander the Great have been up this mountain. So have Amir Timur's clan and his army. The shrine at the top of this mountain, Dom Babur (Babur's house), was built by Zahiruddin Babur, a great-grandson of Timur. He claimed the throne at the age of fourteen and went on to establish the Mongol dynasty in India. To get to it, we walk through a park and then a gateway that marks the entrance to a steep set of stairs. It's a good half hour walk to the top, where you see a spectacular view of the city of Osh. Down below lays the city's main cemetery with elaborate headstones that mark the veneration of ancestors. On the way to the summit we pass a number of trees, their branches loaded with little pieces of rag tied to them by hopeful pilgrims. I have seen the same thing on some of the holy sites around Bishkek.

The Wahhabi women of the south

The shrine at the top of the stairs is a very small windowless room. An Uzbek imam at the far end is reciting verses from the Koran to a handful of worshipping women seated on a bench. We just take a peek, but do not enter, and walk on to the other side. Here, facing the valley below, a piece of rock six feet wide with shiny, smooth surface lies horizontally on the side of the mountain. It has a gentle slope and I see people taking turns to slide on it.

"Is this a game?" I ask Samira.

"No," she says, "if you lie on that stone, make a wish and slide three times; your wish will come true." She encourages me to try it for myself. I feel like a child at a playground. "No, I feel silly." I decline. There is shrills of laughter from a fat woman who has just stepped off the wishing stone, helped by a young man. The small crowd around us are a mix of young and old, male and female. There is a holiday atmosphere, and a kind of relaxed spirituality. We go back to sit on a stone bench and gaze at the view of Osh as the sun sets over its expanse of low-rise buildings and gardens. This is a city nearly three thousand years old; a crossing point for caravans on the Silk Road. Through the ages merchants, explorers and warriors took respite in its ancient and medieval houses and caravanserais. Sadly, none of them remain today.

Back in the park at the bottom of those steep stairs, I notice a large yurt selling handicrafts. It is filled with small rugs, various types of embroidery and colourful wall hangings made of felt. I buy a few items as souvenirs and have a chat with the woman running the shop; it turns out she is a great-granddaughter of Kurmanjan Datka. She tells us many of her descendents still live in the area. Afterwards, we go to a small *chaikhana* serving drinks. It has the usual collection of carpet-covered wide wooden benches. The place is very quiet; only one other bench is occupied by a group of locals. Samira orders *kumis*, and I try it for the first time. The fermented drink has quite a pungent taste that takes getting used to. I switch to my green tea, ignoring the *bubu*'s advice. The sun has now set and the sky is dark blue with a few puffs of white cloud here and there. The ground around us is a carpet of green grass, and there is a gentle breeze in the air. I lean on a cushion in this delightfully serene surrounding, thinking what a romantic setting it is. I should bring Suleiman here tomorrow and sit with him, holding hands.

Hearing his voice this morning had sent waves of excitement through me. Now I am asking myself, shall I let him stay the night? And if so, what about his wife? She is called Dilora, the enchanter of hearts, though it seems not in his case. Still, what about his responsibilities for her and the two young girls? Am I in the way of that? The thought of it casts a dark shadow over my happy mood. I am gripped by guilt and confusion. Perhaps I should just make myself unavailable for the day. If he comes all this way and doesn't get to see me, he will be pissed off, and I won't enter an unwise affair. I could go and visit Elizabeth in the morning, then come here and spend a few hours until it gets dark. It will be rude and unkind of me, but perhaps better for both of us in the long run. But wait a moment; I begin to reconsider. If this couple lived in the West, they would have long been divorced, or more likely, never married. I shouldn't make a hasty decision. I'll wait till tomorrow to see how I feel about it.

***

Oh, what a morning it turned out. I was up since 4 a.m. with stomach cramps and bouts of vomiting. After my fifth visit to the toilet I managed to fall asleep for a couple of hours. When I woke up, it was past 11. Bloody hell! He may be here soon. But I did not feel like getting out of bed; my legs were no longer my own. Finally I managed to drag myself to the bathroom for a wash and got dressed. Soon there was that knock on the door. My man had arrived. "Hi Sima *janim*." He hugged and kissed me on both cheeks, then stood back and said, "You look so pale. What's up?"

I told him about my stomach condition.

"Oh, damn," he said. "I would have come earlier if I knew ... Let me go and get you some medicine."

"I was just about to make some tea," I motioned him to sit down.

"No, no . You don't move. I'll make it." He dashed into the kitchen.

"Can you find the tea bags?" I called out.

"Yes. I've got everything."

After we had the tea Suleiman went out promptly to look for a pharmacy and to buy some groceries. I told him I wasn't able to eat anything just yet, but later I could have a little boiled rice with plain yoghurt. Before he left, he said, "You go back to bed, *janim*. I will prepare the food for you."

I lay on the sofa, thinking, yesterday I was considering avoiding him. Today, I am more than grateful for his presence. Is fate playing me?

It was now an hour since Suleiman had returned from the shops. Another sugary tea, the tablets and some more sleep had perked me up. I went into the kitchen to see what the nice smells were about. He had just finished preparing two dishes, one for me, rice boiled in chicken stock, and another one, rice cooked with fried chicken, onions, tomatoes and some spice for him and for me when I felt better. "It's light," he said. "I cooked it without the chicken fat. I also stewed some apples for you."

"That's really kind of you, all this trouble, on my account ..." I was impressed.

"No trouble at all. I thought you may want to avoid restaurant food for a couple of days."

"Where did you learn to cook?" I asked.

"In America. And now, for the last two years in Tashkent I cook for myself and sometimes for friends."

"What about the woman you lived with over there?"

"That was only in the second year. Before that I was on my own for over a year. Anyways, Lizi didn't like cooking that much. I did more than her."

After we'd sat down to eat, I thanked him again for looking after me. "Are you surprised an Uzbek man can cook?" he asked with raised eyebrows.

"No I am sure a talented man like you can easily master culinary skills."

"Oh, I like that, my culinary skills ..." He chuckled. "So you think I could get a job in the US or the UK as a kitchen hand?"

"Why not as a Central Asian chef?"

"Sure ... When you open your first restaurant, I will be happy to serve you."

Now it was my turn to laugh. But it did occur to me that Suleiman might have an agenda with me. All the attention he'd focused on me since Samarkand could not be just for fancying me. I knew he was unhappy with his life in Uzbekistan and wished for a way out. Ideally, he wanted to do a PhD in America and get settled there, but how could I help him with that? I wasn't even sure if I definitely wanted to get a job there myself.

***

Later that afternoon we went for a ride around the city. It was a warm sunny day. Along one of the roads there were flower stalls everywhere. Suleiman bought me a lovely bunch of red tulips which I carried everywhere like a young bride. We then went to the Suleiman Park. But this time, I skipped the climb up the steep stairs and went straight to the *chaikhana* in that delightful setting. The weather was now getting cooler, with the sun hovering low in a cloudless sky. I told Suleiman about my brief visit to Kara Su two days ago. This was a market town on the border with Uzbekistan. At one end of the town there was a small monument very close to the border post. Nearby there was a broken bridge over the river that formed the border. I was shocked to find out the authorities had smashed parts of the bridge to hinder the traffic in trade. Chinese goods had been making their way to Kara Su via Bishkek, and onward across the border. The Uzbek authorities were concerned about the adverse effect this had on local production.

"But why break the bridge?" I asked. "Isn't that a juvenile thing to do?"

"It's because there are too many fucking stupid people in power," Suleiman said bitterly. "Our leaders can never co-operate, they are so full of suspicion."

"What a shame. This region is so rich and yet most people are so poor. It hurts to watch."

"Yep ..." he sighed with a solemn expression, and went on to talk about the rivalry among Central Asian leaders.

Soon it was dusk and the *chaikhana* was beginning to empty. Suleiman seemed lost in his thoughts, leaning on a cushion, gazing at the distance.

"I'm cold. Let's go," I said with a pleading smile and made a move to get up. "Sure. If you like." He got up promptly and followed me.

As we began to stroll towards the car, he put his arm around me and asked, "Sweetheart, how do you feel now? Is your stomach better?"

"Much better. Thank you."

"Shall I take you home?"

"Yes please. I am getting hungry."

"That's a good sign," he said, and gave me a kiss on the cheek. The sexual tension between us had surged this afternoon, close to boiling over. Yet this was still a public place and passion had to be contained.

Finally we were inside my apartment. With the door shut behind us, he hugged me like a hungry child and a long kiss followed. "I love you, I love you," he said softly. "I think about you, day and night."

"I love you too," I said, no longer doubting my own feelings. But hunger was now beckoning, so I suggested I should heat up the leftover food for our supper. Suleiman looked at his watch and said, "It's getting late. Will you let me stay the night?"

"Yes, of course."

Earlier, I had offered him the sofa bed in case it got too late to go back across the border. Now there was no question of that. After four months of going without sex I could no more wait for our carnal union than he could. So we ate quickly and washed, then went to bed for a night of loving.

The next morning we were awake early and renewed our love making; more intense and with greater passion than the night before. God! How I had forgotten what it was like to lose yourself in the embrace of a strong young man; one who was full of sweet words, alert to your every pleasure. Afterwards he said to me, "*Asalim*, you have a lovely body. How do you keep in shape?" I told him it was years of exercise, even in Bishkek I found an aerobic class I could attend. As we were now getting very hungry, Suleiman went out to get some food, while I got packing. Once we'd finished with breakfast, he took me to the main bazaar.

This colourful open market meandered along the *Akbura* river bank for a whole kilometre. It is reputed to have existed in this location for two millennia. It would have been one of the main hubs on the Silk Road, with caravans of merchants coming from all over, East and West, to trade merchandise and exchange ideas. Currently it offered goods of varying kind; traditional knives and hats, cassettes and videos, clothing and household goods, huge piles of fresh fruit and vegetables and the most enticing display of dried fruit I have seen anywhere. Being a Sunday, the market was teeming with people: Uzbeks, Kyrgyz, Tajiks and other Central Asians. There were also stalls and *chaikhanas* selling food and drink. At one point we came across the section selling fabrics, including the quintessential Uzbek *Atlas*, a silk fabric with geometric design in rainbow colours.

"Would you like a summer dress made of this?" Suleiman held a roll of finely patterned *Atlas* against me.

"Yes, I did think about it. Shall I take one of these as well?" I picked up a finely embroidered Tajik cap.

"Definitely," he said with a glowing smile. "You will look a real Central Asian beauty."

I thanked him for the compliment and approached the seller to pay.

But as I put my hand in my handbag, he grabbed it, saying, "Let me take care of this. You shouldn't pay for things when you are with me."

I did not like being told what to do, even if it was out of generosity. However, there was no point in arguing. Instead, I decided I shall take him to the Dordogne bazaar when he is in Bishkek and get him a nice leather jacket or something. We have already talked about our next meeting in three weeks, when the CACE convention is once more held in the Issyk Kul resort. He will then come back with me and stay on a few more days at my apartment. Now I cannot wait for these weeks to roll on.

Chapter XVIII

Naryn; capital of bride kidnapping

Returning from Osh, I am loving my apartment, so much more roomy and clean compared to the place I was staying at over there. And no more of those perilous plane journeys. Thank God! On the way back from the airport, I noticed how much more modern Bishkek looked, even if dated and drab. This Russified northern city is 5000 miles from Osh, separated by a massive mountain range traversing across Kyrgyzstan. But the gulf in their culture and history is even greater. That ancient city where caravans met and pilgrims arrived with their bundle of wishes has been spared the Soviet style modernity. The selfish tourist in me well appreciated its quaint charm, stuck in a time warp.

A few days before I went to Osh, Gerhard had phoned, telling me he wanted to come to Bishkek to stay with me for a couple of weeks.

I agreed. He was always good company. But now, given my feelings for Suleiman, and after last night, how could I face him so soon? And what if in an impulsive gesture, Suleiman was to come over a few days early and the two of them met? Not that Gerhard would burst out in a fit of jealousy. He is too dignified for that. He would just bottle it up and show his hurt in another way. But Suleiman? God knows how he would react.

Luckily, I found a solution the next day at our departmental meeting. The head asked me if I was willing to accompany a group of students on a month's field trip. The location was At-Bashi (Horse's Head), a small town south east of Naryn province. It is one of the remotest parts of Kyrgyzstan where ethnic Kyrgyz customs have survived the most, a haven for the anthropologist. When I called Gerhard later that day, I told him I will be too busy until the end of the semester, late in May. After that I was going to accompany a group of students to a remote part of Kyrgyzstan.

"Oh…But you've only just come back. Again another adventure."

"It's not an adventure," I replied tersely. "It's work."

There was an angry silence. Then came the rebuke, "But you are not a youngster anymore. …all this rushing off to unsafe places. …"

"Thank you for *reminding* me."

Damn it, I thought. The man just can't help making me feel older to create parity between us.

***

There is only one more week left before the final year thesis has to be handed in. Zarina came to my apartment last night in a state of panic.

"I am ruined, Miss," she announced, tearful. "If I fail the year,

I have no money for next year's tuition. I will have to leave the university and go back to Naryn."

I had not seen Zarina for over two weeks. She missed her last meeting with me. "But so far your grades are good. You'll pass," I reassured her.

"No, Miss," she insisted. "You fail, if you fail the thesis." She then told me that her father had come to Bishkek a couple of weeks ago for hospital treatment; she had to stay with him and could not do much work on her thesis. She had brought what she had written so far. I reviewed it, suggested improvements and some brief further readings. She was to come back the following afternoon. I would go over everything and get her on her way to completing the work by the following week. "You can spend the night here if it gets late," I offered.

Zarina was not the brightest of my students, but she was committed and ambitious. A lot of her future plans hinged on completing the degree. With that qualification at hand, even if she did not get as far as Texas, she could at least get a job in Bishkek and be independent.

That weekend, as it happened, Zarina was not my only student visitor. Jamila also turned up, looking distraught, but her tears revealed a different kind of concern. Roger was having an affair with a local girl, her mother had reported, telling her the man was unreliable and she should break off her engagement.

"I am not surprised," I said, having my own doubts about him, especially after my last trip to Osh. "You don't need him, if all you want is to get to America. Just keep applying for grants and you'll get there eventually."

"But I love him, Miss."

"Are you sure?"

"I think I do ..." she said with some hesitation.

I did not want to contradict her, even though she had recently expressed doubts about the marriage.

"If I lose him," she continued with a sour expression, "I don't want to go back working in bars and sleep with American soldiers."

"I didn't know you did that," I said, really surprised.

"Yes. Before I met Roger."

Goodness me! What a revelation. Back in the autumn she was claiming to be a virgin when she met Roger, and was concerned that he may not have believed her. Now if her innocence was fabricated, what about her story of abuse? Was that another ploy to seek sympathy? This, I could not ask without seriously offending her. My doubts had to stay on the shelf.

"Be more courageous about the future," I tried to encourage her. "Have you read Chingiz Aytmatov's Jamila?"

"Yes, at school."

"Then take inspiration from her. She was brave and took her destiny into her own hands."

"That was a story, Miss."

Jamila was the eponymous heroine of Aytmatov's best-known, charming novella set in a Kyrgyz village in 1943. A free-spirited and outspoken teenage girl, she was married to a young man serving at the Front. When a stranger came to the village she fell in love with him and eloped, risking severe punishment in the hands of her outraged in-laws and her community. She chose a new life, burdened with war time hardships, in pursuit of love. My dear, pragmatic Jamila, on the other hand, was imbued with the post-Soviet lack of idealism, looking for an easier life with material riches. But who could blame her?

***

Finally, my students have finished their exams and I was happy to see everyone pass. God knows I tutored them enough. The administration, in their lingering Soviet custom, insisted that I should provide a list of 20 questions, out of which they would choose five to give to the students. This would be the case for all three papers. But what were their criteria of choice? None of the staff here have a clue about anthropology or its history. Well, so be it. Soon I will have no more to do with this establishment, and its warped bureaucracy.

Tomorrow I am off to Naryn accompanied by Zarina who will assist me with my research there. It is the eastern, most mountainous region of Kyrgyzstan, sparsely populated. It lies on one side of Tien Shan, on the other side is China. The massive mountain peaks at 6000 metres. That is where, according to local legend, the Gods live. Down below, between the mountain ranges, vast valleys and multitude of rivers run east to west. The longest of them, Naryn River, flows past Naryn city, the administrative capital of the region. It is a small town of 50000 people, almost solely populated by the ethnic Kyrgyz. It was initially built in the second half of the 19th century by Russians as a military fortress to protect the trade route to Kashgar in western China. The beautiful Alpine lake of Song-Kol at 3000 metres is within 50 kilometres. In the summer months, its lush pastures take on a wild beauty with the yurts sprouting like wild mushrooms on the grassy slopes.

Land of Forty Tribes

Zarina was keen on the trip; it gave her the opportunity to visit her family. We took a communal taxi, a Russian Zhiguli, from the long distance taxi rank in Bishkek. I paid for three so we could have the back seats to ourselves. We were on the road for over seven hours and only stopped once, to have our packed lunch; there were no cafés or restaurants on the way. Until Issyk-Kul, the route was over flat land, after which we began to ascend the mountain range. The temperature then began to drop and five hours into our journey, we got to a narrow passage through a gorge, iced up on both sides. The views coming up had been breathtaking; green valleys interspersed with winding roads hugged the side of the great mountain range. Looking at the sheer drop on the side of the road, I was happy that most of the time we were the only car on the move. I did not fancy an accident on these hairpin bends. Fortunately the Kyrgyz driver, a middle-aged man with a droopy moustache was experienced and sane, even if his car's shock absorbers left us with churned up stomachs and sore bums.

We finally got to Naryn city in the late afternoon. There was plenty of light in the sky and a pleasant breeze in the air. Zarina soon found me a room through a friend of hers. It was in a small three room apartment in a two storey block, the tallest in town. We then went for a stroll in the neighbourhood. The place was barely touched by 20th century, except for the name of the main street, Lenin. It ran the whole length of the city close to where my apartment block was situated. On the other side of the street was the town's post office, a one story building painted bright blue. A few hundred metres further up this road was a small square, encircled by a wall of mountains on three sides. In fact the vista of a mountain was never far as we walked around and later took a car ride through the town. This outpost of human civilisation was indeed a settlement on the rooftop of the world, ideal for mountain lovers and climbers.

For dinner, Zarina took me to a hotel restaurant recommended by her friend. The best one in Naryn city, she told me. The old two storey Soviet building had been turned into a 'no star' hotel with cheap, shabby furnishings. The place was quiet, with the restaurant section completely empty. Fortunately the food, regular Kyrgyz menu, was better than I anticipated. I ordered the safe bet *lahman*. After we had finished eating, the waiter suddenly reappeared with a grin on his face, asking if we would like some pancakes. I was full so I declined. "Try it, Miss," Zarina suggested eagerly. "They make them like in America."

"Really?" Now I had to try some, indigestion or not. And yes, what he served us did taste authentic. I couldn't believe my taste buds; American pancakes in Naryn. Whatever next?

On the way back, Zarina dropped me off at my block before she went on to her parents' home. Once inside the apartment, I could hear noisy conversation from one of the rooms and assumed it was the new lodgers in the vacant room. But when I went into my room I found a couple of backpacks lying on my bed. Who were these intruders? I had already paid for this room. Too tired from the journey and not in the mood for arguments, I placed them outside in the corridor, had a quick wash and went to bed. A few minutes later, the door opened and a guy put his head through, looking around. The room was dark; I pretended to be asleep. Fortunately, he must have got the message and soon went away. Afterwards, I could hear the water running in the shower room next door. This went on for ages, during which, the noise and my wariness of the strangers kept me wide awake.

The next morning I woke up late and found Zarina at my door. She told me a group of mountain hikers had arrived at the apartment late last night, and they were off this morning. I told her, "You better get me a key to lock my room, or I am not staying here."

This took some haggling. The landlady was reluctant at first, but with the threat of me leaving she eventually produced one.

We now had a couple of hours before meeting members of an NGO Zarina had specially invited. We could go for a brief walk. On a street nearby there was a small two-room museum; I suggested we visit it. The larger room displayed the contents of a yurt, everything a nomad family would need: cooking utensils, mats and mattresses, a child's wooden cradle, and a beautiful quintessential *shyrdak*. These were embroidered wall hangings with motifs of nature. Next to the cradle there was a very small whip on the floor. "Surely this is not for striking the baby?" I asked.

"No." The museum attendant laughed. "It is used to ward off the *jinns*". These underworld creatures, or evil spirits, were believed in by people across the region, all the way to Iran.

Next door in the smaller room there was a chart with the names of famous *manaschis*. Next to it were a number of photographs of the most eminent ones, dating back to the 19th century. You could see from the display, the prominence of these bards in the traditional Kyrgyz community.

***

In the afternoon, Zarina's friend, Nazgul, and two other girls came to the apartment to meet me. Nazgul was half Uyghur, a plump girl in her twenties with short hair and round eyes. She ran an NGO called Ay Kumar, giving young women advice on bride kidnapping. Ay Kumar was funded by a European organisation, and functioned with the help of half a dozen young female volunteers. They organised seminars, discussing the legal aspects and the victims' rights. There was already a law against *ala kachuu* (bride kidnapping). The girls who attended were given training on how to resist the strong moral pressure to submit from the kidnapper's family. They were advised to immediately report the incident to the police. The problem was the police often did not want to interfere in what they considered a family affair. According to Nazgul, at least 50% of marriages in the region were conducted in this way.

After Nazgul had given me her brief, Jayna, one of the two girls present began to talk about her experience. She was a final year law student at Naryn University, a tall, pretty Kyrgyz girl with flowing long hair. Last November a group of eight young men had kidnapped her. She was very scared at first, but then managed to get them to take her back.

"Did you know any of them?" I asked.

"No. They were all strangers. But the one who wanted to marry me, I had seen before. He had followed me a few times. He was an unemployed young man from a nearby village; he had come to Naryn to find a girl."

"Here if a boy doesn't have a girlfriend," Nazgul commented, "he asks his friends to go searching for one. We call it *andip*."

"It means a chase or hunt," Zarina translated.

I asked Jayna how she was hunted down.

"I was having lunch with my friends in a restaurant," she began, "when the men came in. My male friend from the university knew one of the guys and invited him and the others to join us at our table. But when we finished eating my friend left quickly. Outside, my girlfriend and I wanted to take a *marshutka* home. But the guys insisted on giving us a lift. I refused to go with them. Then all of a sudden they took hold of me, dragged me to a parked car and forced me in. Four of them came in the car with me, the others followed in another car."

"What happened to your girlfriend?"

"She was afraid. A few weeks earlier, she had been kidnapped and taken to a village nearby. Her parents had come quickly to fetch her. But afterwards they had a lot of trouble from the kidnapper and his family, so she didn't want to get involved."

"Did you not shout and ask for help?"

"I did. But the two militia men who were nearby ignored me. I think they guessed it was bride kidnapping, and didn't want to get involved. They had probably kidnapped their own wives."

"If it is one or two men in the dark forcing a girl," Nazgul interjected, "they would think it is an attempt to rape. But when there are a few of them, and it is daylight, then everyone assumes it is bride kidnapping."

Jayna continued, "When it became clear to me what was happening, I kept telling them I was a law student and knew my legal rights. I would report them to the police, and they would be prosecuted. They weren't convinced; so I told them I was a Baptist and could not marry a Muslim."

"Why a Baptist?"

"There are some Baptist converts here and people hate them."

"Did they believe you?"

"No. They just laughed and said, 'when we get to the house, there is going to be a big party to celebrate your wedding'."

"You must have been really scared. Was it a long journey?"

"The man's village was not far, though it felt like we were driving for hours. I was sweating and shaking all the way. I knew I should not cry and let them think I was scared." Jayna stopped and took a deep breath. "Most of the girls who are kidnapped don't know their rights and can't argue logically. They panic and keep crying. There is a phrase in Kyrgyz: *tash doshgon gerinda oor*" (The stone lies where it falls).

"If a girl is kidnapped and is returned," Zarina commented, "it is considered shameful. It diminishes her chances of marriage, especially if she spends a night in the man's house."

"Even if he doesn't touch her?"

"Who knows if he has, or hasn't?" she replied.

Nazgul now described what often happens following the kidnapping. The man takes the girl out of the car and leads her to his house. She should sit behind a curtain and wait for the women of the house to come and talk to her. They usually try to console and reassure the girl. If she objects, they tell her the ancestors' spirit will punish her and she will be doomed to misery for the rest of her life. No one will want to marry her. Sometimes an elderly relative may block the entrance door, or they may place pieces of *borsok* in front of it. This is ritual fried dough offered at religious ceremonies and could inhibit the girl to step on. Finally the grandmother or some other old woman in the family puts the scarf over her head to confirm her as a bride. After this, the relatives come to the house to celebrate the wedding

"So how did you react when you arrived?" I asked Jayna.

"I was determined to get away. When we got out of the car I

walked quickly to the house, barged in, and yelled, I will never marry this man. I will sue you if you don't take me back immediately."

"What was their reaction?"

"They were really surprised to see the way I was behaving. Despite this, an elderly woman came to place the scarf over my head. But I pulled it off and threw it on the floor. They didn't like that at all. They began to curse and kept looking at my short skirt and whispering among themselves. I also told them I worked with an NGO that gave advice to kidnapped girls, and how they could get out of it. I think this really shocked them. Finally, they agreed to send me back home and kept asking me not to sue them."

"How did the man react to all this?"

"He didn't have much choice. His parents told him to send me back. In the evening two of his friends drove me to the city. But I was so upset I couldn't face my parents. I went to a friend's house and spent the night there. I told them about it a few days later."

"How did they react?"

"I am very lucky that my parents are liberal people and don't want me to marry against my wishes. My father is seventy years old, but very understanding of my ambitions. He is an educated man, an engineer."

"Did you hear any more from the kidnapper?"

"I heard that a few weeks later he had kidnapped one of my relatives. She was a first year student at our university, a timid girl. She didn't resist. Now she is pregnant and lives with his family in the village. She can't attend classes regularly, so she bribes the teachers, and is allowed to continue. I never saw that man again, but I heard that his friends were gossiping about me. They said I was a drug addict and a prostitute."

Naryn; capital of bride kidnapping

After Jayna had finished, I asked the girls, what if a kidnapped girl turned out not to be a virgin? Nazgul said that in one such case recently, the girl was returned to her parents with shame and her family had to return the *kalym*. Afterwards the girl was estranged from her family and could no longer live with them; she ran away to Bishkek. But if a man was very keen on a girl he may pretend she is a virgin. In one such case, the groom on his wedding night had made a cut on his leg to produce the blood on the sheet to present to the family.

"But do these enforced marriages last?" I was skeptical.

"Most marriages here last," Nazgul responded, "because the girl often gets pregnant in the first year of marriage. It is the custom here. So she is trapped quickly."

"How about arranged marriages?"

Zarina explained that this was more common among the rich. People of high status considered kidnapping shameful. They preferred to arrange marriage with those of their own class and from an early age. The wedding is also more expensive and the groom's family has to buy the girl a ring and jewels. For a kidnapped bride, however, the *kalym* is less, maybe 5000 Som (100 dollars) and a horse.

***

This is my third and last day in Naryn. In the morning I took a walk in the neighbourhood and discovered the Celestial Mountain Guest House. A small two-storey Soviet construction, renovated to cater for western mountain lovers. It offered basic, but cleaner than usual accommodation. The dining room invited you to imagine you were in a Swiss chalet, with wall-to-wall posters of the Alps. In the gardens behind the building, a couple of large guest yurts had been erected, their backdrop the great mountain range that gave the place its name. The vista was stunning and the air so fresh, I began to feel lightheaded as I strolled back. Later in the afternoon, Zarina brought along a former neighbour, Mairam, to meet me. "She has quite a story, Miss," she enthused.

Mairam was twenty two years old. She had finished high school five years ago, after which she stayed at home helping her mother. She was now six months pregnant with a very big bump.

"Do you think you are carrying twins?" I asked.

"I don't know," she chuckled. "My mother-in-law thinks so."

She began to tell me her story.

One day last year, Kanybek, the boyfriend of her best friend, Tolgonay, had called on Mairam and asked if she would go to his girlfriend's house to get her to come out to meet him. He had three of his friends waiting in a car to kidnap Tolgonay for marriage. Mairam had known Kanybek for some time. He was twenty three years old and worked as a trader in town, earning a good income. She considered him a decent guy and saw nothing wrong with this arrangement. But when she went inside and told her friend the plan, she responded angrily, "No way, I am not coming out."

Tolgonay had previously told her boyfriend, "If you love me, why can't you come and ask for my hand?" But he had said he couldn't afford the *kalym*.

Mairam and Tolgonay now argued for ages, not getting anywhere. So Mairam went back to the car and told Kanybek that she wouldn't come out.

"The bitch!" he cursed. "Why is she messing me about like this? My family have already killed a sheep and invited guests." After some more huffing and puffing, and throwing punches in the air, he pleaded with her, "Please, tell her to hurry up. They are waiting for us." She went back in and tried once more, but Tolgonay would not budge. Mairam finally gave up and went to the car to tell the boys it was no good. Meanwhile, one of Kanybek's friends came up with an idea, "What if you take this Mairam, instead? You know her already. She is a nice girl." The others agreed. When Mairam approached the car, the boys were smiling. They asked her to get in and sit down to have a chat. But soon they drove off, telling her what their intention was. Mairam was shocked and kept protesting, but deep down she felt agreeable to the idea. When they reached Kanybek's house and went inside, a group of his older female relatives surrounded her, saying, "If you reject your fate, you'll be cursed by the ancestors. The stone lies where it falls."

Meanwhile, Mairam's parents had been notified of the kidnapping and came over to the house. Kanybek's parents, dressed in their best attire, greeted them warmly offering food and drinks. In the discussion that followed, Mairam's parents began to like the family, pleased that they were not poor. In fact they considered Kanybek a good match for their daughter. Mairam was already twenty one, time for marriage, they thought. Later that evening, as they were leaving, they told her, "We are not going to take you back. We agreed to the marriage." The wedding ceremony, she was told, would take place the following week, when guests from both sides could attend.

The following day, just as Mairam was beginning to adjust to her new home, there was a knock on the door. Tolgonay was standing there, angry and tearful. "I am the one who was to marry your son," she told Kanybek's mother. "We have been planning marriage for ages." The woman shrugged and said, "Sorry my girl. It's too late now. Talk to my son." But Kanybek was just as dismissive. "You are in the past," he told her.

After Mairam finished telling me her story I asked her how her marriage was working out.

"I have a happy marriage. He is a good husband," she said with a broad smile.

"Don't you feel unhappy that he loved someone else and only took you out of necessity?"

Mairam sighed. "That was fate ... But now ... he loves me."

After Mairam left, I asked Zarina if this girl was happy with her marriage. "She seems to be. She says she wants to have at least four children."

This fatalistic attitude seemed to be common among the kidnapped girls, not only here in Naryn but also those from Bishkek and Osh. Samira, the final year student at Osh Technological University who was my guide in Kyzil Kiya had done a study of the phenomenon in the area. She considered it the worst case of denying women their human rights, and was appalled by the helplessness of many of the kidnapped girls.

"You know, Miss Omid." she said with knotted eyebrows, "In the weddings here, everyone wants to know the amount of the *kalym*. They always ask the bride's parents, 'how much did you receive for your daughter?"

The notion of women treated as merchandise becomes particularly clear when considering the shame attached to the return of a girl kidnapped for marriage. From the moment she is taken she seems to be the property of her kidnapper, and like soiled goods her return brings shame to her family.

The Soviets had banned the practice but never managed to

eradicate it. And now with the post-soviet rise in ethnic nationalism, although still illegal, bride kidnapping appears to be on the rise. It may be connected to the rise in domestic violence and worsening security situation for women; a phenomenon verified by various United Nations reports. The increasing economic hardships and the authorities' lack of will and resources to enforce the law contributed to this. The educated young women such as Samira and many of my students saw it as a reflection of male supremacy in the culture. I believe the exploitative family relations here is another factor. The *gelin* (daughter-in-law) is seen as a spare pair of hands serving the family. I heard of a number of cases where mothers actually encouraged their sons to kidnap a bride.

When I discussed the subject with one of my Kyrgyz colleagues, Emil, he confirmed that the stigma attached to a girl's return was very real.

"Is this because they suspect sexual encounter between her and the kidnapper?"

"Yes. But in any case, being taken means another man has laid claims on her; she is tainted."

Emil went on to argue that bride kidnapping was rare and happened mainly in the rural areas. "Educated men would not do it," he insisted.

So far, I have not found official statistics on the subject. It is a difficult one to research. In some cases the girl may have consented to a staged kidnapping but will not admit it. She may be having a relationship with the boy despite her parents' disapproval.

In a recent study by a visiting American professor, one third of the men who kidnapped their wife had university education. Among the kidnapped girls, a quarter had consented to their abduction, effectively eloping, whilst three quarters were taken by force or deception, some by total strangers. A disturbing finding of the study was that one fifth of the girls were raped following abduction. Thinking about these forced marriages I wondered about their adverse consequences, such as rising divorce rates, domestic abuse and suicide attempts. Again, there were no statistics on this. Among the 12 cases of kidnapping I heard about at the university, three ended in divorce, two cases involved serious domestic violence and in one case, the young man whose beloved was abducted committed suicide. Then there was that tragic incident last autumn when my student Baktigul's sister drowned in the river, attempting to escape her kidnappers. That case and my students' reaction to it was what convinced me of the need to research the subject.

But where did this tradition come from? There is no mention of it in Manas, and Islam certainly does not condone forced marriages, or acts of kidnapping. Historically, the custom existed in a number of societies around the world, including, in the Caucasus and among the Turkmens. Within Central Asia today, non-consensual bride kidnapping seems to occur mainly in Kyrgyzstan, and to a far lesser extent in southern Kazakhstan. One does not hear of it among the Uzbeks and Tajiks. But if this was a nomadic tradition centuries old, how is it that it has been maintained in the modern, settled society? There is a lot of speculation regarding the origins of the tradition. Some scholars believe that it only dates back to the 19th century, becoming prominent in the 1940s and 50s.

From what my students have told me, the practice was not so rare in Soviet times. A student from the Issyk Kul region, for instance, told me that back in the 1980s both of her uncles had kidnapped their wives. Another one from Osh told me the story of her mother's *ala kachuu* that took place in 1974. She was studying medicine in Tashkent at the time and came back to her village in the Osh region for a holiday. The man who kidnapped her was from a neighbouring village. He had known her from a distance. She did not really know him and did not want to consider marriage until she finished her studies. A few hours after she was taken to his house she found the opportunity to escape through an open window. She then ran to the house of a relative of her father nearby. But as luck would have it, a little girl living in the house opposite had spotted her jumping out of the window and noted the direction she went. Being a small village it did not take her kidnapper's family long to trace her and bring her back. And that was the end of a medical career for the woman. "That is a real shame," I said to my student.

"They get on well now," she replied. "But before, whenever my mother was unhappy, she would say angrily, 'If it wasn't for that little girl ..,"

***

Later that evening Zarina asked if I would like to visit a shaman. "No thank you," I told her. I didn't really believe in fortune telling.

"But Miss, she is the best in Naryn. People come from far away to consult with her."

I thought about it for a moment. I was interested in the subject matter and wanted to know more. The one I met at the bazaar in Osh did not impress me; she looked like a beggar. But this one, Zarina assured me, was a professional who ran a practice from home.

Shamanism in Central Asia is an ancient religion that considers sacred elements of nature, such as animals, trees, mountains and rivers. The word shaman originated from northern Siberia, meaning the knowledgeable one. He/she could mediate between the world of spirits and humans. In Kyrgyzstan they are called *bakshi* or *bubu*. In the pre-Soviet days when shamanism was strong, shamans were leading figures in their community and considered holy. They performed ceremonies to heal the sick, or bring about rain and other desired outcomes. During the ceremony, dressed in animal skin and a hat of feathers, a shaman would chant, play the drums, dance, gesticulate and go into a trance to undertake his/her spiritual journey. They had a lot of similarities in their acts and way of dress with their counterparts among the indigenous Americans.

With the spread of Islam, shamanistic beliefs and ceremonies lost their potency and what remained integrated with the new religion. Then following the establishment of atheism under the Soviet rule, shamans were denounced as charlatans and shamanism branded as backward and regressive. Its beliefs and practices, nevertheless, continued through the 20th century. In the rural areas the female shamans, *bubus*, became guardians of the faith teaching girls and young women a version of Islam syncretised with old shamanistic beliefs. An example of this was the emphasis on visiting shrines, and the choice of location for them. Another one is the custom of tying torn rags to branches of trees around holy places. I saw this on the climb up the Suleiman mountain and in the vicinity of the shrine by the Issak Ata sanatoria near Bishkek. In the post-soviet era, shamanism has once more gained popularity. Whether it is the revival of tradition, the new poverty, or the loss of state provisions, shamans are increasingly referred to for an array of problems, physical, psychological, and financial.

***

Naryn; capital of bride kidnapping

The *bubu* we were visiting today lived in a one storey house dug into the side of a rocky mountain on the edge of town. Nearby on the other side of the road was a small mosque, its outer walls covered with colourful Kyrgyz motifs, distinct from Islamic symbols. I was told it had been built only a few years ago with Saudi money. However, the peeling plaster of its white walls and staircases hinted at a lack of maintenance money. Today unfortunately the building was closed; I could not view its interior. I took a few pictures of its unusual appearance and wondered how much of a juxtaposition of Islamic and Kyrgyz art adorned inside of the building.

After the mosque we walked a short distance along the asphalt road then continued on a desolate patch of grassy land that stretched to the base of the mountain. At the far end, standing by itself was the *bubu*'s house. It backed onto the steep, rocky mountain face. There were no other habitats, far and wide. In the fading light of the early evening, the place had a ghostly feel about it. When we knocked on the front door, a Kyrgyz woman in her forties appeared. She was wearing a dark, ankle-length dress and a black scarf wrapped around her head. "Welcome," she greeted us with a faint smile. I could see from the way she stared at me with her sharp black eyes, she was as curious about me as I was about her. "Come to my work room," she said, and shuffled along a narrow corridor. We followed dutifully. The room had white washed walls, with no décor, a large oval table that could sit a dozen people, and a number of chairs.

Once we were seated, I asked her what type of clients she dealt with.

"All kinds," she replied, "young and old; some have money worries and some have psychological or health problems. But I don't touch the alcoholics. That is beyond me." As for her method of diagnosing, she explained, she checked the person's pulse and examined their hands and eyes, then used cards or special stones. She also consulted the Koran and asked for Allah's guidance. For physical ailments she had an assortment of herbs in stock which she gave out as needed. In some cases where the person had had bad fortune and their life was in a bind, she assumed that an ill spirit, *jinn*, had taken hold. To dispel it, she did a special ostracising ceremony dressed in a white robe that had motifs of nature sewn on. She would then ask the person to kneel down, head bent, as she circled them, chanting prayers. After this she would pick up a small whip with which she would gently hit the person seven times to dispel the *jinn*.

I asked the *bubu* if I could have a look at that outfit.

"No, you can't." She said firmly.

Zarina then asked the woman if she would look into my future and foretell what lay ahead. The *bubu* took out a small book of Koranic verses and read a few in her Kyrgyz accent. At the end of each one, she would lift her head and look into my eyes, making me feel uneasy.

"You are going to get married in 2004," she said finally.

"That is only next year," I said to Zarina with disbelief. "How does she know I am not already married?"

"I told her."

"You shouldn't have. Tell her you misunderstood. She is married already."

But the *bubu* didn't buy that. She gave me a skeptical look and said, "I can see that you were married once, a long time ago. Now you want to marry again."

"Ok. Ask her who this new man is."

"I can't tell you exactly ..." She paused, then stretched her shoulders and looked up to the ceiling. "There are many stones on the path you will take. Think carefully before you make any final decisions."

Well, there was no point in quizzing her further. This shaman seemed to have reached the limit of her otherworldly perception. It was time to leave. As for her prediction, I could not see the possibility for, or seriously consider, marrying one or the other of the men I was currently involved with. Still, tomorrow I will be back in Bishkek. I shall see what is in store for me then.

Chapter XIX

East meets East

It's June and Bishkek is blooming; so much greenery everywhere, I am reminded of the English countryside. Yesterday I discovered a small park nearby full of flowering bushes in full bloom. I sat on a bench feasting my eyes on the sea of colours and the grace of willows in mourning. I thought I should bring Suleiman here when he comes over. I could imagine him sit beside me, his arm around my shoulder, listening to my tales of Naryn. We would chat and chat about our lives and sketch out plans for the future. He is going to stay at my apartment for a few days and we shall go to the mountains together. In Bishkek we are both single and free to love.

Most of my colleagues are heading home at the end of the CACE convention next week. It is to be held once more at the Aurora hotel in Issyk Kul. All the sponsored teachers from Kyrgyzstan and

Uzbekistan will be there. I can't wait to see him again, but wonder how we can keep our affair away from prying eyes. I don't think he is as bothered about it as I am. I can just imagine tongues wagging, "She's got herself an Uzbek toy boy". When we first met at last year's meeting I could not imagine a romantic entanglement with any of those guys, let alone a passionate love affair with one who is firmly shackled by ties of marriage and fatherhood.

Oh God, what am I going to do? My contract with the university is at an end and I am due to return to London by the end of the month. The tenants at my London flat will be leaving then, and Jamie will be back from university. I have not seen him since January, the longest we have been apart. I am anxious about my boy, and dearly miss my London life. Tomorrow I must go and book the flight back. But the thought of leaving him behind wrenches my heart. He is in my thoughts day and night.

***

Last night Jamila appeared at my door, her cheeks pale as the moon above. What kind of trouble is she in now?

"You remember that *bad* uncle I told you about?" She mumbled, her eyes welling up. "He had arranged it."

"What? Which uncle?"

"The one who ..." she gasped, "did bad things to me. They said he was now in Bishkek and was waiting for me at his friend's house. He had an important message from my mother."

"Who were these people? Did you know them?"

"No. There were three. The one who wanted to marry me, I think worked for my uncle. I saw him once, last time I was in Osh.

Can you imagine …" she said tearfully. "If I couldn't run away, they were going to drive me to Osh, and …"

"Come on. You are safe now." I gave her a hug. "Let me make a coffee. You can tell me afterwards."

From what Jamila had told me, her father died when she was ten. The following year her maternal uncle had moved into their home. He was a stern character but kind to Jamila. He often hugged and kissed her, buying her little presents and calling her "my beauty". Often when she was told off by her mother, he would back her up. "You really spoil that girl," her mother would complain. During the summer break, when she was just twelve, he offered to take her on a short holiday with him. He had a yurt in the Alai Mountains, just south of Osh. Jamila took delight in joining the children of her uncle's friends, running around and playing games. In the summer, the Alai Valley was covered in velvety green grass. The sky would be turquoise blue and the grass would shimmer in the bright sunlight.

Here she felt a sense of freedom she had never felt before. She learnt to ride horses, tutored by her uncle. In the evening they would visit the other yurts, or have guests for whom Jamila would cook on a paraffin stove, aided by her uncle. At night they slept on a quilted mattress on the floor of his yurt. Then one night after copious amounts of vodka he began to touch her in ways he should not have. She tried to pull away from him, but was held down by his firm grip. He kept telling her that he loved her very much, and she should not reject him. The next morning he told her that the love between them had to remain a secret. Her mother was already jealous of his love for her and this would really upset her. She may send her away to live with her aunt in the village, an unhappy prospect Jamila could not face. She felt ashamed and confused, and decided not to mention her experience to anyone.

A few months later the *bad* uncle had married for the second time and moved out. As the years went by she resented and feared him more and more. A few years ago his eldest daughter had married the son of a very rich businessman. A powerful local Mafiosi, he had some of the southern politicians in his pocket. Following this, Jamila's uncle was able to extend his network of rich and powerful friends, becoming influential in his own right. There were rumours that recently he had found himself a new source of income in drug smuggling. This was a lucrative business, originating in the poppy fields of Afghanistan, then transported across Central Asia to Russia and beyond. Unhappy with the idea of his favourite niece marrying an American, he now wanted to resolve the matter in a particularly Kyrgyz way.

***

The next morning I went to the local shop to buy groceries for breakfast. Standing at the gateway to our courtyard was a large man with heavy moustache, possibly an Uzbek, smoking furtively. As I went past I could feel his piercing stare following me. I looked away, trying to ignore him, but felt quite uneasy. When I returned the man had changed position, now standing very close to the entrance to our apartment block. Again, I tried to ignore him and made a dash for the door, my hand trembling as I turned the key.

Inside, Jamila was watching TV and attempting to read a magazine at the same time. "I am going to open this balcony door to get some air in," I called out from the kitchen.

"No, Miss. Please ..." she ran behind me. "It is not safe."

"Why? It is daylight and we are not on the ground floor."

"You don't know these people." Jamila's face was tense with fear. "Relax my dear, and please call me Sima." I tried to seem calm. "Anyway, did you get hold of Roger?"

"I couldn't this morning. But last night he promised he will get a flight today and come. If he doesn't …"

"Then you stay here as long as necessary. If you want I can call the police for protection."

"You must be joking Miss. I mean Sima …" Jamila shook her head. "The police won't do a thing."

"What do you think Roger can do?"

"He is a man and he is American. They won't touch him."

"Okay, we'll wait," I agreed reluctantly.

What a fucking situation, I thought. My last days in the country, and here I am, hostage to an archaic, misogynistic tradition. When I took Jamila on for thesis supervision, I did not bargain for any of this.

Late that afternoon Roger finally turned up. He looked clearly shaken. The heavy lines around his mouth had deepened. "Are you alright sweetie?" He asked as he held her tight and kissed her. "Did they hurt you?" Jamila shook her head and a tear rolled down her cheek. Her face was lightening up. "I am gonna stay with you until the fuckin marriage is done," he announced and kissed her again. He had already called the American consulate for advice and was given a number to contact if there was any trouble. He believed the situation was now under control and he could keep Jamila safe until his return from Issyk Kul. He had arranged for her mother to come to Bishkek to stay with her during his absence. We chatted some more and had tea. Then before leaving, Roger gave me a hug and said, "Thanks Sima. You are a doll."

***

It is my third visit to the Aurora, a fading Soviet beauty with its delightful gardens and outdated rooms. I try to dispel the memory of my previous visit to relieve my conscience. I had enjoyed my time here with Gerhard. Then we parted, with me as ever suspended in that yo-yo of a relationship, yearning to find the 'right' man. But now that I am on the wrong side of 50, can I afford to spend more years with another unsuitable partner? God knows how long it will be before my new love moves on to fresher fields and younger flesh. How will I recover from that? Oh, damn it! I should take my cue from the men here and enjoy what is on offer today. The broken heart can be mended later. Can't it?

On the coach journey to Issyk Kul I sat next to Suleiman, discreetly holding hands. It was a strain keeping the passion under wraps. I asked about his daughters. He told me he'd only seen them once since his return from Osh. "Don't you miss them?" I asked.

"I do, but ..." Unhappiness rippled through his voice.

"And how is Dilora?"

"Ahh, the same bullshit, all we do is row." He added in a hushed voice, "I've got to get a divorce. But she won't let go."

"I guess she still loves you."

"It's not love ... It's obsession. She is fucking selfish." There was a sour expression on his face as he turned his head away, gazing at the road ahead. "It's not just her," he added, "our mothers also can't take it."

I knew that Suleiman's family, being of rural background, did not take to the idea of divorce lightly. Besides, there was that special bond between the two mothers, having grown up as fictive sisters. Nonetheless, wouldn't Suleiman's mother prioritise her son's happiness? He didn't seem to think so. After a long silence he moved his head close to mine and whispered, "Honey, let's not talk about my situation anymore. I love you very much and that is all that matters."

It was midday when we arrived at the hotel. At the reception the staff were acting confused, arguing among themselves. Bina, the CACE administrator for Central Asia, was the event organiser. She had confirmed the booking by fax and phone. "So damn incompetent," she grumbled, her back turned to the Kyrgyz receptionist. The woman was nervously shuffling through a large pile of papers. She then disappeared for quite some time, finally returning with a bunch of keys and a list of names. The men were to share two to a room. The two couples got double rooms and the remaining three women were given a single room each. I was much relieved to have some privacy at last. Suleiman's eyes were filled with excitement as he followed me to my room. How sweet it was to be alone together at last. Inside my room, as we kissed and caressed, all my doubts about the future melted away like butter in the sun. But our time was short; we could only make hurried love. The first meeting of the day was due in 20 minutes. As I got up to refresh myself, I pointed to the single bed in my room and said, "We won't get any sleep on this tonight."

"I can hire us a double room if you want," Suleiman suggested.

"Oh, no. That will make it too obvious."

"We'll work something out." He winked, going out.

***

The meeting was to discuss the year's experience and what further resources CACE could bring to the respective universities. I took my turn to speak about the shortage of library resources. At present there was often only one copy of the essential text book; it had to be shared by the whole class. In the American universities, students were expected to buy the books on their class reading list. Over here, even if they were available locally, a great majority could not afford them. We dealt with the matter by producing multiple handbooks of photocopied chapters; nobody talked about the copyright infringement. I also mentioned the lack of bursaries to help the very many students who struggled financially.

"Why don't you come up with some fundraising suggestions?" The European head of CACE turned to me, his voice booming across the large hall.

Yes, I had some ideas, but there was no point in mentioning them. I was not coming back in September. Reza then stood up and began to elaborate on his ideas for next year. He would be returning here. I just sat back and let my mind drift. Was Suleiman telling me the truth about his relationship with his wife and family? And if so, what was to become of Dilora and her chances of love and remarriage? Most men in this part of the world sought a virgin wife, ideally younger than themselves. Even worse, what would become of his little girls abandoned by their father? I kept mulling over these worrisome thoughts, struggling to keep track of what was being said.

After the meeting we had some free time before dinner. Suleiman asked if I fancied a swim in the hotel pool. He was going to join Reza, Emil and a couple of the other guys for a dip. I said I may join them later. Then on second thought, I decided not to. I would watch them for a bit then go for a walk on the lake shore. This evening none of the women were in the pool, except Rosy, the Canadian teacher who had come from Kazakhstan. She was a tall blonde, much fancied by my male colleagues. They were playing about in the water, with Rosy the centre of attention; only Reza seemed to linger at the edge of the pool, impervious to the excitement of others. Then all of a sudden a race started. Four male colleagues, including Suleiman were straining to keep up with Rosy. Splash, splash you could hear the noise of limbs dropping into the water in an uncoordinated effort. Rosy's smooth strokes, meanwhile, carried her past everyone to the edge and back. She was a clear winner. "Come on. One more time," they challenged her. A second ferocious attempt by the men resulted the same. "Fuck it," came the admission of defeat by Emil, "You … have had special training," he blurted in between much panting. "We don't live near the sea," Suleiman said aloud. "Neither do I," Rosy responded, as she began splashing back at Suleiman. A water fight then ensued among much laughter. Emil and the other two guys joined in. The pool was now getting too noisy. Let the kids play on, I thought, I will head for the beach and catch the last of the sunset over the lake.

From the entrance of the hotel, the beachfront was a short walk through birch trees along a gravel path. It was a quiet time, hardly anyone around. I took my shoes off and began a leisurely walk over the soft sand, wallowing in the gentle breeze that stroked my face like a tender lover. The sun was now far gone in the horizon, soon to disappear for the day. I hastened back over the pier, and leaned on the wooden barriers to catch the breathtaking view. On the other side of the crystal clear water stood the snow-capped Tien Shan, its summit piercing the darkening blue sky, and in the foreground, green and brown covered lower mountains. A huge red dish was now slowly descending behind the massive mountain, puffs of pink clouds scattered in the sky. Standing here, bewitched by the calm and beauty of the place, I could just imagine how dazzled the early nomadic tribes would have been arriving here for the first time. Having long journeyed and fought their way through freezing steppes and barren lands in the north, they had arrived at this warm lake, the Issyk Kul. This was a sacred lake the Gods had rewarded them with.

Back in the hotel, I had to rush to get changed and go for our evening meal. When I arrived downstairs in the dining hall almost everyone was into their second course. I picked up my meal and went to sit next to Suleiman; he had kept a seat for me. "Where have you been? I was getting worried." He gave my hand a gentle squeeze under the table.

"I went for a walk."

"In the dark? By yourself?"

"Yes. Does it matter?"

"It's not safe. Anyways, why didn't you want to join us? I thought you liked swimming."

"You weren't swimming." I kept my eyes averted. "You were all getting excited with Rosy."

"You were not jealous. Were you?"

"No. Why should I be?" I said without meaning it.

"*Asalim* (my honey)," he whispered in my ear, "you are the only one who excites me."

"Sure." I replied and carried on eating. He let pass the skepticism in my voice, and began to talk to Alfonso and Rosita.

A brunette woman in a red dress, with matching bright red lipstick had just come into the hall; she joined the diners a couple of tables ahead. I was reminded of the woman I saw the last time I was here; she was with the jolly Jews celebrating their company's anniversary. The boss had invited Gerhard and I to join them for dinner. I remember him taking numerous pictures of her. It was a joyful night with lots of music and dancing; recalling it, I was touched by nostalgia, laden with guilt. Oh, forget it. I tried to deflect my mind to the happy state I was in with my adoring lover. Who knows how long this would last.

***

The second day of the convention began with more talks and discussions, this time mainly in workshop groups split by the subjects taught. This was just as well. Suleiman and I could have a break from each other. The passion of the night before was too raw and distracting. After lunch we had a short concluding session, then a couple of hours of free time before the evening barbecue party on the beach was to commence. Out on the corridor leading to the staircase that went up to the rooms, Suleiman asked if I would join him and a couple of the guys for a quick drink at the bar. I told him I was going to have a little nap first. Afterwards, I would love us to go for a walk in the gardens. I wanted to show him my favourite spot by the pond. It was a place I considered the most romantic corner of the world. "Darling don't drink too much before the party," I pleaded.

"I am only having one drink," he assured me. "Come and meet me when you are ready."

I headed to my room thinking he couldn't have had much sleep last night, either. But perhaps he doesn't need it.

***

It was now past five o'clock, in another hour the sun will set and daylight would begin to fade. This was my last chance to visit the gardens. Tomorrow morning straight after breakfast, we are to

354

head back to Bishkek. But where was Suleiman? There was no sign of him in the bar. There were a few colleagues, including Emil and Alfonso. I asked them where he might be. "He went to his room to get some sleep," Alfonso informed. Then whispered suggestively, "I think you wore him out last night." I tried to ignore the comment and looked away. Alfonso was a close friend of Suleiman, but still, he shouldn't have bloody said anything. Ah, these men. They are all the same. I felt angry and embarrassed, yet thinking that I shouldn't be so bothered about discretion. He was the one with a ring on his finger, even if he'd stopped wearing it.

Just at this point Roger came into the bar area. "Hi Sima," he waved at me, looking cheerful. I went across to him, glad to get away. "How you doing? Are you enjoying the CACE extravaganza?"

"I love the location," I told him. "I wish we could stay a few more days." He offered to buy me a drink. I asked for an Efes beer, a German lager produced in Turkey, popular here.

"Have you heard from Jamila? Is she alright?"

"She is fine. I spoke to her this morning. She told me she is not going out until I get back."

"You mean the poor thing is incarcerated for two days?"

"It's not that bad," he shrugged. "Her mother is with her. I'll be back tomorrow afternoon."

Roger went on to talk about the wedding. Marrying across cultures is never easy, he observed. He had learnt a lot about the Kyrgyz culture, but some of it he didn't like. "This *kalym* business … " he shook his head with annoyance, "how can you set a price on a girl?" Jamila's mother had set the *kalym*, an apartment in Bishkek, which he could not afford, though it would only cost a fraction of the price in his home town.

"What does Jamila say about all this?"

"She just says it's our custom. You have to pay a *kalym.*"

"It sounds awful. But if you love her, …," I paused for a reaction; there was none. "I guess you'll just have to barter for her."

"I've known Jamila longer than you have." He looked straight at me. "She is fragile. She was abused as a kid, doesn't have much experience with men."

Goodness! I better hold my tongue. Did he know about her waitressing job at the American Bar and episodes with the GIs? Perhaps not. But I was not going to spill the beans. Whatever that cute face of hers and those innocent-looking eyes could get away with, good luck to her. She needed his help to escape the hardships of life in this country. Nonetheless, despite my concerns for her welfare, I could see his vulnerable side. Perhaps he wasn't quite as smart as he thought he was. That girl was certainly ambitious and shrewd with it. Watch out Roger!

Finally, after nearly an hour of waiting at the bar I set off for my walk in the gardens. I did not want to go into Suleiman's room in case his roommate was there. Let the bugger sleep away the precious time we have here. Then by the time I reached the pond the light was fading and the sun had utterly vanished. Being early summer, there were none of the autumnal colours, the green, yellow and gold that stood so vividly against the backdrop of the majestic Tien Shan and its snow-covered peaks. That was a spectacular view perfectly reflected in the crystal clear waters of the pond. Now with the warm weather the trees were in full bloom, though the snow on the mountain's summit had not melted. The picture postcard view was just as amazing. The quiet calm of the place, devoid of visitors, was delightfully soothing. I sat alone on the solitary bench, and could not help remembering my last visit, with Gerhard beside me. "Thank you for bringing me here," he had said, his face glowing with appreciation. "So beautiful, ... It reminds me of the Alps ..."

Sitting there by myself, I couldn't help thinking, if I truly ended it with Gerhard I would badly miss our outings together: walks in the countryside, visiting museums and galleries and the opera. Could Suleiman ever sit patiently watching a performance of Puccini's arias, or trail through art exhibitions? These and other damning thoughts were crowding my mind. I felt really disappointed sitting in this lovely spot by myself. Why couldn't he keep up with our arrangement? Bloody unreliable Central Asian man. He just wasn't interested, I guess.

Finally, seeing that it was getting dark and I needed to get ready for the party, I left the area and began to approach the hotel. Then as I got close to the staircase leading to the lobby, I noticed Suleiman hurriedly walking towards me. When he reached me he asked, "I went all over the gardens, looking for you. Where is this damned pond?"

"It's too late now." I gave him a cross look and moved away. He followed me and apologised profusely, then said, as if in repentance, "I'll sleep in my room tonight and get up early tomorrow for our walk."

I kept my cool and did not respond. He put his arm around my shoulder, kissed me on the side of my head and apologised again.

***

Land of Forty Tribes

The barbecue party was held on the beach near the pier. The nearly full moon shone bright over the lake, gentle waves flapping onto the sandy shore. A generous supply of beer and Georgian wine was laid out on a large table lit up by generator powered lamps. The food, grilled meat and variety of salads were served by the hotel staff from an adjoining table. A sound system had been set up with a couple of the guys from the group organising the music, a mix of popular numbers. Once the dancing started, I was one of the first to join in. Suleiman shied away, saying he needed more drinks. After a few numbers I approached him again, "Come on big man. You have to join in." He smiled and shook his head, saying, "I can't dance, not like you." I took his hand, pulled him towards me and began dancing, holding onto him. After some hesitation, he followed my cue; I could see he had a good sense of rhythm. Then when a Latin number came on, he really got into it, twirling me, and at times lifting me in the air like a child. "I am feeling dizzy." I protested, laughing and panting. "You will sleep well tonight," he said in my ear with a quick kiss.

Well, I did get to sleep quickly once I hit the pillow. I had left the party at midnight, leaving Suleiman drinking and chatting to Rosy and a couple of the guys. One of them had just produced a large bottle of vodka they were sharing. I don't know how long I had been asleep before I suddenly woke up, feeling the impact of a heavy arm flop onto my shoulder. Fuck! Who is this? Didn't I lock the door? The room was dark. I struggled to sit up to see the intruder. "As … salim … my Cindella …" I heard Suleiman's slurred voice. In the sliver of light through the curtains, I could see his eyes were shut. "You've come to the wrong room," I said aloud. There was no response. So I just lay next to him, hoping to get to sleep. As minutes went by, the heavy breathing turned into a drilling noise. "Go to your room," I finally shouted and began to push him off the bed. He shifted a bit, then came a bang followed by him groaning, "Ahh …" He was on the floor. He then stood up slowly, sat on the edge of the bed, rubbing his arm and mumbled, "Y …you don't love me anymore."

"No, not in this state." I got up and accompanied him to his room.

***

The next morning I was late getting up. When I got to the dining room, most people in our group had already left, only Roger and another guy remained. I went to sit next to them, ignoring Suleiman; he was sitting by himself a few tables away. Once my companions left, he came over, "Bon appétit. May I join you?" he asked, looking pale and a little dispirited. I nodded keeping a solemn face. He asked what happened last night. He vaguely remembered coming to my room, then going to his and being sick. He had woken up this morning, with a sore arm and a headache. I told him he'd given me a fright coming into my room in the middle of the night and hopping into my bed. I had to send him back to his room, but afterwards couldn't sleep for ages. "Why did you drink so much?" I reproached him.

"I'm really sorry. I don't usually," he mumbled. Seeing the skeptical look on my face he added, "I swear on my children's life … In my family no one drinks heavily. We are not like Russians …"

Soon we were invited to board the coach. I let him sit next to me, in the hope of a more convincing explanation. A few minutes after we were on the road, the driver turned on the radio and Russian pop music filled the air. We could then talk without being heard by others.

"Now tell me the truth, why did you get so pissed last night?" I began.

"I already said I'm sorry."

"Yes, you did. But I want some explanation."

"Ahh, ..." He took a deep breath. "Where can I start? You know my situation ... I am trapped in a marriage I hate, and I have responsibilities I can't ignore. My life is wasted."

"Oh, come on. You are being dramatic."

"I'm just telling you how I feel," he said, irritated. "I hoped you'd understand."

I lowered my gaze and said nothing. After a long silence he continued, "Basically, I made a big fucking mistake three years ago when I came back and didn't ask for a divorce right away. I had to return because it was a condition of my fellowship, but after two years I could have gone back, married Anna, and obtained a Green Card. She kept writing to me for ages..."

"Do you still love her?"

"Oh, that is long finished." He said in a sorry voice. "You know, my grades were very good, I could have got a scholarship for a PhD. Instead, I am stuck here in this shitty situation."

Suleiman did not often talk about his unhappiness living in Uzbekistan. But I could imagine the experience of life in America had sharpened his awareness of the massive corruption in his country and the prevailing undemocratic relations. In Indiana, tradition and cultural norms were respected, not obeyed. There were no *mahalla*, neighbourhood committees watching over your every move, and parents did not impose life decisions on their children. The sense of freedom over there had made him feel like a new born. I was aware of all this. Now seeing the pained expression on his face, I said kindly,

"You can still apply to universities over there. It's not too late."

"You think so? It's been five years since my Masters."

"Yes, I am sure. You are a very intelligent man and ambitious. You'll get there."

"You are very kind," he said smiling, and kissed the back of my hand. "But if I hadn't come back ..." he looked deep into my eyes, "I would have never met you."

There was such a loving look in those ebony eyes, no more words were needed.

***

We have three more days together in Bishkek, before Suleiman returns to Tashkent. Afterwards I will have a day to pack and get ready to leave for good. When we arrived back yesterday afternoon, he looked around my flat and asked about the paintings on the walls. I told him I am taking them back, but the three in my study I had to return to Gerhard. "Are you going to see him immediately you are back?" he asked abruptly.

"No ... I don't think so. I'll just have to arrange to send him his stuff." Gerhard was in fact planning to be in London when I arrived. But there was no point in arousing Suleiman's jealousy, telling him that. Instead I quickly went on to talk about the art of western style painting in Central Asia and how it was influenced by the Soviet school. Every republic had its own classical arts school, training generations of fine painters. I had seen some very good oil and water colour paintings in Baku and now in Bishkek.

"I have a good friend in Tashkent, a painter," he informed me. "If I knew you were interested, I would have taken you to his gallery."

"Maybe one day in the future."

"Not maybe. Definitely. Don't tell me you are never coming

back," he said with a worried expression.

"Of course I will come back. I loved your country; you've such rich history and culture."

"You haven't seen half of it yet. Come soon and I take you to all the interesting places."

***

This morning we set off early for the Ala Archa national park in the AlaToo Mountains at the foot of the Tien Shan; it is only a 40 minute car ride. We hire a taxi to take us there and back. What an amazing place, with a river running through a gorge, alpine forests on both sides and the most wonderful vista of mountains ahead. In winter skiers use the slopes and in the summer hikers, mountain climbers and picnicking families come for a day or longer. Today, though, there are hardly any people around. The calm of the place is most refreshing. We trek for an hour on an easy route, then climb over scattered rocks and boulders for another half hour, by which time we reach an old wooden bridge. It stretches over a very steep fall and shakes every time you move. I take a few steps and stop, not feeling safe. Suleiman is further ahead; he turns back, takes hold of my wrist and says, "You can make it. Just don't look down." As he guides me slowly, I picture myself in one of those action movies, a weakling female in the jungle rescued by a strong man, but I'm no Jane. Fear is fantasy, I tell myself, and focus on the breathtaking views; it's worth the stress. What a pity; I spent a whole year in Bishkek and this is my first trip here.

We are back in town late in the afternoon. We pick up some groceries on the way and I cook a dish of spicy rice with lentils and raisins. He likes it and wants to know more about Iranian cuisine. I tell him there are a number of Iranian shops in my part of London; I will cook him a fancier dish if he comes to visit me. "Inshallah …" he says wistfully. I suggest he should come in August, when the university is closed. There are so many places I want to show him. He has never been to the UK.

"Maybe," he says and pulls me onto his lap.

"I am going to really miss you when I go back," I say in earnest.

"Oh, sweetheart …" His fingers stroke my face and run down my neck. "The thought of you going away, and not seeing you again is killing me. … That was the reason I was drinking."

"Maybe one of the reasons, but …"

"Oh please, don't imagine I am an alcoholic just because of that night. Even if I was, your love would cure me."

Yes, my man is a charmer, but I am pretty certain his feelings for me are genuine. "Why don't we make a definite arrangement," I suggest. "Let's set a date for you to book a flight."

"I'll see." He forces a smile. I insist, and he admits that he owes his brother money from two years ago; he will have to work through the summer and into the academic year to finish paying it back.

"Just come for two weeks as my guest. I'll pay for your ticket."

"Oh, no." He shakes his head. "I can't let you do that."

I know that my paying would hurt his male pride, so I say, "You know I don't subscribe to gender stereotyping. Just consider it a gift between lovers," and give him a kiss on the cheek. He laughs, saying, "You are one determined lady," then draws me into a long kiss.

This morning Suleiman had asked me if I would consider applying to renew my contract here for another year, or see if I could get a job in Uzbekistan. Then we could both apply to the universities in the US for the following year. I told him there was ageism in the western academia, and at my age I could not afford wasting another year. Besides, there was no guarantee we could find positions in the same city or even the same state. America was a vast country. Hearing all this, he said with a sigh, "It's a shame. I wish things were different."

"So do I. But don't forget about my son. He also needs me over there."

"You must let him find his own way, don't try to always manage him." Suleiman's tone was assertive in the way men are with their partner's son. I said nothing but began to wonder how it could work out with the three of us living together. It took years for Gerhard and Jamie to adjust to each other. Now finally there is some harmony between them. Jamie respects Gerhard's seniority and social position, not to mention the material benefits he brings. How is he going to react to a young Central Asian man suddenly taking over his mother's heart?

I ponder these thoughts and more, when we lounge on my sofa late in the evening. We are watching a Russian language movie on a Kyrgyz channel. I can only catch some sentences; Suleiman has to translate most of it. Ten minutes into the film, his patience has run out. I am only relayed bits and pieces, some of which I have already figured out myself. Actually I am not really watching. I keep wondering, how am I going to face Gerhard when I return. I have been cool towards him recently. I could not really discuss separation in a long distance phone call. As soon as I am back I'll have to tell him straight: it's over. There will be a lot of heartache. After a decade, neither of us really wants to let go. But then what? I don't want to go back to my London life before Bishkek: constant arguments with

Jamie and worries about him. This time I won't even have a part-time man around. I'll be going to bed alone every night, dreaming of Suleiman, 5000 miles away.

***

Today was our second day together in Bishkek; we went shopping for souvenirs. Once we got home we listened to CDs of Uzbek and Kyrgyz music I had bought to take back with me. I love the haunting melodies of Kyrgyz songs. It is nomadic music, traditionally performed by travelling musicians, *manaschis*, and shamans. The Uzbek music, I found had similarities with Iranian; both influenced by Indian and Arabic music, a lot of lively rhythms. "What kind of music do you like?" I asked Suleiman.

"All kinds … But I don't know much about jazz or hip hop."

Through his Soviet education, Suleiman had learnt to appreciate western classical music and performing arts, though he was not as keen on them as I was. Before independence, Central Asian music, as with local languages was considered inferior to Russian by the educated population. Today, western and Russian pop music were the most popular.

"What about Uzbek music?" I asked

"Sometimes … You hear it a lot on radio and TV. It's good for dancing." He wiggled his shoulders.

"Alright then, let's try some."

I played one of the Uzbek CDs and we began to dance, while laughing, kissing and cuddling. There was such joy in the air I wanted the moment to last forever. It was a very warm evening, an arousing heat that sharpened the desires. Drenched in sweat we

365

stopped and showered together, barely fitting into my small tub. Afterwards we went to bed and made mad love, with pleasure and excitement rippling through every fibre of our bodies. My enjoyment was complete. Here was a man who complemented me in more ways than any other I had known. We were not only great in bed, but on a par intellectually, never short of topics to discuss, each of us learning from the other. Could he become my life companion, despite the culture gap and age difference? He did not think the former was significant, or the latter mattered. But then as a man, time was more on his side. He could marry me, establish himself in the West and once tired of me ageing, still have many good years ahead. These were the uncomfortable thoughts I often battled with.

Later when we sat at a lively Turkish restaurant, I hinted as much.

"What if we were in a permanent union? Do you think you would still fancy me when you are my age and I am already sixty five?"

He took my hand in his, looked into my eyes and said, "*janim, asalim* ... my love for you is eternal ... pretty as you are I love you more for your mind."

"I love you too," I said, grinning.

The waiter had just brought our order. Once he left, Suleiman lowered his gaze and continued with a resigned expression, "But I don't know how I could prove it to you ... Because of my situation; you think I am only after an exit visa."

"No. I know you really love me."

He nodded, "You said yourself, it should be possible for me to get a scholarship in America and move there. But I want to be with you, for always."

"Well ... I guess where there is a will, there is a way."

East meets East

***

Today is our last day together; we'll have to make the most of it. Tomorrow morning he will take his flight back to Tashkent and our ways will part for God knows how long. We both feel depressed, but avoid the subject. He prepares a breakfast of eggs and sausages with tomatoes and fresh bread he has just bought. I keep him company, reciting and translating verses from Hafiz, the great Persian poet of the 14th century. I have a copy of his *Divan*, book of poems, on my bookshelf. He looked at it the first day he was here and said he'd read a few of his verses in the Russian translation. He wished he could read the original. I told him that in Iran, the *Divan* is used as an oracle. People seek advice from the Sufi sage when facing life's crossroads. He was well known in the old European literary circles. Goethe admired him greatly, and Edward Fitzgerald called him the best musician of words. "Read me that first verse again," he asks.

"The path of love appeared easy at first."

"Whence came the hardships."

He shakes his head and remarks, "Don't we know it." After I read him another verse he says, "It sounds so melodic in Farsi. I'd love to learn the language, and visit Shiraz and Isfahan."

Shiraz, famous for its rose gardens, was the home of Hafiz and Saadi, the other great Persian poet of a century earlier.

"Learning Farsi will be easy for you. You are so good at languages," I tell him.

"Will you teach me some?" He pulls me into an embrace, stroking my hair.

"Sure. When you come to visit me." We kiss.

But our happy mood is soon shattered. Just when we are ready to go out, the phone rings. I walk quickly to my study to answer. It is ten in the morning, 5 a.m. in London, too early for Jamie to call.

"Hello. Sima?" I hear a man's croaky, dim voice I do not recognise.

"It's me, Gerhard," he clears his throat.

I'm startled. "Where are you? Are you in Bonn? It must be very early over there."

"Let me see … It's just after 6 a.m."

"Is everything alright? You don't sound good."

"No … Something terrible happened last night …"

My heart sinks. "Is Jamie alright? What happened?"

"Thomas … Thomas had a car crash. He almost died."

"Oh My God … that's dreadful."

"We've been in the hospital all night. The doctors say …" He sounds tearful.

"What do they say?"

"They say … he may never walk again."

"Jesus, … I'm really sorry. How did it happen? What are his injuries?"

At this point Suleiman comes into the room and stands next to me. "Who is it? What's happened? " I cover the receiver with my hand and tell him that Gerhard's son has had a very bad accident. "I'll talk to you later." I gesture him to leave the room. He hesitates, and goes out reluctantly.

"Do you have someone with you?" Gerhard asks.

"No," I reply, feeling uneasy. This is no time to bring Suleiman into the picture. I go on quickly to talk about the accident.

Thomas, the youngest of Gerhard's children was his baby son, rather spoilt and naïve for his age, though I got on well with him. Last autumn when Gerhard was visiting me, there was all that worry and debate about the young man's bankruptcy and the possibility of his going to jail. But this is a much more serious situation. He has concussion and a very serious back injury. He will have more tests done, but the doctors are not very hopeful. "Look love," I try to soothe him, "the doctors in the hospital may be telling you the worst to warn you. I am sure you'll get him the best medical care. They do wonders these days."

We go on to chat about my flat in London, Jamie, and Gerhard's other two children. I sense that talking to me; he is a little comforted. This is the least I can do for him. But with Suleiman within earshot, I have to keep the call short. Finally, before we end our conversation, Gerhard says, "You know, I had booked a flight to London for tomorrow. I meant to hire a car to pick you up, with your luggage. We could also do some touring together. But now …"

"Forget it. Jamie can meet me at the airport. I will come to see you as soon as I am back."

"Oh, I hope so. I really need you here." There is a plea in his voice I can't ignore. I want to send him a kiss over the phone, knowing how upset and anxious he must be. But I restrain myself. I just say, "Take care love. I'll see you soon." After I put the receiver down I remain seated for some time, digesting the sad news. When I go into the lounge, I find Suleiman in a pensive mood, looking dejected. He gets up immediately and says he is going to the internet café to make a call to his brother, Marat. Suleiman works part-time as a manager for his brother's warehouse. He has been away for a week and wants to know what is happening back home. "You'll find out tomorrow. Why the rush now?" He ignores me, puts his shoes on, and leaves.

I sit by myself, reflecting on Gerhard's disturbing news and my feelings for him. His sad voice and the news of his son has really upset me. I thought I had stopped loving the man. Is this the false sensations of an amputated limb, or does old love never die? Whatever it is, Suleiman is suspecting something he is not happy with. What did he hear exactly?

***

"Where have you been? You've been gone three hours," I greeted him angrily on his return.

He ignored me, went straight into the sitting room, and slumped on one of the easy chairs. He then began reading a Russian language newspaper he'd brought in. His indifference was irritating. I had meant to spend a couple of hours today sorting out my research notes and packing the books and articles I wanted to take back. But worrying about him, I could not concentrate. When I told him about it, he simply said, "Then get on with your work. I'm going out soon to make another call."

I swallowed my annoyance and went back to my study. If only we had left the flat a few minutes earlier, before that phone call … The thought was gnawing me. But how could I blame Gerhard for wanting to share his sad news? He still loved me in his own way; I had not told him yet about the new man in my life. That trauma, I would have to face in a few days time. For now, I had to remedy the situation with Suleiman. After some minutes of brooding, I went to sit with him and asked gently, "What is wrong?"

"Nothing," he said tersely.

"You are not being truthful."

"Don't fucking tell me I lie," he yelled, "I am not the one who …"

"What?"

"Oh, forget it," he tossed the paper aside as he rose to his feet, ready to leave.

I wanted to have a candid talk and got up to stop him.. "Just a minute," I took hold of his arm. He looked away as he shook his arm free, giving me a hard push. I stumbled and fell. "Ouch," I moaned. My right leg had taken the impact and began to hurt. Hearing the noise, he came back into the room. "What happened?"

"You pushed me hard and I fell."

"I didn't push you," he said defensively.

"No you didn't. The fairy did," I rebuked him.

He ignored my remark and helped me get up and sit on the sofa. I began to rub my leg. "Are you alright? Do you want to lie down?" He asked with downcast eyes. I almost laughed, thinking his anger with my assumed guilt had put *him* in the guilty spot. The man had an aggressive side, I was not comfortable with. I had to get him to disclose his anger "Why don't you go and make some coffee?" I suggested. "We need to talk."

"What is bugging you exactly?" I asked, when he came in with the coffees. He fidgeted a bit, took a sip of his drink and said, "You still love him. Don't you?"

"Why do you imagine that?"

He ignored my remark and went on, "Once you get back, you are going to forget all about me."

"What is all this about? I've told you I'm finished with Gerhard."

"That's what you tell me … maybe even tell yourself. But the way you talk to him … I know you miss him."

"Oh, for God's sake …" I had to once again explain and justify my reasons for remaining friendly with the man I had shared my life with for so many years. I reminded him about the practical issues to sort out, like the flat in Brighton. He had paid for most of it, but let me have an equal share. Finally I said, "Over the years, he's been kind and generous to me. I can't just dump him like a used rag."

"I never said you should," he frowned.

I could see that trust was a major issue here and tried to reassure him, saying, "But I have never felt about him, the way I feel for you."

He remained quiet, staring out of the window. After a long pause he looked at me with a resigned expression and said, "Maybe ...but he has all the cards. I have none. Once you are over there, he'll work his way back into your heart, if not your bed."

"Oh, for fuck's sake," I shouted. "Just because he is well off ... You think everything revolves around money. I know it does over here but not where I come from."

"Bullshit! You're talking nonsense," he snapped and left the room.

"Suit yourself. I don't care anymore." I shouted, as I heard him leave the apartment.

But that was a big lie. Deep in my heart and with every bit of my body I cared for him. Why else was I crying? This morning I had woken up in his arms, intoxicated with love, oozing with vitality and full of hope. I was lying next to a man I had known, not for months, but for centuries. He had turned around my emotionally barren life and I was swimming in a sea of happiness under the blazing sun.

Now a few hours later, that glowing mirage had vanished. Was I seeing the other side of him: jealous, possessive and too proud for his own good? How did I get myself into this goddamned, hopeless love affair? So many barriers to overcome, could there be a future for us?

I wiped my tears and moped around the flat for a while, then decided to focus on getting ready for my departure. In a couple of days I would be seeing my son and my old friends again. There was also the prospect of getting that job next week. Still, I felt restless. I needed a cigarette. The old Russian woman across the road sold them from a stand. I would just buy a single stick to avoid temptation with a whole packet. I had more or less stopped smoking since Osh, and felt better for it. After I came back I sat on my balcony, took a deep drag and gazed at the lovely view of Tien Shan in the distance. I began to feel strangely calm, as if the thought of ending our relationship had lifted a big weight off me. If we continued, I told myself, in time the distance would erode the attachment and kill the passion. Was this why he was reacting so unreasonably?

An hour later Suleiman was back. He came into the sitting room where I was and said he had met Emil on the street; he could stay the night at his place if I didn't want him around.

"It's our last day together … and we are fighting." I said, my eyes welling up. "I don't want you to leave like this."

He kept standing by the door, glum faced and finally said, "I am sorry I lost my temper earlier … I've been thinking … I keep making you unhappy. I am no good for you."

"Why don't you sit down?" I pointed to an armchair facing me. "Maybe we should communicate better, and have more trust in each other."

He sat down, leaning forward, and held his head in his hands. After a long silence he began, "I know I should not be jealous of your friends, but …" He raised his head, fixing his gaze on me, "if I do wrong, it's because I love you too much … It's like a fire inside me and I can't control the flames."

His dramatics brought a smile to my face. I got up and gave him a kiss on the cheek. "Shall we call the fire brigade?" I humoured him. We both laughed and he kissed me back.

That evening, I suggested we do something joyful. There was a performance of Rossini's Barber of Seville at the opera house. It was a comical opera that would lift our spirit. I told him in London I could rarely afford it. After the show we went to a local restaurant to have our last meal together. On the way, we walked holding hands. Love had conquered the earlier tiff between us. Whilst having dinner, he told me that in his last couple of years of school in Tashkent he had been taken with his classmates to see a number of opera productions. "We were given the back rows," he said, laughing. "We sat there; gossiping, making noise and get told off ... We boys didn't really have any interest. We just wanted to impress the girls." I asked if he liked tonight's performance.

"Yes. I saw it already; three years ago. We went with Dilora. She is more keen on the opera than me."

"Really?" So she was not as unsophisticated as I had imagined; a whiff of jealousy ran through me.

"You know, we have a nice opera house in Tashkent, better than here. When you come over," he said eagerly, "I will take you there. Sometimes the singers come from Russia or Ukraine."

"Maybe over the Christmas holidays; let's see how the job situation turns out. But first you should come in August. You promised." I went on to suggest that we both look for a scholarship for him for the following year. But this was far more possible in the US than the UK.

We had now finished eating and were sipping the last of the Georgian wine. There was a gloomy silence between us.

"Don't you think our situation is a bit hopeless?" he began. "You don't want to come and live here, and I have no possibilities over there."

"It's not that I don't want to …," I protested.

"I know *janim*, I don't blame you. If I were you, I wouldn't want to leave London to move here. I just want us to be realistic. …" He paused, looking away, then looked into my eyes and said, "You are a very attractive single woman and I am a single man in need of female company. How long do you think we can keep it up?"

I looked past him at the remaining diners talking and laughing noisily; their carefree enjoyment irritating me in my miserable state.

"So what are you saying? You think we should end it now?"

"I don't know," he stared at his glass, lines of sadness etched around his mouth. I could not talk. I pressed my lips and did not blink, lest tears would fall onto my cheek. Deep down I agreed with him, but I was not ready to give up. There was always the option of marriage that we had not discussed so far.

"Okay … What if we get married?" I made my unromantic proposal. "You can get some work in London, and do your PhD part-time. I will eventually get a teaching post, or some other job. We'll manage financially."

He stared at me for a moment, not showing any emotion. I was surprised. I'd expected him to break into a thankful smile.

"You give me this ideal scenario, make it sound easy. But marriage shouldn't be out of compulsion. It wouldn't work."

"How is it out of compulsion if we really love each other?"

"Because it is the circumstances forcing you to propose to me."

"To hell with the circumstances." I threw my hand in the air. "I know that I love you and you will bring me happiness … You are a remarkable man."

"Well …" he took a deep breath. "What can I say?" Before he could go on, the waiter approached our table with the bill and automatically placed it in front of Suleiman. I grabbed it quickly, thinking that it was my turn. The last couple of times he had paid. He took the bill out of my hand and said, "Please let's not argue about this again."

"Alright," I conceded, thinking he won't be able to keep up his chivalry with London prices.

After the waiter had finished with our table, I looked at him directly and asked, "So ... What do you think?"

"Oh, marriage ... You know that I am still married, he teased. You'll just have to wait." We both laughed.

"Let's go home and celebrate," I suggested. I still had a bottle of vodka in my drinks cabinet.

***

This morning we made it to the airport just in time. Last night we had stayed up until the small hours, drinking and chatting about the future, the opportunities for him in London, and about our children. He was concerned whether my son would approve of him. I said that the introduction had to be gradual. Over the past couple of years Gerhard and Jamie seemed to get on well. I now had to deal with Jamie's disappointment over our breakup. As for his daughters, he wanted them to go to a good school and learn English properly. He would take on any amount of work he could get and send money for their care. "In Tashkent, sometimes I worked three jobs," he said. "But teaching was the one I really enjoyed."

Finally the dreaded moment arrived. Both of us in tears though his were mostly held back. "See you in August," I shouted, as he approached the passport control gate. He turned round and blew me a kiss. "See you," he shouted back and moved on quickly. I stood where I was for some time, my face awash with tears. A number of passengers came past, mainly Kyrgyz, Uzbek and a few Russians. They stared at me pitifully. An irrational feeling of doom had descended on me. Was I ever going to see him again? All the negatives ran through my mind: a plane crash, a serious car injury on Uzbekistan's rough roads; entrapment by his family; or a sudden opportunity for him in the States, and we drift apart. I stood for some time, engrossed in my feeling of loss, before I noticed the driver waving at me. He was waiting to take me back to the city.

Once I was home, I moved around the flat aimlessly. I had hardly done any packing. The stuff I had accumulated over the year needed sifting through; things to give away and items to take back. A day and a half of tedium lay ahead; I wasn't in the mood. As I pondered, the phone rang; it was my colleague Nazira, from the politics department. I hadn't seen her since the end of the semester. She wanted to meet up later. I told her I had no time; my packing was well behind schedule. She cheered me up, saying she would come and help.

***

"You must be happy you are going home," Nazira said soon after she arrived. "Yes …" I replied hesitantly.

"You don't sound sure." I told her I had a lot to deal with over there; a job interview, repairs to my apartment, sorting out my son, and whatever else problems that may have accumulated in my long absence.

"What about your German friend?" Aren't you excited to see him?"

"We are not together anymore."

"Since when?" She was surprised. She had met him one evening when we went out together for dinner, and liked him. I told her I had been unhappy with the relationship for a long time and now living apart for almost a year, I realised it was over for me.

"That is a pity. He seemed a nice man, real gentleman."

"Yes. But there is more to love than good manners."

"I know," she nodded, giggling. "Sex has to be good too." She then asked, rather excited, "Have you met someone new? Who is it?"

I told her briefly about Suleiman. "An Uzbek man?" She sounded skeptical. "You are used to European men. They are more honest and considerate with women than Central Asian men."

"I know all that, but he is different. He treats me with a lot of love and respect."

"Can you trust him? He may say things just to impress you." I shook my head in disagreement. "Anyway," she went on, "You are not coming back here next semester. How are you going to keep contact with him? "

"We'll see." I left it at that, not wanting to mention a possible marriage, lest she thought me a fool for considering it.

***

This is my last day in Bishkek Clara came early in the morning to help me finish the packing. I gave her all the stuff I wasn't taking back, toiletry, kitchenware, and the quality radio/CD player I had bought when I first arrived. She told me Nina was over the moon about it. This was something they could not afford. The clothes I gave her also went to Nina. They were two sizes too small for Clara. Not to disappoint her, I gave her some money to buy herself a gift from me. She has been so kind and helpful; I am going to miss her. I have lived a comfortable, leisurely life here, no housework or property matters to bother with. It's been the life afforded someone from a rich country coming to work in a poor one, a kind of colonial existence. Even though the colonies are gone, the exploitative swap of labour and resources persist today. Recently I have been thinking a lot about my own part in this. Did teaching theories of culture to a few privileged students really raise the knowledge capital in this desperately poor country? Perhaps not, but at least I did encourage them to question gender relations and the position of women in their own society. These are the areas where Central Asian countries rank very poorly.

As I was mulling over these thoughts, the phone rang. I ran to pick it up. Suleiman had not called so far to say he'd got back alright. I was getting very anxious.

"Hello Sima *janim*" Hearing his voice at once perked me up.

"What happened yesterday? You didn't call."

"*Asalim*, you have no idea how busy I was. As soon as I got back Dilora called. My daughter, Gulzada had been ill for a few days and was getting worse. The doctors in Syrdarya are an ignorant bunch. I had to bring her here to see our family doctor."

"What was wrong with her?"

"We feared pneumonia. But thank God it wasn't that. It's a bad flu."

"Who is looking after her now?"

"I took her and Dilora to stay at my mother's for a few days. Gulzada needed more tests done today." He interrupted for a moment, talking to someone, then continued, "I am sorry honey ... What was I saying? Oh, yes. I wanted to say that you don't realise how much you love your children until something goes wrong."

"Darling, I know the feeling. If there is anything you need from

London, medication, or anything ..."

"No, no. I don't need anything. Except ..."

"Yes?"

"I need you and your lovely self beside me," he said in an emotional voice. "Yesterday on the way back I thought a lot about us and decided I would immediately go to see Dilora and tell her I am definitely applying for a divorce. We have been living apart for nearly two years. It should be easy to get it through the courts. But given the situation, I couldn't mention it."

"No, you have to wait until Gulzada gets better. I guess you can't tell your family just yet, either."

"Hell, no. My mother again was going on about me and Dilora getting back together. She told me I should earn more money and rent a decent apartment so they can come back and live with me. The children need their father, blah, blah ... But you know that I don't love her ... I love *you* ..."

Yes, the girls did need their father; how could I be the cause of wrecking their family life? "Look," I said with a heavy heart, "maybe you should give yourself time and reconsider the whole thing. Your mother has a point. If you love those children so much, you are never going to be happy living far away, with me, or ..."

"Stop, stop ..." he cut in. "My mother, above all, thinks about what the relatives, and specially the *mahalla*, will say about her son getting divorced. I told you this already. In this God damned country we are a slave to reputation. Sometimes I feel our *mahalla* dictatorship is worse than the state one, and we live under both."

We had been talking for no more than 15 minutes when the connection was broken. "God damn the bloody phones in this country," I cursed. We had not said goodbye properly. I best call him from London I decided, and joined Clara. There were three pieces of embroidery wall hanging and four paintings to de-frame and pack. Two of these I was to return to Gerhard, the man with all the aces. Thinking of him, I felt a blast of anxiety. How was I going to give him up for a man with no financial assets and tons of responsibility? But there was no delaying it. Once we met, I would have to reveal my love for another man. After that there would be no going back. The life I will lead may become more austere, but hopefully more enjoyable, with greater promise. Marrying Suleiman could be the greatest venture in my life, but when did I ever shy away from adventure?

I had come to the rooftop of the world, searching for my Turkic roots. I go back having discovered a vast corner of the world for decades hidden from western view, a region with amazing history, diverse cultures, wonderful nature and friendly people. The gift that I take back from this world is the love of a man who has met the East and the West in me. No matter what the future holds for us, I shall cherish this gift for ever.

Epilogue

Over the past decade Kyrgyzstan has witnessed two revolutions and a major inter-ethnic clash in the south of the country. The first revolution in 2005 led to the overthrow of President Akayev. A southerner, Kurmanbek Bakiev, was then elected as the new president. In the following years corruption and nepotism of the new government gave rise to growing discontent. Then in January 2010, during the height of winter weather, the government introduced massive increases in utility prices. Large demonstrations were held across the country calling for nationalisation of the privatised energy companies and withdrawal of price increases. Later, on the 7th of April that year protest rallies in Bishkek led to violent clashes between the security forces and the crowd, resulting in 100 dead and many more injured. There was also large scale looting and destruction of government offices. Bakiev was then forced to flee the capital, taking refuge in his hometown of Jalal-Abad, after which he fled to Belarus.

The following day a new government was formed by Rosa Otunbaeva from the social Democratic party and a former ambassador to the US and the UK. This was for a period of six months until parliamentary elections were held in October 2010 and a new government was elected. Otunbaeva, meanwhile maintained the function of the president. Kyrgyzstan's political turmoil, however, was compounded in June that year by the interethnic clashes between the Uzbek and the Kyrgyz population in the south of the country. The events left at least 1000 dead and many more wounded. Over 100,000 fled for the neighbouring Uzbekistan. The rioting and fighting had begun in the city of Osh where nearly half the population are Uzbek, then spread to Jalal-Abad and the neighbouring small towns and villages. Among the factors that contributed to these tragic events were the Kyrgyz resentment of the Uzbeks' higher economic position, the Uzbeks sense of discrimination by the politically dominant Kyrgyz and provocations by members of Bakiev's former government.

In July 2010 a new constitution was drafted and ratified in a referendum. It established a parliamentary system whereby the leader of the majority party would be the prime minister, with the president the head of the army, the border guards, the intelligence service and the public prosecutors. He/she would be elected for 6 years, with no right of return. In December 2011 new presidential elections were held and Almazbek Atambaev from Social Democratic Party was elected. Otunbaeva did not participate in the election. She had successfully overseen the transition from Bakiev's increasingly authoritarian regime to a more democratic system with greater political and press freedom. Kyrgyzstan could now claim to be the sole country in Central Asia not run by a despot, but ruled through a freely elected assembly.

In terms of social changes in Kyrgyzstan over the past decade, a major development has been the large scale migration of workers to Russia. Their remittances have made a considerable contribution to the national budget. In Bishkek this has manifested, among other things, in a building boom. City limits have extended with the addition of new housing settlements. Number of cars on the road have also greatly increased. Traffic jams and air pollution are becoming familiar features across the city. However, the economic situation is currently volatile. With the Russian Rouble greatly losing its value and the recession in Russia, some of the workers are returning home. The national currency, Som, has already devalued by 20%. The anti-Central Asian sentiments of many Russians is also making work in Russia less and less attractive. The return of workers could create social unrest and political instability if not met with increased employment opportunities. China could acquire a significant role in this. It has already invested in development projects in Kyrgyzstan, such as road building and support for banking through the Asian Development Bank.

Currently a major debate facing Kyrgyzstan is the question of relations with Russia. The government and the older generation are often loyal to Russia and favour the idea of joining the Customs Union (composed of Belarus, Kazakhstan, Armenia and Russia). The opposition parties and the educated young, on the other hand, are more oriented towards Europe and the US and favour closer ties with them, rather than with Russia. In recent months distrust of Russia and opposition to the Customs Union has grown due to that country's expansionist policies in Ukraine and its annexation of Crimea. The Kyrgyz value their independence and fear domination by Russia, their former colonial masters. Until today, the Kyrgyz government still has not fully joined the Eurasian Customs Union.

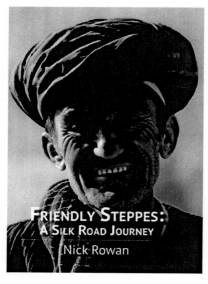

Friendly Steppes: A Silk Road Journey
by Nick Rowan

This is the chronicle of an extraordinary adventure that led Nick Rowan to some of the world's most incredible and hidden places. Intertwined with the magic of 2,000 years of Silk Road history, he recounts his experiences coupled with a remarkable realisation of just what an impact this trade route has had on our society as we know it today. Containing colourful stories, beautiful photography and vivid characters, and wrapped in the local myths and legends told by the people Nick met and who live along the route, this is both a travelogue and an education of a part of the world that has remained hidden for hundreds of years.

Friendly Steppes: A Silk Road Journey reveals just how rich the region was both culturally and economically and uncovers countless new friends as Nick travels from Venice through Eastern Europe, Iran, the ancient and modern Central Asia of places like Samarkand, Bishkek and Turkmenbashi, and on to China, along the Silk Roads of today.

RRP:£14.95
ISBN: 978-0-9557549-4-4

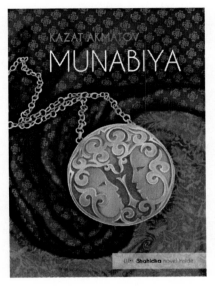

Munabiya And Shahidka
by Kazat Akmatov

Recently translated into English Akmatov's two love stories are set in rural Kyrgyzstan, where the natural environment, local culture, traditions and political climate all play an integral part in the dramas which unfold.

Munabiya is a tale of a family's frustration, fury, sadness and eventual acceptance of a long term love affair between the widowed father and his mistress.

In contrast, Shahidka is a multi-stranded story which focuses on the ties which bind a series of individuals to the tragic and ill-fated union between a local Russian girl and her Chechen lover, within a multi-cultural community where violence, corruption and propaganda are part of everyday life.

RRP: £12.95
ISBN: 978-0-9574807-5-9

KAZAT AKMATOV

THIRTEEN STEPS
TOWARDS THE FATE
OF ERIKA KLAUS

"Thirteen Steps Towards
the Fate of Erika Klaus"
by Kazat Akmatov

Is set in a remote outpost governed by a fascist regime, based on real events in a mountain village in Kyrgyzstan ten years ago. It narrates challenges faced by a young, naïve Norwegian woman who has volunteered to teach English. Immersed in the local community, her outlook is excitable and romantic until she experiences the brutal enforcement of the political situation on both her own life and the livelihood of those around her. Events become increasingly violent, made all the more shocking by Akmatov's sensitive descriptions of the magnificent landscape, the simple yet proud people and their traditional customs.

Born in 1941 in the Kyrgyz Republic under the Soviet Union, Akmatov has first -hand experience of extreme political reactions to his work which deemed anti-Russian and anti-communist, resulted in censorship. Determined to fight for basic human rights in oppressed countries, he was active in the establishment of the Democratic Movement of Kyrgyzstan and through his writing, continues to highlight problems faced by other central Asian countries.

RRP: £12.95
ISBN: 978-09574807-6-6

Finding the Holy Path
by Shahsanem Murray

The Kyrgyz-British novelist Shahsanem Murray was born in Kyrgyzstan and settled in Edinburgh, UK after marrying her husband Gordon Murray. With a degree in Philology and speaking three languages fluently, writing is a natural past time for her. After completing a translation of one of her Uncles book from Kyrgyz into both English and Russian two years ago, she then set about writing her own first novel. This first novel can trace its roots and influences to many aspects of her life. Clan cultures in both Scotland and Kyrgyzstan along with travelling to many corners of the world provided a framework for a story through the ages and the continents of the world. Whilst a keen interest in Politics, International Business, Poetry, Films and Art provided threads and strands for back-stories and sub-plots as well as many factual references and content. Outwith writing Shahsanem works with a number of colleagues to arrange cultural events, and endeavours to promote Central Asia throughout Scotland and the UK

RRP: £12.50
ISBN: 978-09927873-9-4

100 Experiences Of Kyrgyzstan
Text by Ian Claytor

You would be forgiven for missing the tiny landlocked country of Kyrgyzstan on the map. Meshed into Central Asia's inter-locking web of former Soviet Union boundaries, this mountainous country still has more horses than cars. It never fails to surprise and delight all who visit. Proud of its nomadic traditions, dating back to the days of the Silk Road, be prepared for Kyrgyzstan's overwhelming welcome of hospitality, received, perhaps, in a shepherd's yurt out on the summer pastures. Drink bowls of freshly fermented mare's milk with newfound friends and let the country's traditions take you into their heart. Marvel at the country's icy glaciers, crystal clear lakes and dramatic gorges set beneath the pearly white Tien Shan mountains that shimmer, heaven-like, in the summer haze as the last of the winter snows caps their dominating peaks. Immerse yourself in Central Asia's jewel with its unique experiences and you will leave with a renewed zest for life and an unforgettable sense of just how man and nature can interact in harmony.

ISBN: 978-0-9574807-4-2
RRP: £14.95